"*Station Eternity* balances both the science fiction elements—meeting aliens, understanding how to work with them—and the mystery elements very evenly; it genuinely works as both genres (and works best as both). I'm already looking forward to however many more of these stories we get, because it was just so much fun."

—*Locus*

"Mur Lafferty proves once again that she has the rare talent to blend and bend the sister genres of mystery and science fiction. . . . Smart and sassy, here's the book that will blast you to orbit."

—James Patrick Kelly, winner of the Hugo, Nebula, and Locus Awards

PRAISE FOR *SIX WAKES*

"A taut, nerve-tingling, interstellar murder mystery with a deeply human heart."

—NPR

"An exquisitely crafted puzzle box that challenges our thoughts on what it means to be human—*Six Wakes* is a sci-fi murder mystery of light speed intensity."

—*New York Times* bestselling author Scott Sigler

"This is a great book with so much going for it: clever structure, wonderful characters, and a fiendishly clever puzzle that you'll roll over in your mind for months after you close the covers."

—BoingBoing

"Mysterious and tense . . . I wish I wrote this book."

—*New York Times* bestselling author Chuck Wendig

"Lafferty delivers a tense nail-biter of a story fueled by memorable characters and thoughtful world-building. This space-based locked-room murder mystery explores complex technological and moral issues in a way that's certain to earn it a spot on award ballots."

—*Publishers Weekly* (starred review)

"Lafferty delivers the ultimate locked-room mystery combined with top-notch sf worldbuilding. The puzzle of who is responsible for the devastation on the ship keeps the pages turning."

—*Library Journal* (starred review)

ALSO BY MUR LAFFERTY

• • • •

The Midsolar Murders

Station Eternity

CHAOS
TERMINAL

MUR
LAFFERTY

ACE
NEW YORK

ACE
Published by Berkley
An imprint of Penguin Random House LLC
penguinrandomhouse.com

"Gravity is Stupid" by Devo Spice. Used by permission. All rights reserved.

"Needs of the Many" by the garages. Used by permission. All rights reserved.

"Take the Fire Back (Prometheus Has Left the Building)" by Worm Quartet,
copyright © 2022 by Timothy F. Crist. Used by permission. All rights reserved.

Library of Congress Cataloging-in-Publication Data

Names: Lafferty, Mur, author.
Title: Chaos terminal / Mur Lafferty.
Description: First edition. | New York: Ace, 2023. | Series: The Midsolar Murders; 2
Identifiers: LCCN 2023010242 (print) | LCCN 2023010243 (ebook) |
ISBN 9780593098134 (trade paperback) | ISBN 9780593098141 (ebook)
Subjects: LCGFT: Science fiction. | Detective and mystery fiction. | Novels.
Classification: LCC PS3612.A3743 C53 2023 (print) | LCC PS3612.A3743 (ebook) |
DDC 813/.6—dc23/eng/20230306
LC record available at https://lccn.loc.gov/2023010242
LC ebook record available at https://lccn.loc.gov/2023010243

First Edition: November 2023

Printed in the United States of America
1st Printing

Book design by Alison Cnockaert

To Joe Magid, Eric Smith, and Eric Daniels
for shenanigans in high school

and

the Drunks in Space for shenanigans now

PART ONE

I'm resigned to my fate so I'll state in plain words
If gravity's so great, explain birds
It's a force that tries to drag everything down
So why's the moon keep going round and round?

—"Gravity Is Stupid" by Devo Spice,
written by Tom Rockwell

1

SENSE ENOUGH TO COME IN OUTTA THE RAIN

A SENTIENT SPACE STATION *should have perfect tempera-ture,* Mallory Viridian thought. *This has got to be far below freezing.* When the station imitated weather, it should be Los Angeles weather, not Pluto's bloodred snow. And when it was helping a resident, it should produce a pleasant flat walk, or even something downhill, not an uphill, snowy, windy trek that gave one frostbite.

The fact that there could be people aboard the station who wallowed in frigid, bloodred snow like a pig in slop, she refused to consider.

It was possible, she thought, squinting through the crimson swirls, that the massive space station was just in a bad mood.

Red snow stung the exposed skin on her face. Her ears ached. She shoved her hands deep into her jeans pockets and shivered. Her destination lay at the top of a freaking mountain—a *fabricated* mountain—inside a cave, also fabricated. She wanted to rest, but the risk of dying of hypothermia on the way felt very real.

She probably should have put on a coat, but she hadn't thought she needed it. The station took care of its residents. Why would she suddenly need to travel through a deadly storm to go to a meeting?

This isn't worth it.

When Mrs. Brown calls, however, you answer. The tiny woman had a steel spine and a personality that filled a room, yes. And she was more than capable of protecting herself and those she loved with deadly force, sure. But she was also the human host who had a direct connection with the station itself, so when she asked to speak to you, you answered.

The cave loomed ahead, a dark cut in the harsh red drifts all around her. She was almost there. Probably. She didn't know what she'd do if it wasn't there. This was a great place for someone to lure her to an ambush. Or, more likely, according to her experience, lure her to watch someone else being killed, giving her a new murder to solve.

Her fingers and toes tingled with the beginnings of frostbite, and Mallory gritted her teeth around her rubber oxygen breather to keep them from chattering. How much damage would Eternity allow her to suffer? And good Lord, why? Would she let Mallory die here? Mallory didn't think so, but she wasn't entirely sure.

Almost there.

Station Eternity liked her, that much she knew. She probably wouldn't let Mallory die of hypothermia. Eternity's whims overrode everything—except, perhaps, Mrs. Brown's own whims. Mallory wasn't entirely sure how the symbiotic connection worked. Mrs. Brown didn't seem to know much either.

The snow got deeper as she got closer, until she was pushing through knee-deep powder with a crusty layer of bloodlike ice on top. She gritted her teeth and pressed on, the muscles in her thighs hot and threatening to turn to loose rubber and then seize into a massive cramp. *What is going on? Am I being punished?*

The cave opening shimmered in front of her and then appeared much closer than it had been previously.

Inside, Mrs. Brown paced, hands on her hips.

"I guess you took the long way around?" she demanded.

MRS. BROWN HAD sent her a message that morning. Mallory had been going through the list of new clients to her detective agency, dismayed at the lost items, the stolen items, and the requests to find incomprehensible things for aliens—including, apparently, a lost day.

Reading a message from Mrs. Brown asking to see her that afternoon was at least something she could understand and be interested in doing.

Mallory wasn't too fond of solving murder cases, but it was what she knew, and she hadn't known how, well, boring it would be to do other detective work. Or, admittedly, how difficult it would be to investigate alien crimes done to aliens by aliens.

The weird thing was that Mrs. Brown had requested that Mallory meet her in a place she had never visited on the station. After getting the information, Mallory approached the wall terminal and pulled up a complex 3D map of Station Eternity. She had a bizarre impulse to rotate the map to look for a secret port that she could torpedo and blow it up, à la Star Wars. She shook her head to clear the connection; she had no desire to blow up Eternity. Where would she go then?

Like the Death Star, Station Eternity was the size of a small moon. Unlike the Death Star, it had no planet-killing ability (that she knew of, anyway).

Mallory moved the station around until she found a small glowing dot. "Now, where are you?" she asked, trying to puzzle out the map. She ran her finger over about three-fourths of the sphere, dulling the brightness. The dot lay amid a large open area on the station, one of the places that tried to mimic various planet biomes to give the illusion of home to visitors. This one looked extremely hostile for humans and—

"Oh, come on, red snow?" she said aloud. "Is that even a thing? Can I survive that?"

The globe spun in front of her, mute. After a moment, an image of Pluto popped up, along with a paragraph about the red methane snow in the Cthulhu region.

She shook her head. "Methane atmosphere and red snow? I can't survive on Pluto."

Another image popped up of a full-body protective suit. She rolled her eyes. A suit? She wasn't going into total vacuum or anything.

Eternity wouldn't kill her. She grabbed a jacket and an oxygen breather from the closet by the door and headed out.

MALLORY PUT THE last of her strength into galumphing through the snow to the cave. As she reached it, her legs gave out and she collapsed onto a dirt floor beside a campfire.

Mrs. Brown strode over to her and stood above her head, looking down. She looked slightly ridiculous in a big puffy coat and a homemade knitted cap. "Well?" she asked.

Panting, Mallory didn't move, just glad to be out of the wind. The fire's heat penetrated faster than a normal campfire would have, underscoring that, despite the exhaustion and the frigid temperatures, the station kept her as cold or as hot as it wanted to. She slowly sat up.

"What do you mean?"

Mrs. Brown frowned. Her light brown skin creased further and she pulled her cap off. Mallory sat back, sliding away from her a little bit. Mrs. Brown was a tiny prim grandmother who was also a three-time murderer—or a three-time self-defense killer, depending on whom you asked. She had been visiting Eternity with her granddaughter when the station's last host had been murdered. The station needed a host to communicate with its many residents and visitors and was in shock and distress after the murder. Mrs. Brown had stepped in to take over before the station could tear herself apart and kill everyone on board in a panic.

Mrs. Brown was always perfectly pleasant to Mallory, despite the two of them having a "history," as Mrs. Brown liked to call it. She was polite and proper, and Mallory knew she would suffer zero fools. She defended herself and her loved ones with deadly efficiency, and she both inspired Mallory and scared the shit out of her.

"I mean that the station is making this frozen hellscape for us to meet in," Mrs. Brown snapped, gesturing to the weather outside the cave.

"You didn't instruct her to do this?" Mallory asked.

"I hate snow, why the hell would I do that?" She glared at Mallory. "Why aren't you wearing a suit?"

"I— Why are you asking me? Can't you ask the station?"

"The station is saying that everything is fine," Mrs. Brown said. "She just said we had to meet here. She won't tell me why."

"Why did you want to see me?" Mallory asked, scrambling to her feet. "Maybe that will shed some light on the issue."

Mrs. Brown bent over and a tree stump rose from the floor to fit exactly where her butt landed when she sat back. Mallory shook her head in wonder.

"I wanted to tell you I was leaving for a bit, and I'm taking *Infinity*."

"You couldn't tell me this in your office?" Mallory asked. "Or mine?"

"I asked Eternity to give us a place where I could talk to you in private," Brown said, gazing out at the blizzard.

"What do you mean, private? How is this more private than any other room?" Mallory asked.

"Unless you squirreled them away in your pockets, the Sundry couldn't have followed you here, correct?" Mrs. Brown asked, referring to the insect-like alien that made up a hivemind that had taken a marked interest in Mallory.

"Oh. You're right," Mallory said. No insect could fly through that frigid methane nightmare. "But why keep stuff from them?"

"I don't know. Eternity suggested it. When I ask her why, she says everything is fine." Mrs. Brown shook her head. "I'd say she sounds like my grandmother when she was angry, but Eternity has never shown passive aggression before. I wanted you to know I was leaving, Eternity didn't want the Sundry to know, so this cave was her solution."

"Won't they know when you leave? They know pretty much everything that goes on around here."

"They won't know where I'm going," Mrs. Brown said. "Eternity felt strongly about this."

"That's so weird," Mallory said. "So where are you going?"

"A planet called November. Apparently it's an area of the galaxy where the sentient stations are born. I need to go there to learn more about all this." She gestured vaguely to the walls of the cave. "It's not just a matter of learning more about her. Eternity is still acting sickly after that disaster from a few months ago. I don't have the understanding to fix everything, so I'm heading to November. They tell me I can learn more about host relationships when your best friend is the size of a moon."

Mallory's gut sank. "Won't Eternity freak out again if you leave?" The scars, both internal and external, were still fresh from when Eternity's host had been murdered. In a confused panic, she had killed or injured many people unfortunate enough to be in her way. The thought of what the station would do if she lost another host terrified Mallory.

"Not if you help," Mrs. Brown said. "While I'm gone, Eternity will take a little nap." Seeing the look on Mallory's face, she smiled. "Oh, don't worry. Her life support and other necessary functions will be just fine, but she won't be able to communicate much. I need someone to look after her. I need you."

"You're hiring me to babysit a space station?" Mallory rubbed her forehead. "There has got to be someone else aboard who's got more experience with all of this. Hell, Xan would be better than me. Why don't you ask him?"

Xan was like Mrs. Brown; he was a human connected symbiotically to Eternity's daughter, the sentient spaceship *Infinity*. Both humans had deep mental and emotional communicative experiences with the aliens, which Mallory envied. She, too, had a symbiotic relationship with an alien race, but it wasn't nearly as healthy.

"I need Alexander for something else," Mrs. Brown said primly. "I want you for this."

Mallory shook her head vehemently. "No way. I don't know how your relationship works, or even how the station works. All I know is what goes wrong when she loses her host, and it's very bad."

"But she's not losing me. I'm going away for a bit, and then I will be back. She'll be asleep, mostly." She cocked her head curiously. "You really don't know why I'm choosing you?"

Mallory shrugged. "No, honestly."

Mrs. Brown clasped her hands together like a preschool teacher about to tell a story to a wiggling class. "Something's off with Eternity. The need for this cave, and saying 'it's fine,' and worst of all, wanting to steer clear of nosy insects tattling to their hivemind. She can't tell me what's off. So, I need someone to watch over her and keep the Sundry out of it."

"Why is she suddenly worried about the Sundry? I thought they got along," Mallory asked, extending her hands to the fire. The cave itself was quite warm, but her fingers were still red with cold.

"You don't seem to have done any research regarding the Sundry's role in the universe," Mrs. Brown said. "This surprises me, considering your experience with them. In fact, I thought they would have told you themselves."

The Sundry. A brilliant, complex hivemind that had come to Earth when Mallory was eight and stung her, giving them a human's eyes to look through, and giving Mallory an inexplicable ability to be drawn toward pockets of high probability of murder. She had left Earth because she was tired of murders, but it seemed that death had followed her to Eternity. On Eternity she had learned about her connection with the Sundry, which had explained her curse/gift a little better. But she hadn't agreed to the connection, and the hivemind terrified her. She had touched it mentally only a few times, and the deluge of data had been overwhelming. So, while Mrs. Brown and Xan had friendly connections with the station and a ship, Mallory was symbiotically connected to a scary hivemind of bugs she was allergic to. Not the ideal relationship.

"Communicating with them isn't fun," she said grimly. "And I can't really trust them. They don't see me as an individual; I'm just another sensory input device."

"Mallory," Mrs. Brown said in her patient-grandmother voice. "Sometimes we have to do what we don't want to do in order to learn things. You have a direct line to a near-omniscient hivemind. Don't ignore that because they were mean to you."

Resentment flared inside Mallory, but she knew that reacting would sound petulant. "If you're so eager to get access to the hivemind, why not let them sting you?" she asked lightly.

Mrs. Brown smiled. "Because I have you." She waved a hand as if hurrying the tense moment past them. "And I have enough to deal with connected to Eternity. And about her, she'll be mostly asleep. She'll keep life support going, and the elevators, monorail, atmosphere, water reclamation, energy; all of that comes from involuntary systems, like our circulatory systems. Think of it like watering a plant while your grandmother is out of town on a cruise."

Yeah, a three-time-murderer grandmother whose plant is a giant station that is sustaining thousands of lives, no biggie.

Mrs. Brown had killed two men in self-defense when she was a young woman, and a few decades later, she had murdered her second husband. She'd killed him in self-defense, but then had tried to cover it up. Coincidentally, her case was the first murder Mallory had ever solved. Mrs. Brown went to prison for ten years. Currently she was technically breaking parole by living aboard Eternity, but humans were desperate to ally with alien races, and, ex-con or not, Mrs. Brown was connected to a sentient space station. The station and everyone on it would be quite upset if humans extradited her, so the federal prison system concerned themselves with just about any problem rather than appeal to bring her home. Mallory figured this made Mrs. Brown the most powerful human in existence.

Mrs. Brown gestured for Mallory to follow her, and they went to the back of the cave, which transitioned slowly from rock and dirt to sleek metal.

"Damned if I know why you don't wear an environmental suit," Mrs. Brown muttered. "You don't have the sense to come in out of the rain." She reached the end of the cave and put her hand on the wall.

"I honestly didn't think Eternity would try to give me frost-bite," Mallory said as a door opened in the cave wall, sliding back to reveal the interior of one of Eternity's many elevators.

"But she told you to wear one, didn't she?" Mrs. Brown said. "You need to listen."

"Fine, the next time Eternity says I will be in a subzero room, I'll put a coat on," Mallory said with a smile.

Mrs. Brown didn't smile back. "Don't be smart, girl. You know what I mean."

The door closed and the lift began to move laterally, then drop into the depths of Eternity.

* * * *

MALLORY WAS GETTING tired of the riddles. She was exhausted from the hike and just wanted to go take a hot shower.

"Next time, you think Eternity could give me a lift to the secret cave? That'd save a lot of effort and frostbitten fingers."

"You're letting the environment distract you." Mrs. Brown faced her and looked up, hands on tiny hips. "You haven't asked the biggest question, Detective."

Mallory raised an eyebrow.

"Why did I ask you, of all people, for help when you're connected to the very beings I'm trying to keep this information from?"

Mallory crossed her arms and thought. It was a good point. Brown had asked for the person who had the biggest connection to the Sundry to hide something from them. Mallory didn't connect with them voluntarily, and she didn't think they could just spy through her eyes and ears if she didn't let them, but she wasn't entirely sure how much the hivemind could take from her if they wanted to. "Yeah, I'm wondering that. So what's the answer?"

The lift came to a stop. Mrs. Brown smiled at her like a dad pulling a station wagon into Disney World. "You're about to see something amazing, and I want to enjoy it while you do. Have you ever wondered how the station operates, how she knows everything that happens?"

Mallory shrugged. "No more than I wonder how a car or computer works. If it works, I don't worry about it."

"The station has symbiotic connections with more than me," she said. The doors opened. "And the Sundry have more connections than just you."

Mallory stepped out of the lift onto a catwalk with a shaft going up and down beyond her line of sight. Around them swarmed Sundry, both blue and silver, creating glittering patterns as they crisscrossed. The noise was almost overwhelming, the buzzing of thousands of wings.

"Holy hell," Mallory said, barely hearing her own voice over the noise.

Mrs. Brown pulled Mallory back into the lift, gently but firmly. The doors didn't close, and they stayed watching the orb created by the constantly flying bodies.

"Easier to hear in here," Mrs. Brown shouted.

"Why are they working together?" Mallory asked. "I thought blue and silver didn't get along."

"The ones with the luxury of being a stand-alone hive can have principles," Mrs. Brown said. "The blue up top are content with gathering data like magpies and shiny things. The traveling silver are always on their way somewhere, but they like dropping in and messing with the blue. I do think they exchange information even during their little skirmishes. But down here, the station needs data and action. It needs communications and navigation. Both Sundry help with all of that."

Mallory stared at the swarm. "What happened when the station nearly self-destructed? Where were they then?"

"Most of them died. There was a port breach."

"How did you replace them? How did I not know about this?"

"I spoke with both silver and blue queens while you were recovering from your injuries," Mrs. Brown said. "They each offered a segment of their population to help out while these queens worked on building up the population again." She waved out at the swarm, then pointed high up a slick wall where two massive paper nests hung, adhering to the wall. "Queens can work hard to build up their population when they're focused on it. They also called some in from other areas, some other stations. And you probably didn't know because you were actively avoiding connecting with the Sundry after you healed."

"Yeah, okay, I need to learn more about them," Mallory allowed. "So, what do I do with this info, exactly? I mean, this is amazing, but I can't do much to affect it."

"You just need to connect with Eternity from time to time. She will tell you if she needs anything. I wanted to show you this because you wondered why I chose you instead of Xan. He connected with *Infinity*, but you connected with the Sundry, who also connect with the station."

"How do I connect with Eternity?" Mallory asked.

"I like to go into my garden and just sit there," Mrs. Brown said. "It's in the Heart. I can get you a cutting of her vines for your apartment so you can do it in private."

Mallory was silent while the lift doors closed, cutting off the incessant humming. The thought of another intimate symbiotic connection with the hivemind made her want to leap off the catwalk and call in dead to work. But she suspected Mrs. Brown thought she was whining, and, deep down, she agreed with the old lady. She tried to sense the Sundry at the edge of her awareness where they usually lurked, but felt nothing.

"Oh, there's one more reason I didn't ask Xan to help out," Mrs. Brown said. "He's going to be mad as hell at me in a little bit."

"Why?" Mallory asked, trying to imagine her quiet, slow-to-anger friend losing his temper.

"I told you, I'm taking *Infinity*. I'm essentially kicking him out of his apartment."

"Oh, no," Mallory said.

"He knows that he doesn't own her. And she will do what her mother tells her to." Mrs. Brown's tone held an undercurrent of unsaid "if she knows what's good for her."

The lift opened to Mallory's hallway. She stepped off but turned when Mrs. Brown held the doors open. "One more thing, dear," she said. "There's another shuttle from Earth coming in a few days. I will try to be back by then, but if I'm not, try to welcome them as best you can."

Mallory nodded, distracted. Her head had started to pound, and she fought a wave of dizziness.

Mrs. Brown watched her for a moment as if expecting something. Mallory stopped rubbing her forehead and asked, "Anything else?"

"No, nothing. Take care of yourself and take care of my station, dear," she said, and the door closed, that curious look finally shut with it.

She trudged down the hall, her room feeling too far away. She shivered, even as sweat broke out on her forehead.

"Christ, what's wrong with me?"

She paused at her apartment door; an audible commotion drifted down the hall from around the corner. Several voices cried out in fear and annoyance, answered by a loud buzz. She recognized the sound at once: a Sundry swarm. A soccer riot had nothing on a Sundry swarm.

Before she could run down the hall and investigate, the swarm rounded the corner and zipped over to Mallory. Hundreds of silver Sundry buzzed angrily, forming a tight little ball in front of her.

"Whoa, what's going on?" she asked, holding up her hands and trying to hide the tremor in her voice. She understood these aliens a little better than most others, but they still scared the shit out of her. And she couldn't hide her fear; these insects could taste her pheromones on the air and know exactly how she was feeling at any time.

Trying to hide her fear was a hard habit to break, however.

The buzzing of hundreds of wings formed words. "Confuse. Obfuscate. Veil. Possible crossroads lie ahead, we don't understand but want to help."

Mallory leaned back from the mass of insects until she

bumped the wall. "But you don't help anyone. You do things that suit yourselves."

The swarm altered slightly to stay a few feet in front of her. "Help. Aid. Support. It has been known to happen," they said.

Mallory glanced around. Blue Sundry usually had a few scouts with her at all times, but she hadn't seen any since she had begun the ridiculous wintry trek to the meeting with Mrs. Brown. Blue Sundry typically didn't like to be around when silver were, especially when their numbers were vastly different.

The Sundry had two factions: the blue insects typically gathered and stored data in their hivemind, and the silver often did more active things, but she hadn't figured out what motivated them. She'd never seen them work together until she saw what powered much of Eternity. Which was probably for the good of everyone else, since a unified group with that much power would be terrifying.

Mallory was connected on a symbiotic level with only the blue Sundry. She had been stung by a silver Sundry a few months earlier and had touched their hivemind, but that connection had faded over the next few days. Her theory was that connections could be made only with the young. The blue sting had happened when she was eight, and the silver had happened when she was thirty-one.

Silver Sundry usually didn't approach her unless they had some kind of demand, and the blue often stepped in to deny them before she could ever respond. Hearing from them now, with an apparent altruistic motivation, was bizarre.

"What do you mean by 'crossroads,' and why are you the ones warning me and not—" Mallory was interrupted by an angry buzz.

"Visit. Join. Farewell. Come see us in the shuttle bay if you need help," the silver swarm said, and moved as one into the ceiling ventilation shaft. "Caution. Confusion. Worry. Don't wait too long."

"Why not wait too long?" she shouted after them. "What's going to happen?" But they were gone.

2

LAW, ORDER, AND TINA

ABOUT ALL XAN Morgan had to his name these days were the clothes on his back, a cell phone good only for the books saved on it, the change in his pockets, and the friendship of (and residency within) a sleek copper sentient shuttle named *Infinity*. Luckily some of that was changing now, with his brother, Phineas, promising to send him a substantial care package on the next Earth shuttle. Unluckily, his brother couldn't send him an apartment, because his current digs were far from Eternity.

He'd barely had time to grab his toothbrush before Mrs. Brown shooed him out of *Infinity*, saying something about a trip she had to take, and Eternity would set him up with a nice apartment, and by the way, the new ambassador is arriving soon and would he be a dear and show her around and help her out however she needed it? Then she took off in his best friend. He'd stood in the shuttle bay and stared at the departing ship, *Infinity*'s regretful apology fading in his mind.

Landlords in the US weren't allowed to kick people out for their own convenience. Of course, they did anyway—Xan had friends who had been tossed out of their apartments—but at least you could challenge that in court if you could afford to.

His temporary room provided by the station wasn't bad, but he hadn't realized how lonely he would be without *Infinity*, so he spent a lot of time at his friend Ferdinand's bar. Currently he was at the bar reading a book while waiting for his lava drink to cool. Ferdinand had modified it to suit a human palate, but it still took a good half hour to cool off before he could drink it.

Ferdinand was a Gneiss, a massive rock alien, stoic but loyal and somewhat friendly. Better than no one. He tried not to think about the near-constant mental presence of *Infinity*.

Ferdinand's bar resembled a cave. It seemed to change according to his mood, being dank and dark some days, and well lit and brightly colored other days. Possibly it reflected Eternity's mood instead, Xan thought. Currently the stone walls had veins of rubies running through the light gray walls, with electric light sconces lighting the walls.

Very few alien races other than Gneiss populated the bar. Xan and Mallory went there for the company instead of the food, very little of which they could eat. His Gneiss friend, made of dark gray shale with silver veins streaking through him, was shorter than most Gneiss, while taller than most humans. Usually calm while everyone else was freaking out, Ferdinand was vibrating audibly.

"Are you all right, Ferd?" he asked, frowning.

"Things are getting complicated," Ferdinand said. "You will see when they get here. Mallory is on her way."

"They" meant Stephanie and Tina, Xan assumed. Two other Gneiss, they had visited their home planet of Bromide to meet with some officials there. They had broken some rules a few months back while on Eternity and had to go home to testify or get punished or something.

Xan wondered what they would do to punish a princess who was in line to rule a whole planet, when that princess had turned herself from a giant statue into a fully armed mech. He couldn't imagine Tina allowing herself to be put in jail. Or accepting any punishment, really.

Stephanie was less blatantly chaotic than Tina, but no less disobedient, since she too had transformed from humanoid to another form. Stephanie had chosen to become a space-worthy shuttle capable of carrying oxygen-breathing life-forms, more useful and less obnoxious than Tina, but it made her physical body limited to the shuttle bay, while Tina still stomped around the station.

The next person to enter the bar was not Gneiss, however, but Mallory. She had dark circles under her eyes and her messy hair was messier than usual. She looked so tired Xan felt exhausted in sympathy.

"What the hell happened to you?" he asked.

"Just a bad day," she said. She slowly climbed onto the stool next to Xan. "A bunch of bad days, actually. Not sleeping much. Ferd, can I have something warm?"

Ferdinand, still vibrating in a way that meant he was having a lively discussion on a frequency only Gneiss could understand, put a stone mug the size of Mallory's head in front of her, full of bubbling lava, then turned to go into the bar's storage area.

"Uh, thanks?" She stared at the drink. "It's going to take me a few hours to get through this. If I can even lift it. What's with him?" she asked Xan, putting her hands around the mug.

"I think Steph and Tina are back," he said. "But he won't tell me anything else. And she . . ." He paused here, the sudden hollowness in his chest startling him.

"And *Infinity* usually gives you the inside scoop since she can understand what the Gneiss are saying," Mallory finished for him, nodding. "You miss her?"

"Yeah. A lot."

"How's the room Eternity gave you?"

He shrugged. "It's fine. I still feel off since they left. It's been over a week. Did Brown tell you how long she'd be gone?"

Mallory shook her head, wincing at something. "No. She did

say there's a human shuttle coming in soon, and she wanted to be back for that but couldn't promise."

Xan braced himself for the freak-out Mallory usually had when she would be around a group of people—he had thought she was exaggerating at first, but he'd seen enough murders happen around her to realize her fears were very valid—but she just sat warming her hands again.

"A human shuttle?" he asked. "And you're cool with this?"

She shrugged. "Yeah, I guess. I mean, I'll have to help Adrian play diplomat, and I feel like crap, so I hope I don't have some kind of alien flu, but it'll be good seeing some people around. And aren't you expecting a care package from Phineas?"

"Mal?" he asked, baffled. "What about your whole 'worry about the inevitable murder' thing? You usually freak out at this point."

She sat, puzzled for a moment. "Oh, yeah, I guess that could happen. I haven't been around a group of humans in a while. I must have forgotten about it."

He stared at her. She had been so sick of murders happening around her that she had left Earth for Station Eternity in a desperate attempt to remove herself from humanity. But then the station's host was murdered, and the violence rippled out from there. They still weren't sure of the death toll, since many had been spaced when Eternity's hull had cracked. Xan had lost a good friend during that time and nearly lost his brother.

Mallory had avoided the next few ships, keeping away from any groups of humans she saw. But just ignoring the possibility? That was shockingly unlike her.

"Guess what?" came a booming voice behind them.

Both humans winced and turned around at the same time.

Tina stood in the door of the bar. Twelve feet tall, dusky pink shale, friendly, lower-than-normal intelligence but higher-than-normal self-awareness. You could possibly say she had a heart of gold in her chest, but really it was a heart of whatever stone you'd most associate with chaos. She was a princess, but Mallory and Xan had privately worried about her eventual subjects, as Tina had none of the diplomacy, restraint, and intelligence that good leaders possessed. But alien politics was far beyond their understanding. Maybe it would be okay.

When Eternity had been falling apart as a result of the cascading events following the first human shuttle arrival, Xan's old army buddy Calliope had been stabbed, and Xan had held her hand while she bled out. While most people donated their bodies to science, Calliope'd had another idea. Her final wish had been to donate her body to . . . Tina.

The humans had just learned that the rocky Gneiss could absorb biomass to hasten their own healing, or, if they weren't injured, their literal evolution to a different form. This was how their friend Stephanie had changed into a shuttle; when Calliope died, Stephanie was already in the process of absorbing a different murder victim to transform herself. Calliope was highly impulsive, headstrong, and a lover of chaos, so she had asked for Tina to take her body instead of asking Xan to return her to Earth for burial.

Tina, who was also impulsive, headstrong, and a lover of chaos, had taken the gift without a second thought and transformed from a lumpy statue-like humanoid to a much larger battle mech, complete with weapons, a jet pack, and the ability to hang out comfortably in vacuum. She was utterly delighted with her new form.

That had been a wild time. They hadn't had the luxury of thinking their actions through (or, to be honest, thinking Tina's actions through), and if anyone had been able to stop and think about it, they would have realized this was a terrible idea. Xan would have been more comfortable with a toddler who'd found a knife and a kitchen torch than with Tina armed with a rocket launcher. Xan also suspected that Tina had ended up with some of Calliope's personality along with the energy from her biomass.

As much as he had liked his old friend, amplifying her personality inside a very powerful alien was not a choice he would have made.

But no one—including the Gneiss—had known this would happen; the action of absorbing alien dead bodies was generally looked down upon by the Gneiss, who had ended that barbaric practice thousands of years earlier. The ruling body back home were furious that not one but two of their kind (and one of them a princess) had done this blasphemous, forbidden action.

A few months back, Ferdinand had left Eternity to get some advice from trusted people on Gneiss worlds, but eventually returned with a summons for Stephanie and Tina to appear on Bromide for trial.

And now they were back. Ferdinand was annoyed, and Tina was loud. (But Tina was always loud.)

The other Gneiss turned as one to see her, then turned back to what they were doing. Tina wasn't terribly popular—she was loud for humans, which meant she was inescapably obnoxious to the Gneiss, who usually spoke in low vibrations. Still, she was fond of the humans, Stephanie was grudgingly her friend, and Ferdinand had an inexplicable devotion to her.

"Welcome home, Tina," Mallory said. "You don't have to yell."

"You sound like them!" Tina said, still loud, pointing at the other Gneiss in the room.

Xan wasn't an expert in alien body language, but he knew the Gneiss better than any other species, and Ferd was stiffer than usual when he emerged from the back room.

"What are we guessing?" Xan asked Tina.

"You haven't guessed yet!" she complained. "Here's a hint. We need to borrow *Infinity*. Can she give us a ride?"

"'Us'? Who is 'us'?" Mallory asked, looking from Tina to Ferdinand. "And why can't Stephanie take you where you need to go?"

"'Us' is me. I'm royal, remember?" Tina asked.

Without prompting, Ferdinand put a bucket-size crystal goblet full of a gray bubbling liquid on the counter. Xan turned away from the acidic smell, his eyes stinging.

"And Stephanie is too exhausted for another deep space trip," Ferdinand said. "Isn't she, Tina?"

"Yeah, we rushed her pretty damn fast," Tina agreed, crossing the room in four strides and lifting the goblet with her mighty fist.

"You rushed?" Xan asked, almost afraid of the answer. "Does that mean the meeting was bad?"

"Oh, it was a disaster," Tina said agreeably. "Total fucking disaster."

Xan glanced at Ferd. "So that's what's got you so mad," he said. "Yes."

XAN HAD NEVER seen his friend this frazzled, and the guy had been sturdy through a lot of shit.

Ferd surprised him by topping off both Xan's and Mallory's scorching-hot drinks, making them undrinkable again. He then picked up both drinks for them. "We need to talk. Shuttle bay."

The humans hurried to catch up to him, with Tina following. The bar was a few floors away from the main shuttle bay, where their friend Stephanie was hanging out, probably yelling at her grandfather, a sullen, monarchy-loving square shuttle. He had evolved over time like Gneiss were supposed to do, not in a day like Stephanie had.

Tina outpaced the humans easily, knocking Mallory out of the way in her hurry to get beside Ferdinand. Xan caught Mallory's arm, startled by how fragile she felt.

Even though the humans couldn't hear the Gneiss, Xan assumed they were arguing.

Stephanie was docked at the far end of the shuttle bay. Xan

looked automatically for *Infinity*, the empty feeling returning when he remembered she wasn't there. Unlike *Infinity*, who looked to be made of shiny bronze, Stephanie looked like a statue of a sleek shuttle carved from adobe. A fissure opened in her side and massive stairs descended. They were better suited to the Gneiss, but Tina reached down and picked up Xan and Mallory in her two fists and tossed them like rag dolls into the ship.

"Fuck, Tina, we're not pets!" Xan protested, rubbing his hip where he had landed. Mallory just groaned where she lay and held her head.

"I was helping!" Tina said, scaling the stairs. Both Gneiss stepped over them, heading for the cockpit. Xan helped Mallory up and they followed.

"Did you hit your head?" he asked.

"No, I just have a headache," she said, stumbling a little bit. He caught her elbow until she steadied herself. "I just need some rest. I've been feeling run-down a lot lately. It started right after my meeting with Mrs. B."

"Must have been some meeting," he said.

They entered the cockpit, where Ferd sat in a captain's chair. Tina lurked by the windscreen, a thick piece of diamond that showed a swimmy view of the shuttle bay outside as ships took off and landed. A small bench sticking out from the wall looked the right size for humans to sit on.

"Hello, friends," Stephanie said around them. The floor vibrated uncomfortably as she spoke, more slowly than usual.

She's spent, thought Xan.

"Tell them what happened," Ferdinand said.

"I wanted to tell them," protested Tina.

"I'm sure you'll add your colorful commentary," Ferdinand said. "But we need to get the story in less than three days, if time is a factor here."

Tina lapsed into silence, pouting. "Fine."

STEPHANIE'S DESCRIPTION OF the home planet of Bromide was definitely beautiful, but clearly deadly to humans. It had raging, thick mercury seas and an atmosphere of sulfur and methane, with yellow clouds roiling overhead, dumping acidic rain and mercury onto the planet below. Right after they took in the beauty of the scene, humans would die as their lungs burned away.

"I still think you should visit sometime; it really is pretty," Tina interjected.

"Tell me why you didn't go, again?" Mallory asked Ferdinand, ignoring her.

"Good question," Xan said. "You're level-headed. Don't your people have the concept of a lawyer?"

"That word is not familiar to me, so probably not," Ferdinand said. "And I, particularly, was forbidden from accompanying them."

"Sounds like they set you up to fail," Xan said. "If they wouldn't let the most logical one of you accompany them."

Stephanie was calmer than Tina, but that calmness had hidden her serious mad-scientist energy. Gneiss appeared to humans to be calm and slow—even stoic and boring—but inside Stephanie's statue-like purple body was a scheming, wild mind. And if she had an idea, she would decide and act on it. She had been the first one to absorb a murder victim to begin her transformation to a shuttle; something that usually took Gneiss hundreds of years to complete had happened in the span of a few minutes.

Yeah, the Gneiss had definitely set Tina and Stephanie up to fail.

"As beautiful as the surface is, most of our people live in a cave system within the mountains," Stephanie said. "Trials are held in a dormant volcano. We like ceremony, and there's nothing so grand as standing inside a hollow mountain and proclaiming that your traditions are law."

"The judge was a real asshole," Tina said. "He was made from the dominant rock compound on the planet, bromide, and was a blocky, important son of a bitch. Didn't even bother looking bipedal. This guy actually rolled! He was a cube, but he tried to roll." She laughed but stopped when no one joined her. "What? He's stupid!"

Xan thought of Phineas, the bizarre sport of his family. Phin had a love for liberal arts, poetry, cooking, and hip-hop and would probably eat this shit up.

"The other elevated Gneiss like us, the ships, were also in attendance," Stephanie continued. "Everyone from my own grandfather to the twins Eric and Erica, my cousins who became armed ships of black and white marble. Even the matriarch."

She paused.

"Are we supposed to ask about her, or just be impressed she was there?" Xan finally asked. "I'm not getting the relevance."

"The matriarch is a four-thousand-year-old Gneiss named Premee who evolved into a massive battleship. Rumor has it that she waged war on carbon-based beings in order to consume them, and she's one of the reasons the tradition was changed."

"So a war criminal?" Mallory asked.

"When you evolve into the biggest battleship your people have ever seen, and you sleep all the time, people don't try to punish you so much as use you as a cautionary tale," Stephanie said. "You'd think she would be on my side, but she rarely wakes up for anything and was only there as a spectator."

"Until the shooting started, at least," Tina reminded her.

"Hang on, the shooting?" Xan asked, staring at Tina. He hated admitting it, but he felt somewhat responsible for Tina, since he still saw some Calliope in her. The Gneiss hadn't said any part of the dead person's personality would stick around after a Gneiss absorbed them, but Tina now seemed impulsive on a disaster-seeking level, very reminiscent of Calliope.

Calliope would have loved knowing she was part of a huge chaos mech.

Both Gneiss had transformed using ancient techniques that Gneiss had used when the people were less friendly with alien species and would consume their bodies after battles. Steph and Tina didn't quite understand everything going on and were even worse at explaining it to humans.

"We're getting ahead of ourselves," Stephanie said. "When the trial started, they said the crimes were blasphemy in accelerating the natural progression of things, taking the biomass of another species without permission, insulting our ancestors, assault on the sleeping, provocation of our betters, revealing our ways to the lesser, soft species, transformation to a forbidden form—"

"That's a lot more than you said you were charged with!" Mallory said.

"They had time to think up new ones," Ferdinand said.

"But are they all traditionalist and fussy like this?" Xan said. "I mean, every single Gneiss group on every single planet? There have got to be billions of your people; surely someone thinks differently."

"We're a special case," Stephanie said. "Tina is royalty and I'm considered part of her entourage, even though I've never said I wanted that role. So I'm a bad influence, and she's going to rule a planet someday."

"I expect that if only Stephanie had transformed without permission, word wouldn't have even gotten back to Bromide," Ferdinand said. "Tina's situation is what concerns them."

"What's funny is that people on Bezoar are very laid-back," Tina said. "They won't have a problem with me being like this."

"Sounds like you really committed the high crime of 'not the way your parents did it,'" Mallory said, leaning her head against Stephanie's wall and closing her eyes.

"That's it exactly!" Tina said. "I got up and said that on Eternity, I have had more fun and learned more about the universe than any other time in my life! Stephanie and Ferdinand and our human friends listen to me and treat me like an equal. Unlike all of you!"

That wasn't exactly true. Stephanie had not hidden her disdainful opinion about Tina in any way. She thought Tina was not terribly smart and possibly a danger to them all. Stephanie was a fair person, though, and had fully admitted when Tina had been helpful and loyal, and Tina had saved Stephanie, Xan, and Mallory when she had launched her new mech form on a suicide mission to force a Gneiss shuttle to stop attacking them. Stephanie's shuttle grandfather was a monarchy-loving obsequious toady who broke off his attack on them to save Tina, which was her plan all along.

Her friends had admitted that they hadn't thought she was capable of this level of manipulation.

Stephanie's grandfather considered himself a hero now, even though he had caused the dangerous situation in the first place. He now spent his time in the shuttle bay telling the story of saving the princess of Bezoar to any ship listening, even ones that weren't sentient, "just in case."

Stephanie was utterly disgusted with him.

But the group had new grudging respect for Tina, even though she was wilder and more chaotic than ever, now that she had weapons and had been influenced by a soldier who was a gestalt of skills. Calliope had been terrible at individual skills and very, very good at doing things all at the same time.

"You said all this at a trial?" Mallory asked, lifting her head to stare at Tina. "And Steph let you?"

"Tina was determined to make her case," Stephanie said. "She's a princess and has to learn to speak for herself someday."

"And this seemed like the best time to let her do that?" Disbelief dripped from Mallory's voice.

"You weren't there," Stephanie said.

"Then it got really cool!" Tina said. "Stephanie started yelling, she said, 'Honored judge and other distinguished or whatever! The real question here is not whether blasphemy laws have been broken, but that the laws are antiquated and pointless. Achieving a higher form has always been a goal of our kind. How have Tina and I broken that? Where in your holy texts does it say that we must adhere to a specific timeline while waiting to evolve and ascend?' Or something to that effect."

"That was pretty much verbatim," Stephanie allowed. "But they didn't listen. They said the past was barbaric, it encouraged the devouring of lesser races, we moved beyond that, we're peaceful—"

"Even though we didn't kill anyone to take their biomass!" Tina said, stamping her foot. "But they were all, like, 'And you think that everyone who wants to ascend will follow that rule? You think the people on Bezoar won't start hunting the lower life-forms to get off that planet?'"

"Why did they single out that planet?" Xan asked.

Tina ignored him. "And I said, 'Because supporting the people of Bezoar is my future. And I plan on setting up a deal with the humans for them to supply us their dead so that every one of my subjects who wishes to ascend can do so!'"

"And that's when the shooting started," Stephanie said into the shocked silence.

"LET'S BACKTRACK A minute. Why are you suddenly sending dead bodies to Bezoar?" Xan asked.

"Yeah, we haven't heard you say anything about it besides it's a shithole planet," Mallory added.

Xan nodded at her. "And what was that about having a deal with humans to take our dead? I'm not sure who on Earth would agree to that."

"I was bluffing," Tina said. "But it is on my list of things to do when I get my diplomatic shoes on and go stomping around the galaxy."

Shoes? Gneiss didn't wear shoes. There was definitely some Calliope in Tina.

"Have we never told you about Bezoar?" Stephanie asked. "Bezoar is a prison planet for more races than the Gneiss. It's a terrible place, so no one wants to claim it, but it sustains life, more or less, for oxygen breathers, so that's where most ship their unwanted."

"Yes, it's been a shithole prison for hundreds of years," Tina said.

"Why does a prison planet need a queen? Shouldn't it have a warden? Someone in security?" Xan asked, trying to imagine Tina as a prison guard.

"Not everyone there is a criminal. It's less a punishment and more a place to put people you don't want," Ferdinand said. "There is a group there who try to make the planet more habitable. Tina's family manages those."

"So, yeah, they didn't like that," Tina said impatiently, "and one of the terrible twins fired on us, and then Steph was all, 'I'm out.' So she flew off and I followed her. They tried to fire on us again, and old Granny Premee got really mad and started spinning and throwing her escape pods at us, but we dodged and stuff, and got out of there! It was awesome!"

Xan noticed that the translation bug attached to his auditory nerve gave more inflection to Tina's voice than to those of the other Gneiss. Something else he wondered if Calliope had anything to do with.

"You say it was awesome because you didn't get hit," Stephanie said.

Mallory sat up in alarm. "Are you okay?"

"Yeah, I'll get it fixed," Stephanie said. "Didn't appreciate it, though. Always hated those cousins. It wasn't as clean as Tina implies, but we got out of there, I got her aboard, and we got back here as fast as we could. But I can only assume they're sending someone after us."

"Which is why we need to get out of here. I figure Bezoar is our safest place to be. Can *Infinity* take us?"

Mallory and Xan exchanged a look. Mallory nodded to him to deliver the bad news.

"Sorry, Tina, but no. *Infinity's* gone. Mrs. Brown needed her. We don't know when she'll be back," he said.

"Well, shit," Tina said.

"And let's just gloss over the fact that you were going to leave Stephanie here to deal with the coming mob," Mallory said.

"Oh, she'll be fine. I'm the one they want," Tina said. "They're really scared about what I'll do with Bezoar if I take the throne."

They weren't the only ones.

"I guess I'll have to figure something else out," Tina said, and left the cockpit.

3

. . .

THE RELUCTANT HOSTESS

THE HUMANS LEFT Stephanie with Ferdinand still aboard. Stephanie said she needed to rest and talk to Ferd, while Mallory was worn out from whatever minor bug was bothering her. The headache was killing her by this time.

Xan exited the shuttle in front of her, took two steps to the right, and then stopped as he realized *Infinity* wasn't there. "Damn," he muttered.

"I know you miss her," Mallory said. She wondered if anyone would ever miss her like that.

"I just wish she'd said when they were coming back," Xan said.

"That's rough," Mallory said. She'd checked on Eternity a few days after Mrs. Brown had left, and things had been calm. But after she got sick, days passed where she just forgot about Eternity altogether. "Right now I'm going home to crash—" Her watch, a gift from the station herself, beeped, and she swore. It was a message from Adrian, asking if he could come visit her.

"Do you have to let him in?" asked Xan, looking at her watch as she frowned at it.

"Mrs. Brown asked me to help with the incoming humans, so I'd better see what he wants." She rubbed her head again, then messaged him to come see her at her apartment.

"I'd offer you some painkillers, but my medicine cabinet flew away," Xan said.

"I've got some back at my room." She heard a rushing in her ears like there was a mountain creek nearby, and stumbled against the wall. Xan righted her, worry creasing his face.

"You don't seem okay," he said from very far away. She squinted at him. He seemed to be behind a haze of green, like a filter had been raised between them.

The dizziness passed and she took some deep breaths. "I'll be fine. I'll see Adrian and then go straight to bed, promise."

"Okay," he said doubtfully. "We don't know what kinds of bacteria and viruses aliens have that can kill humans. Don't be a hero here, Mal."

She waved her hand at him. "I'll be fine."

MALLORY PAUSED OUTSIDE her apartment. Her legs ached and she longed for a tub to soak in. It struck her, the strange things she missed. Potato chips. Bathtubs. Trashy celebrity gossip. Eternity had approximated a human apartment well, but there were still some luxuries that Mallory had never known were luxuries until she didn't have them anymore. Like tubs and gossip.

She went inside, opened a bottle of wine, and right after she collapsed into her chair, the door dinged.

She hadn't seen Adrian, the former Earth ambassador, very much since the time when his ambitious attempt to take over as Eternity's new host ended in such horror and bloodshed. He had turned out to be woefully opportunistic, but not a murderer, but it didn't make her like him more.

He had mellowed considerably—a near-death experience can do that, she figured—but he was still an abrasive pain in the ass. He kept to himself, and she was fine with that. But there were four permanent resident humans aboard the station, so they should attempt to stick together.

She opened the door.

Adrian stood there, arms crossed. His messy brown hair hung in his face, something he hadn't bothered to change, since he hid the mess that was his eyes with a bandage.

"Come on in," she said.

A small silver drone with scorch marks and a few dents hovered near his shoulder, bumping him on occasion. The drone herded him, pushing him in the direction it wanted him to go. When he stopped, he held his hand out and the drone plopped into it with a sound of decreasing whirring that sounded like a sigh.

Adrian had gotten rid of his three-piece suits and was now clothed in a long robe, like an extra from an American movie about a white Christ. Mrs. Brown had offered to get him better clothes, but apparently he was embracing this attempt to be humble. Mallory would have bought this new personality if he had dropped some of the attitude, but that might be requiring too much from him.

"Do you want some water or wine or something?" she asked. "I opened some red."

"Red is fine," he said. Mallory pressed a mug into his hand. His hands felt around the mug, identifying it as not-wineglass, and he smiled slightly. "Wine in a mug? How hospitable. Have you gotten your full dinette set purchased?"

Mallory snorted. "I'm waiting for the wedding registry to do that. And, Adrian, you served me recycled tea bags once. You're a pot, I'm a kettle. Now, what can I do for you?"

"There's a human shuttle that's arriving soon, and we are throwing a reception for them," he began.

"I know, Mrs. Brown told me," she said, motioning him to speed it up.

"With the station's host out of town, welcoming falls to us," he said importantly. "I am hosting the party Saturday and would like you to co-host it with me, as the other legitimate human representative."

Adrian resented Xan for arriving on the station when he, Adrian, was supposed to be the only human there. He also resented Mrs. Brown for connecting as the station's host when Eternity had nearly killed him, but she was too powerful for him to disdain openly.

"Sure, I'll help. What do I have to do?" she asked, rubbing her face in an attempt to wake up.

"Just look less rumpled than you usually do, comb your hair or something, be friendlier than you normally are," Adrian said. "We can welcome them as they come in. I've gotten a Gurudev restaurant to host the party; they've been the most open to carrying our food and drink. Then, you know, mingle. Welcome people. Apologize to them that the station's host isn't here to welcome them."

Mallory laughed. "So many backhanded compliments, so little time." She frowned slightly. "I don't think there were any compliments in there, actually. And, Adrian, I'm not going to help you shit-talk Mrs. Brown to people from home. Nice try, though."

His mouth went flat. "Fine. Come for the free booze and food."

"I'll be there. Where is it?"

"Green Grasses restaurant," he said. "Come by my apartment and we'll go together." He paused. "You look like hell, by the way."

She bristled. "Come on, cut me some slack. I'm not feeling great, and then Tina—" She frowned at him. "Wait a second, I thought you lost your sight when you tried to jump into Eternity's driver's seat."

He still had a blindfold over his scarred face. A thin smile spread across his lips. "You're usually quicker than that. Devanshi has been working with the translation device technology—"

"Just call it a Babel fish, Adrian," Mallory said, downing her own mug of wine. She referred to the little fish from *Hitchhiker's Guide to the Galaxy* that lived in people's ears and translated for them. "It's easier that way."

"That's not what the aliens call it," he said stiffly. "Anyway, using that tech with the Sundry's information on human anatomy, we have a prototype of eye tech for me. There's a small implant here"—he lifted his messy bangs and pulled his blindfold down about an inch to show a small gold disc embedded in his forehead—"that receives data from a camera in Sprocket." He gestured to the drone, which had taken flight and perched on Mallory's lampshade.

Their Phantasmagore friend Devanshi's specialty, since leaving security, was drone programming, but this was above and beyond impressive.

"Isn't that awkward, though, seeing yourself from the outside?" she asked.

"I did vomit a few times before getting used to it," he admitted.

"Why not just put a camera on your person?" she asked.

"I'm trying to get used to seeing things from all angles," he said.

"Or creep on other people," she said, frowning at him. "Do not send your little drone into my room, Adrian."

He snorted. "That is so far outside my plan for this." He turned to face the door, and the drone came to life and whirred toward him. "So you're good to host the party with me? Just like that?"

"Why do people keep treating me like I'm a soufflé they're afraid to walk around?" Mallory said, rubbing her forehead. "Yes, I'm fine, I will help you welcome the humans. Anything else?"

"No, nothing," he said mildly. "I wanted you to know we will have some doctors coming. If there's anything you—or Xan—need, they might be able to help."

"I'm fine," she said, annoyed at the subtle request for personal information. Then, without irony, she said, "I've got a mega headache. Are we done? I need to lie down."

She pushed the button to slide the door open, but Adrian stopped in the middle of the doorway. "I have to ask, Mallory. I expected you to worry about your whole murder thing with the arrival of the shuttle. But you don't sound like you're carrying on about inevitability and the probability of bloodshed like you usually do."

She shrugged. "I've had some kind of low-grade bug, so I'm not getting that anxiety spike anymore. Who knows? Maybe I'm mellowing. I'll see you Saturday."

The door closed behind him and she staggered to her bed and lay down on top of the covers. She closed her eyes but opened them when she heard some buzzing.

Above her, two blue insects held tight to the ceiling. They resembled Earth wasps except they were as long as her thumb and much, much smarter. As she looked up at them, they buzzed their wings briefly at her.

"Hey, gals," she said. "Nothing interesting to see here. I'm just napping." They buzzed and flew off, but Mallory knew they wouldn't go far. The insects followed her all the time, whether in public or private, bedroom or bathroom. They patrolled around the ceiling of her small apartment every time Mallory came home. Mallory never knew what they were checking for, and even if they wanted to, they usually couldn't tell her, since she would need at least four of them to communicate. Two was the usual number of her companions. She found that if she concentrated, she could tell them apart, and sometimes even tell their moods. But right now her head hurt too much to wonder about them.

MALLORY HAD MADE a sort of truce with the Sundry. Her grudge lurked in the back of her mind like a cousin in an ill-fitting suit refusing to dance at a wedding.

Sundry stings were excruciating, the knifelike stingers cleanly injecting venom in at least five—she'd lost count after that—quick jabs. Mallory had no idea if she was an outlier, but she was pretty sure it was the first encounter with the Sundry that caused her allergy to bees when she was a child.

What she didn't know until her second sting was that the Sundry venom, which already had several medical uses, could connect their hivemind to their victim (if the victim survived). According to the Sundry, it was this connection that caused Mallory to be subconsciously attracted to places where murders were likely to happen. She was drawn to pockets of strife and able to spot important clues that most people overlooked (to law enforcement's irritation and embarrassment). Mallory didn't quite understand it, but she wasn't that eager to do more research. She'd been connected to the hivemind, trying to stop the serial killer, when her body nearly died. The hivemind had been all too willing to hold on to her, and it had been a close call to get her body breathing again and her mind returned to where it belonged.

The temporary sting had given her a frightening deluge of information that was nearly impossible to sift through to find anything useful, like reading all of Wikipedia in a minute. She had wondered if she could communicate on a nonverbal yet not overwhelming level without being stung, but didn't trust the Sundry to let her experiment.

Everything humans had been told about alien symbiotic relationships indicated they were all consensual and beneficial to both parties. If she concentrated on the hivemind, sometimes they were able to use her as eyes and ears, and she could be just another scout to study an area and a situation, but that was a one-way benefit. She didn't know what she got out of them using her senses.

On rare occasions, usually when she was about to fall asleep, she could gently touch the scouts in her proximity, getting another view of her surroundings through their compound eyes. But she refused to attempt more than that, actively resisting entering the always-hungry maw that binged on information all the time.

Her two scouts flew back into the room, perching on her dresser, buzzing their wings in alarm. But Mallory only had a moment to register this before falling asleep.

She woke up three days later, in the medbay.

4

NOT MY CAT, NOT MY ROCKING CHAIR

MALLORY WAS MIA. Ferdinand was spending a lot of time with Tina. With *Infinity* gone, Xan had had nowhere else to turn, so he knocked on Stephanie's hatch to air his frustrations.

"So your concern is our friends aren't upset enough?" Stephanie asked after he explained what was going on. "I'm actually relieved that Tina has calmed considerably."

"You know how Mal gets when she's around a group of humans. She's like a cat in a room full of rocking chairs. And since you got back, Tina has been really relaxed about the fact that she can't get off the station and run away. Aren't your people coming for her? Shouldn't she be worried?"

"I need about another day of rest and then I can take her away," Stephanie said. "I asked around the bay; no one wants to give her a shuttle and risk angering the Gneiss ruling body. Not even my grandfather will obey her on this."

"But you can't take her far, can you?" Xan asked. "Not somewhere that they can't follow, so you'll keep wearing yourself out running, and they will eventually catch up with you." He thought for a moment. "Maybe she knows being caught is inevitable and has made her peace with that."

Stephanie laughed. Gneiss laughter was not something he heard very often, and the sound always startled him. Her voice was like rocks grinding together. "You know Tina. She has never made peace with anything. Accepting a bad situation is boring to her. Fight, run, or trick—that was her motto growing up."

"Trick?" he asked. "Was she smart enough for that?"

"Rarely," Stephanie said. "But she considered it an option. I'll see what Ferd says about her, and see if I can get anything about her state of mind. But what about Mallory? She's not worried that murder is coming to the station again?"

"She doesn't seem to be. I figured she'd be coming to you to ask for a ride off the station," he said.

"Maybe she only gets worried when there definitely will be a murder," Stephanie mused.

He shook his head, gazing out her diamond shield to the shuttle bay. "No, there's not always a murder, but she's always worried about it. Something is weird."

"Have you talked to her?" Stephanie asked.

"Not in a few days," he said. "I figured she's getting ready for the reception."

"Tina and Ferdinand are coming," Stephanie said right before there was a pounding on the bottom deck.

"You didn't tell me there was a party," Tina accused her when they came aboard.

"You know there's no party until you get here," Xan said.

"You flatter me," Tina boomed, towering above him. "Keep doing it."

"Hey, Tina, are you worried about the Gneiss following you here, since we can't get you off the station in time?" Xan asked.

"Not really," Tina said. "I've gone cuckoo. This whole place is cuckoo."

"I guess you can get wildly Zen about it, sure," Xan said after an uncomfortable pause.

"I'll be fine," Tina said. "I think I'm finally learning!"

Xan looked at the captain's chair (a polite addition Stephanie put in the cockpit since she was technically her own pilot), the place where he had decided to look when addressing the person who was the ship itself. "Steph, are you worried about retaliation?"

"Kind of," Stephanie said. "I have some thoughts on how to deal with it, but I don't have the option of getting in another shuttle to get out of here."

"Don't worry about it. I have it under control," Tina said. She patted the chair.

"Never pat me again," Stephanie said.

MALLORY WASN'T ANSWERING messages sent either to her watch or to her home terminal. He tried contacting her new office terminal and then tried visiting her new office, situated near the main marketplace and park area. Finally, he knocked on her door.

No answer. He was starting to get worried.

"Eternity, is Mallory home? Can you tell me if she's okay?" he asked out loud, but the station didn't respond. She didn't always respond when the humans asked for things (which was another reason why he missed *Infinity*), but he really didn't have high hopes this time since Mrs. Brown was gone.

He messaged Stephanie on his watch. "She's not answering the door. I can't find her anywhere."

"I'll ask around the Gneiss to see if anyone has seen her," Stephanie replied. When they spoke among themselves through vibrations, Gneiss communication was usually public. Not a lot of secrets in that community, he guessed.

"Xan can't get into a room?" he could hear Tina asking over the link. "I can help!"

"No, do not bust any doors down, Tina!" Xan said. He left another message for Mallory and then went to his own temporary room.

He paced the floor a moment and then swallowed his dislike and made a call on the wall terminal.

"What do you want?" Adrian Casserly-Berry was never happy to see or hear Xan. He stood at the other end of the video call, head bowed, with a drone hovering by his shoulder. He had traded his robes for a suit, and his messy hair was tied back.

"I can't find Mallory anywhere, so I wanted to see if she was with you. You've got that reception thing soon, right?"

"Tonight, yes," Adrian asked. "And Mallory had better be here for it."

"Yeah, your threats don't carry a lot of weight if she's not around to hear them. Let me know if you hear from her, all right?"

There was silence on the other side, Adrian's head still bowed.

"Adrian?" Xan asked. "You okay?"

"I would say I can't believe she would leave me in the lurch like this, but I can believe it," he said, his shoulders tight. "I have to go meet the shuttle shortly. What am I going to tell them? The station host is gone, the mystery writer is gone, and the only ones left are the AWOL soldier and me. Mallory is untrustworthy."

Brave card for him to play considering he had jumped at the opportunity to leave his ambassador position to take over the station when it presented itself. But Xan had learned a bit about diplomacy himself in the last few years.

"I'd hoped you might be concerned about her, but if you're so worried about being the only human to host your reception, I was also calling to tell you that I'll be there," he offered.

Adrian chuckled bitterly. "In your bloodstained T-shirt and dirty jeans? No, thank you."

"My brother is sending me a package with the shuttle," Xan said. "I'm also supposed to meet the new ambassador. Mrs. B's orders. But if you don't want my help, that's cool."

He raised his hand to terminate the call, but Adrian lifted his head and held up his hand.

"No, wait," he said, sounding like the words were hard to form. "If you can look presentable, and we don't find Mallory, then, yes, I'll take your minuscule offer."

"Can't wait to see you at the party, Adrian," Xan said dryly. "You must be a real hit in social situations."

He severed the call and tried to check with the station logs to find out when the shuttle from Earth would arrive, but Eternity didn't respond. He shrugged and picked up the novel he had borrowed from Mallory, one of her murder mysteries.

He put it down after a moment. Where the hell was she?

AN HOUR LATER, Tina pounded on his door. He knew it was Tina because it was loud and it sounded like the thumping was coming from near the ceiling. Also, it was obnoxious.

He jumped up and opened the door before she could dent it.

Tina stood there, huge right fist raised to pound again, with Mallory draped over her left forearm. Mallory looked terrible, worn-out, sweaty, and unconscious.

"What the hell, Tina?" he blurted. "Where did you find her?"

"She was in her room, like you said," Tina said. "I tried to talk to her and wake her up but she didn't move. So I remembered that humans should move when you poke them, and I brought her here."

Xan winced as he saw the bruise starting to flower on her cheek. Tina's pokes were not friendly things, no matter the intent behind them. He felt Mallory's head and found her burning with fever.

"We need to get her to the medbay," he said. "Can you carry her?"

"Carry her?" Tina asked. "I can do more than that!" The jets on her back fired, scorching the metal floor and raising her a few feet in the air. "Let's go!"

"You don't need to do that, you damn fool!" Xan yelled as she zoomed down the hall. He ran to catch up.

Tina rounded a corner and then yelled in surprise. More people yelled, and there was a great crash.

When Xan caught up, Tina was sitting on the floor, leaning against the dented wall. The jets on her back fired a few times and then guttered out. The Gneiss trio she had run into lay a few feet down the hall, toppled like bowling pins.

At least she ran into someone as hard as she is, Xan thought, but then he checked on Mallory.

She had a bump and a cut on her forehead, which trickled blood. "Christ, Tina, you're going to kill her trying to get her to medbay! And I ain't your mom, but no jet packs in the hallway! Someone's going to get hurt. Give me Mallory and you apologize to those people right now."

"I was just being fucking metal," she said, a petulant tone coming across the translator.

"I know. That's the problem," he said, lifting Mallory off her forearm.

THE MEDBAY WAS a mess, with wall terminals blinking and confused medical staff running around trying to get data out of any device.

Chaos or not, the Gneiss orderlies who spotted him efficiently came by to take Mallory from him and put her on a bed. Xan was gratified to see some doctors he knew had treated humans before. One approached him, a short Gurudev named Pax.

"What happened this time?" she asked.

"I don't know. She's had a headache, then I didn't see her for a few days, then we found her passed out like this."

"And the facial injuries?" Pax said, touching Mallory's face lightly.

"You've met Tina, right? Giant, even for a Gneiss, enthusiastic about everything, including trying to wake a friend up?"

"Ah, I've heard of her," Pax said. "The problem right now is our medical systems are down. I can examine her as best I can, but I probably can't make a real diagnosis until we get back online."

"Hell," he muttered. "I'll be back to check on her in a few."

HE PINGED STEPHANIE. "Has the human shuttle arrived yet?"

"It just got here. I don't recommend coming down, though. It's chaotic."

"Chaotic? How?" he asked. The only time he'd seen the shuttle bay chaotic was when thousands of aliens were trying to leave Eternity at once.

"Traffic control went down, and the poor Phantasmagore had to manually help land the shuttles that were already on their way in. There are a bunch of shuttles outside still, and no one knows what's going on."

"Station comms are down, medbay is down, now traffic control," Xan muttered. "Eternity must really be missing Mrs. Brown."

Xan went back to his room to get cleaned up. Tina sat inside his door, curled up as best she could on his bed. The bed, designed for a human's weight, had collapsed.

"Tina. What are you—How did you—" He took a deep breath. "Why?"

"I didn't want to make the medbay more cuckoo than it was," she said. "So I thought I'd wait here. It's a small room, so I had to curl up."

"And bust my bed, thanks," he said.

"You're welcome," she said. "Is Mallory alive?"

"As far as I know, but medbay systems are down, so they can't do much for her now."

"Everything's cuckoo," Tina said. "It'll get better."

"Sure," Xan said with a shrug. "You need to leave; you're too big for this room, and I need to clean up and get changed. If my package gets here in time, that is."

She perked up, raising her head. "You need something? I can help!"

"I don't think you can get my package for me, Tina, don't worry about it. They'll deliver it," he said, stripping off his T-shirt. "But you do need to go."

"No, it's already done, you'll have your package! I'll see to it!" Tina rolled awkwardly off his bed with a mighty thump and scooched across the floor until she could unfold herself in the hall, which was made to accommodate all sizes.

"Tina, don't—" he said. Then he sighed. With three long strides, she was gone.

"Like she said, everything's crazy right now," he muttered, and closed his door, making sure to lock it.

When he got out of the shower, he found a large box sitting neatly inside the door.

5

WARNINGS, LIKE DREAMS, DON'T MAKE SENSE UNTIL IT'S TOO LATE

THE PLEASANT STEWARDESS, complete with little hat and tight pencil skirt, pleasantly handed Mallory a flute of pleasant champagne and a pair of binoculars. "Don't check the closet, please," she said pleasantly.

This is pleasant, thought Mallory.

She took her seat beside her tenth-grade homeroom teacher, buckled her seat belt, and looked out the window with the binoculars.

The lenses were green, giving the world a swimmy, sickly hue. When she pulled them away from her face, she saw mountain ranges below the plane. When she put them to her eyes again, she saw her best friend from high school, Amy, shielded by a boy.

Mallory couldn't see the boy's face, but she was simultaneously pulled toward him and repelled by him. She wanted to look past him to see her friend Amy Valor, but he kept shifting, and she couldn't see around him.

Behind Amy loomed a door large enough for Tina to get through, garishly colored pink, with blood droplets beading on the door like sweat.

From far away, a voice said her name. She wanted to ignore it, focus on the boy's face, or find out what Amy was hiding in the closet.

"Mallory."

She thrashed on the bed, hands tangling in the soft sheet that covered her. Her chest constricted, cutting off her breath. She gasped, feeling like a fish flopping on a hot dock.

Confined, hot, dark, can't breathe. One yearning, sharp pain in her chest, like falling in love at fifteen, and then—

—severed—

Then nothing.

"WE DON'T KNOW what is wrong with her," a voice was saying. It was flat and emotionless, an alien speaking through the translator bug, which often failed to parse emotional inflections. "Her system seems stable, however."

"She looks terrible," a voice said.

"She's sick," another voice said. "This is medbay. Did you miss that part?"

"Just let me have a moment with her, okay?"

"No, she needs a sedative, and you need to leave."

"Fine. Tell her I dropped by and I'm looking forward to seeing her."

"I will. Get out."

"I am really looking forward to it, Mallory." The voice was soft and slid into her ear like a small boning knife sliding into a neck, severing an artery and ending a life. Then it was gone.

The body is in the closet. It's in the closet. There's blood. The closet. He's in the closet and you need to find him.

She thrashed again, the hot taste of blood on her tongue.

"Humans are strange," the alien said, smoothing the sheet over Mallory. A flat, cool disc was placed on her forehead. "This should calm you down."

The images left her; she breathed better, and slept.

• • •

"SOMEONE CAME TO see her. A human. She's still out."

Mallory opened her eyes. She felt exhausted and dehydrated. Hair stuck to her forehead and she brushed it away with impatience.

A Phantasmagore face peered down at her. Scrunched low, Tina's bulk stood beyond the nurse.

"Am I in medbay?" she croaked, looking around.

"You've been dead for a few days," Tina supplied.

"No," the nurse said, looking at Tina. "Just unconscious."

"What's wrong with me?" she asked, looking down at her body under the sheet, trying to find an injury.

"We don't know, but you seem to be all right now," the nurse said. "We've had some diagnostic difficulties of late."

"Absolutely cuckoo around here," Tina confirmed. "But things are getting better. You're awake. Now Xan can stop worrying and the ambassador can have you join him. Did you hear? There's a party tonight!"

"Tina, why are you here?" Xan asked, his voice tired. Mallory craned her head off the bed to see him as he slid with difficulty past Tina's bulk.

"Who came to see her?" he asked the nurse.

"I don't know, humans look the same to me," the nurse said, looking at a tablet. "Ask her."

Mallory grimaced and tried to sit up. Xan came to the bedside.

"Jesus, you scared us," Xan said. "What the hell happened to you?"

She blinked a few times. "No idea," she said. "How did I get here?"

Xan paused, then said, "Tina and I brought you—"

"I would have brought you faster than he did, but we had a disagreement," Tina said.

Xan glared at her, then looked back at Mallory. "You weren't answering any comms and I was worried about you. Tina got into your apartment and found you unconscious. The computers have been going a little wild since Mrs. B left, so the docs here didn't know what was wrong with you."

She accepted a cup of water from the nurse. "How long was I out?"

"I don't know when you passed out," he said, "but it's Saturday."

"Jesus," she said. She pushed her sweaty bangs out of her eyes, fingers touching the cool disc on her forehead. "Uh, what's this?" she asked, picking at the edges with her fingernails.

"It regulated your temperature," the nurse said. "Leave it on for now."

"I think I'm okay," she said. "The headache's gone. I just feel like I need a shower and some real sleep."

Xan shook his head. "You're going to want to be around tonight. We need you at the Earth reception."

"I can't call in sick?" she asked incredulously.

"You can," he said carefully. "I just said you will want to be around tonight. Or maybe you won't, actually."

"Xan, people don't think real clearly after a coma," Mallory said, groaning. "Or at least I don't. What are you talking about?"

"An old friend of yours was on this shuttle," he said. "That's all Adrian said, but he thinks you should be there."

"A friend?" Mallory asked, thinking. She hadn't left many friends on Earth. Her lack of friends was one of the reasons she had decided to leave.

"Adrian was mad that you were out of commission." Xan grimaced. "That fucking guy."

"Great." Mallory scrubbed her face with her hands and took a deep breath to try to wake up. "Do I have time to shower and make a late entrance, or would Adrian rather me be on time looking like this?"

Xan grinned at her. "Get the shower. I'll tell him you're coming."

As he left, she got off the cot, gingerly putting her feet on the cold metal floor. The nurse brought her shoes and socks to her.

"Did I hear you telling Xan someone came to see me? I think I remember that," she said.

"Yes, a human came to see you a few hours ago," the nurse said. "I don't know who it was."

She tried to think back to the voice, and the anxiety it had ignited in her stomach, but it was a haze. "I can't remember," she said.

"Probably doesn't matter," Tina said helpfully. "Want me to take you to your apartment?"

Xan poked his head back into the room. "Do NOT let Tina take you anywhere. Tina, we talked about this."

"I'm helpful!" Tina said. "Didn't I rescue her?"

"You did," he said. "But wait till she asks how she got those bruises."

ETERNITY'S SOCIAL AREA for most oxygen breathers resembled a park, if it was drawn by a human child with crayons. The trees were purple, the sky was a dull orange with a fake sun crawling across it, and the green area was surrounded by a wide walkway and a series of smaller kiosks and larger freestanding buildings for restaurants and services (the classic doctor, dentist, the Gneiss filer, which Mallory kept meaning to ask her friends about—what did they file there?), and a few art galleries from different races. Many of the restaurants were clumped together, with a general outdoor seating area like a mall food court, only classier and more alien, with many different sizes of furniture.

Mallory stood outside the Gurudev restaurant, pretending she was a Phantasmagore and blending into the background. It failed immediately when Adrian met her at the door, wearing a three-piece suit, his blindfold, and his little drone on his shoulder. "Figured you'd be late," he said.

"Thanks, Adrian, I'm feeling a lot better," she said.

"Actually, I'm surprised you're here at all. I expected you to have a panic attack and run away."

His hurtful comment aside, Mallory realized what was missing: her anxiety. She was used to approaching crowds of people with a sick feeling of dread, expecting murder and mayhem to follow.

She shrugged. "Yeah, I don't know. Maybe it's because I was sick. Do you want me to leave? Because I could really use some more rest."

"Nice try," he said. "You're not getting out of here. I need you."

"Have you met the ambassador yet?" she asked.

"Not yet," he said, taking her arm and pulling her inside. His little drone chirped from his shoulder. "I've been waiting for you."

Mallory sighed. Adrian's passive-aggressive abilities had just gotten stronger.

"Mrs. Brown didn't tell me anything about the ambassador," she said. "What do you know?"

"Why would she tell you?" Adrian asked, sniffing.

"Because she left me in charge of Eternity." Mallory spoke faster to cover up Adrian's offended huffing. "Not in a political way or anything. I just need to check on her if things go wrong. That's all. I figure since she left something that huge in my hands, she might tell me of other big things to keep track of.

"Do you know who it is?" she added. "The ambassador, I mean."

"No, I didn't recognize the name," he said. "J. Brass or something. I assume he'll introduce himself at the party."

"How do you know it's a him?" Mallory asked.

Adrian stood there as if the other possibilities had never

occurred to him. If he'd been able to, she was sure he'd be staring at her blankly.

"Never mind," she said, shaking her head.

"I need to make sure of something," he said, stopping and facing her. "You usually get uptight about going to a party. That murder thing you have going on and all."

"That murder thing you have going on" was an interesting way to put it. But he was right: now she was actively attending a gathering with a lot of humans, and that sometimes ended in murder, in her experience. But it didn't really bother her tonight.

"I don't know," she said. "Nothing has happened in a while, so I haven't thought about it much."

"I find that hard to believe. Wouldn't you be most confident right after a murder happened? Because you knew some time passes between them?"

Is this guy trying to wind me up any way he can? "Not quite true. I have had murders happen one after the other before."

"You should just be on alert all the time," he said with a note of finality.

"I've spent most of my adult life like that," she said. "I was hoping I could relax a bit tonight."

"Just don't scare the guests, okay? Especially don't talk about what happened with the first Earth shuttle."

"I'm not a moron, Adrian," she said mildly. "Anything else awkward you want to ask me before you release me?" she asked as they walked toward the bar. "We have time for you to get another dig in."

"I'll let you know if I think of anything," he said dryly.

Mallory laughed, surprised. Had Adrian made a joke? She wasn't going to ruin the moment by asking.

The restaurant in question was run by the Gurudev, skinny humanoid aliens that were a bit smaller than humans, with bark-like skin. They often wrapped themselves in brightly colored fabric, and Mallory assumed there was a class or occupation indicator within the patterns and colors of the wraps, but Gurudev seemed offended when you asked them species-specific questions, so Mallory didn't.

Mallory had recently learned that the Gurudev had at least four different genders, and many felt other aliens' use of specific gender pronouns was strange, although some did adopt them if they were going to be working with other races frequently.

Mallory got herself and Adrian glasses of wine from the bar. "It seems they really are ready to host some humans," she said, handing him the wine.

"More or less," he said. "I'm worried they still don't have all the food right. Just tell me if you see anything moving on the plates."

"Oh, no, really?" Mallory said, laughing.

"I'm not kidding," he said stiffly.

"I didn't think you were. Still funny," she said, remembering the time she had been served a plate of green leafy vegetables and was glad to finally have a salad, only to realize the greens were a shield so that the real meal, caterpillar-like creatures, would feel safe and not try to run off the plate immediately. When Mallory had tried to eat the greens, the waitstaff had run to her in horror to stop her.

"It looked like kale," she'd said numbly, her eyes fixated on the orange caterpillar the Gurudev server tried to encourage her to eat.

"Ambassador, it's lovely to see you," said a Gurudev behind them. It was Morn, the owner of the restaurant. They looked at the wine that the humans were drinking. "It's a real pleasure to host your event here. You will tell them that this is the first official human event on the station, right?" they asked.

"Yes, it is, and we're so glad you could accommodate us. Did the shipment of Earth supplies make it here all right? Do your chefs need any help with the final preparation?" Adrian asked, his voice gaining his smooth ambassador lilt, which he dropped entirely when speaking with Mallory.

Morn confirmed everything was in place to make the humans comfortable, and pointed to several of them that were not getting ill. Mallory refrained from pointing out that that was a low bar to clear.

The restaurant was decorated in pleasing, subtle shades of slate and blue, frequently used colors by the Gurudev, as Mallory understood it. The walls bulged in some areas, as if something in the next room over had swollen and distended the wall, and thinned to appear almost translucent in other places. In the swollen places, it was decorated with darker blue swirls. One partition in the middle of the main dining room was a mural of a distant city—Mallory assumed a Gurudev city, based on the odd shape of the buildings.

Like most on the station, the restaurant was built to suit a wide variety of sizes of patrons, from the huge Gneiss to the small Gurudev. The tables and chairs were of all sizes, but mostly fitting the humanoid-size beings. The wall around the exit was a complex blue-and-black swirling pattern. In areas where aliens would prefer Phantasmagore to not disappear, they often made complicated designs on the walls to make it harder for them to blend in. This was often seen as an insult and lack of trust in the Phantasmagore, and they often took offense at complicated patterns.

The restaurant had a few rooms, including one with the bar and a large area for people to mingle, and a quieter room with tables of several different sizes. A buffet of food lined the wall between the rooms, the size of the tables indicating which race should take from it.

Mallory guessed about twenty humans were there, mingling with aliens who were probably diplomats and taking their awkwardness in stride. She spotted Xan and Ferdinand talking to a tall Hispanic woman about forty years old, with her long hair in a stylish bun held by two crossed silver sticks.

If Ferd's here, Tina's likely close by. But while the ceiling did accommodate a ten-foot Gneiss, Tina was even larger, so it was too low for the modified Gneiss to comfortably move about. Mallory was surprised Tina wasn't lurking outside, wanting to mingle with the visitors, yelling advice and opinions through the door.

She took a step toward Xan, but Adrian grabbed her arm and led her away from the bar. "No, you know that one," he said. "There's someone else you need to talk to."

"Who?" Mallory asked, but Xan and the tall woman intercepted them.

"Adrian, how come you haven't met your replacement yet?" Xan asked, indicating the woman. "This is Jessica Brass, former WNBA star, current Earth ambassador to the station."

"Ambassador Casserly-Berry, I've been looking forward to meeting you," the woman said, stepping forward with confidence. She stood expectantly in front of Adrian. Mallory realized she was waiting for him to initiate a handshake, since she assumed he couldn't see her.

Adrian paused, and Mallory wondered if he was debating whether to divulge that he had a way to see her. He finally reached his hand out, and she took it, pumping it once.

"It's a real pleasure," Jessica said. "You had a historic position in the path of Earth-alien relationships, and it will be a challenge to follow in your footsteps."

She smiled, and Mallory shook her head internally. This woman was good. Adrian's tenure on Eternity definitely was historic, but that wasn't always a good thing. And it would definitely be challenging to repair the damage he had done.

"I hope we can set up a meeting in the coming days. I have so many questions," Jessica added. Then she quirked her head toward the bar. "How about we talk now over a drink?"

Adrian frowned and then sighed. "Fine. Let's get a drink. Mallory, your friend is in the next room," he said, gesturing vaguely.

"Hi, I'm Mallory, no one important, but nice to meet you," she hastily introduced herself, shaking the hand of the ambassador, who smiled an insincere politician's smile at her.

"Ms. Viridian, I have read about you. It's a pleasure," Jessica said, and followed Adrian.

"Huh," Mallory said, watching them go.

"What?" Xan asked, also watching her.

"She didn't sound pleased to meet me," Mallory said.

"It's her first day on the station. Cut her some slack," he said. "So, you going to face your past or whatever?"

"Apparently," she said, grimacing. "You want to come with me?"

"I think I'll get a beer," he said. "Phineas sent me some, and I want to make sure Adrian doesn't serve it to everyone. Or try to kill Jessica. Yell if you need me or someone dies or something."

"Very funny," she said.

"I'll save you a beer," he said with a grin.

Feeling very alone, Mallory stood in the doorway and scanned the quieter room.

Her stomach dropped when she spotted three people sitting at a table. One looked up and locked familiar eyes with her. She took a step back, the "flight" response taking over her executive function briefly. But then she saw the person's companion, whom she also knew. And then the third person turned around.

Well. Shit.

Amy, her best friend from high school.

Parker, Amy's brother. Amy's *twin* brother she'd completely forgotten about, like he'd never existed.

And beside them sat a man in jeans, a blue SBI jacket, and a brown-and-white ball cap. SBI agent Donald Draughn, Mallory's old tormentor, watched her closely, grinning when he saw her pull up in shock.

6

· · ·

OLD GHOSTS

WITH *INFINITY GONE*, Xan found it hard to focus. He had heard veterans talk about phantom limb syndrome; how strange it was to feel a very real sensation but see nothing but empty space where your foot used to be. He'd completely taken for granted the ship's constant presence—they didn't even communicate all the time, but he always knew she was there.

Now he felt off, out of balance, wrong.

He stood in the polite wings of Adrian and Jessica's conversation, trying to focus on them. He'd been thrown when she walked into the room. He'd been a huge fan of hers when he followed basketball, ever since she showed promise as a Tar Heel point guard.

Now she showed every bit of sly skill that she had used as the captain of the basketball team, asking Adrian pointed questions but giving vague answers herself. *What is this woman doing as alien ambassador? She needs to run for office.*

For all he knew, this was one step on her way to public office.

"So, Mrs. Brown, where is she now?" she asked.

Adrian grimaced. "She had to leave and said it was something to do with the workings of the station. She left it in Mallory's hands in the meantime, but we don't anticipate any problems.

Eternity is just in hibernation, where her services still work but we can't make direct requests to her," he said.

"If you anticipate problems, then they're not problems, just expectations," Jessica said, sounding like one of Xan's sergeants, who claimed there were no accidents. "What if there's an emergency?"

Adrian frowned, and Xan stepped forward. "The different residents of the stations make up the security, medical, and emergency teams, just like any city. We ask something from Eternity maybe once a week or so, and she doesn't always answer," he said. "If there's an emergency, then emergency teams will take care of it."

Jessica looked at him briefly, then turned her focus on him entirely. "I was led to expect to meet the ship and her host," she said.

"And you will, when Mrs. B gets back," he said pleasantly. "She can't be gone long. Eternity can't be without a host forever."

"What if something happens to her while she's gone?" Jessica asked.

Xan thought of anything daring to hurt Mrs. B. If something rare came across that she couldn't handle herself, *Infinity* would no doubt protect her.

"She'll be fine," he said. "So what about you two? When is the official handoff of power?"

"Oh, don't be crude, Xan," Jessica said with a friendly smile. "You make it sound like I'm wrestling a gavel from Adrian's fist."

She doesn't know Adrian well, does she? he thought, and, again, despaired at the lack of a sense of amusement. He didn't know if he'd ever get used to *Infinity* being gone.

"ARE YOU WORRIED your people have sent another assassin to do what the last one failed to do?" Ferdinand asked. He held a massive mug full of something that radiated intense heat.

Xan picked up a beer from a tray on the bar. (The beer Phineas had sent was safely put away in the kitchen, Morn assured him.) "A little. Eternity said she wouldn't let it happen, but it doesn't seem she's paying much attention to anything right now."

"I understand it's not in the humans' best interest to murder you," Ferdinand said. "You're in a powerful diplomatic situation with your connection to *Infinity*."

"A lot of the time, humans aren't too concerned with consequences," Xan said. "We're a very short-term-focused species."

"While the Gneiss are usually long-term focused," his giant friend said. "I think it's why Tina will make such a good leader."

Xan choked on his beer. "Wait—you think Tina is going to be a good queen? You and Stephanie keep saying she's a moron."

"She isn't very intelligent," Ferdinand allowed, focusing his gaze on the restaurant window next to him. "But I am learning she has good instincts, even though they're short-term, fast-thinking instincts. She'll be a different kind of leader, and I think our government needs a shake-up."

"When do you think people will arrive to take her and Stephanie into custody?" Xan asked. Ferdinand had been quiet about the supposed incoming Gneiss retaliation, and Tina hadn't been around much except when he saw her after Mallory woke up.

"I don't know," Ferdinand said. "Tina told me not to worry about it."

"And you trust her?" Xan said.

"I will have to at some point," Ferdinand replied, looking back at Xan. Two small bright points shone from his deep eye sockets. "There's no good time to start trusting someone."

Xan considered this, then nodded. "Point taken. Are you always so wise and chatty when you're drinking?"

"Yes."

"I'm going to check on Mallory. She disappeared," Xan said. "You know, look for dead bodies and shit."

Xan passed by awkward-looking humans, some of them staying very firmly away from the aliens, others delightedly chatting with them. He stood in the doorway leading to the dining room. Mallory sat at a table in the middle of the room with three humans.

Mallory looked like she'd aged years in the few minutes they'd been apart. Her skin was pasty pale, and her lips were pressed together as an older white man talked to her. Dark circles were under her eyes, accentuated when her gaze passed between the man and the two other people at the table. She looked like a deer about to bolt.

The other two white people were around his and Mallory's age, the woman with blond hair and blue eyes, and the man with dark hair and green eyes.

He grabbed a chair from another table, then plopped it down beside Mallory and sat.

"Hey, folks," he said pleasantly. "Anyone dead yet, Mal?"

"That's not funny," she said. "Not in front of this group, anyway."

"I figured I'd check. You look like you've either just seen a murder or are worried you're the next body. What's going on?" He glanced at the three other people at the table. "I'm Xan." He held his hand up in a wave but didn't extend it to shake.

Mallory pointed to the older man. "This is Agent Draughn of the North Carolina SBI. He investigated several of the murders I helped solve."

"You mean the guy who thought I killed Billy before I left Earth? The one who at the same time assumed you'd killed everyone in the cases you investigated?" Xan asked.

Mallory winced, but it wasn't a hidden fact. The agent shifted uncomfortably in his seat and then glanced at the blond woman, then back at Xan.

"I had to follow the evidence," he said stiffly.

"And that," Mallory continued, pointing at the blond woman beside her, "is Dr. Amy Valor, my best friend from high school. And"—she glanced quickly at the man sitting quietly beside Amy—"that's Parker Valor."

"Also a friend from high school," Parker said, and held his hand out to shake. Xan shook it.

"So when Adrian said you had an old friend here . . ." Xan said, raising his eyebrows.

"He meant one of these three," she said, shrugging. "Or maybe all of them. Who knows, with Adrian."

"So what brings y'all to Station Eternity?" Xan asked, deliberately allowing his Southern accent to come through.

Might as well make them feel at home. Ish.

Draughn cleared his throat. "I'm taking a leave of absence, and I thought a vacation would do me some good. I haven't taken PTO in a few years, and I had the money and time saved up. And I wanted to see how Mallory was doing." But as he talked about Mallory, he was looking at Amy.

"And Parker and I are working at UNC now, and we're part of a research team to learn about extraterrestrial life and the diplomatic possibilities," Amy said. "I have to say, Mallory being here was a real shock."

Parker looked at his sister, frowning, then to Xan he said, "Yeah, there's a whole group of us from UNC: biologists, social scientists, a basketball coach for some reason . . ." He rolled his eyes.

Amy slapped Parker's arm. "You said you'd be nice."

"He is a coach," Parker said mildly. "I'm stating facts."

"So what do you study?" Xan asked, pointing to Amy.

"Quantum physics," she said. Her eyes flicked to Parker. "It was luck that they picked both me and Parker to come."

"I'm the bug guy," Parker said.

Mallory's head snapped up. "You didn't tell me that."

"You didn't ask," he said, shrugging. "You asked a high-pitched, 'What are you doing here?'"

"Yeah, and you should have answered, 'Studying bugs'!" Mallory said, pale and visibly shaking.

"Are you okay?" Xan asked in a low voice.

Mallory flinched, then schooled her expression. "Yeah. We were just catching up."

"What about the three of you, how do you know each other?" Xan said, pointing to each of the newcomers. "Did you make friends on the shuttle?"

Amy cleared her throat. "I met Agent Draughn here at a spousal grief support group. We learned we have a similar interest in alien life, so we stayed in touch; he came over when I had dinner parties, so he met Parker and our other relatives. When I told him that Parker and I were coming here, he said it was time for a vacation."

"A spousal grief support group?" Mallory asked, studying Amy. "I'm so sorry. What happened?"

"I was married for a brief time," she said, looking down at the table. "He died. I found a lot of help with the group."

"You also learned to play softball," Draughn said with a smile that Mallory had never seen. It looked odd, as if someone had tried to change a doll's expression. "Don't forget that."

"Softball?" Mallory asked, squinting.

"We had a lot of fun with softball, yeah," Amy said. She still stared at the table. Parker watched her curiously, then put a hand on her shoulder.

"Fun times with the grief group. You don't hear that a lot," Xan said.

Mallory pointed from the older man to the younger woman. "So you're dating?"

Draughn laughed and sat back in his chair. "You have to go straight there, don't you? Of course we're not. I'm old enough to be her father. But I figured, if you're going into space, what's better than going with people you know?"

Mallory shifted in her chair. Xan could almost smell the discomfort coming off her in waves.

No one said anything for a bit. Xan looked around the table. Draughn watched Amy, who looked at her hands. Parker looked at the ceiling with a clear, curious gaze. Mallory stared at the table.

"I've heard the Sundry are pretty much everywhere around here? Not like normal insects; I mean, you can see them?" Parker said. "And the blue is the dominant sect here?"

"Usually, yeah," Mallory said. She glanced at the ceiling. "And you'll see silver from time to time, but the blue are definitely dominant." She frowned to herself and looked like she wanted to say something else but thought better of it.

"I think Adrian wanted you to welcome some of the other humans, Mal," Xan finally said, and Mallory was on her feet immediately.

"Let's go," she said.

"Can we get that beer sometime, Mallory?" Draughn asked.

"No, I mean, only because there's not a lot of beer on the station. But yeah, sure." She pulled out a pen and scribbled something down on a napkin. "That's how to find me on the station. Or message me. I'll see you around."

And then she practically shot out of the room.

"MALLORY, WAIT UP!" Xan said, catching her elbow as she left the dining room. "What has spooked you so bad? Are you getting the murder-feeling thing?"

She shook her head violently. "No, that's not it. I can't explain, I just had to get out of there."

"So that was the SBI guy who ruined any hope of a career you had on Earth?"

She nodded miserably.

"What about the other two?" He looked past her shoulder to where Parker was still watching them, catching sight of them through the doorway.

"I don't know. Amy and I were close in school, and then she and her family moved away." Mallory stared at the floor.

"And the other guy?"

Her face flushed. "Her twin brother, Parker. And I'm really confused because I'm only now remembering he exists. All I know is he makes me really nervous."

"You don't remember your best friend's twin brother?" Xan asked, laughing.

She flushed. "I know. It's— I don't know what it is." She got a faraway look on her face, trying to remember.

"What do you think they're all doing here, really? Doesn't look like Draughn is here to keep investigating you."

"I don't know," she said miserably. "I saw them sitting together and my brain screeched to a halt. Then they were asking me to sit down and all started talking to me. I felt like I'd been hit by a truck or something."

"Let's get you out of here," he said. "I'll cover with Adrian for you." They started walking toward the door, but he slowed down, thinking. "There's a big coincidence thing happening here. Doesn't that usually happen before a murder? You should see if you know anyone else here. If something happens . . ."

"It won't," she said. "I'm not feeling any of the usual things."

"Still," he said. "Who came with that group? Did you meet any of them?"

She sighed in frustration and backed up until she bumped into the blue wall. She looked around the room and finally pointed to a tall white bald man in sweat pants laughing with a few other people who were wearing clothes that looked like they were bought on a professor's salary, not a diplomat's or rock star's.

"That's Oscar, in the sweat pants. I think he's the basketball coach Parker was talking about. He's talking to some other people who work with Amy at the college."

She kept scanning the room. To Xan, it looked like most of the rest of the humans were rich, probably some minor celebrities, or people who were famous for being rich.

Her eyes lingered on Oscar's shiny head, and then she bit her lip. "I'm sorry, I really need to get home."

XAN WALKED WITH her outside, determined to get her home before Tina found her and "helped."

"I've never seen you like this," Xan said. "Mallory, what are you so scared of? We've faced worse things! What's worse than your aunt trying to kill us? Getting spaced? Getting stung by the Sundry? You've dealt with so much more than old ghosts in a bar."

She pulled up suddenly, then glanced down at her hand, still bearing a small scar where the Sundry had stung her. "I did, didn't I?" she asked. She glanced behind them as if to make sure no one was following, then took a shaky breath. "Shit, Xan. Parker! Amy's brother! How could I forget my biggest high school crush? Fifteen years can't erase something like that. I remember him, and that Amy wouldn't let me date him."

Xan twisted his mouth sardonically. "What, were you in high school?"

"Yes, Xan, that's exactly why," she said flatly. "I think he may have had feelings, but we never talked about it. And then when they moved, I forgot him. I mean I forgot he existed. Entirely. Who does that? Who forgets an obsession from high school?"

Xan stepped back, rubbing his chin. "That's fucked up. But while you're worried about your friend cockblocking you from her brother, you're not worried that your friend is now hanging out with the guy who cockblocked your career?"

She laughed weakly. "That's crude."

"Am I wrong?"

"Well. No." Her breathing was returning to normal, and the wide-eyed, likely-to-run-straight-off-a-cliff-in-panic look had left her face. She took a deep breath. "I actually don't know what was going on with me. I was just hit with this desire to get the hell out of there. I'm doing better now. I think I need some rest."

"Want me to walk you back?"

She shook her head. "I have to think. I'll be okay, don't worry."

"That's what everyone says right before they get into a situation that you should worry about," Xan said.

She waved him off with a laugh and entered a lift.

"Oh, yeah, something's not right," Xan muttered, then went back to the reception.

7

. . . .

TINY MURDERS

MALLORY STARED AT the two blue Sundry perched on the back of her couch. "Hey, can we get two more of you in here? I'd like to talk to y'all."

Sometimes she felt like the Sundry sent two scouts to be with her so that they could get info on her but she couldn't ask questions in return. The hivemind needed at least four Sundry to form words that Mallory could hear.

The Sundry didn't move except to flick their wings. Mallory sighed. "I will have to go talk to the silver if y'all don't help me out. Is that what you want?" The scouts still didn't move, and Mallory waited about five minutes to see if the hive would send more. When no one else arrived, she put her jacket back on and left to talk to the silver. The blue Sundry didn't accompany her.

Mallory went to the shuttle bay. Silver Sundry were more dedicated to action, not data gathering. But without constant connection to the blue hivemind, they had to be basing their actions on something else.

While the blue Sundry lived in the beautiful park area of Eternity, their massive, dainty (in appearance) paper nest lodged in a tree that resembled a giant weeping willow, the silver Sundry were forced to live on their shuttle—which was also a paper nest, just in the dank shuttle bay and not a pretty park.

Turf wars are ugly all over. Mallory stood outside the nest. "Hey, silver? Can we talk? I need to know what you were warning me about. I mean, probably has something to do with the humans that are here, but what, exactly?"

A dangerous buzz sounded from inside. No words were formed, but any human could identify that stay-away sound.

"Hey, you told me to come around, and I'm doing that, and . . . now what? Did I miss my window?" She knocked on the nest, making a soft *pumpf* sound instead of a sharp knock.

When nothing else happened, she stepped back and heard a crunch. She'd stepped on a silver Sundry.

She leaped to the side, terrified she had killed it. She crouched down to get a closer look. It was definitely dead, but next to it lay three more that she hadn't stepped on. Now that she noticed them, dead silver Sundry were visible everywhere. Bodies littered the floor of the shuttle bay around the hive shuttle, and a few others glinted off ledges and the tops of other shuttles.

"Are you guys okay? What the hell happened?" she asked, knocking on the soft hull again.

No answer, just the stay-away buzz.

Had the blue and silver been fighting to the death? Or was this the crossroads they had been warning about?

"Hey, I want to help, what can I do?" she asked.

No answer.

She looked around her feet in frustration and then carefully gathered all the silver bodies within reach and placed them as respectfully as she could at the foot of the hive. Aliens had different views of death than humans, and she wasn't sure if the Sundry mourned, but it felt wrong to leave them there to be stepped on.

The silver bodies glittered like jewels. She chewed on her lower lip, then went to see Stephanie.

"DID YOU SEE or hear anything?" she asked, sitting in Stephanie's massive captain's seat.

"Nothing," Stephanie's voice came over the speaker. "I've been monitoring the sub-space communications to track the approaching Gneiss. I'm having some trouble with triangulation."

"So there's a massive death event in a public area and no one saw anything, not even the sentient ships?" Mallory asked, shaking her head in frustration.

"We don't all just sit and stare around the shuttle bay," Stephanie said. "There's a lot more to do now, with sending messages across space and speaking to other ships and other Gneiss. The ones who will talk to me, I mean."

"Fine. If you do hear of anything happening, let me know?" Mallory asked.

Stephanie paused. Then she said, "If I can, I will. But there are strange things happening with our navigation, and that's taking most of my attention right now."

"Navigation? What's going on?" Mallory asked. "I thought we were just orbiting Ariadne and ships come to us."

"We have to monitor other ships' navigation," Stephanie agreed. "But something is off with Eternity's personal trajectory.

"It's like she's trying to escape orbit."

THE PARTY WAS still going on, even though the light had faded to dusky shadows and the park had cleared out. Before she told Xan anything, she wanted to check with the blue Sundry in their hive.

She spotted another human under the fronds of the willow, staring up at the nest. Mallory hung back, edging close to a fluffy bush. She couldn't hear what was said between the person and the

Sundry, if anything. The person shifted then, and Mallory could see she had long blond hair and wore slacks. She just stood still, watching the blue Sundry buzz around the outside. Then she shook her head and walked away.

Mallory's breath caught in her throat. Amy? What was she doing out here? She'd said she was interested in the Sundry, but lurking around their nest at night didn't sound like it was a diplomatic visit.

Once she was gone, Mallory jogged up to the nest to see if she could tell what the woman had been looking at.

The entrance to the hive, large enough for most aliens, including Gneiss on the smaller side, was always guarded but usually open. Now it was closed, completely papered over.

"Guys, what's going on?" she asked. "There are a bunch of silvers dead in the shuttle bay and I haven't heard from you in days."

None of the blue Sundry replied. Some exited the top of the nest and flew down to her, circling her. The fake moonlight glinted off their blue bodies, then they flew higher, out of sight.

She ran her hands through her bangs, pulling them out of her eyes. "Weird shit is going on, guys. The last time weird shit went on, lots of people died. I would like to avoid that. But I don't know what's going on!"

Nothing.

MALLORY PEEKED through the open door of the restaurant but didn't immediately see Xan among the reception attendees. He hadn't answered the message she'd sent him either. Telling herself that Eternity's navigation was handled by people who had a lot more knowledge and authority than she did, she walked into the park across the way and found a bench where she could think.

Her mind drifted to the new humans aboard the station.

The last time she had seen Agent Draughn, he was trying to neg her into staying on Earth. Which was damn funny since he'd spent a decade trying to get rid of her by either threatening to put her in prison or encouraging her to move out of state.

They'd sat at a bar the afternoon before she left. She had allowed the final meeting just to tie up loose ends in the most recent murder she was helping him solve/interfering with (depending on whom you asked).

"You know what gets me about you?" Draughn's voice was gruff and unfriendly, sounding like he was trying to permanently alter his voice to sound like Tom Waits. That kind of vocal dedication required careful tending with cigars and scotch to achieve the proper grumble.

"Yeah, because you constantly tell me," she said. "I interfere with authority. But if you have something new, please, tell me." Her hands tore at the edges of the damp napkin under her beer bottle, but she kept her gaze level.

He had bought the drinks, so Mallory couldn't complain too much, but free beer didn't make her obligated to hear a lecture on her shortcomings.

"Yeah, you interfere. What makes you think that alien cops aren't going to be just as mad as I am when you interfere with their cases? They'll probably get madder since you're a human."

She took a drink from her ale. "Just like you get mad that I'm a civilian? Listen, Don. I am going off planet in hopes to get away from murder. I'm not going off to start an interstellar detective agency."

He went on as if she hadn't spoken. "And you just stand there and let the clues come to you. You don't ask for help, you don't listen to anyone else's advice, you're like this passive sponge just soaking in clues until there's enough to wring out a solution."

"And this is bad? I thought you wanted the cases solved," Mallory said with a puzzled smile.

Agent Draughn had investigated her after learning her

connection to several murders. He'd interviewed former friends, family members, and coworkers. He had accused her of at least two murders, accused her of messing with crime scenes, and actively blocked any attempt she made when she tried to get into law enforcement or private detective education/certification. He wasn't her favorite person by far, but to be fair, he was one of the few who talked to her without a drop of fear coloring their communication, and she liked him a tiny bit for that. But only a tiny bit.

"But why are you bringing this up? You don't like me. I know that. I'll be out of your hair soon enough. Did you just want to bring me here to insult me?"

He apparently wasn't done. "You don't even write your own books. You wait until a murder happens and then write about that. Have you ever tried to write a real mystery?"

She stared at him. "That's— What the hell are you talking about? I'm doing the only job I can do that will make me money and keep people safe. The material is right there. Why wouldn't I use it? You"—she jabbed her finger at him, narrowing her eyes—"you were the one who blocked my attempt to do all this the 'right way.' And now you're giving me shit for doing the last little bit of income earning I can do. What the fuck, Draughn? What new insult have I given you?"

He frowned as if he had forgotten the torpedoing he had done to her career aspirations. "Why don't you investigate people, try to find clues in the first place, stop the murders before they start?"

"You want me to interview every stranger I see to assess them for murder likelihood?" She rolled her eyes. "Do you not remember every interview you've made me sit through? What I've tried to do in the past, what's happened when I try to warn people or stop a murder from happening? People think I must be connected to it to know that it's going to happen. On the other side, people think I haven't tried to help at all before something terrible happened. You act like giving people warning just hasn't occurred to me."

Draughn surveyed her, his ruddy face getting redder as she spoke. "Maybe."

"I don't owe you a debate or an argument," she said. "Whatever you think of me, I really don't care anymore. I'm gone. You will never have to see me again, you will never have to deal with my 'meddling,' or my causing the murders, or my inability to listen to you and your wonderful advice, or whatever you don't like about me today. It's going to all go away tomorrow!" She started to slide out of the booth.

"Hang on, sit down," he said, motioning her to get back in the booth. "I'm doing this for your own good."

"Are you negging me to stay? Do you have any idea how patronizing you sound?"

"I just think you should work here to make your life better. Not run away. And we"—he swallowed all of a sudden, like the words were sticky in his throat—"need you."

Mallory laughed in surprise, the anger like bitter medicine in her mouth. "No." She took her bag and slid out again.

He waited a moment longer, and when she didn't elaborate, he asked, "'No,' what?"

"'No' is a complete sentence, Agent Draughn," she said. She grinned tightly at him. "I don't owe you an explanation. And telling me you need me now is far too little, far too late." She fished a ten out of her pocket and put it on the table. She waved to the bartender, who had always been nice to her (if she drank while the bar wasn't busy and didn't cause any murders), and left without looking back. She hadn't expected to see Draughn ever again.

And now he was here.

"I THOUGHT YOU left." The deep voice startled her out of her thoughts.

Draughn stood a few feet away, arms crossed.

"Jesus, Draughn, what are you doing lurking around the park like a goddamn creeper?" she snapped.

"I was going for a walk," he said. His face was in the shadow of a nearby tree. "I just saw you here. Thought I'd say hi."

He just fixed her with that stare. She shook her head in disbelief. "Draughn, what are you really doing here?" she asked. "Have you gotten new state funding to come to space and blame me for whatever new murder you can't solve?"

"No," he said. "Everything isn't about you, Mallory. I told you I'm on sabbatical. It's purely coincidental that we ran into each other."

Mallory rolled her eyes. "I don't believe in coincidence."

He looked around the park like it was a disappointment. "I got your letter, incidentally," Draughn said, not looking at her. "Surprised you thought to let me know your weird little bug secret. Nice to find someone else to blame it on. Is that what you're doing here? Talking to the bugs?" He gestured to the massive willow tree about twenty yards away that contained the blue Sundry hive.

"Yeah. That's what I did. Blamed it on someone else." Her eyes narrowed. "I thought you should know that I figured something out about why murders happen around me. Sorry I wasted the effort."

After the violent events on Eternity that ended with several humans and aliens dead, Mallory had written to Agent Draughn and a few other people on Earth, explaining what she had learned about her connection with the Sundry and the frequent murders in her life. It had taken her considerable time to reword the first-draft line that read "So you were fucking wrong, and I was right, and I hope you feel really bad about yourself because you're a garbage person" into something polite, and she'd been proud of her attempt.

The words had apparently landed as well as she'd expected. It had felt good to write them, though.

"I was hoping to see some of this connection with bugs," Draughn said. "But I don't see any right now."

"I'm not a trained monkey for you," Mallory said. "Besides, they're dormant right now."

He made no indication that he detected her lie, continuing to stare at the tree.

"Besides, do you actually want a murder here?" she added. "I thought you were on break."

He grinned at her. "Don't be ridiculous. Of course I don't want a murder. What kind of law enforcement agent would I be if I hoped for a murder to happen?"

She glared at him, then asked slowly, "Why are you here, Don?"

He finally threw his hands into the air and dropped them. "Fine. My wife died a few months ago, so I took some time off."

Mallory looked at her feet. "I'm sorry."

He shrugged, an "I'm over it" gesture. "I met Amy in a grief support group. She'd lost her husband. We started talking about what we did for a living, and then started to talk in a more social capacity. I met her UNC friends, and when they told me about their trip, I thought it sounded interesting. My being here has nothing to do with you." He tapped his chin—his tell that he was about to attempt cleverness. "But now that I have you here, I want you to leave me and all the humans aboard the station alone."

She fixed him with a stony stare. "Tracking me down to tell me to leave you alone? That's a new one."

"I thought you had gotten my message when you ran out of the party," he said. "Then I saw you lurking out here. Waiting for I don't know what."

"You tell yourself that's what was going on," she said, rolling her eyes. "I'll be over here not bothering you, which I've been do-ing since you got here. I am happy to leave you alone. But you have no right to tell me I can't talk to the others."

He frowned at her. "What? Why?"

"You're going to stop me from catching up with old friends?" She said it with a smile, like it was something she wanted to do, like something that would be easy. She didn't want to. Good God, she didn't want to. It had felt like there was a negative force field around Parker and Amy, making her want to run the hell away. The idea of approaching them again made a cold sweat break out on the back of her neck.

But she had learned a while ago that when instinct told her to run, it was a better idea to face the problem. And what she felt with Amy and Parker was a lot more than the awkwardness fifteen years of silence brings.

"If I have to," Draughn said.

"You don't have any authority here, Don," she reminded him.

Draughn sighed like he was disappointed in her. He shook his head slowly, but something caught his eye near the willow that held the blue hive.

Parker had moved toward the hive. She hadn't even seen him leave the restaurant. Now he stood in front of it, outside the willow tree branches. From this distance, she normally couldn't hear sounds from inside the hive, but when Parker approached, the buzzing intensified to the point where it was audible.

But she couldn't feel the Sundry inside.

Parker glanced over at Mallory and Draughn and the fabricated moonlight caught his blue eyes. Memories of intense high school emotions surfaced, and she fought a surge of loss and regret. She got a sense of falling, only this time she clasped a hand slick with blood, and if she was going to die, well, at least it wasn't going to be alone.

HANDS WERE ON her shoulders, turning her over. Soft, feathery grass tickled her neck. She opened her eyes to see Eternity's full moon projected onto the sky.

Then a head eclipsed the moon, and Parker was looking down at her, his hair hanging in his face. Draughn's hands were on her shoulders, gentle and firm. He stood up when she opened her eyes.

"Holy shit," Parker said. "Are you okay? What happened?"

"I was gonna ask you that," she said, rubbing her forehead. She touched her nose; while sore, it wasn't broken or bleeding. Draughn helped her sit up, then her eyes met Parker's and she scrabbled backward, colliding with Draughn's knees. She rolled to the side and struggled to her feet. "God, I've got to get out of here."

"I don't think you should do that, you need to—" Parker said, but she was on her feet and running. Nausea roiled in her stomach like an asp. When was the last time she'd eaten anything?

What the actual fuck am I doing? Xan was right, she had faced worse things than regrets from her past. This panic was not like her. She bent over, hands on her knees, closing her eyes and taking in deep breaths. She looked back, expecting to have to explain herself to Parker and Draughn, but they were gone.

This isn't like me. None of this is like me. The thought caused another spike of fear in her chest, but she coldly squashed it. Something weird was going on, and she couldn't run away, no matter how much she wanted to. She had to go back into that reception.

She went back into the party and finally spotted Xan by the bar, talking to the ambassador. She walked up and, with an apologetic nod to Jessica, pulled him away.

"What's wrong?" he asked. "You look like you've seen something rise from the dead."

"That's how I feel. Something weird is going on." Mallory rubbed her eyes.

"Yeah, I know that. I'm the one who told you that, remember?" Xan asked.

She put her face close to his and whispered, "There are a bunch of dead silver Sundry in the shuttle bay. Stephanie didn't see what happened to them because she's more concerned with something bigger. Something about Eternity."

His eyes got wide. "Shit. The blues aren't telling you anything?"

"I can't get anyone to talk to me. But the bigger thing Steph is worried about is that Eternity is moving."

"What do you mean, 'moving'?"

"Steph says it's like she's trying to escape Ariadne's orbit. What happens if she does that? *Why* would she do that?"

"I have no idea. Maybe she's running after Mrs. B and *Infinity*. Maybe they called her. We can ask navigation about it."

"Huh," Mallory said. "I hadn't thought of that." It sounded reasonable. And definitely less scary than any other possibility. "But there's something else. Something weird with me. I'm not scared of this party." She bit her lip for a moment, then shook her head. "No, I'm fucking terrified. But not like the usual there's-going-to-be-a-murder fear. I'm used to having my senses heightened and expecting a murder. I don't feel any of that. I'm just this basket case when it comes to the people I know from Earth.

"But I know—*I know*—that when people come together like this, with connections, and I'm around, a murder is going to happen. I need to meet some more humans. I need you to keep an eye on the ambassador. Her dying would not look good."

"You're acting like a spooked horse," he said. "Do you need my help when you're interviewing people?"

She shook her head violently. "No, I don't need help," she said. "I need you to watch the ambassador."

"Get some wine, at least. That might relax you," he said doubtfully, handing her a glass.

"You don't have to tell me twice," she said, taking it.

They looked for the ambassador and saw her talking to Ferdinand. "Ferd won't let anything happen to her," Xan said.

"Amy and Parker came with a whole group," Mallory said.

"Some people from the university. Professors. A coach. I don't know if Draughn is connected to any of them."

"Let's find out," he said.

She raised an eyebrow at him. "'Let's'?"

He pointed to Jessica and Ferdinand. "You think I could protect her better than Ferd over there?"

She sighed. "All right. Let's go."

"Maybe we can stop the murder this time," Xan offered.

Mallory made a strangled laugh.

He shrugged. "Worth a try, isn't it?"

"I suppose," she said.

8

HAVE YOU TRIED REBOOTING?

MALLORY HAD TO meet more humans, and she had to face Parker. She could tackle both since Parker was talking to the bald man in the sweat suit. Was this Oscar?

The men stopped talking when Mallory and Xan approached. Mallory introduced Xan. Then she forced herself to make eye contact with Parker. "Sorry I've been weird. I've been sick this past week, and I'm not feeling great right now."

"Nothing catching, I hope!" his bald companion interrupted with a booming laugh.

Mallory winced slightly but went on. "No, not catching. Just trying to explain my behavior. I wanted to meet some of the new Earth visitors. Who's this?"

"This is Oscar," Parker said, his forehead still creased in worry. Mallory's heartbeat was loud in her ears, but she firmly told herself she had to stay where she was. Parker turned to ask Xan a question while Mallory held her hand out to Oscar, who shook it.

Oscar was tall, white, bald, and built like a truck. His sweat suit was one of those high-end deals, looking like slobby leisure wear, but when you see the brand name you know he spent twelve hundred dollars on it.

He also wasn't letting her hand go, but kept shaking it. His hand was massive and moist with sweat. It engulfed hers like a fleshy prison. He smiled, sly and knowing, as if he already knew what she looked like with her clothes off and was waiting for just the wrong moment to tell her.

"Oscar Daye," he said. "You may have heard of me."

"No, we don't get a lot of news here," she said. She looked pointedly at their hands.

He didn't let her hand go. "What did you say your name was again?"

"I didn't," she said slowly. "I'm Mallory." She pulled her hand. He kept smiling at her, his grip tight.

This is the kind of guy that gets mad and calls women whores when they say no to dates.

"Mallory," he said thoughtfully. "I have heard of you, actually. Amy won't shut up about you."

She glanced at Draughn, who had returned to Amy. She talked about Mallory to this guy, but not to Draughn? "Yeah? What does she say?" she asked, yanking her hand free.

"She didn't say you were so touchy!" he said. "I was just shaking your hand."

Xan and Parker stared at them.

"What's going on?" Parker asked Oscar.

Oscar shrugged. "I was just fooling around."

Mallory rolled her eyes. "Parker, is this the basketball coach you mentioned?"

"I also run a website," Oscar said, frowning at being talked over.

"Something predatory? Celebrity gossip?" Mallory asked.

"You have heard of me!" Oscar said, delighted. "But I'm bored. Parker, where's the cuter twin?" He turned his back on Mallory and walked toward the dining room.

"Hang on, you're not nearly good enough for my sister," Parker protested, and made to follow him.

"Wait." Mallory caught Parker's arm. It was only her iron will that made her not jerk her own hand back. It wasn't an electric shock she felt, but something deeper, a current that tightened the muscles in her arm.

Parker, however, was just fine with a violent shudder and pulling away. "Jesus, what was that?" he asked, rubbing his forearm where she had touched him.

"I don't know," she said. "But it looks like we have to talk." She handed Parker a card with her information—and how to use station communications. "Contact me tomorrow. Please."

"Sure," he said, meeting her eyes for a beat too long. Then he followed Oscar.

Mallory staggered on her feet but regained her balance. Xan dragged her to an empty table and made her sit down. "You look like shit. This really is getting to you. What happened back there?"

"I have no idea," Mallory said, her own words sounding slurred to her ears. "I have to go home. I can't do any more tonight. Whatever this is." She took a deep breath. "Keep an eye on them. You're right. There are too many coincidences going on here. Someone's probably going to die tonight."

9

. . . .

MEET THE HUMANS

RIGHT INSIDE THE door, Jessica was talking to the man who Mallory had pointed out was the obnoxious coach, Oscar. Their heads were close together, and he was laughing, but she looked deadly serious.

They both looked up, surprised, when Xan walked in. "If you wanted privacy, there are better places to get it than right inside the front door," he said mildly.

Oscar boomed out a laugh. "Nah, she's not my type. I like them petite, you know what I mean?" He made an exaggerated hourglass shape with his hands, then elbowed Xan.

Xan made a disgusted noise and glanced at Jessica, anticipating outrage, but she just watched Oscar with a cool, calculating look on her face.

"Just be careful, Oscar," she said. "Remember what I said."

"Yeah, I know," Oscar said. "Sheesh, can you relax for once in your life?"

"I will if you stop relaxing and take things seriously. How about it?" she asked with a tight smile. "This is serious. Don't fuck this up."

"Fine, fine," Oscar grumbled, glancing at Xan. He went to the bar and got a beer.

"Jesus," she said with a sigh. "Those Tar Heels who came here in a group. They're a lot."

"What do you mean?" he asked.

"There's that fuckup; he's loud, obnoxious, and is convinced everyone loves him. And if you don't love him, you can't take a joke."

"I know plenty of guys like that," Xan said. "What makes him special?"

She watched Oscar, her lips pursed. "I have to think about diplomacy. Everyone here needs to make a good impression, show the aliens that humans are worth working with. If we were going to present the best of humanity, we didn't do a good job."

"The last time y'all sent the best of humanity, most of them died," Xan reminded her. "There are plenty of people who aren't worth working with, in all species. But I thought there were plenty of smart people on this trip. Lots of professors?"

She faced him, her dark curls bouncing. "Have you met them?"

"Not really," he said. "I met a few folks from UNC. I went there for a few years. Never graduated."

"Yes, you left school to enlist, didn't you?" she asked. At his startled expression, she smiled, tight-lipped. "I do my homework. But let's go meet more people. You can tell me what you think." She grabbed his hand and dragged him toward a few humans standing by the buffet.

The two white men looked to be in their late thirties or early forties. One was short with thinning blond hair and blue eyes and wore a smart, tailored gray business suit with a red tie and a gold wedding ring. The man next to him was tall and built, with curly red hair and brown eyes. He was about as tall as Xan and looked uncomfortable in a black button-down shirt and khakis. He also wore a wedding ring.

Jessica presented Xan like a present. "Folks, I want you to meet one of the permanent residents of the station. This is Xan Morgan." She looked at him suddenly, appraising. "What would we call you? You're not a soldier anymore. A pilot?"

He flinched, not expecting his personal information to be the first topic of conversation. "Sure. I'm a pilot, that works." He gestured to the humans. "Who are we talking to here?"

She pointed first to the man in the suit, then to the tall man. "Reggie and Dr. Max Valor-Cole," Jessica said. "Reggie is a lawyer specializing in alien law."

Reggie shook his hand, meeting his eyes and pumping his hand twice, a handshake that Xan would bet he practiced before some kind of networking seminar. "Not alien law, exactly, but how the US law has changed in response to First Contact. I'm eager to learn more about the folks on board here to take back and present to Congress."

"A lot of Valors here," Xan said. "I guess that's not a coincidence."

Reggie nodded. "My younger twin siblings, Amy and Parker, are also here."

Max Valor-Cole stuck out his hand. "I'm the better half. I teach experimental psychology at UNC."

Xan shook his hand with interest. "Are you here in a professional capacity?" he asked. "Or are you a plus-one?"

"The university sent me, if that's what you mean," Max said. "I study human behavior and, now that I'm here, how alien contact affects it."

"He'll be on another job soon," Reggie said, an edge to his voice. "Going from registered nurse to professor of psychology— that's a step down, if you ask me. In one job he saved lives. In the new one, he teaches frat boys about luck."

"As he so lovingly stated," Max said, casting a side-eye over his shoulder to Reggie, "I study luck, among other things, in my profession. He doesn't respect that part of my career."

"That's really interesting," Xan said. "I'd love to talk more about that."

Beyond Max and Reggie, Xan saw Oscar approach a human woman from behind. She was young and Black, with long braids hanging down her back. She stood with a certain confidence that made him wonder if she was with the academics from UNC. Then Oscar cupped his hands over her eyes and said, "Guess who!"

The woman immediately drove her elbow back into his stomach. Oscar staggered back, doubled over. "Christ, it was a joke!" he croaked.

"I told you not to touch me," she said calmly.

Reggie went to Oscar's side to steady him, saying, "You really should listen to people, man. It might save your life one day." He didn't look too sympathetic, but Max stiffened slightly when Reggie touched Oscar.

"Careful, Lourdes," Oscar said to the woman, straightening and attempting to get his bravado back. "You don't want the world to know what I know, do you?"

"I doubt you know anything that would inform anyone of anything, you moron," Lourdes said, but she left the room, heading into the restaurant section.

Oscar gave a smirk to Max and then sauntered off.

"What was all that about?" Xan asked, looking around at the group.

"I think it's pretty obvious," Reggie said, returning to them. "Oscar tried to hit on some people outside our group. Most everyone here was used to his bullshit, but he tried it on some strangers and it didn't go well. Somehow he still thinks he's charming."

"Do you all know him from UNC?" Xan asked.

"No," Reggie said as if it pained him. "I work with him. On a professional level."

Before Xan could ask for more clarification on the odd statement, Max interjected.

"His sister invites Oscar to her dinner parties, and I see him around campus."

Xan raised his eyebrows. "Really? UNC's a big school."

"You'd be surprised how small it can feel," Max muttered. "I'm going to get a drink."

Reggie stood there with Xan and Jessica, the awkwardness building. Xan wondered if Max was the social glue holding the group together.

Finally Reggie broke the silence. "Oscar has a talent for ruining things. I apologize for my colleague."

Xan shrugged. "Why are you apologizing? You're not the asshole here."

"Guilt by association, I suppose," Reggie said, his eyes on the floor. He looked tired all of a sudden. "Ambassador, when is your speech happening? I'd like to get Max out of here. He is double fisting the Merlot right now."

Jessica looked at her watch. Xan whistled when he saw it. Phineas had told him about this watch; it was a new galactic Fossil watch that kept time for seven places on Earth and also for the twenty-eight-hour day that Eternity kept. Only three existed when Phineas had told him about it.

This one had a mother-of-pearl face and the image of the time projected onto it from a microscopic projector. Xan couldn't even fathom how much it cost.

"Right about now," Jessica said. "I think folks are getting tired. Human folk, anyway." She gestured to the various humans who had wandered into the room.

Agent Draughn stood at the bar, chatting with Oscar and looking rumpled, like a partially deflated balloon. The twins, Amy and Parker Valor, conferred closely, glancing at Oscar; then Amy approached the two men, looking friendly and at ease. Max and Reggie were near the doorway to the larger restaurant room, looking tense and frustrated as they argued in low voices.

Just for a moment, Xan had a sense of what Mallory must feel when she was in this situation. *Mal's right; if someone dies tonight, it's probably going to be Oscar. And I don't know what to do to prevent it.*

Mallory would know what to do. He had to get her back here. As Jessica tapped her fork on her glass for attention, Xan slipped past the arguing couple by the door.

"It's not my connection with Oscar we need to worry about," Reggie was saying as Xan walked past. "I've seen how you look at him."

Outside, he took a deep breath. He pushed a button on his watch to contact Mallory and saw the watch was dead. It had zero charge. *Infinity* always charged everything that needed it, and he had forgotten that he had to do it himself when she was gone. He went back inside to a wall terminal by the bar, ignoring the Gurudev waiter who tried to stop him. He poked a few buttons, but the terminal remained black.

"Comms are down, sir," the Gurudev said. "I could have told you that, had you asked."

He barely heard Jessica finish her speech. There was polite applause from the humans, rumbling from the Gneiss, and the Phantasmagore flashed their skin a number of pleasant shades of blue and green. And the Gurudev didn't respond at all. Jessica would have to learn how different species showed their appreciation. He hoped she wasn't expecting a standing ovation.

He watched Oscar polish off his beer and saunter toward the other humans, holding two steaming mugs of a Gneiss liquor. Now he was drinking alien booze, which was never good if you didn't know what you were drinking. Xan had to stop him.

But then Jessica was in front of him, smelling like flowers and wine. Her hair was loose now, flowing down her back in messy dark waves. She toyed with one of her hair sticks, frowning at it. "I lost one, dammit. Keep an eye out for me? They were a gift." Then she looked up at Xan and smiled. "My job here is done. I'm exhausted, and this station is still a maze to me. Walk me home?"

He looked around her, trying to keep track of Oscar's bald head, but it disappeared behind a huge Gneiss.

"I don't think now is a good time," he stammered.

She crossed her arms. "Mrs. Brown told me that you were my liaison here. I need a walk home, and frankly, I don't trust anyone else."

I could at least keep her *safe*, he thought, and sighed. He was probably jumping at shadows, since Mallory wasn't here to jump at them. None of these academics looked like they were going to snap and start stabbing people. He sighed again. "All right. I'll walk you home."

10

· · ·

THE MURDER MALLORY MISSED

MALLORY COULD MAKE it home. She could do that much.

Home. Showered. The stench of anxiety and fear had finally left her, and she could breathe easier. She lay on her bed and stared at the ceiling, remembering Amy in high school. And trying to remember Parker.

But why had she forgotten him in the first place?

Once she had touched his shirt, the memories came flooding back.

In school, Amy had been a little bossy, harsh at times, but a good friend.

Mallory was a shy kid, even more so once her mother had died and she had to live with her aunt, who firmly put her in the "other" column when it came to immediate family, even though she was Mallory's guardian. Mallory had been fine with another girl setting their social rules.

Until it came to Parker, that is.

She'd fallen for Parker's wide green eyes, and fallen hard. But Amy was protective of her "little" brother and believed firmly in the rule that you do not date your friends' siblings or exes.

"It's ancient friend rules! Older than time and high school it-self," she had proclaimed importantly.

So Mallory kept her distance. But every time she saw him in the halls, or hanging out at Amy's house, he was looking at her.

Do amazingly hot people know they're amazingly hot? How can he not know that I pretty much die inside when I see him? she wrote in her anonymous blog one night. It sparked a lively debate, which pleased her, but the answer itself didn't matter. Whether he meant to or not, he was invading her head and taking up residence there.

Amy eventually noticed and got mad. She surprised Mallory by getting mad at Parker, not herself, and told him to lay off her friends. She cited more ancient rules. She yelled. She even cried. Things were tense for some time, and Mallory decided if she and Parker dated and then broke up, she'd probably lose both of them, so she lied and said she was interested in a basketball player named David.

This was a mistake. Amy also had a crush on David. Mallory had committed to the lie and stayed away from Parker. But she still dreamed about his eyes, and looking at him was still a painful jolt.

Parker was one of those lazy good students: he made average grades, excelling in things he loved and squeaking by on things he didn't care about. He'd had little ambition until he discovered biology. In all other classes, he was the crafty one, cutting corners, pulling pranks, and losing points on tests for being a smartass in-stead of answering the questions. He'd also been funny, kind, and chaotic. Also accident-prone.

Mallory remembered a very weird argument he and Amy'd had, when Amy was telling him he had the worst luck in the world and he needed to be more careful. Parker had been playing Fris-bee in the school parking lot and a car hit him. While they waited for the ambulance, Amy berated her brother.

"I don't know if you're a moron or have the worst luck in the world!" she yelled as the EMTs were putting him onto a stretcher.

Amy got into the ambulance with him, still yelling, while Mallory watched, stricken.

"Worst luck?" Parker had said as they loaded him in. "What are you talking about? I got hit by a car and only broke my leg! That's amazing luck!" he'd said. His face was still pale, but he was smiling at the time.

"Your head is bleeding," Amy said, waving her arms. "You could have a concussion! You could need stitches!"

He laughed at her, then met Mallory's eyes as the ambulance doors closed.

At graduation, Amy was salutatorian and got a full ride to Elon University to study physical therapy. She was seated up front with the top ten. Mallory was twelfth in the class, which sounded impressive but got her absolutely nothing in the way of academic perks. And she was seated at the end of the alphabetical line as usual.

This put her directly beside Parker, and for the first time, they were put together by outside forces, where Amy couldn't separate them. Amy didn't even know, since their names, Viridian and Valor, were usually separated alphabetically by a boy with the unfortunate name of Landry Violence. (Who had once explained to Mallory that his dad had changed his name from Cowart to Violence before Landry was born. "It was a hypermasculine thing. He blames the 1990s but doesn't want to go through the trouble of changing it back.") But Landry hadn't shown up to graduation.

She had never been this close to Parker for such a lengthy time, and it was driving her to distraction.

She caught him glancing at her sidelong, and when the principal started giving his speech, Parker leaned in and whispered in her ear, "Hey."

Her entire face had heated up at that one word, but she swallowed to keep her composure. "Hey. Where's Landry?"

"I paid him five hundred bucks to stay home today," he replied, nonchalant.

She whipped her head around to stare at him, nearly upsetting her mortarboard. "You what? Why?"

He smirked at her. "Why do you think?" he asked. "She's already told me I can't dance with you at prom."

Amy had told Mallory the same thing, which was starting to get old. "Yeah. Me, too," she whispered, frowning. "But why did you spend so much just to sit here at graduation? It's not like we can talk much or anything."

"Worth it," he said, and then faced the principal again with a faux-attentive look on his face.

She tried to stop smiling but couldn't, and tried to pay attention to the speeches. She looked down at her lap; the program had gone damp in her hands and she'd been idly shredding it. To stop herself, she put her hands down by her legs and took a deep breath. *He should not have this much effect on me,* she told herself sternly. *He's just a guy and you're both going to different colleges soon anyway.*

Her breath caught in her throat when she felt the hesitant touch of a finger against the side of her hand. His touch was hot, almost painful. Was that reality or just her perception? She had no idea, but she opened her palm and let him twine his fingers with hers. Nobody's touch, no kiss, no hug, had affected her like this. The world had become just Mallory and Parker, and all she could do was keep herself from throwing herself at him in the middle of graduation.

Mallory had thought her face couldn't get more flushed, but when Amy got up to give her speech, Mallory was sure that she was staring right at them. Parker gripped her hand tighter during Amy's speech.

They reluctantly released each other when they had to stand

to receive their diplomas. And when graduation was over, the spell was broken. Amy joined them with their grandmother, who commented that the heat of the day was starting to affect Mallory. Parker had somehow stayed cool the whole time, not even looking at her as they removed their hats and robes.

Prom was the following weekend. They had gone in a group of people, but with different dates, and barely spoke all night.

Then high school was over. Whatever tension remained between the three of them was buried by external forces, namely, the end of high school, Parker and Amy moving north, and college. Mallory had considered trying to keep in touch with them, but she had started to experience more and more murders happening around her, and she felt it would be safer for her friends if she stayed away.

She told herself she was keeping them safe. Then she was telling herself that she was keeping Amy safe, Parker fading from her mind.

Disappearing entirely. Until now.

AND DRAUGHN? WHY was Draughn at the station?

He was in his fifties, but she knew he still aspired to transfer to the FBI. He had told her he wanted the job mainly so he would have the resources to really investigate Mallory and truly find out why she showed up in so many local murders. Mallory doubted the feds held data back from state agents investigating multiple homicides and told him so, and he had just yelled at her that she didn't know anything about it.

She did know. She'd done the research when she had started to put Draughn into her novelizations of the murders she solved (under a different name, of course). She didn't tell him that, though, because he didn't need another reason to dislike her.

She couldn't shake the feeling that Draughn was there for her, for some old grudge, instead of just for a break like he had claimed.

If Draughn was friends with Amy, she had to know that he had tracked Mallory's association with murders for years. Amy had to be lying about not knowing Mallory was on the station. She'd poorly faked being surprised to see Mallory, and any human coming here had to know the names of the only four people on board.

Four Sundry flew into the room through the vent shaft.

"Threat. Danger. Confusion. Old threat and new threat and old threat and new . . . new . . . new . . ."

She jumped up. "Tell me what's going on! And where the hell have you been? There's dead silvers all over the shuttle bay, and no one will talk to me!"

The silver Sundry had come to warn her earlier, and they never made an effort to warn people. It was probably due to their lack of experience that the warnings were enigmatic and therefore useless. Mallory needed concrete details, which didn't often come with communications with the Sundry.

She tracked them as they flew around the room. "Things are weird on the station, and there are a lot of people from my past here. I already know things are scary and confusing. Tell me something I can use."

"Unknown. Unknown. Distress. Confusion. Unknown." The Sundry landed on her bed as one and Mallory had a weird feeling of a teen friend flopping down to tell her a miserable secret.

"How can you not know? You know everything."

"Unknown. Unknown. Chaos. Chaos. Unknown . . ." The chant continued with growing intensity, until the Sundry took flight again, buzzed once around the room, then left through the vent.

"Hey, I'm not done!" she yelled into the shaft.

A few final words echoed down the shaft: "Unknown. Confusion. Chaos. Chaos. Chaos."

"Shit. Now what?" she said.

She would have thought she was too worried to sleep, but her recent days' adventures had taken a lot out of her, and she dozed off at last.

· · · ·

MALLORY FELL INTO a troubled sleep, dreaming of angry colors. When she was growing up, she had imagined colors with personalities, with Red as a dominant, kind of mean leader, Blue as a standoffish bookish person, Orange being the party animal no one took seriously, Yellow being a force for good and fairness, and Green being the one that always flew under the radar, a trickster god of the visual color spectrum.

Not that she called Green a trickster when she was ten. She called it the hider. Green was good at hiding in plain sight because it was everywhere there were plants.

In her dreams, the colors argued, and she didn't know what the topic was, but they were all very distressed. Then Orange began pounding its fist on a tablet to get attention.

Pound pound pound.

Pound pound pound.

Mallory struggled to wake up. The pounding was real, someone at her door.

"Christ, what is going on?" she yelled. It had to be Tina. She still didn't understand how people needed sleep, and her gentlest knocks sounded like they could bring a wall down.

"Tina? Is that you?" she asked, pushing the button to let the door slide aside.

Draughn stood there, eyes wide, face covered in blood.

"Mallory. Help," he whispered, and fell forward into her arms.

"Shit," she blurted, trying to catch him and lower him gently to the floor. He was much bigger than her, and there was no way she was getting him farther into her apartment.

"Eternity, please call security," she called in desperation.

There was no answering tone to indicate Eternity was there to help.

Swearing, Mallory did a quick check of Draughn's body, looking for the wound. He had a nasty cut on his face, which oozed blood, but he otherwise looked fine. *He must be in shock. Or concussed.*

His left hand was swollen, and Mallory inspected closer. Tiny punctures dotted his palm, with some silver and blue smeared bodies.

"Oh, God, Draughn, what did you do? There's got to be a swarm somewhere."

Were any communications working? She poked at her watch to try to rouse Xan, but he didn't answer. Ferd was also not answering. Mallory gritted her teeth and then contacted Stephanie.

"Steph, can you contact Tina? I need some help and I can't get anyone else."

"I can do that. But you might want to get up here. There's a Sundry swarm in the shuttle bay. And something else—"

"I know there's a swarm," Mallory snapped, getting a blanket to cover Draughn, "but I've got a bloody human collapsed in my apartment right now and I can't contact security. Can you just send Tina?"

"It's difficult to contact security right now," Stephanie replied. "When you can get through, they just tell you that everything is fine."

"Fine?" Mallory asked, startled. "Fuck. Okay. I'm going to call medbay. Thanks for getting Tina for me."

"She may not come," Stephanie warned. "She's distracted by something."

"Great," Mallory muttered. "I'll deal with it, then."

She ran to the fridge and got some ice out of the freezer. She wrapped the cubes in a dish towel and put it on Draughn's hand.

Draughn was a big man. Instead of going through the embarrassment of attempting to move him, she got a rag and held it to his head.

"Now what?" she asked aloud.

She tried not to think about what it meant that Eternity wasn't allowing emergency messages. Or what was up with Eternity. Who else could she call who might help her? Were any calls connecting anywhere?

Ugh. There was one more person she could get, but she hated to do so. Adrian lived a few halls over, and it wouldn't take a lot of time for her to run to get him. And he might know how to get in touch with Devanshi, his Phantasmagore friend who used to be on security.

Draughn stirred and tried to pull his hand away from the ice. Mallory held his arm in place.

"No, dude, you need the ice. You're wearing a catcher's mitt." She ran another dish towel under water and then wiped some blood off his normally ruddy face. On the third pass of the cold cloth over his cheeks and forehead, he opened his eyes. She applied pressure to the cut on his head.

"Draughn, what happened to you?" she asked, trying not to let the strain show through in her voice, knowing she shouldn't get him excited again.

He winced and put his hand to his head. "Fuck, what hit me?" he asked. Then he saw his other hand and his eyes went wide.

"I don't know. You showed up here, covered in blood, and passed out," she said, gesturing to her apartment and the bloodstains on her floor and her clothes. "You've clearly been stung by Sundry. You had their guts all over your hands, which doesn't bode well, by the way."

"Can I have some water?"

"Draughn, what happened?" she insisted, but she did jump up to get him water. She held his head as he drank. "If you have a concussion, you may be nauseous. Take only a sip."

He struggled to sit up, the cloth falling from his forehead. It immediately started to bleed again. He fumbled it back to his head and sipped at the mug she handed him.

"Tell me what happened. Is anyone else hurt? I can't contact security, so we'll need to go help whoever else is injured." *Or dead, but please don't be dead*, she thought.

"No, not you. Don't need your help."

Mallory bristled. "You just came here in the middle of the night, covered in blood, asking for help. And now you don't want help? Sitting on the floor and drinking my water and staining my washcloths with your nasty blood. It's not the time to go back to old habits." She took a deep breath and softened her voice. "Look. I don't know what happened here tonight, but you came to me asking for help. So let me help."

"I don't know." His hands shook, spilling water over the edge. "There were bees. Wasps. Huge bugs."

"Sundry," she corrected.

"Whatever. We were closing down the party. We had jet lag, or space lag, and none of the humans were really tired. Most of the aliens had gone. Then the wasps were there, then the body fell out of the closet, and it was chaos. I tried to swat them away, but they just attacked me."

"Yeah, like they do on Earth if you attack hornets," Mallory said.

"They stung me and I—don't remember much after that."

"If you got injected with Sundry venom that many times, I'm surprised you're still alive," Mallory said.

"God, the dreams I had when I was out," he muttered. "I saw my first day at the SBI. I saw my promotion. I saw you and one of your murders. I saw—" He grimaced. "Then it was like I was drowning in light. I couldn't breathe."

"Sounds like typical dreams to me," Mallory said impatiently. "Did you say something about a body?"

"No, these were much clearer than dreams," Draughn said. "I had your address in my pocket, so I came here."

"What about the body, Draughn? And the other humans? Were they in the room with the swarm?"

He squinted. "I remember Amy, Parker, that obnoxious coach, and the gay couple."

"Whose body fell out of the closet, though?"

"I don't remember," Draughn mumbled. "You should let security handle it," he said faintly. "Don't get involved."

"I told you I can't. And if you wanted that, then you should have run to security. And if you're well enough to be an asshole, you're well enough to at least stand up. Come on, Agent."

He didn't move. His eyes fluttered closed and he slumped over to the side.

She knelt by his head and slapped his cheeks, gently, then harder. "Dammit, no, don't pass out on me again!"

He was out. He was breathing, at least, but Mallory remembered that concussion victims were supposed to stay awake, so passing out again wasn't a good thing.

Relief washed over her when she heard a pounding coming down the hall, a sound that usually irritated Mallory (and most Gneiss, since "hurry" was a swear word in their language). But now she welcomed the sound. The cavalry—an unreliable, giant pink cavalry—was on its way.

The door slid open. "Xan won't let me use my jets in the halls," Tina said by way of greeting, sticking her head in. "Stephanie said you needed me! Me! I'm so excited!"

"Thanks for coming," Mallory said in relief. "Can you take this man—carefully!—to the medbay? I can't lift him and the security comms aren't working."

"I can do that! I thought you were going to ask me something difficult or cuckoo," she said.

Mallory forced her shoulders to relax. "No, in this case the favor I need is simple, but really important. Will you do it?"

"Sure," Tina boomed. She reached down and grabbed Draughn by his feet.

"Carefully!" Mallory warned as Tina tossed him in the air and caught him. The man groaned.

"Tina!" Mallory said. "Do I have to tell you again that we're much more fragile than you are?"

"Fine," Tina said, draping Draughn over her arm with exaggerated care. She paused. "The medbay has technology more advanced than anything you have on Earth. Why are you worried?"

Mallory froze, startled by the intelligent question. "Uh, they told me the medical databases were down. That was one of the problems the station's been having. With no human doctors here, and no human medical databases, there's not much the medbay can do."

"Oh," Tina said. "That makes sense. I'm ready. Let's go."

"I'm not going," Mallory said. "I need to figure out what happened to Draughn and if anyone else is hurt."

"But I was going to tell you all sorts of cuckoo things," Tina said, a plaintive note coming across the translator bug.

"You can tell me all the crazy things you want when this crisis is over," Mallory said, pulling a jacket over her pajamas and following her out the door. "But now is the worst time. Please get him to the medbay soon."

"Fine," Tina said, and started pounding down the hall.

Something pulled at Mallory's mind as she watched Tina run off, but she couldn't figure out what was bothering her. She'd think of it some other time. She had to figure out what Draughn was running from.

LUCKILY, ADRIAN'S APARTMENT lay between hers and the lift she needed to get back to the park.

Adrian, to his credit, took her panic seriously and contacted Devanshi immediately with a tool similar to the one Mallory and Xan shared. People could develop private comm channels on devices between friends that didn't need the station comms relay to transmit, but Mallory didn't have Adrian on hers. She'd reasoned that she'd never need it.

When they'd met her, Devanshi had been high in station security, but she had quit after the events of last fall. She missed the entirety of the action with the serial killer Mallory and her friends were catching because she was trudging around the station trying to find someone to take a very wounded Adrian Casserly-Berry off her hands. She saw that as a sign that security work wasn't for her. Now Devanshi had become a hardware and software expert, designing drones like the one that helped Adrian around. Mallory didn't know her that well, but Adrian seemed to trust her. And he didn't like anyone.

Devanshi had been vital to figuring out what was wrong with Eternity at that time by using a drone to connect with her on a more basic level.

Mallory told them what was going on with the humans. "And I figured someone in the know needs to find out why security isn't responding. Can you do that?"

"Security is probably dealing with the problems with station navigation and comms right now," Devanshi said.

"Wait, you know about the problems with the station?" Mallory asked, staring.

"Of course I do. Hundreds of people do," Devanshi said, cocking her insectoid head.

"Did you think you had privileged information?" Adrian asked. His tone would have withered her, but she had so little respect for him she ignored it.

"That's rich, coming from you," she said. "I didn't think I was special because I was the only one who knew. I thought I might be one of a few who knew because no one is doing anything about it!"

"With the station not responding, it's hard to do anything,"

Devanshi said. "But you can see how they're likely very busy and can't bother themselves with a small attack."

"Devanshi, this wasn't a small attack," Mallory said, frustrated. "It was a Sundry swarm. They aren't supposed to swarm and attack people like hornets from Earth! Don't you think that's weird?"

Devanshi's skin started to change color, mixing in with the tan wall behind her. She was either thinking hard or frightened, as far as Mallory understood Phantasmagore. "Then all of these things are connected, possibly also to the movements of the station and the comms problems."

"The medbay is also having trouble with their databases," Mallory said thoughtfully. "Do you really think they're connected?"

Adrian laughed, a mean sound. "Don't you? Isn't that what you're always saying, that connections just form around you like children playing ring-around-the-rosy?"

Mallory ignored the cruel tone. He was right. She could almost see unrelated things connect in her mind's eye as she contemplated the murders she solved. She used to be able to, anyway. Right now nothing occurred to her.

"I have to go," she said. "You're probably right that they're connected. Can you get in touch with your friends in security and see if they know what's going on? If only to put our minds at ease. If stuff is connected, then it's possible we can help each other."

"We'll do that right now," Devanshi said.

"'We' will?" Adrian asked.

"Come on, Adrian, you don't want to lose a chance to be a hero just because you were fussy," Mallory said, then ran toward the lift.

THE RESTAURANT WAS in chaos. Morn, the owner, stood at the wall terminal trying to contact security and medbay. The view was surreal, since the translation bug wasn't great at conveying emotion, so the energy in the room was frantic, with Gurudev servers running to and from the room with the tables, the owner at the terminal, and all the voices completely deadpan.

"I can't raise security, I can't raise medbay, and the humans abandoned their own. They're monsters." The Gurudev turned away and fixed its compound eyes on Mallory. "You are here. Go get your people."

From the dining room, Mallory could hear loud buzzing.

"How many are in there?" she asked, glancing through the doorway. She couldn't see anything but the occasional blue glint.

"Three humans. Two are not moving," Morn said.

Still not sure what she was supposed to do for a Sundry swarm, especially since they didn't seem to be listening to her on any level, she edged to the doorway.

Her breath caught in her throat. In front of an open closet door, two bodies lay on the floor, one face up, one face down. Oscar's bald head and large white tracksuit were very obvious, and beside him lay Amy in a tangle of blond hair, blood trickling from a wound on her head. She was very pale.

But the most shocking thing was Parker. He sat, dazed, in the middle of the room, staring at the blue Sundry that swarmed around him. His blue eyes were wide and vacant as the large insects made complex patterns in the air. Then, as one, they flew into the ventilation shaft and disappeared. Parker swayed slightly, blinked, and then focused on Mallory.

"Mallory?" He looked at the bodies on the floor and scooted backward in alarm, and then shot forward to check on Amy.

"Are you okay?" she asked, approaching.

He didn't answer her, just touched Amy's face gingerly. "We need Max, someone get Max." He didn't appear to be stung or in any distress, or any bleeding distress, anyway.

Mallory checked to see if Amy was alive. She was out cold, but breathing. Then she looked at the second body.

Oscar was dead. No question about it; a puncture wound leaked blood from the left side of his chest, staining his tracksuit. No weapon was readily available, but they were in a restaurant, the best place to kill someone with a knife and throw it into a dishwasher to scour away the evidence.

There was less blood than she expected. The strike must have killed him instantly and the blood hadn't had the heart behind it to push it out its new exit hole. Oscar's smug face had turned to slack horror in death, and Mallory felt a familiar regret; he had been a creep, but he hadn't deserved this.

A few feet beyond him, Amy lay with her head now in Parker's lap. His anguished eyes met hers. "We need help!"

Strangely enough, the remaining Sundry in the room ignored her, circling Parker and landing on Amy several times, then taking off again. Then a few landed on Mallory, and she had a swimmy feeling of vertigo, but then they took off and left the room.

She looked up at Parker again. The urge to run overcame her once more, but she closed her eyes and breathed deeply.

"I'll get some help," she said.

PARKER SAID HE had worked as an EMT in grad school, so he was able to look at his sister and determine that she was likely concussed. They got her on her back and Mallory was able to convey a message to medbay through Tina, who was only too happy to not be a human taxi anymore.

Morn had begrudgingly handed over a red tablecloth when Mallory explained the human need to cover dead bodies, in part because of respect, but also because they were often disturbing. It didn't bother her, since she'd been around more dead bodies than most, but she still adhered to the classic procedures.

Parker sat at a table beside Amy while Mallory gave a cursory look at the area for footprints or anything weird or out of place.

She'd never been to Morn's restaurant before the party, so she wasn't sure of the usual layout, but having an actual closet in the dining room seemed weird. It was a large closet, full of cleaning supplies and bolts of colorful cloth. An overturned bucket had spilled something clear, shiny, and viscous on the floor. Mallory touched it with her fingertip gingerly; it was slick. She thought she had seen Gurudev food made with this substance, but on the other hand, would they store it in a bucket in a closet?

She went back to Parker and sat down across from him, the anxiety building again. She was getting tired of this. "So, what did I miss?" she asked with a bitter smile. "I came in at the end."

"I'm not sure," he said, not looking at her. "We were talking about getting ready to go, but someone noticed that Oscar wasn't around. We looked for him and assumed he went back to his room early."

"Oscar didn't seem like the kind of person to leave a party early without telling anyone," Mallory said. "He would either stay till the end, or brag loudly that he was leaving with a woman."

"You got it in one," Parker said, glancing at the covered body on the floor. "Then a lot of things happened at the same time." He frowned. "Don opened the closet and Oscar fell out. Don caught him and put him on the floor, but it was clear he was dead already. We ran up to see what was going on, and then—"

He broke off, his eyes going glassy again.

"The swarm?" Mallory prompted.

"Yeah, the swarm," he said. "They just flew in, and there was chaos and noise, and the next thing I knew, everyone else was gone except for you and—" He gestured vaguely to the two people on the floor.

"Did you get stung?" she asked, eyes raking over him. He wore a black button-down shirt and black slacks, leaving only his face, neck, and hands exposed. They could have climbed inside his clothing, but Sundry rarely did that when there were ready targets available.

"No," he said.

"Doesn't look like Amy did either. Draughn got stung several times. I'm surprised he survived."

Parker looked shocked. "Don? You saw him?"

Mallory told him about Draughn showing up, injured and stung. "So you didn't see what happened to him and Amy to get those head wounds?"

Parker shook his head. "Once the—the Sundry arrived, I don't remember anything."

Mallory looked around the room again. Usually things started to coalesce at this point; she could see how things could have worked together, possible vectors to form this eventual result. There was nothing. "Who else was in the room when all this happened?" she finally asked.

"Everyone from the college, Reggie, and Don."

"And who was from the college?" Mallory asked patiently. She pulled a notebook out of her jacket pocket.

"There's Max, of course, our older brother's husband."

She blinked at him. "Wait, you have an older brother?" She tried to remember, and had a dim memory of Amy referencing a brother who had already gone to college and was rarely home. "Oh, right. Reggie. He's five years older?"

"Six," Parker said. "I don't know if you ever met him. He's doing lawyer things now. Max is an experimental psychologist professor with us at UNC."

"And they were all in here, and they all ran," Mallory said, writing in her notebook.

"They were in here when we found Oscar's body, and they're not here now," Parker said. "That's all I know."

"What about before all this? Who was spending time with Oscar, who was drinking a lot, did anyone seem upset at anything?"

Parker thought for a moment. "After you met Oscar, he went to hit on Amy. I followed him because I know he can be a charming bastard when he wants to be."

"Doesn't Amy know how you feel about him?"

Parker shrugged. "Yeah, but you know. Pheromones. Oscar has never had a problem getting dates."

Something went ping in Mallory's brain, but before she could connect the dots, the stomping of Gneiss feet came into the restaurant. Four massive bodies, all wearing armbands with five stars, indicating medbay personnel, approached. They held coffin-like pods between them.

Parker jumped up. "Are you here for my sister?"

"Which one is a sister?" one of the orderlies said.

Mallory pointed to Amy. "This is his sister. She's alive with a head wound, as far as I can tell." She pointed to Oscar. "He's dead."

"We'll leave that one, then," said the Gneiss in front, a grayish blue with gold accents running through them. "We don't have time or room for wet, dead bodies."

"What's going on?" Mallory asked.

"Comms are down station-wide. Security keeps telling us that everything is fine. Navigation tells us that everything is fine. And our xenobiology database is down. And there is one human in the medbay already that we don't know what to do with."

"Is he conscious?" Mallory asked.

"Not when we left, no," the Gneiss said.

"Will you be able to help her?" Parker asked.

"We can stabilize her, stop that wet mess that is coming from her head, see if she has any other damage," the Gneiss said. "But we can't do much until the database is back up."

"We have to take this one in now," the Gneiss said bluntly. They loaded Amy into one of the pods, working efficiently and with a lot more care than Tina ever gave.

"I'm coming with you. I can help with medical questions," Parker said.

The Gneiss headed for the door, the one in front saying over their shoulder, "No. We will let you know when she's stabilized. If comms are working. Things are too chaotic."

To Mallory's surprise, Parker accepted that.

"Wait, no, you can't leave that garbage here," Morn said, pointing to Oscar's body as the Gneiss left the restaurant. "Who will get rid of this?"

Mallory sent messages to Xan and Devanshi on their private network, hoping their personal connections could bypass the broken comms. Help would be good. So would information. Then she sat back in the chair with a sigh.

The constant fear spikes Parker seemed to cause were exhausting. It wasn't as bad as it had been earlier that night, but she was done with anything demanding her attention other than murder. She'd reached her limit. "Looks like I have a crime scene to investigate. You should go back to your room."

Parker laughed, a slightly hysterical noise that sounded half like he was choking. "And leave you here alone? With a murderer around?"

She rolled her eyes. "This isn't a rare course of events. I'll be fine. And I work better alone."

"Didn't you just call your friends for help?" he challenged, leaning forward over the table.

"I can't carry injured people to the medbay by myself," she said. "But when it comes to the crime scenes, I'm good on my own."

"But—" Parker betrayed his own objections with a yawn.

"Go back to your room. Or go to the medbay to be with Amy. I'll contact you tomorrow. I'll have more questions."

He stared at her with hurt in his blue eyes, and then turned and left.

Besides, she thought bitterly, *you're a suspect, too.*

And here we go again.

PART TWO

We brought you fire, dumbed it down so you could
    understand it
But now you think it's magic, you're taking us for granted
You used the very tech and platforms that we created
To spit disgust and spread distrust of everything we've ever stated
Now we can research for years, present our data in reams
But if your mother's plumber's meth dealer sends you some memes
Despite the lack of proof you think they're just as valid as fact
So now we're forming a pack
We're gonna take the fire back

       —"Take the Fire Back (Prometheus Has Left the Building)"
          by Worm Quartet (featuring Devo Spice),
             written by Timothy F. Crist

11

. . . .

NEW SUNDRY AND OLD FRIENDS

XAN HAD EXHIBITED willpower of mammoth proportions by leaving Jessica Brass, star point guard, new ambassador to the station, and terrifyingly attractive woman, alone in her apartment after he walked her back.

After she had given her speech at the restaurant and made tense coffee plans with Adrian for the following day, she had asked Xan for a nighttime tour of the station since she wasn't sure how to get back from the restaurant.

"Mrs. Brown asked me to help you however I can," he said. "Want me to show you the park?"

He pointed out various restaurants and shops, then the Sundry nest in the trees on the edge of the park.

"How many live in there?" she asked.

"I don't know, but it's got to be hundreds, possibly thousands," he said. "Mallory would know."

"I've read about you," she said with a smile. "You have quite the file."

He stiffened. "And?" he asked.

"There are people back home who would really like to see you come home in handcuffs," she said. "There are others who want you to come home a hero. I've spoken to both and told them that our diplomatic efforts with the station hinge entirely on treating you well. I've also reminded them that you could easily abuse this, and you haven't done so."

Xan smiled bitterly, looking at the full moon. "It hasn't occurred to me. I guess they told you about God's Breath and the attempt to fuck up the station?"

She laughed, her head tilted and dark hair flowing down her back. "It took some pushing, but yeah, I found out about that. I assume Elizabeth Brown knows that humanity's hope for diplomacy with aliens hinges on her? If she hadn't joined with Eternity, I can't imagine any alien race being welcoming to us." She paused. "That's another person who they would like to come home either in cuffs or to a parade. Or to be dissected and studied."

Xan shuddered. "I can imagine. That would be a monumentally bad idea."

"I am aware," Jessica said. "And then there's Mallory, with her unique ability and connection to the hivemind of the Sundry."

Xan paused, then looked at her. "And? What about Mallory?"

"She's just fascinating, that's all," Jessica said. "Connection to all that knowledge. It makes her powerful."

"She hates it," he said flatly. "She doesn't trust the Sundry, so she doesn't access the hivemind much. It's overwhelming for her."

"That seems like such a waste!" Jessica said. "But to know that, you two must be close?"

"We're friends," he confirmed.

"Just friends?" she pushed.

"That's pretty personal," he said, getting annoyed.

"Well, out of four people on the station, only two are young and attractive; seems like it would be a foregone conclusion," she said lightly.

"That's pretty cold, Adrian can't help the way he looks," Xan said.

"I meant Adrian is unattractive on the inside," Jessica amended. "And stop deflecting."

"Mrs. Brown is busy all the time, and Adrian already hates me and Mal. We didn't want to risk animosity between the two of us. Mal and I . . ." He paused, searching for the words. "We need each other in more ways than romantically." He also didn't feel a huge need for love in his life since bonding with *Infinity*, but Jessica didn't need to know that. Mallory understood their connection, which was the only thing that mattered.

They entered an elevator occupied by a few Gurudev. Xan was grateful for a distraction and showed Jessica how to work the basic controls to get home. "Usually Eternity won't let you get lost if you're just going home," he explained, "but right now we don't know how much she's aware of."

"So there's nothing between you," Jessica said, arching a perfectly shaped eyebrow.

"Yes, we're not anything more than friends," he said flatly.

She turned away from him to the doors, taking on the standard elevator etiquette. "Good."

Heat flooded his face and he fought to keep his cool. The Gurudev exited the elevator on the next stop, and then they were alone.

She was tall, nearly as tall as he was, and with heels, she was slightly taller. She glanced over at him and smirked.

"I'm glad Elizabeth assigned you to show me around," she said. "Will I see you in the morning?"

The unstated suggestion sat between them like an invisible force field. He cleared his throat. "I can come by to get you for breakfast if you like. There are a couple of good places you should try.

"Oh, and no one calls her Elizabeth. She's Mrs. Brown to everyone. And, uh, she's not someone you want to piss off."

"Is that so?" Jessica said mildly, as if she didn't give a shit about this topic.

The elevator arrived on her level and they exited. "I need to go back to my room and give Mal a call. Make sure she got home all right."

Jessica touched the button to open her door, keyed to a subtle and unique biological signal. "Is it true that Eternity will modify the apartment to my needs? Like, tub instead of shower, or large bed instead of small?"

Xan refused to rise to the bait again. "Yeah, typically. Again, I don't know how accommodating she'll be while Mrs. B is gone, but eventually your room will fit you to your specifications."

She stepped closer to him. He resisted the urge to step away. This woman's sheer personality was a lot. He had known that when he'd seen her play basketball and didn't doubt she'd be an excellent diplomat.

She smelled like lavender and wine. She smiled, close-lipped, a small, knowing smirk. "I hope we spend some more time together, Xan. I'd love to get to know you better. You're extremely attractive."

For a hot, breathless moment, he thought she was going to kiss him, but she gave a little wave and stepped into her apartment.

"Fuuuuck," he muttered.

He'd planned on going back to his room, but Jessica had thrown his mind into turmoil, so he went for a walk through the corridors of Eternity.

Ever since he saw her first postgame interview, he knew that Jessica was the kind of woman you admire from afar, knowing if you got too close, you could get burned. But Xan had spent a good deal of time hoping he could test that theory. What was a little burn between friends?

But there were complexities to work through, and whatever he might want, he knew that falling into bed with the new permanent resident of the station the first night she got there would likely end very badly.

He thought of the last time he'd been with someone, and then purposefully thought of something else. Anything else.

"YOU SHOULDN'T HURRY," Ferdinand said. "Your people have such a small energy store."

Xan hadn't realized he was walking fast until Ferdinand pointed out that he was rushing when he came into the bar. "Yeah, got lost in thought," he said.

"It's time for you to be dormant now, right?" Ferdinand said. The Gneiss found sleep a waste of time and were baffled by the species who needed it. They did go dormant to rest on occasion— in fact, there was an ossuary on a lower level of Eternity just for sleeping Gneiss—but not regularly.

"I don't think I'd be able to sleep now," he said, rubbing the back of his head. "Can I get something to drink?"

"Of course," Ferdinand said. He went into the kitchen behind the bar.

Xan climbed up onto the barstool created for people his size (a barstool that required a few rungs of a ladder to get on but put him at the proper height at the bar) and placed his forearms on the surface.

The bar was made of black obsidian, always sleek, always cold. He liked how the chilly shock grounded him. The bar itself was usually pretty warm, thanks to the heat of the drinks Ferdinand sold, but the actual tables and bar had the heat-sucking ability of stone.

A movement caught his eye down the bar. Five large wasps crawled over the obsidian, touching it briefly with their antennae. The appearance of Sundry was not strange.

Their color was. These wasps were green.

His eyes grew wide. "Now, what the fuck are you?" he asked.

Despite his question, the wasps didn't react. Another buzz sounded from a shelf close to the ceiling, where three blue Sundry sat atop a jar of some kind of goo the Gneiss enjoyed floating in their alcohol. The green wasps froze, then buzzed their wings fiercely, an obvious challenge in the sound. The blue Sundry buzzed in response and then took off over Xan's head, through the open door of the bar. Four of the green wasps took off after them, leaving one behind.

Xan leaned as far as he could off his barstool to get a closer look at the remaining wasp. "What was that all about?"

Ferdinand returned with Xan's drink. He had recently stocked some cups that fit human hands better, even though he couldn't really understand how humans could enjoy such a small amount of drink. He had also turned down the heat on the human-potable drinks to "cold" to a Gneiss.

"I thought you would be with Mallory," Ferdinand said.

"Why does everyone think that?" Xan asked, irritated, but then he realized Ferdinand just meant proximity.

"Because she asked for help," Ferdinand said. "Stephanie said she couldn't get in touch with you, so she had to ask Tina for help."

"Shit," Xan said, looking at his watch out of habit. He had forgotten it was still dead. "What's going on?"

"Another murder, I expect," Ferdinand said. "She tried to contact me, too, but I thought that all comms were down, so I turned everything off."

Xan stared at him. Whenever he thought he and Mallory had started to make close friends with the Gneiss, they would say something that would underscore the stark differences in their mind-sets. "Where is she?"

Ferdinand paused, and Xan felt a minuscule rumble through the floor as he communicated with Gneiss around the station. "She's back at the party. Which I suppose isn't a party anymore."

He dimly appreciated Ferdinand's subtle humor but didn't have time for it. He jumped off his barstool. "I need to go."

"There's no current emergency; you can finish your drink. I made it cold just for you," Ferdinand said. He paused again, then said, "Besides, she's on her way here."

"YOU STILL LOOK like hell," he told Mallory.

"Are you trying to butter me up for a reason?" she asked, eyebrow raised. She sat on the barstool next to his, dark shadows under her eyes and her hair mussed. She had a small blood smear on her forehead, just visible beyond her bangs.

"Sorry. Just concerned," he said. "What happened?"

She told him of Draughn ending up in her room, of the return to the restaurant, and of her friends. When she told him about Parker's strange encounter with the Sundry, she pulled her bangs out of her eyes and held on to them as if she could pull an answer from her own brain. "But the thing is, Xan, they won't talk to me! What were they saying to Parker?"

"Did you ask him?"

"Not exactly. I asked him what happened, that was all." She let her hair go and it fell back into her eyes. "Anyway, he went to medbay to be with his sister and I looked around the crime scene."

While she was talking, four green wasps flew back into the restaurant and joined the other on the bar, all of them pointedly looking at Mallory and Xan. He glanced at them, then back to her.

"I was letting Steph and Ferdinand know what was happening when they said you were here, so I wanted to come see you."

He frowned. "You left the crime scene?"

She shrugged. "Sure. Nothing was going on there. The restaurant owner said he'd lock it."

Xan slid off the barstool and landed in front of Mallory's stool.

He glanced at Ferdinand, who was serving a table of Gneiss. "Something is wrong here," he said.

"Obviously," she said, looking down at him. "And where were you tonight, anyway?"

"My watch died," he said. "I was walking Jessica back to her room." His cheeks got warm, but he didn't elaborate further. "Then I came back here. Right when Ferd said you were looking for me, that's when you walked in."

"So you and she left before the murder?" Mallory mused.

He rolled his eyes. "No, Mal, she's not a suspect."

"She could be. The murder victim was stuffed into a closet," she said. "We don't know when he died."

"Well, let's go figure it out," he said, gesturing for her to come off the stool with him.

"What?" she asked.

"You wanted my help, let's go look at the body," he said.

"No, I don't need help," she said. "I just wanted help with getting the wounded to medbay. I can solve this on my own."

"Can you?" he asked. He was dimly aware of the green wasps taking off from the bar. "You didn't ask a suspect an obvious question, you left the crime scene; you're usually better than this, Mal." He shook his head. "Something is wrong with you. You're off your game."

"If all you're going to do is insult me, I'll head back to the crime scene, then," she snapped. She jumped off her stool and landed next to him. "Alone."

The green wasps flew over and circled her once, then exited through the restaurant door. Mallory stalked out after them.

Xan looked around at the Gneiss in the restaurant, at his friend, who had returned behind the bar. Had no one else seen the green wasps? He wondered if the aliens just tuned the Sundry out in general.

Xan was not a xenobiologist, but he was aware of only two

kinds of Sundry. What he did know was that they were territorial and didn't mix, so if there was a third faction here, he couldn't imagine the blue or silver welcoming them.

But Mallory, who was symbiotically connected to the Sundry, hadn't batted an eye when the green ones appeared.

12

. . .

HUMANS ARE DELICATE IN BODY AND SOUL

ONE LACERATION OF delicate human flesh, some relatively simple bruising, one concussion of human brain, which admittedly is one of the better-protected organs that you have," a Gurudev doctor said, approaching Mallory. "You're lucky our databases came back online. We would not have known how to treat them and would have euthanized out of efficiency."

Mallory made a strangled sound, then coughed. "Yeah, we're going to unpack that later. In the short run, don't just up and kill humans if you don't know what to do. Call one of us to see if we can help." They stood outside the room set aside for the humans, now housing Amy and Draughn, with Parker at Amy's side.

"I'm glad there were no more injuries," Mallory said. "And Amy wasn't stung at all?"

"No, there is no venom in her system," the doctor said. "The male patient"—he gestured to Draughn—"who arrived earlier did have considerable venom in his hand. We are still unsure what species delivered the venom."

"The room was full of blue Sundry. I figured one of them stung him?" Mallory asked, frowning.

"No," the Gurudev said. They gestured to the wall where multiple terminal screens showed what Mallory supposed were very smart alien sciencey things, but she was neither a scientist nor an alien, so she had no idea what the various glyphs and symbols indicated. "We have blue and silver Sundry venom well documented, and we've been able to synthesize it both for healing purposes and to create an antivenom to treat accidental or attack stings. This venom is similar, but with enough differences to indicate it came from somewhere else."

"Have you tried giving him the antivenom for Sundry anyway?" she asked.

"That is a very bad idea," the doctor said. "Some Phantasmagore doctors tried using silver antivenom on a blue sting once. It dissolved the patient from the inside out. That was a messy day. I can't even imagine the damage it would do to your species."

Mallory held her hands up to stop the doctor from telling her more. "Okay, okay, you know your job and I don't. I get it. Is he going to be okay?"

"He is stable," the doctor said. "We are continuing to study the venom. Both patients are resting. You can talk to them tomorrow."

She paced a couple of steps, then stepped back to the impassive doctor. "Can I talk to my friend who isn't injured? The woman's brother?"

"I have no jurisdiction over him," the doctor said, as close to a shrug as Mallory had ever seen an alien communicate.

The doctor went into the room, and Parker soon came out.

"They told me how she is, but can you tell me in English?" she asked with a rueful smile.

"She woke up, doesn't remember much," he said. "The docs said she should sleep and gave her something." He looked over his shoulder, forehead creased. "You're not supposed to sleep after a concussion, but they said they knew what they were doing."

"What about Draughn?" she asked.

He made a face. "They put his hand in this sandwich bag

thing that's full of goo, and it's tight around his wrist. I can't tell if the goo is healing or the bag is a tourniquet or what."

"Both, probably," she said. "The doc said they couldn't identify what stung him. But I saw the room full of Sundry. What else could have stung him?"

He looked away from her. "I don't know," he said.

"Parker, they were swarming around you but not attacking. And you say you lost whole minutes of the murder. What was going on there?"

"I don't know," he said again. "This is all really weird. We were supposed to come here and meet the aliens and see you—"

"Me?" Mallory interrupted. "I thought you didn't know I was here? And you knew where I was for years back on Earth! Why did you wait till I was light-years away to come find me, and then lie about why you're here?"

He made a frustrated gesture with his hands. "There's no point keeping up the lie now. Of course we knew you were here. And when we got the chance to come and meet some of the races, it was a perfect-storm kind of thing. To be honest, I didn't—" He rubbed the back of his head. "I didn't want to remember you," he finally said, part defiant, part angry. "I spent years trying to forget you."

"God," she said, stepping away from him. "We can't talk about this right now."

He gave her a funny look. "But you asked. You asked specifically about you and me."

She blinked at him. "You're right. I'm sorry. But Oscar, remember Oscar? He's dead. Someone attacked your sister and Draughn. Can we talk about last night?"

"Sure. That's a much safer topic," he said quietly.

MALLORY'S MEMORIES OF Amy and Parker were fractured, angry, tender. There were the memories of her old friend, support and love and tears in school. Growing up was hard, and they'd been there for each other. Amy's grandmother, who raised her and her brothers, had given the teen Mallory more parental love than her guardian, her aunt. And this was before Mallory knew her aunt was a sociopath and serial killer. Amy's grandmother was still murder-free, as far as she knew.

But the day she had looked into Parker's green eyes and really noticed him, the bottom of her stomach fell out. Blood rushing in her ears, the shock nearly painful. His hair was black, the opposite of Amy's blond hair. They looked like the sun and moon, like he was her negative.

He was quiet, studious, always someone to gauge a situation before acting. And still he had the worst luck of anyone Mallory had ever known.

He'd had multiple injuries: fractures, lacerations, stitches, and one knocked-out tooth by the time he was fifteen. And yet he also had managed to find money in the cracks of sidewalks; if there was a limited amount of something, he would often get the last one; and near the end of their senior year, Amy had confided in her that Parker had told their grandmother what numbers to buy for the state jackpot lottery, and they had won. Amy wouldn't say how much, but her college education, as well as Parker's, and their brother's student loans, and their grandmother's debts were all taken care of. Their grandmother moved them north after that, which was when Mallory had lost touch with them.

As her memories of Parker came back, the day of the car accident became clearer. Mallory had watched the ambulance take him and Amy away from her and then spent a sleepless night trying to get Amy to answer her texts and wondering what the hell had happened.

The next day at school Amy avoided her. Parker wasn't there.

The day after, Mallory had cornered Amy and asked what she had done that made Amy so mad when they had been fine the last time they'd been together. Amy had avoided her eyes, very unlike her, then spat out, "You were all he wanted in the ambulance."

"What are you talking about?" Mallory asked.

"He was wild with pain. He kept asking where you were, why you weren't there with him," Amy said, her words pouring out.

Despite the hope that leaped in her chest, Mallory had tried very hard to focus on Amy. "He was in a ton of pain. Why did you trust anything he said?"

"Because I looked at his phone after they knocked him out with painkillers. It's full of unsent texts to you. He's been too afraid to send them."

Mallory just stared at her blankly. Amy slid out of her corner and backed away from Mallory. "He's my twin, Mallory. He's been my best friend other than you. And I may as well not have been there with him at the hospital. You're not even dating and I'm already disappearing. If you two get together, I won't have anyone!"

Mallory had carefully knit their friendship back together and assured her that Amy wouldn't be "third wheeled."

She'd tried, very hard, not to pay attention to Parker during this time. She really didn't want to lose Amy as a friend.

But God. Those eyes.

MALLORY AND PARKER sat in the balcony above the surgery room in the medbay. Nothing was going on below them, so it was a quiet place to sit and talk while still letting him be near his sister. "Tell me about Oscar. I only met him briefly. What was your connection to him?"

"Oh, I can't stand him—couldn't stand, I mean," Parker said. "He has—had—a real job as a basketball coach, but he was working on being a bodybuilder slash protein drink influencer. His big side hustle was working on launching a celeb gossip site. I know him through the university, but also because Reggie works with him on the same content site. It's called the Trash Heap."

"Reggie? Your stuffy-suit brother who can't relax one muscle ever? Writes for a trashy news site?" Mallory asked, baffled. She didn't know their brother well, but Amy had mentioned him as being stuffy and unfun. "What does he have in common with someone who's doing protein-drink influencing, bodybuilding, and celebrity gossip?"

"Reggie's changed a lot since First Contact," Parker said. "Still can't take a joke, but he got obsessed with aliens from a legal point of view. Now he's editor of the legal channel of the site."

"Legal? What does that have to do with celebrity gossip?" Mallory said. "I figured those kinds of people would want to stay away from any legal expert."

Parker nodded, settling back on the massive chair he occupied in the dimly lit observation balcony. "His section of the site covers trashy lawsuits, but his true passion is changes in the law dealing with alien involvement. He even quit his law practice to study the effect that aliens had on new laws on Earth. The Trash Heap noticed his antiquated blog, which was a time capsule of 2015 site design, and brought him on board with all the current tech. He writes all the legal crap while more attractive people, who have a lot more charisma than he does, are the face of the channel."

"Sounds like you don't like your brother," Mallory said mildly.

"I don't like what he's become, and thought he had more integrity than to contribute to crap that eclipses actual news," Parker said. "The only good thing about the Trash Heap is they don't try to hide what they are. But you'll never hear Reggie say the name of his employers. He's too good for that."

"Yeah, well, McDonald's burgers are terrible but they still sell more than quality burgers do. Sometimes people don't want the best, they want the easy thing that will give them a moment of happiness." Mallory thought for a beat. "Oscar was trash. But you sound like you really hate him. Why?"

Parker sighed and looked away for a moment. "Killing Oscar was a victimless crime."

Mallory raised her eyebrows, but let him continue.

He set his jaw. "You'll find out from someone, it might as well be me. No one will miss him. Oscar's told everyone, at some point or another, that he had been practicing his hacking skills on people he knew. He implied he had read texts, emails, personal files. He didn't elaborate on who he had stuff on, or what exactly he knew. I think he liked to see people squirm." He glanced at Mallory. "Everyone's got secrets. Telling someone you know what their secrets are is enough to make anyone paranoid."

Mallory settled back on the couch, thinking. She wondered what Parker's secrets were. "Did he blackmail anyone?"

"He didn't blackmail me," Parker said carefully.

"I thought he was your friend," she said. "You were hanging out at the party, weren't you?"

He gave a bitter smile. "Sure. We had to tolerate him while he was alive, but now he's dead and we can say what we really feel. The dirty laundry he's been hoarding is going to come out eventually. Might as well hear it from me."

A blue Sundry flew into the balcony and landed on the back of Mallory's couch, crawling and investigating with its antennae. Mallory glanced at it, and something tickled at her brain. She ignored it.

"Is it possible he was bluffing? Does everyone believe he had dirt on them?" she asked.

"He was convincing. He had that way of talking that made you believe him," Parker said, watching the Sundry.

"Oh, don't worry about her, she won't hurt you," Mallory said. "She's just investigating."

He laughed. "I'm an entomologist, Mallory. Insects don't scare me."

She winced. "Right. I just remember that most people are terrified of wasps as big as their thumb. I know I was."

He leaned forward. "When we get a chance, I'd love to talk to you about your connection with the Sundry."

A realization hit Mallory like a punch to the gut, and she had a momentary sensation of being unable to draw air. Her eyes went wide as she stared at the Sundry, just a bug waving antennae at her.

Fuck. That's what's wrong. My connection to the hivemind. It's gone. It's completely fucking gone.

WHAT FELT LIKE terrified, frozen minutes was only seconds, as Mallory snapped back to herself. It all made sense—she'd felt ill, then alone. Her reactions to the murder were nothing like they had ever been. She didn't have that feeling of looking at a jigsaw until the pieces of the crime just clicked together. She didn't have any details of the crime scene stand out larger than others. And she couldn't sense the Sundry at all. Not even this one.

Without the Sundry, she was just a regular old boring person playing at detective, like Draughn had always accused her of being.

Her spine felt like it had been replaced by a floppy hose full of frigid water. She forced herself to sit up.

Parker was still looking at the Sundry.

"Yeah, happy to talk about that," she said, trying to keep the shaking out of her voice. "But let's deal with the murder first, okay?" she asked. She sounded weak and far away.

"You okay?" he asked, glancing from the Sundry to Mallory's face.

"Totally," she said, and cleared her throat. She thought hard.

Before now, making connections between suspects and victims had come naturally to her. Like touching her fingertips together and feeling the sensation in both digits. "So tell me about how all the people in your group are connected. How do Agent Draughn and Oscar fit in with a bunch of professors?"

"Draughn is Amy's friend from the support group," Parker said, watching another Sundry join the first one. They flew from Mallory's couch to Parker's sofa. "Amy invited him to a few dinner parties and we got to know him. And Oscar was an assistant coach for junior varsity basketball. I think a bio professor met him while studying the team for sweat bacteria or something, and then he just got to know more people in the faculty. Then he started hanging out with us at lunch. Reggie met him separately online."

The Sundry crawled toward Parker's hand, which rested on the back of the couch. He didn't flinch when she investigated his skin, eventually crawling into his palm.

"How did you all end up here?" she asked, staring at the insects. "I get the academic people, but not Oscar or Draughn."

Parker opened his mouth, and Mallory held up a hand to stop him. "I don't buy Draughn's story about being on a leave of absence. Sorry."

"But that's what he told us," Parker objected. "If he has another reason for being here, I don't know what it is."

"Well, if he attached himself to Amy, then her research is probably important to something he's investigating. If he wakes up, I'll try to get it out of him. And see if he knows why he and Amy were attacked."

And why you weren't, she didn't say.

"What about Oscar?" she said. "Why did a basketball coach–news hound come here with a bunch of academics?"

He looked her straight in the eye. "I have no idea."

Was he lying? She had no idea. God, she was tired. She rubbed her face. "All right. That's about all I need for now. Can you give me the full names of everyone you are traveling with? I'll talk to them tomorrow."

Parker gave her the list, spelling out everyone's names. Mallory wrote down everything he said, and a few notes of her own.

> *Parker Valor (prof entomology) "killing Oscar was a*
> *victimless crime" Really?*
> *Amy Valor (prof quant. physics—wasn't she going to*
> *be a physical therapist?)*
> *Reggie Valor-Cole (lawyer)*
> *Max Valor-Cole (prof experimental psych)*
> *Agent Don Draughn (SBI, PITA) "sabbatical"*
> *Oscar Daye (coach/gossip/trash/dead)*
> *?? Jessica Brass (bb player, ambassador) Connection*
> *w/ others??*

Parker went downstairs to sit with Amy again.

Mallory sat in the balcony for a long time, thinking. She fell asleep on the couch, noticing a few Sundry buzzing around her as she drifted off.

13

. . .

ANATOMY LESSONS

REALLY HATE BEING in the vent shafts in the middle of the night," Adrian said from behind Devanshi.

"Tell me what else you hate, Adrian," Devanshi said as they crawled through a service tunnel made for drones.

While it had oxygen, it was frigid and definitely not meant for life-forms. It was big enough for larger drones to drive and fly through. Devanshi had thought it would be a good way to get around the station if they couldn't count on the infrastructure.

"I hate the fact that I'd rather be stuck in an elevator than crawling through this witch's birth canal," he snapped. "I hate the cold. And I hate that we're doing this while Mallory Viridian is off playing detective, and probably very warm."

Devanshi had learned early in their friendship that she could easily distract Adrian by encouraging a litany of things that he hated. The human was fragile and bitter, but she had a fondness for him that she couldn't explain.

". . . but you know what I hate the most, today?" he concluded.

"I have no idea, please tell me," she said, coming to a juncture in the tunnel. They could go straight or veer to the right.

"I hate that I have one of the finest linguistics brains of my generation, but I'll never learn any alien language," he said. "This damn bug in my ear does all the work for me."

Devanshi blinked at him and cocked her head. "If you grew thick fur from that fragile skin of yours and were warm all the time, would you be sad you'd never have to wear coats again?"

He made a movement with his squishy face that she had learned conveyed a negative emotion. "What's that got to do with anything?"

"Something that took effort once no longer takes effort. Why be sad that you don't have to go through years of learning about another language and culture to understand someone, when you can do so in an instant?"

"I liked learning languages," he said quietly. "Besides, I think that the bug leaves out things in translation, like emotions, sarcasm, vernacular speech, and culturally specific things. If we went through the effort of learning the language instead of relying on the bug to do it for us, then we would learn more about the other races."

"But fewer people would understand each other on the whole. Not everyone has the knack for languages that you do. But"—she thought for a moment—"I could probably disable your bug, if you want to learn languages."

His head snapped up. "You can? Why did you never tell me this before?"

"Because no one has ever wanted it!" Devanshi said. "You are asking for work and complication when the rest of the sentient species will be able to understand each other easily."

"Goddammit, I don't have anything else to do," he said. He panted hard, his breath making white puffs in the air.

She pointed to the tunnels ahead. "Well, you do now. This one will take us into security. This one will take us farther into the center of the station."

"What's in the center of the station?" he asked.

She still couldn't read the emotion in his voice (perhaps he had a point in that case), but she imagined he was feeling some trepidation. The last time he had gone to a forbidden place in the station, he'd been attacked and blinded by the station herself. He had always been careful to not step out of line with her since then.

He had only agreed to enter the tunnel with Devanshi because she told him that if he wouldn't help her, she would have to ask one of the other humans. And Adrian would not let Mallory or Xan succeed where he failed.

"Why should we go to security?" he asked. "What can we do that they can't?"

"Take these tunnels around the station, for one thing," Devanshi said. "And if comms are down and security is not active on the station, I am guessing they're locked in."

"Your species can crawl up the walls. Why can't they take these tunnels like we are?" he asked.

"I was high-ranking security when I was active," she said. "Not everyone knows about these tunnels. But whatever the reason, they're not using them. So we need to check on them. Or figure out what's going on at the center of the station."

"Security, then," Adrian said. "I'll stay the hell away from any off-limits station areas, thanks."

She had known he would decide this, but she figured he would like the option to choose. She didn't want to go to the center of the station either. The Sundry were obviously still running the basic things just fine, or else they would have run out of life support by now.

THE DRONE TUNNEL warmed up as they went from the uninhabited areas of the tunnels to the vents that led to the inhabited areas. Security, unfortunately, was accessed by a vertical tunnel that Adrian couldn't manage without a rope system.

"I'll send the drone down," he said, bunching up his shoulders. "I'm not good with authority anyway. If I have something to say, I'll say it through the drone."

Devanshi had just hooked up an audio transmitter to the drone, in case Adrian had to talk through it. She crawled down the dark tunnel toward the vent to security, Adrian's drone buzzing above her.

Through the vent, security presented as confused but not yet in a panic. Some Gurudev were testing comms on various frequencies, and two Gneiss argued with a Phantasmagore about whether they should knock the door down to get out.

But they don't know the other things going on, since the comms are down anyway, Devanshi thought. *Won't they be delighted to learn the wet humans are spilling themselves all over the station again. On top of the other problems, of course.*

Her long fingers made quick work of the catches inside the vent, and she dropped it on the floor and crawled out, clinging to the ceiling. She didn't bother blending in; her fellow Phantasmagore would have been able to spot her easily, and besides, she'd already dropped the vent to clatter on the floor.

"What the— Devanshi?" It was Osric, her old partner. He had not taken her retirement well, and hadn't spoken to her much since she had left security. "What the hell are you doing? Breaking in while the room is full of personnel?"

She dropped gracefully to the floor and looked for the security head on duty. It was a Phantasmagore named Juliette, whom she had met a few times.

"Comms are down," she said bluntly.

"We know, we're working on it. The station says everything is fine, so we're not too concerned," Juliette said. "Do you mind telling me why you're breaking in?"

"Maybe because someone took it seriously that we're trapped here," said one of the Gneiss by the door. He was a short fellow, made of chunky gold metal.

"There's no emergency, so—" Juliette said, but Devanshi cut her off.

"The medbay databases were offline for a good part of the day," she said. "They only recently came back online, but who knows how many patients suffered or died because of that? There was a murder a few hours ago at the human party, as well as a Sundry attack. And the station is off course. She's left orbit. The traffic controllers in the shuttle bay say that navigation is just telling people everything is fine, over and over again."

Juliette turned several shades of bright colors, ending with silver, blending into the metallic wall behind her. She looked over at the door.

"Yeah, Benjamin. Break it down," she said. She looked at Osric. "After they get the door down, take Benjamin and Ashley to navigation. Break that door down, too, if you can't get in. I'll go check on the medbay. The rest of you, monitor comms to see if they come back online, but be ready to go if someone needs us."

Everyone started to move as a well-oiled machine, starting with the Gneiss pounding on the metal door.

"What about the human murder?" Devanshi asked.

"You know the humans best, don't you? You check it out," Juliette said.

"I'm not in security anymore," Devanshi protested, matching Juliette's shade of silver.

"And yet you got in here to get us while we did nothing," Juliette said. "It appears we need you. Be the human expert, check on the murder, see if their ambassador is still alive."

"And if she isn't alive?"

Juliette went a few shades of red in frustration. "Then make a report or something. They always seem to manufacture something going wrong when bigger things are happening on the station. I have never met a species more desperate for attention. If she's dead, she won't be going anywhere, and we'll handle it later."

From above Devanshi came an electric sigh. "I don't know who I'd rather talk to less, Mallory or the new ambassador," said Adrian.

Before she could answer, the Gneiss stopped pounding at the door. "Captain?" Benjamin asked.

"What?" Juliette demanded.

"We can't get the door down."

THE LESS BRAWNY security officers inspected the door. It was bowed outward now and would not slide back into the wall the normal way anymore, even if they could get control over Eternity's automated door systems. The Gneiss were normally more than capable of displacing a door if they had to, but this one wouldn't pop free. The metal was strained, stressed to the point of almost breaking in some places, but still, it wouldn't budge.

"I can get us some help from the outside," Benjamin rumbled.

"What good will that do?" Devanshi asked, pausing on the ceiling before she crawled out. A few of the other Phantasmagore had started to follow her, only to be ordered back to the floor by Juliette.

"I'll send people out the emergency exit when I'm ready," she said.

Devanshi was mostly into the tunnel when she asked her question, head poking out of the ceiling. She forgot that, not being part of security, she wasn't part of the discussion.

"If you contacted other Gneiss, they would just knock the door back in, which would get you nowhere," Juliette said, agreeing with Devanshi.

"Imprisoned Gneiss must report their capture to the ranking leader on the ship," Benjamin said. "So I'm doing that."

"You're not imprisoned!" Juliette said. "That's ridiculous."

"I can't get out. I'm held against my will. I'm imprisoned," Benjamin said stubbornly. "If I can't break a door down, then someone is holding me against my will. It's physics. And diplomacy."

"God save us from Gneiss diplomacy. Now what?" Adrian asked. He flew his drone over to the door, where it hovered above the officers' heads.

"Help is coming," Benjamin said after a moment.

The room went silent as they waited, and then the comms whirred to life, emergency beeps and messages lighting up the terminals on the tables and desks. The door didn't burst open so much as fall outward to clatter on the hallway floor, as if it had grown tired of being a door.

A large pink head poked into the room.

"Hi, guys!" Tina the Gneiss said. "I heard you needed help."

14

. . . .

WE DON'T TALK ABOUT TINA

ALLORY WOKE WITH a stiff neck, shivering slightly. She'd spent all night on the couch in the medbay observation balcony. She stumbled down the stairs and asked the first person, a small Gurudev, if there had been any change to the humans, and they said a curt no. She checked in on the humans, finding Parker asleep on the chair next to the bed. She bit her lip, looked at him a moment longer, and then left.

She needed to go back to her apartment, but the shuttle bay was closer and she wanted to check with the silver Sundry to see if they had anything else to say.

She knew she should connect directly to the blue hivemind, or connect with the station herself, to find out what was going on, but she wanted to exhaust every possible avenue for information first. It was overwhelming to plug your small human brain into a larger alien consciousness, and she only wanted to do it if she had to.

Of course she remembered she had a murder to solve, but if she didn't figure out what was going on with the Sundry, the murder of one human that no one liked would pale in comparison.

In the shuttle bay, she said a brief hello to Stephanie, who didn't reply to her. Back in the corner, the Sundry ship still sat there, a space-worthy paper nest. It usually had busy insects flying around it, but now it was quiet.

The pile of dead Sundry bodies Mallory had left by the ship was gone. Had the station's drones cleaned them up? Was Eternity aware of this massacre?

If the drones are still working, that is.

The hive was silent. A tear was in the side, flapping in the slight air current in the quiet shuttle bay. Normally, worker Sundry should have been flying in and out, checking the shuttle, repairing it, or going out for food. Someone would have taken notice of her, come to investigate. But nothing.

"Hey, silver, you guys okay? I need some help," she said to the fragile-looking ship.

There was no answering buzz, no Sundry coming out to meet her.

She crossed her arms. "Dammit," she muttered. "I'm finally getting what's going on, lots of you are dying, but I don't know what's killing you. Is there anyone left in there to tell me what's going on?"

Nothing.

AT THE CLOSEST lift, Adrian stood waiting for her.

"Okay, creeper," she said. "What are you doing here?"

He sighed. "Confirming a theory. You're going to the blue Sundry hive, right?"

"I wanted to go to my apartment, but yeah, by way of the park. How did you know?"

"Just answer," he said, sounding tired.

"Yes. Now you tell me what—"

"I will tell you everything. Or people who understand it better than I do will tell you." The lift doors opened in front of them. "But after we visit the Sundry. Let's go."

Mallory glared at him but boarded, and pushed the buttons to take them to the park where the blue hive still sat. The key panel emitted a squawk. She tried to type in a few more things, but nothing worked.

"May I?" Adrian asked.

The shock of the polite request had Mallory stepping back. He took the drone that clung to his shoulder, inserted a cord in one end, and then inserted the other end to a port on the terminal.

"I got some override codes from Devanshi," he said before she could ask. "She thought this might happen."

The lift lurched to life, stuttering a bit.

"I don't like that," Mallory said, holding the railing that ran around the three walls. It was much larger than an elevator on Earth, with fuzzy walls and floor, something between carpet and fur. She tried not to think about it very often, but just now she realized it was warm. The whole lift was warm.

"I thought we were supposed to get the hell off elevators when they do this," she said. The elevator car stuttered more as it attempted to go along its path toward the park.

"Yeah, but that's driven by mechanical devices, right?" Adrian asked. "Eternity is driving this."

"Is she?" Mallory shouted. The vibration was getting loud and it felt like they weren't moving at all now.

"Yes. And she doesn't want us to go to the park."

The heat and stuttering increased, but Adrian stood there impassively, waiting, and Mallory had to mirror him.

Everything calmed and the lift began to slide smoothly along toward the park.

"You overreact to everything," Adrian muttered. But then the doors opened to chaos.

They were at the entrance to the park, but Mallory could barely see anything. A full wall of blue Sundry swarmed right in front of the lift exit.

"What the hell?" she shouted. "What is wrong with you?" She reached out her hand, suddenly wanting her connection back, as irritating as she found the insects.

Adrian flattened himself to the wall, and his arm shot out and grabbed her shoulder. He jerked her back with surprising strength, and the drone chirped from its tether to the controls. The doors slid closed.

"They looked ready to attack!" Mallory said, heart pounding. "Why weren't they just talking to us? They were acting like—"

"—ignorant wasps from Earth," Adrian finished. He was very pale. "They wanted to keep us out of the park. That was a warning. And why would you think you could talk to them?"

"They were pretty mad, but I can usually sense their overall emotions. But nothing's there! At all!"

The lift sprang to life again. If Mallory and Adrian hadn't been against the wall, they would have fallen. It traveled farther away from the park at a speed Mallory hadn't experienced before.

"Mallory, what did you say you saw when the doors opened?" he asked.

"Just this angry wall of blue," she said. "I thought your drone eyes would have registered this."

"Then Devanshi was right," Adrian said. "Good God."

Mallory slid down the furry wall and closed her eyes. "Someone. Please. Tell me something."

"I can't explain it all, but I will tell you the one thing I know for sure," he said. "Those insects you saw weren't blue. They were green. I don't know what they were, but they weren't blue Sundry."

"I'M NOT USED to you being this quiet," Adrian said as they approached Ferdinand's restaurant.

"I don't have anything to say," she said dimly. "Not right now."

"That's a relief," Adrian said.

She surprised herself by laughing. "I honestly appreciate you providing the one constant in my life right now. Whatever happens, I can count on the fact that you'll be an asshole."

"Things are getting strange," Ferdinand said when they walked in. The bar was dim, with a few Gneiss sitting around at tables and Xan staring at the wall terminal behind the bar. Ferdinand's comment startled Xan out of his focus, and he looked at Mallory and smiled.

"Tell me about it, Ferd," Mallory said. "What's happening now?"

"Security was locked in their offices with no comms. They have finally been freed and comms are back up. And now Tina's on her way here," he said.

Xan frowned. "What does that have to do with anything?"

"I'm thinking it has to do with everything," Ferdinand said. "But I will let her tell you."

They heard Tina much earlier than they saw her. Not her footsteps, but her complaints.

"Why am I in trouble?" Tina asked. "I saved everyone!"

Tina ducked her head and walked placidly into the restaurant with Devanshi beside her. Adrian left Mallory's side to stand beside his Phantasmagore friend.

Mallory went to Xan. "Do you know what's going on?" she asked.

"No idea," he said.

She looked at the floor for a second, then back up at him. "I'm sorry I was a pain. I've figured out what's wrong with me. I—"

"I am unjustly imprisoned!" Tina yelled.

Mallory laughed at the thought of the relatively tiny Phantasmagore beside Tina being able to imprison her. Devanshi wasn't even with security anymore. Tina had clearly come of her own free will, despite whatever complaint she made.

Ferdinand stepped from behind the bar and stood in front of Tina. The floor began to vibrate in the secret way the Gneiss talked to each other, and within a minute, every patron had left the restaurant. They were alone.

"Now we have as much privacy as we can get," Ferdinand said. "Although I'm fairly sure all the Gneiss will figure out what's going on shortly."

"What *is* going on?" Mallory asked. "Tina, what did you do?"

"Oh, what did I do? I didn't do anything but rescue you from your apartment when you were passed out. I did nothing but deliver Xan his package inside his door from the human shuttle when the shuttle bay would have taken hours to do so. I have been carrying injured meat sacks around all day—which is work definitely below my rank, by the way—because you're my *friends*."

"Hang on," Mallory said, frowning. She was remembering Tina appearing when Draughn was in her apartment, the door sliding open for her. "How did you get into my apartment—"

Tina continued. "I got the medbay databases working again so your fragile little bodies could get medical care! I freed all the security folks on the ship from where they were locked in! And I got comms working again! Me! The dumb one!"

"How did you do all that?" Xan asked, eyes wide.

"Tell them what else you did, Tina," Ferdinand said. He sounded like an angry parent who was trying to get their kid to understand something, channeling their rage into a teachable moment.

Tina stayed silent. The floor thrummed slightly, the Gneiss talking back and forth. Xan wondered if Stephanie was weighing in.

"How did you get into our apartments, Tina?" Mallory asked. "You're not bio-linked to the door."

"She did it the same way she let security out of their locked offices," Devanshi said.

"Which is?" Mallory prompted.

The wall speaker crackled to life as Stephanie's voice came into the room. "We should start at the beginning. May I introduce to you Queen Tina of Bezoar."

The humans stared, dumbfounded.

"When did this happen?" Mallory asked.

"Did your mom die or something?" Xan asked. "I thought it's really hard to kill your people."

"Nah, royalty usually gets tired of ruling after a few hundred years," Tina said. "I mean, my mom is still on the moon Nugget, where she's been vacationing for a few decades, but she gave me the crown after I told her what happened on Bromide. She's proud of me, guys! Me! I am queen of Bezoar now!"

No one responded.

"Aren't you proud of me, too?" she said, sounding puzzled. "Did I not tell you? I meant to! There's just been a lot of stuff going on. But I'm really excited. You have to come visit! Bezoar is a really big planet, with an inhospitable atmosphere to most, but under the storms and unbreathable air and thick vines covering the whole planet, it can be quite hospitable. And the cave structures are epic."

"You said your mother was vacationing?" Xan asked, shaking his head. "Who's been ruling the planet?"

"There aren't a lot of people to rule," Tina said. "Other species dump their criminals on the planet. And they survive as best they can. The worst of them, we inter into the mountain to think about what they did for a few thousand years. Mostly political prisoners, but a few blasphemers. Not a lot come out alive, now that I'm thinking about it. Only Gneiss. I should look into that."

"What do people do when they get there?" Mallory asked, trying not to sound outraged. "Do they die? Are they really trapped in the mountain? And it's just anarchy and chaos on the planet with no one in charge?"

"Oh, I'm sure there have been some leaders rising up and then brought down. Not sure," Tina said.

"Has anyone ever broken out?" Xan asked.

"Huh. I don't know. No one has ever told me," Tina said thoughtfully. "I guess I should look into that, too."

"You rule space Australia," Xan said, shaking his head. "Amazing."

"Congrats and everything, Tina, but what does that have to do with what's going on here?" Mallory asked. "The station is breaking down and then inexplicably fixing itself, and we're way off course. I don't even know if *Infinity* can find us when they come back."

"Oh," Tina said. "Don't worry about Mrs. Brown. She and *Infinity* are both connected so tightly to Eternity that they can't ever lose her. And if they could, we could just tell them that the station is going to Bezoar."

"What the fuck, Tina?" Xan yelled.

"I told you." She looked at Ferdinand, then at the speaker, including Stephanie. "Didn't I tell you?"

"You told us, in a way," Ferdinand allowed. "But you forgot not every Gneiss will get your references, and not every alien will have it translated perfectly."

"I told you things were cuckoo," Tina said. "How else can I make myself clear?"

There was a knock at the restaurant door, and a human head poked inside.

"Parker?" Mallory asked, completely flummoxed.

"I thought I saw Mallory come in here, so I followed, then I heard you talking. I might be some help here," he said.

"CUCKOOS REFER TO any animal that displaces another," Parker began. "It takes over a nest another animal built, or it forces another animal to raise its young. Most people are familiar with the bird cuckoo, but the concept ranges much wider than that."

"Like other planets, even!" Tina supplied.

"Exactly," Parker said. "There are a few Earth species of wasp with cuckoo tendencies. A queen covers herself in pheromones to make the native wasps think she's just one of their own species, and then she infiltrates the nest and lays her own eggs. After that, it's a matter of weeks before her eggs hatch and her new army helps her take over the entire hive. It can happen in a matter of weeks, before the native wasps even know there's an enemy inside."

"From what I can gather from history," Stephanie spoke up, "Sundry Cuckoos are much less intelligent than the blue or silver. They are closer to the wasps you know on Earth. But they're still powerful. All the power of the hivemind can't help the Sundry if they can't see who is infiltrating them. Generations ago, entire hiveminds were being wiped out. So the Gneiss got involved, since we can't be stung, or affected by pheromones. We rounded up all the Cuckoos we could, killed the ones we couldn't, and dumped the survivors on Bezoar."

"Why doesn't anyone else aboard know about this?" Mallory asked. "Xan can't be the only person who saw the green wasps around."

"That I don't know," Parker said. "But in our case, humans didn't know enough about the station to know what alien life-forms were out of the ordinary to see. They told us we would see large silver or blue insects, but they didn't say that we *wouldn't* see other colors."

"As for those who would know, this happened generations ago," Stephanie said. "That's Gneiss generations. Most of us assumed that the Cuckoos just died out on Bezoar."

"The other sentient species forgot about them once they weren't being infested," Devanshi said. "I found only vague references to them myself."

"What about the Sundry hiveminds?" Xan asked. "Surely they remembered."

"I'm betting the Sundry were like anyone else," Mallory said, shaking her head. "People don't like to remember the time they were beat by the dumber, weaker opponent. Sweep it all under the rug and move on."

"It turns out that the only Gneiss who remembered the Cuckoos were Tina's family," Ferdinand said. "And I'm not sure how much her parents paid attention."

"Right!" Tina said. "I thought everyone else knew what I was talking about when I saw them aboard. I knew they would take a little time to take over, and the station might have some problems along the way, but things would smooth out."

"And when you figured out what they were doing, what was the first thing you did, Tina?" Ferdinand said.

Tina rumbled quietly.

"The humans can't hear you," Ferd pressed.

"Look, no one else would take me to Bezoar! And they wanted to go there anyway! I thought if they helped me, I wouldn't have to put anyone out, just get the Cuckoos to take the station there when they were done taking over, and I'd be home and be safe where the home planet bullies couldn't bother me anymore. Or bother Stephanie either!" she added defiantly, as if she had her friend's welfare at the front of her mind the whole time.

We're going to Bezoar. Mallory stumbled, caught by Xan's hand. She felt dizzy. "And what I've been feeling, for weeks, that was the Sundry dying around me?" she demanded.

"Sounds likely," Tina said, not looking at her.

"And you just let them die?"

"I can't stop a hive from procreating! It's pointless to halt it!" Tina said. "It's not like the blue are gone entirely. There are plenty of Sundry in other places. You can go play with those hiveminds."

"Tina, how did they get aboard in the first place, if they were imprisoned?" Devanshi asked.

"They said their queen snuck aboard a shuttle the last time one landed on Bezoar," Tina said.

Mallory and Xan looked at Ferdinand, who had traveled to Bezoar last fall.

"Oh, shit, Ferd," Xan said.

The stoic Gneiss made no movement or noise. Mallory wondered if he was angry, or retreating inside himself in shame. Then something occurred to her. "Tina, what's to stop the Cuckoos from getting on other shuttles and starting to take over the other hiveminds in the galaxy?"

"That would be catastrophic," Devanshi said before Tina could. "Countless planets have treaties with Sundry hiveminds to run vital systems. If they were displaced or killed, it would have galaxy-wide repercussions."

"They're really not that bad," Tina said.

"Tina! They killed hundreds, maybe thousands, of Sundry! They took over the station!" Xan shouted. "How soon until the life support starts shutting down?"

"Oh, you are so *dramatic*," Tina said.

"THE OTHER SUNDRY see them as belonging, or as a non-threat," Mallory muttered to herself. "How many green Cuckoos have I seen in the past week that I thought were blue Sundry who wouldn't talk to me?"

"Good question," Xan said.

"It's pretty creepy knowing I still can't tell the difference," she said. "They really do look blue to me."

"Well, if the blues are mostly dead, then you can guess if you see blue, they're probably fooling you," Xan said.

Mallory winced.

"Their control of the station is why reports said that things were fine when people tried to contact security, or navigation," Devanshi explained. "The Cuckoos were making sure no one would raise an alarm with anything that could hurt them or stop their takeover. They don't have a sophisticated language, so they couldn't weave a more complex fabrication, so they just locked everyone out of comms."

"So what do we do now?" Xan asked. "Go in there with a bunch of cans of Raid, or what?"

"Insecticide will harm the Gurudev and other sentients aboard Eternity," Devanshi said. "Besides, the Sundry still provide the involuntary systems aboard the station."

"And there aren't any blue or silver to take over if we could get rid of the green," Mallory said, understanding. "It's like someone took out Eternity's heart and replaced it with another one. Wherever it came from, she still needs a heart."

"So what do we do?" Xan said.

Mallory shrugged. "We still have a murderer on the station. I need to figure that out. Except." She bit her lip.

"Except you lost your magical Sundry connection that lets you solve murders," Adrian said, sneering. "Whatever will you do without your powers?"

"Shut up, Adrian," she said.

"Looks like you'll have to leave it to station security," he said, clearly enjoying himself.

"Impossible," Devanshi said. "Security are wrestling with communications and other station problems."

"Mrs. B would ask Mallory to do it regardless," Xan said. "You've got tons of experience with this, Mal. Don't let some dead bugs drag you down."

Mallory felt stunned and empty. She crossed her arms over her chest and hugged herself. "First," she said, clearing her throat, "I don't see anyone else stepping up to do it, so until they do, I'll be interviewing the humans and trying to figure out who killed Oscar. I'd prefer to do it without your snark."

"I can look into histories about how people dealt with the Cuckoos, if I can find anything," Devanshi said. "I'm lucky I remembered this much, to be honest."

"Stephanie, can you try to contact *Infinity* and Mrs. Brown?" Xan asked.

"I can do that," she said. "I'm also getting my strength back. I can go out hunting for them in a few days."

"We don't want you to go too far, not while the station is in transit," Devanshi said.

"I am available if people have questions regarding insects," Parker offered. "I know that the Sundry aren't Earth wasps, but this Cuckoo behavior is very similar to what I've studied."

"Thanks," Mallory said. Her own voice sounded very far away. "I'll let you know. For now, I need to get some stuff done. I'll be in touch."

"Can I walk you home?" Parker asked, standing up with her.

Mallory wanted to say yes because she wanted to ask him more about the Cuckoos. She wanted to say no because he was a friend and could likely get lost or murdered on his way back to his room. She wanted to say yes because she missed those eyes. She wanted to say no because he was still a suspect. There were a lot of feelings, but she was mostly tired. And she had to get to work. "I'm not going home. I need to prepare my interviews."

Parker looked hurt, but he masked it quickly. She sighed, unable to hide her own disappointment. But she'd had people close to her be murderers before, and she didn't want to reignite her relationship with Parker just to find out he was responsible for all this.

"Then just give me a second in the hallway," he asked.

She motioned for him to follow her. She met Xan's eyes on the way out, and they both looked at Tina and then back at each other. No one was saying it aloud, but Mallory had the sense that they were all wondering: What else was Tina going to get into on the way to Bezoar?

15

DEFINING LUCK, PARKER STYLE

AFTER ALL THE chaos of the night, the hallways were strangely serene as Parker faced Mallory across the hall.

He didn't say anything, just watched her, her tired brown eyes inquisitive as she waited.

"You wanted to talk about something?" Mallory finally asked.

He had wanted to talk to her. He'd wanted to tell her everything. But now his tongue felt too big for his mouth and he wasn't able to formulate a thought.

"It's good to see you again," he said.

"It's been a long time," she agreed. "I was really anxious last night, but I'm a little more stable right now. I'm sorry I didn't create the best reunion for us."

He shook his head. "Not important," he said. "I know you'll want to talk to me about the Cuckoos, and the murder, but between us, I have to ask: Why didn't you return my messages after we moved? It was like you fell off the face of the Earth. I didn't know if you had died, or blocked me, or what. And I had no idea what I'd done wrong. Then last night you acted like I was a monster."

She stared at her feet, frowning. Then she looked up, confused. "Last night I was terrified of you. Like unreasonably, animal-instinct fight-or-flight-or-freeze terror. Seeing you just made me want to run."

Made her want to run? That would only happen if— Something clicked in Parker's mind. He realized what he'd done. He felt bad, but it definitely wasn't the right time to explain. "And now?" he asked.

"Now I'm not afraid." She surveyed his face, stepping closer to him. "I don't get any of the fear I had earlier. Your eyes—"

She grabbed his shoulders and pulled him close, staring at him. Her eyes were full of confusion and wonder. "Oh, dear God."

"Mallory, what's going on? I just wanted to ask about the summer after graduation," he said, pulling back.

She took a step away from him. "Your eyes are green. I remember now. They're not blue like Amy's. They're green. I don't know what's going on." She rubbed her face with both hands. "Look, I'm sorry that I didn't respond to you. I don't think you'd believe me if I told you what was going on. We can talk about it more later, but I really have to go."

"Hang on, can't we talk about this? I've been waiting for years to ask you."

Mallory stepped another few feet away. "Parker, I didn't ghost you, I didn't avoid you, I didn't block you. I forgot about you. Completely and entirely. Seeing you last night wasn't just the shock of seeing an old friend. It was seeing someone I forgot existed."

And she ran down the hall, away from him.

PARKER WAS THE luckiest kid in the world.

Amy had been born first, and she'd been bigger, tearing their mother. Parker had been an afterthought, coming out feetfirst as the doctor tried to staunch their mother's bleeding. He'd been slick with maternal blood and fluid, sliding through the nurse's hands to fall to the floor.

Right after he slid through, someone hit a tray of tools, sending them flying. A heavy speculum came down to land in the nurse's hands instead of a newborn.

After the chaos subsided, and his mother was getting a transfusion, and they'd carefully inspected him all over to see if he had more injuries than bumps or bruises, the nurse reflected that if she hadn't dropped the baby, the speculum would have landed right on him, doing God knows what damage to the tender infant head.

Early childhood was uneventful. He watched his twin grow bright and friendly and popular, while he was content to be the shadow twin and spend more time with bugs and books and science experiments.

As he grew, childhood held the usual insect stings and scrapes and cuts and broken legs and burns and dog bites and cat bites and bird bites and hamster bites that most kids get. He was always lucky that he didn't get hospitalized, or lose too many school days, or have to go home too early from summer camp.

He was lucky that his mom didn't die after she'd gotten so sick when he was a kid. Then he was lucky that he and his siblings got to live with their grandmother, who was the best, while their mom recuperated.

In school he was a student who loved what he loved and ignored what he didn't. While his science teachers praised his mind, his GPA stayed a solid C through high school. He excelled at pop quizzes and multiple-choice tests. He was accused of cheating on the SAT because he was a 2.0 student with a 1600 test score. He took another test, alone, and got a 1560. (He never told them he had purposefully gotten a few wrong. No one would believe he just got lucky—twice—while taking a vast multiple choice exam.)

HIS BEST FRIEND was named Matt. Parker's luck had continued when he had broken his ankle and been on crutches. After school one day, he had hobbled around, bored, since the lab was closed and Amy was staying late for band practice. He wandered to the baseball game and figured it was something to watch at least. He sat in the stands next to a boy he vaguely recognized.

The kid was there alone, wearing an old T-shirt that said THE GARAGES in bold letters, under a leather jacket. Like a lot of the theater kids, he'd applied "guy-liner" better than Parker's own sister. He looked painfully out of place.

"Matt, right? Haven't I seen you with the theater kids?" Parker asked as he sat down. "What are you doing at a baseball game?"

The boy heaved a heavy sigh and, without looking at Parker, said, "I could ask you the same thing. Aren't you a science nerd?"

"Fair," Parker said. "My sister is at band practice and she's my ride. And the lab is closed, because yeah, science nerd. Your turn."

The kid shrugged. "Okay. My ride isn't here either. I left theater rehearsal early because I refused to kiss my sister."

"How did that come up?" Parker sputtered, trying to find a connection between incest and high school theater.

"I was cast as Seymour in *Little Shop of Horrors*," Matt said. "My sister tried out for Audrey when I asked her not to. She fucking got the part. I hate her. I can't stand her in the next room at home, I sure as hell am not going to pretend to fall in love with her in front of the whole school. When I refused to kiss her, Dr. Carrol kicked me out of the show. My brother won't pick us up for a few hours, so I had nothing else better to do."

"Couldn't you have edited the scene for a hug or something?" Parker mused.

"Oh, no, Dr. Carrol is pure with the theater, she will always do as the author intended." His voice took on a high, flawless, upper-class Connecticut accent. "'If you think you know this show better than Howard Ashman, then by all means, please, improve on it!'" He fished a vape pen out of his pocket and sucked on it. The scent of sickly sweet oranges filled the air. "It's all just bullshit, man. I'm not committing incest even for the theater. I'm dropping out of school soon anyway."

"Seriously? Dropping out doesn't get you far in life," Parker said.

"How many billionaires completed college? Nearly none of them! High school is just bullshit legacy planning to make us into factory workers, only the US doesn't have factories anymore, so they're wasting everyone's time."

"I'm pretty sure most billionaires finished high school at least," Parker said. "And they don't become billionaires because they drop out. They usually inherit the money or are sociopaths who don't care who they step on along the way."

"Whatever," the boy grumbled.

"I'm Parker," he offered, feeling awkward but not sure what else to say.

"I know," the other guy said. "I've seen you in English class." He paused, and Parker figured he had nothing else to say, but then he spoke up again. "You a math nerd, too?"

"Yeah," Parker said, hesitantly.

"Do you know Algebra II? I don't know what the fuck Mr. Taylor is talking about."

"Yeah, mostly," Parker said. If he were being honest, he'd say he went through Algebra II when he was a sophomore, but he figured Matt didn't need that much information. Numbers were always easy for him. "What's the problem?"

"Everything. I don't get a goddamn thing about it. I'm close to flunking."

"Is that why you're dropping out?"

"What's the point? I flunk and my dad gets super pissed. If I drop out, I can move out and get a job somewhere."

"Do you need help?" Parker ventured.

Skeptical side-eye. "You offering?"

He and Matt had become close friends, Parker helping Matt with academics, Matt helping Parker with confidence; he wasn't very good at talking to girls. Or boys. Or teachers. Anyone, really.

Matt's mother, who had walked out on his dad, returned to town, and after a short but nasty custody battle, moved him in with her and enrolled him in a different school. He emailed Parker to say that after the drama settled, his mom put him in therapy and he was feeling less dark than he had felt in years. They had stayed in touch and still hung out.

Matt got a scholarship to Appalachian State, which shocked him to his core.

On move-in day, he sent Parker an email that Parker still had saved. Matt wrote:

> P– Since we don't have the same school yearbooks,
> you have to get an email from me. I wanted to say that
> you made me stay in school, which was really boring,
> you asshole. But here's a secret. The day we met, I was
> in a pretty shitty place. More was going on than just
> Little Shop. Stuff with my dad. Some home shit had
> gotten real bad. You were one of the few people who
> just talked to me. You helped get me out of that bad
> place. I passed algebra because of you. I'm here at ASU
> because of you. I can't ever pay you back, but if you ever
> need me, say the word. –M

Parker's memory was nearly perfect, but he squashed some memories down so they would stay hidden, some things he wanted gone so he could enjoy his day-to-day life. After he read Matt's yearbook message, he couldn't help but remember the bulge in Matt's jacket pocket that day, coupled with visiting Matt's house to study a few days later and seeing the arsenal displayed proudly on the wall of his dad's garage. They had never talked about it, but Parker wondered what Matt's plan had been that day.

He'd been really lucky.

· · ·

HE AND AMY grew apart; she decided along the way that he was lazy, since he lacked ambition, while he just said that when he became a scientist, no one would care how good his grasp was of the War of 1812.

Amy excelled in everything, considering careers in art and medicine. Parker had laughed at both, since she paled at the sight of blood and her drawing was rudimentary at best. They had their usual sibling rivalries, but that came to a head when Mallory entered the picture.

Mallory was the only thing in Parker's past that he would consider bad luck. He had first thought it was perfect, his sister bringing this girl into his life, but Amy was selfish and guarded her friendship closely. He was barely able to talk to Mallory, but when he did, they got along, laughed at the same things, like they fit together perfectly. Her smile was wide and contagious, and he was finally interested in something other than science.

She'd had some bad luck of her own, with her mom dying, and her aunt didn't seem like a great substitute. A few other people had died before he met her, when he'd never even been to a funeral. She told him their senior year that she thought her life could finally start in college. She didn't say it, but she implied that she thought they might be able to date if they were away from Amy.

Reggie came home for Christmas their senior year, and Parker had tried to confide in him.

"You want to date Amy's best friend? Are you masochistic?" Reggie had asked him, slapping him on the side of the head.

"Why?" Parker asked. "Why is that so bad?"

"Let's say you ask her out and she's not interested. Now she's uncomfortable and won't want to hang out with Amy so much so she doesn't have to see you. Or a happy ending: Let's say you two start dating. You won't want to go on dates with your sister, so you both cut Amy out. Then let's say you break up. You don't want to see each other at all, so she stops coming over. Whatever you do with this girl will affect Amy. Tread carefully, bro."

"How do you know so much about this?" Parker asked, amazed.

"I tried to date my roommate's brother," Reggie said with a sigh. "I'll never make that mistake again. The last month of senior year was a real shit show."

For Amy, he had kept his distance. He and Mallory were friendly, but that was it.

They had that one moment at graduation, when he had managed to sit next to her for two hours, holding her hand, dizzy with the intensity of his feelings. He had thought something might happen at prom when he, Amy, and Mallory had gone as part of a group of seven.

Parker's date was Kelly Parker, who joked, "If Parker and I got married, I'd make Parker take my name so he would be Parker Parker!" After the third time she said it, Parker was looking for the exit of whatever room they'd been in. One time he saw Mallory laughing at him, like they were sharing a private joke. And all he wanted to do was make her laugh more.

The evening ended with them sleeping on the floor of Matt's mom's basement. Matt had been Amy's date, but only so Matt could go to prom at his old school. Amy was just relieved she could stop talking about her fake boyfriend, Calvin Shuttle, whom she and Mallory had invented to keep their nosy grandmother from trying to set her up with boys from church.

No one else in their group was dating seriously, but Kelly had been giving Parker eyes during the night, making him feel awkward and seek conversation with anyone but her.

He had struggled to sleep that night on the floor. He had asked Mallory to dance once, and she had turned him down, looking up at him and saying it wasn't a good idea, glancing at Amy dancing with Matt. Then she had looked at him and said, "We can't. I want to. But if I let myself get that close, then"—she bit her lip—"then I won't be able to play it cool anymore."

That told him what she felt about him more than any swaying to pop songs could, and he was giddy and frustrated for the rest of the night.

In Matt's basement, Parker could almost feel her sleeping in the same room as him.

He heard a muffled giggle and a hissed whisper. He slowly turned his head and saw Matt's spot on the basement couch was occupied by two people. He thought it was Mallory, and his stomach tore itself in two for a moment, then he recognized the giggle.

Amy. Amy was hooking up with Parker's best friend. After all Parker had tried to do to avoid hurting her by keeping his distance from Mallory, she was sucking his best friend's face off. Christ. Parker was in a shadow behind the Ping-Pong table, so he sat up and looked around the room in disgust. Was everyone hooking up? Was he the seventh wheel?

Brown eyes caught his attention. Mallory also was awake, sitting outside her sleeping bag. She sat against the wall, her face expressionless. She was staring right at Parker.

She couldn't see him, could she? Of course not. He hated the idea of being watched while he slept, which was why he had chosen this dark corner. But her eyes watched him unerringly. He moved slightly, and a small, wry grin flickered across her face. She looked meaningfully at where Amy and Matt were making out on the couch. He followed her gaze and nodded. He didn't know if she was trying to say something with that pointed look. It could have meant anything from "check out the horny teens" to "after everything we've done to be good, off Amy goes with Matt."

In his mind, he created multiple alternate universes where he crawled silently over to her, sat beside her on the wall, and just enjoyed her presence. Or he moved aside to invite her over beside him, and he could kiss her in the safety of the shadows. Or he could loudly tell Amy she was an asshole for making him stay away from Mallory while she just got felt up by Matt, proclaiming his love and alienating his sister forever in one fell swoop.

Sometimes in these universes he texted her, sending amusing notes or animations. Sometimes he texted her what he really felt. Sometimes he told her to meet him outside and they made out under the stars.

But despite all those admittedly great ideas, he stuck with the coward's one. He and Mallory watched each other for what seemed like an eternity. Then Amy got quietly off the couch, and Mallory's eyes closed. Was she faking, or really asleep? He never knew. But the moment was over.

PARKER WAS LUCKY when his grandma died, because his mom had come out of her coma and was finally ready to take care of them. He and Amy were adults, but it was still nice to have a home to come back to when the semester was over. But Mom had to move for her rehab and her new job, and northern Virginia might as well have been light-years away if your crush wouldn't respond to your messages.

He tried to reconnect with her over the first year of school, when he was home, when he was in school, when he visited Amy at her college, but Mallory never answered his emails or texts. She either blocked him on social media or stopped posting. He finally took the hint, nursed his broken heart, and moved on.

His luck continued. He got his doctorate, he studied some fascinating things. Graduated with honors.

He had been lucky to be one of only four survivors when Takahashi Memorial Hospital burned down. It was an older hospital, fitted with a sprinkler system, smoke alarm, and fire doors, but little else. It only took a cascade of small failures for a chemical fire in the morgue to run rampant and take over the building in minutes.

Parker had been lying in a post-op pain haze as the smoke drifted through the ventilation system. Somewhere beyond him, alarms were going off and hospital staff began mobilizing to rescue as many patients as they could.

He ended up being the last patient rescued before the building collapsed. Barely. What luck.

He was tired of the pain, tired of other people being tired of his pain. He could anticipate the look on his loved ones' faces when they heard of his latest injury. He hated that look. He watched the smoke billow up the hall and thought for a moment that he could just stay here.

Where do they take those injured when the hospital has burned down? he thought, his head refusing to clear. Maybe this was it. His luck had turned. He would die.

Then his door swung open and a massive firefighter in full gear burst in. He shouted something into a radio and went to pick up Parker.

"Hang on, you don't know what's wrong with me, you could—" Parker's objection was cut off by his shriek when the firefighter's shoulder nestled into his fresh appendectomy incision. He grayed out from the pain, which, in hindsight, was a blessing. Brief memories of a stretcher, an IV, an ambulance ride, and a concerned face that looked like him, but with different coloring. The handsome, blond, serious brother.

"The shit you get into, Parker, you know you interrupted my date with this fire?" Reggie said, swaying with the movement of the ambulance. "Go back to sleep."

Parker obeyed his big brother, like always.

• • •

"APPENDECTOMY. SMOKE INHALATION, bruising, a little bleeding, some torn stitches. Could have been a lot worse."

The words, drifting through the haze.

"He was lucky they found him in time. He was the last one rescued. They don't know yet how many died."

More sleep.

Waking to angry words.

"You're seriously mad at me because I had to help my brother, who was in a hospital that was on fire? No, I'm not putting you first. Compared to my family, I barely know you." Pause. "God, you really are made of drama. Fine, if you must have an answer, yes, I would leave you in a burning building if I had to choose between you and my brother. I would let you die. Feel better?" Pause. Were there tears on the other end? Parker couldn't tell. "If you're going to see my caring for my family as neglecting you, don't call me again."

"I had a birthday present for you, but I think it burned down," Parker said by way of greeting. "Seems I got you out of a bad date, though."

"It wasn't a bad date until I had a personal emergency," Reggie said from the guest recliner by the window. "How are you feeling?"

"If you're dating someone who can't see how important your family is, then that's a bad date. Think if you'd stayed in the relationship, and even married the guy. And then my appendix burst and my hospital burned down." He was going to finish with something pithy, but he started coughing, and Reggie hurried to get him some water.

"Oh, that hurts," he said, wincing. "Remind me not to cough. Did you have a good birthday?"

Reggie gave a bitter laugh. "What do you think?"

The drugs were relaxing him, and he felt like he wanted to give Reggie something special for being there. "How about a secret?" He could usually get Reggie to smile if he told a good story.

"I don't think you should be talking right now," Reggie said.

"I'll tell the story whether you want to listen or not. I owe you a birthday present. How about the tragic love story of me and Mallory Viridian?"

Reggie stilled. "I'm listening."

"NOTHING! YOU'VE BEEN hiding 'nothing' from me for years?" Reggie had raged when he was done. "That is the worst love story I've ever heard!"

"I never said it was a good story. Just a secret I hadn't told you. The fact that the story is so bad is why I didn't want to tell it. Feels like the only time in my life that I've really been unlucky."

Reggie stared at him, then doubled over in laughter. "You experience your appendix nearly rupturing, emergency surgery, almost dying in a hospital fire, but it's that time you couldn't get the courage to talk to a girl that was the really unlucky time in your life. Little brother, you do have terrible luck, but losing Mallory wasn't luck. You just let an opportunity pass you by."

He'd shrugged, just glad he could amuse Reggie. "Meh, I'm over it now. Every few years I try to find her online, but nothing has come up. And she never responds to my messages."

Reggie stared at him like Parker had said that he had always thought Reggie was straight. "You have actively been looking for her and never found her?"

Parker shrugged again, then winced as his bruises gave a renewed throbbing effort. "Not everyone is online."

Reggie shook his head slowly. "How did you ever get your doctorate?" He stood and left the room, still chuckling. Parker listlessly thumbed through the TV streaming services the hospital offered, but Reggie returned quickly, holding a hospital gift store bag. He pulled out a book and handed it to Parker.

"*The Balcony Murders*? What does this have to do with anything?" Parker asked.

"Just showing you that Mallory's been busy since she left college." He pulled his phone from his pocket and pulled up a web site. It was a publisher's mystery series page. The Queen Pen Mysteries. "The novelization of the true adventures of Mallory Viridian, amateur sleuth. Inspired by true events." It appeared that the first book was inspired by events from January 2034.

"Is this real?" he asked, his eyes wide.

"You never found this online? How could you miss this? There are over six books!"

"My heart was broken. I moved on," Parker said crossly.

Reggie stretched and lay back in the recliner. "Just read it. It'll pass the time. Amy should be here to check on you tomorrow."

"Let's talk about your love life," Parker said. "Who were you on a date with tonight?"

A nurse walked into the room, barely following a quick knock. He turned the lights on, making Parker squint. "Good evening, Mr. Valor, I am here to take your vitals," he said with a smile. "Looks like you're one of our new Takahashi Memorial patients."

"I'm always the lucky one," Parker said. "When do people sleep around here?"

The nurse was tall, broad shouldered, with curly red hair. His freckled face was pleasant, and somehow not worn with the usual fatigue shadow that night-shift hospital workers tended to wear.

He frowned in mock concern. "I'm sorry, if you were hoping for a hotel, you clearly made a wrong turn. Maybe program your GPS next time before you check into a hospital."

Parker smiled, yawned, and then held his arm out for his blood pressure to be taken. Reggie fumbled around the recliner, trying to find the button that brought it down, and stood up without any of his usual calm demeanor.

He went to the other side of Parker's bed and cleared his throat. "Any idea when we can take him home?" he asked.

"That's a question for the doctor. They don't let me make any of the big decisions around here," the nurse said. His name tag said MAXWELL. "And I've tried to make them, believe me."

He checked Parker's temperature and stitches, asked about his pain level, and then busily put his cart back in order. "I can give you something for the pain now, Mr. Valor. I can't say when we can let him go, but I can tell you that his vitals are perfect and his incision looks better than it did when he got here. He'll be discharged soon." He smiled briefly at Reggie, his brown eyes kind. "He's lucky to have you here for him. A lot of our patients don't have anyone."

Parker watched his brother closely. He was pale from the stress and lack of comfortable sleeping arrangements, so the slight flush that reached his cheeks was noticeable.

"That's good to know, thank you," Reggie said, and then excused himself to the bathroom.

The nurse smiled after Reggie. "Is he always so formal?"

"Yep, always," Parker said. "But you know, you were right. He's here for me while no one else is. He's loyal. He's here when he should be celebrating his birthday."

"Hey, me, too," Maxwell said. "Mine's December 11."

"That's his," Parker said, delighted at the coincidence. "He's also single."

Maxwell laughed out loud. "I'm not asking for a date. I'm not sure of the ethics of hitting on a patient's next of kin."

Parker smiled. "But you thought about it."

Maxwell wheeled his cart toward the door. "Listen, meddler, you get some sleep and I will check on you before the end of my shift. Be awake around six if you don't want to be startled."

"Count on it," Parker said.

Reggie came out of the bathroom, wiping his hands on a paper towel and closing the door behind him with the towel on the handle, then dropping it into the waste bin by the bed.

"His name is Maxwell and you have the same birthday and he thinks you're cute," Parker said.

Reggie looked immediately offended. "You aren't trying to fix me up with any guy you think might be gay again, are you?"

Parker shrugged innocently. "No, just the ones that you're attracted to."

Reggie made a literal harrumph noise and went to turn the overhead light off. "He wasn't considerate enough to turn the lights off when he left the room."

"Yeah, that's a total deal-breaker," Parker said. "Tall, ginger, handsome nurses that don't turn the lights off are really unattractive."

"Go to sleep, Parker," Reggie said, returning to the recliner and trying to get comfortable.

A little over a year later, Parker was best man at Reggie and Max's wedding. Max was about to graduate with his master's. During his toast, Parker showed off his appendectomy scar, much worse than most due to his unique adventures, and joked that if he hadn't had the good luck to get appendicitis and have his hospital burn to the ground, the two never would have met.

"What I really wanted to tell the two of you is: you're welcome. Now, drink to the happy couple!"

Things were going well. Reggie was married, Amy was going for her second doctorate from Georgetown, and Parker's papers on wasp and hornet activity had just put him on the tenure track.

And then two things happened to twist everything apart: First Contact, and Oscar Daye.

16

A BLOODY MARY WOULD HAVE TASTED BETTER

MAX VALOR-COLE WOKE up angry, still upset from the argument last night. Or maybe earlier that morning. He shook his head. He'd been drunk, and he didn't really understand station time. Before bed. They'd fought before bed.

He'd woken up on the floor, leaning against the wall, with minor burns on his hands, which were coated in a sticky, sweet-smelling substance. He had no memory except of Reggie's furious face before he passed out. His head ached and his hands hurt.

Max smacked his lips and grimaced. He remembered he'd had some of the booze they'd brought from Earth, and then, once well and truly tipsy, had been game to try some alien liquor.

"You're awake," said the voice from the bed. It was an accusation, as if he ought to have stayed asleep.

His husband sat there, cross-legged, glaring down at him. He looked like he had been sitting there all night, waiting for Max to wake up so they could continue their fight. He was rubbing his front tooth with his thumb, the skin snagging on the chip in the left one.

"You know, if you'd have told me I'd be worried about my husband, the medical professional, drinking to excess while in a completely foreign place, including trying drinks that he wasn't even sure if his body would process, I would have told you that you were full of shit," Reggie said.

"And if someone had told me I was going to marry someone with zero interest in my welfare, I'd have run the other way," Max muttered, rubbing his forehead.

Gone were the days when Reggie would hold his head lovingly in his hands, commiserate with him about a hangover or a sour stomach, and run his hands through his hair to soothe his pain. Gone were the "can I get you some Pepto?" or "want me to call work for you?" platitudes. Now the morning-after discussions were all accusations and anger, the fact of drinking to excess carrying with it so much more baggage than "you got drunk last night."

An undercurrent of alcoholism fear. Of blackout questions. Of infidelity accusations.

"What happened?" Max asked, looking at his hands and frowning. "How did I get burned?"

"God, you don't remember anything, do you?" Reggie asked, shaking his head. He pressed on his tooth again with his thumb.

"What happened to your tooth?" Max said. Reggie's lips were slightly swollen, like he had been smacked with something.

"What *happened*," Reggie mocked, his voice dripping with disdain.

Max just waited. Reggie wasn't answering questions, and if Max said anything else, it would devolve into a shouting match about drinking, not including Reggie telling him what happened the night before, and he was very worried about what might have happened.

They both jumped when the wall terminal gave a strange trill. It trilled again, and the men looked at each other, united at least in their mutual confusion. "I think it's the phone," Reggie said.

"How do we answer it?" Max asked, but once he said "answer," the trilling stopped.

"Hey, is this Reggie and Max's room?" asked a woman.

"Mallory, is that you?" Reggie asked.

"Yeah. I need to talk to you guys about last night. Can you meet me for some coffee in an hour?"

"We'll be there," Reggie said. "Just tell me where."

Mallory gave an address that meant nothing to Max, and Reggie wrote it down, then raised an eyebrow at him. "You need a shower."

Max rolled his eyes and got to his feet, wincing at the pain in his hands. He went to the shower without another word.

IN HINDSIGHT, HE should have pressed Reggie for more information before the interview. His husband sat there, coffee steaming in front of him, smiling tightly as Mallory started to talk about the murder.

Max blinked. "Murder? What murder? Who died?"

Mallory stopped talking, then looked carefully from Max to Reggie. "You don't know?"

Max shook his head.

Mallory looked to Reggie. "Do you know what I'm talking about?"

"Oh, yes, I definitely do," Reggie said, glaring at Max.

Mallory ran her hands through her messy hair, wincing as if it pained her. "I haven't had a lot of sleep, so forgive me if I'm getting this wrong, but a friend of yours died, your husband doesn't remember anything, and you let him come into an interview without warning him what it would be about?"

Max felt a small flare of glee when he realized that she was judging Reggie for letting him stumble into a trap instead of putting down Max for blacking out.

"I thought you wouldn't want me to coach him to get our stories straight," Reggie said, looking startled and backpedaling. "What if he's the killer?"

Mallory cocked an eyebrow at him. "Boy, you must be a great life partner to have," she said dryly.

Reggie sputtered, but Mallory faced Max, her eyes tired but kind. "Max. Do you have a hangover?"

"God, do I," he said thickly.

She gestured to a server. "Can you ask Ferdinand what he puts in that 'morning-after' drink he makes for me and Xan?"

The giant rock person grunted in response and wandered away.

"We'll get you feeling better shortly," she said. "Now, last night at the end of the party, we had a chaotic mess. Oscar was murdered and the Sund— some alien insects apparently attacked. They stung Agent Draughn but no one else that we know of."

"Oscar . . . died?" Max asked, his voice sounding far away. He locked eyes with Reggie, whose face dared him to say anything else. Oscar's death meant so much he didn't even know where to start. Freedom for Reggie's career. Security for Max. And a major roadblock in their marriage removed.

Why hadn't Reggie told him Oscar was dead?

Unless he did it. Or unless I did. Max wracked his brain. He was trying to remember. Oscar was being Oscar last night. He had talked to pretty much every human at the party. Spent some solo time with that tall ambassador woman. Then he and Max had gotten a drink together—

"Yeah, I'm sorry," Mallory said. "Were you close?"

Max gave a choked laugh. "'Close' is the wrong word for it. But we knew him well," he said, looking again at Reggie's stony face. He cleared his throat. "How did he die?"

"He was stabbed, but I am thinking he was at the very least drugged, if not outright poisoned, beforehand. There were no defensive wounds on the body. The medbay is trying to analyze the body for toxins now, but the computers aren't running at a hundred percent yet."

"Stabbed. Jesus," Max said, then something occurred to him. "Do they need help in the medbay? I'll know more about the human body than aliens will."

Mallory considered him. "That's true. But you're a murder suspect, and I could just hand you the keys to the candy store for you to destroy evidence if I do that."

"But I didn't do it," he protested.

"How do you know?" Reggie asked. "You don't remember last night."

"Christ, Reggie, are you trying to get me arrested? Is that what you want?" Max snapped, finally losing his temper. He got to his feet. "If you want to interview us, you'll have to do it separately," he said to Mallory. "You can see that he's not going to help you or me in this situation."

"No, Reggie needs to go. Max, you stay. We ordered you a drink, anyway." Mallory closed her hand, firmly but gently, around Max's forearm, and he hissed. She let go immediately. "Are you all right?"

Reggie stood, but neither Mallory nor Max paid him any attention.

"I woke up with these burns, and some sticky stuff all over me," Max said as Mallory gently inspected his hands and arms.

She glanced at Reggie. "What happened to him?"

Reggie shook his head violently, and Max was startled to see tears in his eyes. "No, you want me gone, I'm gone. Clearly Max can handle the interview himself."

"To be fair, Reggie, you weren't helping out much when you were here," Mallory said. "I have an idea what happened to him; we'll work something out. Go cool off, take a walk or something."

Reggie stalked away.

Mallory carefully pulled Max's shirt cuffs over the burns. "Looks like I'm sending you to medbay anyway."

"It's just a minor burn," he said, shrugging and sitting again.

"Not if it's caused by an alien substance," she said. "You don't know what it could do."

The server lumbered back over and put a huge mug of steaming liquid in front of Max. "Thank you," Mallory said, then looked at him. "This is a hangover remedy Xan and I discovered. It's best if you drink it hot, but not so hot it burns you. So you can wait a little bit."

Max glanced at the mug tentatively. Thick black liquid, very much like tar, bubbled slightly. When the bubbles popped, thin strands of red ribbons floated through the black.

He stared in horror as a fat bubble swelled and then burst, sending thick droplets of the stuff to splatter over the rim of the mug.

"Are you sure?" he asked.

"SO WHAT'S UP with you and Reggie?" Mallory asked, savoring her second cup of coffee. She gripped the mug with two hands like she was afraid someone would take it away from her.

"What, that?" Max pointed at the door through which Reggie had stalked. "Every time one of us drinks, all the old arguments come to a head. I guess we don't discuss stuff sober, and it comes out when we drink." He grimaced. "Not the healthiest way of dealing with shit."

"Not really," she said. "What were you fighting about now?"

He sighed, wondering how much he could trust her with. Or how much he could piece together, for that matter. "The question of trust comes up when we drink. Old hurts. New fears." He chewed his bottom lip. "Infidelities. All that."

"Ah," Mallory said, casting a side-eye at him. "Does Reggie suspect you of sleeping with someone last night?"

"I don't know," he said miserably. "Sometimes I think he does suspect, other times I think he's just mad that if I can't remember, then anything could have happened."

"Schrödinger's affair?" Mallory asked.

Max laughed in spite of himself. "Something like that."

"Do you fight all the time about this, or is it just a morning-after fight, and by tonight you'll be happy again?"

Tears pricked Max's eyes as he wondered if he would ever feel happy again with Reggie. He cleared his throat and changed the subject. "You're not going to ask me what I remember about last night?"

She surprised him by looking away, as if embarrassed. "I figured you didn't remember anything."

He gingerly poked a finger at a bubble that hadn't popped in his mug. The bubble didn't break.

"Oh, that's how you know it's done," Mallory said, watching him. "It starts to get a skin."

He looked at her in distaste. "I think I'd rather have the hangover."

She shook her head vehemently. "No, you have to trust me. You've never had anything like this before. Drink it."

He lifted the massive mug with both hands and, wincing in anticipation, he tipped it so the viscous stuff flowed sluggishly toward him.

When it finally met his lips, it surprised him with a sweet, but not overly so, flavor, like honey infused with strawberries. He took a big gulp and savored it, his brain trying to wake up from the hangover, and then a memory hit him like a line drive.

"This is what burned me last night," he said, eyes wide. "I smelled it on me this morning. I must have spilled it on myself before it was ready to drink."

"It's weird; it's medicinal to both Gneiss and humans," Mallory said.

Max shrugged sheepishly and then took another gulp. With each drink, his head cleared a little more.

"You send this back to Earth, and you could make a fortune," he said.

She smiled. "The fourth or fifth time you say that up here, you get tired of it. The medical technology, the space travel, the space suit, even the fashion tech. Some ships and stations are sentient. Everything here could make us a fortune on Earth. That is one reason they're hesitant to work with us. We attach a price tag to everything."

"Are all aliens anti-capitalist?" Max asked with a smile.

"Nah, just like all humans aren't. But we apparently have a level of greed unseen in other races. It's yet another thing that makes them decide we're inferior. Besides, there's something about the galactic economy that is incomprehensible to me. I wonder what economists would say about it."

"Say about what?" Max asked, watching Mallory pour herself another cup of coffee.

She grinned, embarrassed. "I haven't had coffee in a while. So, economy. You know how there were influencers in the teens and twenties? They said that X product was good and suddenly the product would sell out in a night?"

"Yeah, I remember that," Max said, thinking about a few ill-advised purchases he'd made as a kid.

"There's a race called the Silence. They don't communicate with audio at all, but they're more evolved than everyone else put together, apparently. They also control economies. When they want to pay you for services, instead of giving you money, they just increase your worth. If you enter the galactic economy, they take all the things we take into account—supply, demand, education, difficulty, labor-intensive work, price of components, et cetera— but also the gleam."

"The gleam?" Max asked, delighted. "That sounds shiny."

"Yeah. It's the case where we don't have a word for it, so the translation bug does its best. It shows you how shiny you are in the galactic economy. So if you have a widget to sell, you take the cost of the supplies, and the cost of your labor, and the cost of any services you need, and the money to actually make a living, and then you add your gleam on top of it. If the Silence say you're worth more, you are." She shook her head in disbelief. "I did a job for them a few weeks back, so instead of just dealing with credits, I had to get an account in the galactic economy. I had like twenty bucks, or the equivalent, but when they 'paid' me"—she paused to make quotes with her fingers—"the money was worth about thirty. And no actual money had entered my account. I got paid in gleam."

"Sounds like the emperor's new clothes," Max said. "Seems all it needs to tumble down is for someone to point out how stupid it is."

Mallory laughed. "Have you looked at the wealth on Earth? Buying and selling of bad debt? Shorting stock? It's all a hand-waving system that works because everyone believes in it. You need more than one person to say, 'That is fucked up,' for something to change. Besides, people like the gleam."

"Doesn't it make the Silence too powerful?" Max asked, looking around for these aliens. He didn't think he had seen any that were like this alien, but now he was worried.

"Yeah, but they don't seem to care," Mallory said. "There were some major wars a while back, but they have peace now. I haven't done a lot of research. I'm not good with Earth history, so I'm really behind on galactic history."

Max finished his mug. The liquid sat heavy in his belly, but it was a comforting, warm feeling, not a leaden, sick one. "Why are you telling me this? Shouldn't we be talking about Oscar?"

"I wanted to give that"—she pointed to his mug—"time to work. How are you feeling?"

"Better," he said, blinking. "I could use a nap, though."

"Yeah, that's a side effect. If you can afford the time, it'll be the best nap ever. But unfortunately, you don't have the time, because I need to know what you remember of last night."

To his surprise, the memories started to re-form in his head: his own laughter, Reggie's rage, Oscar's smug face—

"I remember," he said. "Reggie's been angry since we got the tickets for this trip."

THE SECRET THAT only Reggie would know, and Max would never discuss with him, was that Oscar's death was a relief. When the opportunity had come up to go to Eternity and study in their various fields, Max had been excited, hoping that if they were away from their day-to-day stresses, they could repair their marriage.

The problems began when Reggie found out that Oscar was coming before he found out Max wanted to go.

"Why is he coming? He's a coach. And who's going to run the site while we're gone?" Reggie raged, pacing the kitchen floor while Max stirred the pasta sauce.

"I have no idea, why does he do anything?" Max said. He put the wooden spoon to his lips and tasted it. Needed more oregano. "By the way," he said mildly. "I've talked to the dean about going as well. She's going to try to clear it."

He wasn't sure what kind of response he expected. He wanted Reggie to be delighted that they were going into space together. But his moods lately were unpredictable.

Reggie stopped pacing. "You? Why? What could possibly interest an experimental psychologist?" He said it like Max's field of study was a joke.

"There are plenty of things that are interesting," Max said, carefully stepping around the main reason he wanted to go. "Aliens, for one."

"And the other one?" Reggie asked pointedly.

"That's not enough?" Max evaded.

"Is it Oscar? Are you going because of him? Did you just now decide to go because I said he was coming?"

The old hurts and anger threatened to rise in his chest, and he took a deep breath, put down the spoon, and gently took Reggie's shoulders. "No. I asked the dean this morning right after we had breakfast with Parker. I didn't know Oscar was going to be there."

Reggie looked frightened for a moment, vulnerable and small. "I really don't want him there. It's hard enough working with him. I can't stand him."

"I know," Max said. "But it's a great opportunity for you. You're making decisions based on business, and doing what you love. A slimy business partner is a small price to pay."

The offer from Oscar had come at a perfect time. With congressional hearings cropping up to discuss alien movement and actions on Earth, and how powerless the humans were to stop it, he had been fascinated to see what would change within the law. Unfortunately, his legal expertise was real estate, and his partners were not pleased about the distractions the hearings were giving Reggie. After a few months of letting his own cases slide, and three warnings, they fired him.

With three months' severance, he went home and continued watching all coverage of the hearings. "Someone has got to care about this," he said several times a day. "It should be me." But he didn't move on it.

Max and Reggie had been dismayed to see Oscar at a dinner party Amy was throwing. They'd pledged to ignore him, but Oscar was hard to ignore if he wanted to be in your face. He had approached them and started bragging about his new website and how he was going to make TMZ Universe obsolete. He said he was looking for interesting content, and that Reggie might be able to provide him with stuff that no one else had. Reggie firmly turned him down until Oscar stated a dollar figure.

"Take it," Max had told him. "I can't support us on my salary and go to school for much longer. Even if I take some part-time hospital shifts."

"You want me to work with *Oscar*?" Reggie asked, skepticism in his voice.

"I want you to work," Max said.

With the requirement that he could work from home instead of in an office beside Oscar, Reggie joined the Trash Heap. To his surprise, he found that he really liked his job. Their financial burden was lessened, and the only downside was Oscar's presence in their life again.

Oscar was a pansexual flirt. He flirted with anyone and everyone and was very good at making people feel as if they were the only person in the room to him. Until he moved to the next person, of course. On the flight to the station, he took the seat between Reggie and a woman he didn't know, flirting with her all the way. She ignored him the best she could, and then flatly told him to leave her alone.

"Tough crowd," he told Reggie with a grin.

"Not everyone likes your attention, Oscar," Reggie had said stiffly, paging through the newspaper on his e-reader.

"But lots of people do, at one time or another, right?" Oscar said, winking.

Reggie said nothing. Max put on his headphones to listen to his audiobook on luck.

Max closed his eyes but opened them again when he felt Reggie shift next to him. Oscar was leaning in and whispering something to him, and Reggie was leaning away, cheeks red and distaste twisting his mouth.

Max removed his headphones and looked at them both. "Oscar, leave my husband alone," he said calmly.

Oscar sat back and held his hands up in surrender. "I was just kidding. Everyone is so sensitive these days."

"Are you okay?" Max asked Reggie.

Reggie stared straight ahead. "I don't want to talk about it."

"But—" Max started.

"No," Reggie said, the clipped word falling like a guillotine blade between them.

Then there had been the party. Max was tired. Tired of the travel and tired of the tension, and tired of the shit Oscar brought into their lives. Tired of having to tolerate Oscar for Reggie's job's sake. And now he had to go to a cocktail party and play nice again.

"Let's not go," Max said, stretching out on their bed while Reggie emerged from the bathroom.

His husband looked at him coldly. "This is important academically, isn't it? Hobnobbing with aliens? I thought that's why you were here."

Max threw his head back into his pillow. "I'm here for you, and for meeting aliens. We'll be here a week; I'll have plenty of time to meet people. I'd just like a chance to stay away from Oscar for once. He can't bother us in here."

"He will always bother us," Reggie said softly, turning his back on Max to straighten his tie in the small mirror on the wall.

"I'm ready to move past it, Reggie," Max said softly. "Please. Let's move past it."

Reggie combed his hair as if he hadn't heard Max. "I'm going. You can stay here if you want."

"And leave you to the wolves?" Max said, trying to lighten the mood, but Reggie didn't turn around. "All right, I'll come with you."

"Fine."

So they went, Max's mind in a whirl of whether he could live another fifty years like this, struggling to communicate or find any warmth within his husband.

The party had been a dizzying clash of colors and strange alien beings, and Max had tried to communicate with them, or watch them, excited to learn body language for entirely new sentient species. He also kept drinking wine, as it kept him relaxed and not constantly glancing at Reggie.

"Trouble in paradise?" Oscar asked when Max was at the bar for his fourth glass of wine.

"Leave us alone, Oscar," Max said with a sigh.

"I thought you should know, Reggie is doing a great job," Oscar said, voice dripping with innuendo.

"Uh-huh," Max said, not looking at him.

"Has he told you about my safety valve?"

Intrigued despite himself, he cocked an eyebrow. "Is this a sex thing?"

Oscar laughed. "No, it's my insurance policy to protect myself. In preparation to collect celebrity gossip, I learned a bit about hacking. I found some interesting stuff about the people around us."

"Great," Max said.

"I found out about you," Oscar whispered. "And your great big lie you don't want your husband to know."

"AND?" MALLORY PROMPTED, when Max didn't continue.

"And what? He was a dick," Max said, looking into the empty mug of disgusting but effective hangover cure. "He ordered two drinks and then just strutted away. He always strutted, God."

"What was he referring to?"

"I have no idea," Max said. "He didn't say what he had on me. Just said he knew, and winked."

"You don't know? You don't have any secrets?" Mallory asked, frowning.

"We all have secrets, don't we?" Max asked. "I didn't know what in my past he had unearthed. I wasn't going to ask—for all I know, he wanted me to lead him toward a secret, or confirm something he only suspected."

"All right," Mallory said. "What happened next?"

Max thought, trying to appear as if the memory wasn't clear and painful. "I asked for another glass of wine. They said they were out. I went to find Reggie, and he was talking to Oscar. They looked angry. Oscar just smirked at me when he saw me coming, so I stopped to talk to Agent Draughn. Oscar was loud and belligerent, said something about sleeping with Amy that night. He'd given Reggie one of the mugs he had gotten, which made me mad. I'd asked Reggie that night if he knew that Oscar was gathering dirt on everyone, and he said I shouldn't be surprised, and that it was my fault that we were involved with his dirty dealings. And"—the memory was painful, more painful than the burns on his arms—"when Oscar just laughed at Reggie, I lost my temper. All I remember is being so angry. So hurt. And then I woke up in my apartment like this." He held out his hands again.

"So you don't remember taking your anger out on Oscar? Or Reggie, for that matter? He seemed pretty mad."

"I don't remember," Max said evenly.

She waited another beat and then sighed. "All right. Let's get you to medbay, then I need to get back to my apartment for a bit."

17

. . .

OPERATORS ARE STANDING BY

MALLORY SAT IN her cushy chair, the one that Eternity had supplied her with when furnishing her apartment. On the side table was a potted plant with a vine trailing out of it. Xan and Devanshi had asked her to please try to connect with Eternity, since she was the custodian of the station. She wanted to tell them that she didn't ask for the job, or the responsibility, but asking anyone else to link with the station could be dangerous.

Xan stood by the door, his arms crossed, watching her. Devanshi clung to the ceiling and also watched her, upside down.

"Are you going to do it or what?" Xan asked. "The sooner you do this, the sooner you can go back to your murder."

She glared up at him. "Give me a second. I want to try meditating to touch any blue Sundry that might be around."

"Again?" he asked, exasperated. "They're not there. Tina confirmed it. I've asked around and no one has seen any blue Sundry for days."

"Confirmed with security," Devanshi said. "They have said no silver or blue living Sundry have been spotted, and that all station systems are up and running again."

"Still," Mallory said, closing her eyes. "I can't help but feel like I'm missing something."

"You—" Xan began, but Mallory opened one eye and shushed him.

She took some deep breaths and released the little bit of concentration that she had been working to develop, a mental wall to keep out any prying Sundry. Now she was open, seeking, willing to make a connection.

Again, something prickled at the edge of her awareness. Again, she couldn't grasp it. *For all I know I'm sensing the Cuckoos.* She wondered if that was possible.

What am I if I don't have this murder-solving sense?

"Nothing." She blew out a frustrated breath. "Fine, I'll do it." The vine dripping from the pot flexed as she said it.

"What can I do?" Xan asked, shifting his weight. He was vibrating like a tuning fork.

"I don't think I need anything," Mallory said, frowning at the innocuous potted plant in her hands. "Supposedly I just let the vine grab me, and I've connected. Just make sure it doesn't strangle me or blind me or something." She shuddered, remembering Adrian's attempt to merge with Eternity.

"We'll be right here," he said.

Mallory extended her finger, hesitated a moment, then reached out her hand and touched the vine.

The reaction was immediate; the vine wrapped tightly around her fingers and then snaked under her sweatshirt, over her forearm. It constricted, and Mallory had a brief moment of panic, thinking about the thorns that Eternity had grown that had taken Adrian's sight. The plant was insistent, urgent, but it didn't hurt her.

With her hand starting to turn red and pulse with her heartbeat, she closed her eyes.

Eternity? Are you okay?

I'm fine I'm fine It's fine we're fine fine fine fine fine—

Mallory pressed. *You don't sound fine. Your Sundry systems have been replaced. You've left Ariadne, we're traveling to a new planet. What can we do? Can we get you to turn around and go back to Ariadne?*

A buzzing sensation overwhelmed her, and the continued insistence that Eternity was *fine fine fine* FINE FINE FINE.

Mallory tried to reach out to touch the Cuckoos directly, but as she tried to direct her attention to the swarm that now made up the center of Eternity, she bounced off hard, returning to her own mind violently. She gasped, opened her eyes, and fell off the chair, landing roughly and twisting her wrist under her. The pot fell from her hands and shattered on the floor next to her, the vine still holding her tightly.

"No, no, let me go, it's not fine, it's not fine," she mumbled, yanking her hand away from the vine. She heaved herself to her hands and knees and then vomited on the floor.

Xan jumped forward, his hands on her back, supporting her.

She sat up painfully and wiped her mouth, grimacing. She pulled the vine, which now showed little resistance, off her arm.

"What happened?" Xan asked. He took a cup by the sink and filled it with water, then handed it to her. His wide eyes never left hers.

"I don't know. It's like someone's been shot but they're telling you that it's no biggie. She keeps saying she's fine, but clearly she's not. There's . . ." She accepted the cup gratefully. He helped her to her feet so she could rinse her mouth a few times, and then she took a drink.

She looked down at the vine, constricting slightly on the floor like a hungry tentacle, and groaned at the dirt and vomit all over her floor.

"I have no idea what to do."

BACK IN THE medbay, Mallory met a Gneiss doctor with blue-gray accents on light gray marble. "This is Dr. Jeremy," said the

Gurudev nurse. "He's looking after Donald Draughn. He was able to work with the Gneiss named Tina to get antidote for the venom."

"This is fascinating," the Gneiss said, sounding animated on a level to rival Tina. "We had thought the Cuckoos long extinct, but with the help of Queen Tina, we were able to cross-reference some old files with the venom sample she provided."

"So Draughn's going to be okay?" Mallory asked. "And anyone else who might get stung?"

"Indeed," Dr. Jeremy said. "Cuckoos are like the Sundry, except they're lazy assholes, infiltrating existing hives, killing everyone inside, and then taking it over. When they do it to a hive on a planet, it's a tragedy. When they do it to a hive in a living space station, it's hijacking. This species now controls every aspect of the station. We should count ourselves lucky that they didn't see a need to kill us along with the Sundry."

"Mallory!" came a yell behind the closed door. "What did you tell them to do to me?"

"I guess Draughn's feeling better," she said. "Did you save his hand?"

"You humans are—" Dr. Jeremy said, but Mallory held up a finger.

"I'm going to stop you right there, Doc," she said, tired. "I know that we're fragile and wet and gross. Can you skip to the part where he's better or not?"

"I was going to say humans are very loud," Dr. Jeremy said. "I suggested removing the fleshy appendage, but he made a lot of noise. It looks like we were able to save it."

"Did they tell you how they got the sample?" Draughn demanded, his voice still muffled.

Mallory opened the door. The agent sat on the edge of his bed, his hand tightly wrapped in bandages, his face red and angry. "How are you feeling?" she asked.

"Fuck you," he said. "I didn't say it was okay to pump me full of whatever they did. And you had no right to allow it."

"No right to figure out what antivenom you needed to save your life?"

"No! I have rights!" Draughn said.

Mallory sighed and crossed her arms. "The thing is, you don't. We're not governed by the laws of the US, or any other place on Earth. You're human, and most things involving humans are in my hands while Mrs. Brown is gone and the ambassador is still getting her feet under her. If I hadn't suggested this, you would have lost your hand, maybe more."

"But do you know how they got it?" he asked, turning the topic. "They wanted a sample of the venom, so this huge beast, like, bigger than him"—he gestured to the doctor—"comes running into the room, shaking the floor and threatening to bring the place down."

"Tina?" Mallory asked Dr. Jeremy.

"Yes, Queen Tina," he said.

"Tina's not a stealthy person," she told Draughn, who just glared at her.

"He said he was honored to have her here and how lucky I was. Then she opened her mouth and about a hundred goddamn wasps flew out! I thought they were going to swarm and sting me to death!"

"Did any of them sting you?" Mallory asked.

"That's not the point," Draughn said. "What the hell kind of joint are they running here?"

"They needed the wasp venom to save your hand," Mallory said. "It sounds like it was a success."

"Where's Amy?" he snarled.

IT TURNED OUT Amy was back in her room, having improved from the concussion she'd gotten from falling. She still had a bandage on her head, but her swelling had greatly decreased.

She welcomed Mallory with a tired smile. "Never a dull moment, huh?" she said by way of greeting. She moved aside so Mallory could come in.

Mallory was startled to see Parker in the room, and heat flushed through her, confusing her.

"Are you here to ask about Oscar?" Amy asked. She shook her head. "Shame about him."

"Don't lie," Mallory said, pulling up a chair. "You all hated him."

Amy dropped the act. "Yeah, we did. He liked people to be annoyed by him. He would rather have been known for being a splinter in someone's hand than a hug."

"I hear he was collecting secrets," Mallory said.

"He claimed to be collecting them," Amy corrected.

"Three people can keep a secret if two of them are dead, you know," Mallory said.

"Thanks, Ben Franklin, that belongs on a coffee mug," Amy said, rolling her eyes. "He was all bluff and threats anyway."

Parker had taken up the only chair in the room, so Amy and Mallory sat on the edge of the bed.

"So you don't think he had the secrets?" Mallory asked.

Amy looked down at her hands. "No, he had the secrets. I didn't think he'd use them, though."

Mallory rubbed her face and tried to avoid looking at Parker. "It sucks that we didn't have any time to catch up before all this," Mallory said. "And now we still can't since I need to find out who killed Oscar."

Amy blinked. "Wow, you're all 'by the book' now."

"I guess we all grew up," Mallory said. She shrugged, uncomfortable. "If I find the murderer, then we should have time to hang out. If I don't, then they might kill one of us, and then we really won't catch up."

"Unless we both die," Amy said brightly.

Mallory laughed, glad for at least gallows humor. "Can you tell me what you remember from the party? What happened there?" She pointed to Amy's head.

Amy looked blankly at the wall like she was trying to remember. "It's like my memory is just pictures, not video. I remember Oscar hitting on me. I remember talking to Don. I was really tired. Someone started yelling, and then the room was full of the green wasps." She gave a quick look to Parker, who didn't respond.

"Did the wasps attack you? Were you scared?" Mallory asked.

Amy shook her head slowly. "They were swarming but weren't hostile. Parker told me that much."

"We knew we had no reason to be afraid of them," Parker said, but he stopped talking when Amy glared at him.

"The other humans were swatting at them and getting them riled up," Amy said, twisting her face as the memory returned. "Then something hit me like a truck and I went down. I didn't wake up till recently." She touched the bandage on her head gingerly. "But I think I feel better than I should."

"The Sundry healing is far beyond anything we can manage on Earth," Mallory said. "You got the good stuff, as I understand it. I think you went down hard. Draughn says he tackled you to protect you when the wasps swarmed the room," she added. "Do you remember him?"

"I guess he was the truck," Amy said slowly. "But I don't remember it specifically."

"So you don't recall seeing anything happen to Oscar?" Mallory asked. "You said he hit on you."

Amy rolled her eyes. "Me and everyone else at the party. I saw him talking to the ambassador. He was looking for your friend at one point. He asked what the deal was with you. He was born twenty years too late, he's prime pickup-artist material." She paused, then frowned. "Was. He was. Anyway, I got used to it, never rose to the bait. He'd slept with too many people I knew; I didn't want to get mixed up in all that. I got used to the idea that Oscar flirting was like Oscar saying hello."

"Did he have any secrets on you?" Mallory asked.

"He said he did," Amy said smoothly. "He didn't say what, and I didn't try to find out what he knew because I didn't want to confirm anything."

"Is there something particularly damaging you're hiding?" Mallory asked.

Amy smirked. "Does any smart person ever answer that with a yes?"

Mallory shrugged. "Worth a try. So tell me how you've been. You guys went to the same college?" She glanced over at Parker to include him.

"No, we went to different schools, but both ended up working at UNC and doing some fieldwork at UNC-Asheville," Parker said.

"Both of you?" Mallory asked. "When was this?"

"A few years ago," Amy said.

"Twenty forty-three," Parker supplied.

Mallory thought she caught a muscle twitch in Amy's jaw. "Where did you do undergrad and grad school?" she asked Amy.

"I started at Elon and then transferred to University of Maryland," Amy said. "Got a second doctorate at Georgetown."

"When did you get married? Draughn said he met you at a deceased spouse support group."

"I met and married Cal when I was at Georgetown," Amy said, sorrow clouding her face. She looked down at the blanket on the bed, a green synthetic creation by Eternity. "He was killed when Hurricane Finnigan hit. We were only married a few months."

"I'm so sorry," Mallory said. "So now you're teaching at UNC and you're here with Parker and Reggie and Max to learn more about the aliens. The Sundry in particular."

"Well, they're fascinating," Parker said. "So like the wasps on Earth, but so much more advanced at the same time."

"So Oscar really had nothing on you, either of you?" Mallory asked.

"He never said specifically what he knew about us," Amy said. "And I've had a pretty boring life, widowed at twenty-nine, academia, still hang out mostly with my stupid brother."

"You're on a space station," Mallory said in a deadpan voice. "You're one of fewer than a hundred humans who can say that."

"Yeah, but I haven't had an interesting life like you! Solving murders! Linking with alien life-forms! And a successful writer!"

"I fell into most of that," Mallory said. "You built your career brick by brick." She pivoted and looked at Parker. "Do you remember anything else from last night that could help me out?"

He lifted his hands, palms up, in surrender. "Nothing, sorry. I'm exhausted from very little sleep in the medbay. My memory is Swiss cheese right now."

"All right," Mallory said. "We can talk about the murder after you get some rest. But I need to know more about these other Sundry Cuckoos. How could one get aboard and just take over a hive? A queen needs eggs to raise an army, which means she's got to mate, right? Did she mate with a blue?"

Parker settled back into his chair and spread his hands, lecture-style. "Cuckoos can't mate with other species. Either a worker smuggles an egg aboard for the other wasps to raise, or a queen herself gets into the hive. They won't attack her because her pheromones tell everyone that she is one of them.

"If she has to, a queen can asexually lay male eggs who will grow up in a few weeks and mate with her, and that's when the egg laying for workers, scouts, soldiers, et cetera gets going. When the Cuckoo larvae hatch, they eat the existing wasp larvae, and when they mature, the adults start killing."

"How long would it take a Cuckoo to take out a Sundry hive? Ballpark," Mallory asked.

"We don't know because they're an alien species," he began, but Mallory raised a skeptical eyebrow. ". . . but if they continue to be like Earth wasps, I'd estimate two to three months."

"Jesus. What if they want multiple hives?"

"The queen lays a queen egg and the process starts again, only this time it's easier since she'll have workers and drones to accompany the new queen into the hive. They exude the one-of-us pheromones and it starts again."

"This is a lot," Mallory said. She got to her feet. "If either of you remembers something about the murder, let me know." She left cards with instructions on how to contact her via station comms on the bedside table.

Parker caught up with her in the hallway.

"Hang on," he said. "I'm sorry."

Mallory crossed her arms. "For what?"

"I— For whatever I did to make you not trust me," he said, looking momentarily confused. "Whatever made you not want to walk with me last night."

"Parker, there's a murderer around—"

"You can't think it's me! You know me! I'm not a threat!" He reached out a hand and she didn't flinch away. "Can't we talk?" His hand touched her cheek.

Images and emotions overwhelmed her, his touch burning her. The fear, the longing, the years apart—

She staggered back just as he yanked his hand away. The naked confusion and fear on his face weren't manufactured. He held his right wrist with his left hand like he had been shocked. "What the hell was that?" he whispered.

One word drifted into Mallory's confused mind and something clicked. "Holy shit." She reached out and, careful not to connect with his skin, grabbed his shirt at the shoulder. "Entomologist. Here to meet with the Sundry. Pheromones. Goddammit, I'm such a moron. Take me to your room, Parker. Now."

. . .

PARKER STOOD INSIDE his door while she went through his luggage. She riffled through his clothes and toiletries quickly, pausing briefly to sniff at some aftershave, then toss it aside.

"Where is it, Parker?" she demanded.

"I don't know what you're looking for!" he said. When her hands fell on his backpack, he stepped forward and tried to pull it away from her, but she yanked it free. She unzipped it and turned it upside down while he stared at her in stunned confusion.

He winced as the contents spilled out. A tablet, a notebook, several pens, and a wooden case about the size of a cigar box hit the carpet. She dropped to her knees and grabbed the box.

The box had a simple clasp, but Mallory still fumbled it, her fingers shaking. Her face burned with the lingering feel of his touch. She didn't know what exactly he knew, or how much he knew. But she had a hunch about one small thing.

The lid fell open, and inside were seven vials about as long as her middle finger, nestled in a thick bed of foam.

"How the hell did you get this?" she demanded, holding the first one up.

The vial had a piece of white tape on it with SLF 00106 written on the outside. Parker reached out gently and took it from her hand. She didn't resist; she didn't want what was inside, she just needed confirmation.

"So you know what this is," he said, his voice low. It wasn't a question.

"Christ, it took me long enough!" Mallory said, running her hands through her bangs to get them out of her eyes. "I wondered why I had such unfounded fear when I saw you the first time. You're on the station to test these, aren't you?"

"We have been working to synthesize wasp pheromones for years," he said, his voice dropping into a matter-of-fact academic tone. The kind of tone Mallory imagined physicists used to describe the atom bomb. "Since First Contact, we have been wondering if we could take the synthetic hormones and have them work on the Sundry. This trip was a test."

"What about me, Parker? Did you know it was working on me? Did you plan on it?"

He looked away from her. "I found out about your involvement with the Sundry only when we got here. Amy told me—"

"Amy?" Mallory asked. "What does she have to do with this?"

He winced as if he shouldn't have said his twin's name. "I doubted it would work on you. You're the only human who's connected with a hivemind. I didn't think your physiology would respond to the pheromones."

"So what's that one?" Mallory asked, nodding to the vial. "Fear?"

"Not exactly. This one is more like 'be intimidated and treat me like a queen.' It's what Cuckoo queens exude to take over a hive." He pointed to the vial marked SLF 00120. "That one is a more visceral fear, designed to create a get-away-from-me response."

"So you were wearing this the night of the party? Like cologne?"

"We had to test it," he said. "The swarm that happened after Oscar's death was proof that it worked. Amy and I were protected—"

"—but Draughn wasn't wearing it, so he got stung," Mallory said, nodding. "Everyone else ran. But what caused the swarm? What about Oscar's death made the Cuckoos care?"

"I don't know," he said, shaking his head.

"What are you wearing now? What did I just react to?" She touched her face and winced. It felt like she had a sunburn, the sting of his touch remaining.

"Nothing," he said, looking at his own fingers. "I don't know what just happened."

"I'm having some problems believing you," she snapped. She pointed to the five vials left in the case. "What about the other pheromones?"

"Rank pheromones, nothing-to-see-here pheromones, then the basic sex, alarm, and death pheromones," he said, pointing to each one.

"Death pheromones? What good are those?" Mallory asked.

"They will ignore you as if you're dead," Parker said. "Another good way for Cuckoos to infiltrate a hive."

"And you were going to test all of these?" Mallory asked. "You didn't think that could backfire? You're in an alien environment, with no ready way home, and you didn't think this could go very, very wrong?"

She held up the sex-pheromone vial. "I don't know whether to be angry with you for coming here under false pretenses, worried that you would take such a goddamn risk, or hurt that you used it on me." She paused. "Or relieved that my reaction to you at the party was fabricated. I thought I was losing my grip on reality."

Parker looked at the vial he still held, as if he didn't hear her.

She stood up. "You know I really can't trust you now, right? How will I know that whatever you're doing, you're not doing with these pheromones behind you? God, I hate how I've given you the marionette strings to mess with me!"

He reached for her again but she stepped back. "Mallory! I would never consciously wear these to manipulate you. I didn't know it would do that!"

"But you're doing it to manipulate the hivemind, and I'm part of that. And you did know that part." She crossed her arms. "Parker. Did you know about the existence of alien Cuckoos when you came here?"

He twisted his mouth like he tasted something sour, then slumped, defeated. "Sit down. I'll tell you."

"SUNDRY CUCKOOS WERE theoretical. When we met with visiting hive diplomats, we asked about their similarity with the wasps on Earth, but that offended them." He winced. "Like really offended them. They ended the meetings and we had to work hard to get them to talk to us again. But we were still making hypotheses based on our knowledge of wasps on Earth. We thought that, except for their intelligence, and size, obviously, the Sundry are very similar to the wasps at home. The Sundry were no help, but, surprisingly, it was during a discussion with a visiting Gneiss diplomat where we learned who would know all about it."

The twelve-foot-tall pink rocket-loaded mech appeared in Mallory's memory, and she groaned. "Tina."

"The very paragon of discretion, we learned," Parker said.

"Go on," Mallory said; an aside on Tina was the last thing she needed right now.

He placed the vial he held very carefully back into the box. "I have to ask, though. Can I trust you?"

Mallory sputtered. "You have a lot of damn nerve asking me that. And what kind of question is that? If you can trust me, I'm going to say yes. If you can't trust me, I'm going to say yes because I want your secrets. Who says, 'No, I will totally tell everything,' when asked that question?" She squinted at him. "I should be asking you the same thing. Now, spill. Does this have to do with what Oscar had on you?"

"Very likely," he said. "I was being honest when I said I didn't ask him what specifically he knew. We've been in secret diplomatic talks with the Sundry and have been trying to replicate their pheromones."

"To what end?" Mallory asked.

He shrugged. "I just do the science."

Mallory rolled her eyes. "So a weapon against the Sundry, I'm guessing. Humans won't stop until they get all sentient species hating us."

"Some aliens have taken up residence on Earth, and there's nothing we can do about it," Parker said evenly. "We discovered the Sundry put some hiveminds and nodes on planets, mostly for data storage or large computing projects. These Sundry are bored and seem to be delighted to do any kind of challenging work. There's such a node on Earth."

"There's a hivemind of Sundry on Earth?" Mallory asked stupidly. "When did it get established?"

He paused for such a long time Mallory wondered if he'd heard her. "Parker?" she asked, and started to ask again.

"We don't know when it was established. We discovered it in 2042."

Mallory felt the blood leave her face. She licked her lips. "But that's—"

He nodded. "Fifteen months before First Contact."

"Holy shit," Mallory said.

"Amy was invited to be part of the first group to contact it. My old mentor, Dr. Shirin Sagapedo, had met her through me and asked for her to join up. She and Amy were part of the initial team to investigate them. After a few months, Sagapedo had a suspicion that most, if not all, of the Vespidae family on Earth are descended from Sundry. Meaning they've been on Earth a lot longer than we previously thought. Even before you encountered them when you were eight. When the node was discovered, we monitored it. After First Contact, we discovered we could communicate with it, and we approached it for data."

"A quantum physicist and an entomologist that wasn't you?" Mallory asked, frowning. "Why weren't you on this mission?"

He smiled bitterly. "I would have been redundant. Dr. Sagapedo was already three times the entomologist I was. Besides,

I was deemed a security risk. Accident-prone and all that. I got to join the team in September of '43. But Amy told me a little of what happened before then.

"Even with the translator, communication started out harder than we expected. They don't seem to want to answer questions without giving them something to compute. But once you give them a job to do, they love that stuff."

"Yeah, I've learned that. Asking 'Will it rain today?' is not as good as 'What are the percentage chances it will rain today, and how much is forecasted?'"

"Right," Parker said. "We started getting some data from the hivemind. It hadn't connected to other nodes in some time, so much of its data was Earth focused, but still, it was more than we'd had."

Mallory whistled. "So why did they keep it secret those fifteen months?"

"Typical government secrecy," Parker said. "Amy would joke they wanted to move the node to Area 51. But 'First Contact' means just with the general population. A small group of people knew that the Sundry were aliens. The scientists studied them for a while, then let some world leaders know. They were a small group, and they kept the secret well. Until Oscar."

"Amy's participation in this secret group that studied Sundry was her big secret," Mallory said, not bothering to ask. "Hang on. All that time in Washington, DC, especially around 2042. She's CIA, isn't she?"

"Of course she isn't," Parker said, not looking at her. "We had some government agencies we were working with, but we're just academics."

"What I can't get is why Amy made up a dead husband," Mallory mused.

Parker went pale. "What? How— Why would you think that? Cal wasn't made up! I was Amy's man of honor at their wedding!

That's a shitty thing to say, and do not say it to Amy. That scar is still fresh."

"You mean to tell me that my best friend from high school, who went through years and years of schooling and has never to my knowledge made an impulsive decision in her life, met and married a man within a year? Hard to believe she lost him in that year, too, but that's actually possible."

"People change," Parker said, his voice tight. "Is this how you solve mysteries?"

"I used to, before parasites killed my mojo," she muttered. Something about all this poked at her brain, asking her to connect two dots, but she couldn't see them yet. She bit her lip and focused on him again. "But back to you, historical and political ramifications of this aside, why are you here, now?"

"To learn more about the Sundry, like I said."

She raised an eyebrow and looked at the box he still held.

"And test pheromones," he allowed. "Meet with Queen Tina to find out what she knows about the Cuckoos."

"Why the interest in Cuckoos?" Mallory asked.

"Dr. Sagapedo believed that if the wasps on Earth shared a distant, non-sentient relative with the Sundry, then the Cuckoos could as well. Through more discreet questioning, we discovered that the Cuckoo wasps had been exiled for their crimes against higher beings, and they were exiled on Bezoar."

"How did your mentor know we'd be hijacked by Cuckoos after you got on board Eternity?" Mallory narrowed her eyes.

"That was pure coincidence. We didn't know they were going to take over Station Eternity. I wouldn't have come if so." He frowned and thought. "No, I probably would have. Never mind."

"You were supposed to be on the first shuttle here, weren't you?" Mallory asked. "The one last November?"

"How did you know that?" Parker demanded.

"Seems like they wouldn't wait to send someone. The government sent an assassin after Xan, after all. But you got lucky again and didn't end up in the shuttle accident that killed a bunch of people."

"I caught the flu, and got it bad," Parker allowed. "Amy still could have come, but I asked her not to. I know better than to ignore signs to avoid major travel. Ask me about Iceland someday."

"If we get out of all of this okay, I will," Mallory said. "But that's a big if. Do you think we're in danger from the Cuckoos?"

"I don't think so," he said. "But I've only studied this in theory."

"Why aren't you more worried about this?" Mallory asked.

"I can't control any of it. Why waste the effort worrying?"

"When did you become a nihilist?"

"I vacillate between optimism and nihilism. Sometimes Buddhism, when I'm feeling more at peace with the fact that I can't do anything," Parker said. "I've been that way since I was eighteen and lost the person I was in love with because of reasons I still don't understand."

Mallory felt her face flush, even as her anger still made her feel prickly. "Back to the murder—"

"Are we not going to talk about this at all? You and me?" Parker interrupted.

"Not now," Mallory said, gritting her teeth. "I have to figure this out. Then we can hash out anything you want. As I see it, Oscar had dirt on all of you, and that's a big reason to kill him, especially if he was going to blow your cover here."

Parker's shoulders sagged. "There are motives, yeah."

"I need you to remember what happened last night," Mallory said.

"I've told you all I remember," he said. "I will tell you if I think of anything else."

"Fine. Have you met with any aliens yet?"

"I went looking for the blue Sundry yesterday, and Amy went looking for the silver. We both failed. We were supposed to meet with the Gneiss today, but that got canceled. So it's not going great. The plan was to search for more Sundry, but then everything went to hell."

"There might still be some silver in the shuttle bay, but they're not talking to me," Mallory said. "Maybe you can make them listen. From what I know now, either the Cuckoos have taken them over, or they know what's going on and they've locked up their hive to prevent anyone getting in. I do not recommend using any of that shit when you go," she added, pointing to the box.

He closed it pointedly and put it on the desk beside him. "No pheromones."

The connection poked at her brain again, and the fog started to clear. Realization dawned on her. She covered her mouth in shock, then dropped her hand. "Parker. You moved when your mom got sick and went into a coma, right? Moved to live with your grandmother?"

He blinked, taking a moment to process the topic shift. "Yeah, what does that have to do with anything?"

"You got sick at the same time as she did, right? Only you got over it fast?" she asked, remembering what Amy had told her.

"Yeah," he said, guarded.

"And after that, you started being 'lucky.' Getting injured or sick and avoiding worse injuries or death. Picking lottery numbers. Helping people meet their life partners."

"What is your point?"

"What were you and your mom sick with? What happened to you?"

"We were in the backyard and disturbed a hornet's nest. We both got stung and went into anaphylactic shock. I came out of it in a few days, but it took her years."

Mallory touched her face where his touch still lingered. "Parker, we haven't touched each other much. You held my hand that one time at graduation, and I nearly fainted. I thought that was just teen hormones in overdrive. When you touched me in the hall, it felt like a burn. But we never touched beyond those times."

"You never touched me," he retorted. "We were both afraid that Amy would freak—"

Mallory shook her head, feeling sick to her stomach. "I don't think it was Amy. Not entirely. You know I was stung by the blue Sundry when I was a kid, which connected me to them. They are all about data and probability. I'm drawn to areas of high probability of murder. I kind of wish it were a high probability of anything else, but that's the hand I was dealt. You had a bad reaction to insect venom when you were a kid. Since then, you've lived a life of a lot of chaos and a little bit of luck. The Cuckoos are a species of chaos. They don't appear to do much themselves, but weird shit happens when they're around."

"What are you saying?" he asked, his face going pale.

"I'm saying that I'm not the only one with a Sundry connection. My personal Sundry theory is that children who are stung get a symbiotic connection. Adults just get sick." She winced and flexed her hand, remembering the sting from the silver Sundry that had put her into anaphylactic shock but hadn't done more than give her a brief connection with the hivemind. "Sick like your mom. You were stung by a Cuckoo as a kid."

He stepped back, his face slack with shock. "That's impossible."

She shook her head, then thought better, and nodded, the whiplash movement making her feel giddy. "It all makes sense. You said the Cuckoos send pheromone messages to the other Sundry, either saying they are something they're not, or they should just be ignored. Ignoring leads to forgetting. And I forgot you entirely."

"But what does it mean that I—" he started, but she waved him silent.

"It's the Cuckoo pheromones! It's possible that when you moved away, whatever was Sundry inside me decided to just ignore the fact that you existed. Maybe it was easier that way. Like the Sundry want to deny the Cuckoos exist, and their inaction is what got us so deep in this shit."

Another piece fell into place. "Last night, you weren't protected from the swarm because of the pheromones—the Cuckoos weren't afraid of you. They were *protecting* you. You saw a murder and panicked, and they came to defend you. Because you're part of their hive." She rubbed her forehead. "Jesus, it all makes sense. We were kept apart like freaking Romeo and Juliet, our Sundry connections pushing against each other like identical magnetic fields."

"But why didn't we just not see each other in high school? It was the opposite for me. Sometimes you're all I saw. Explain that," he said, bright red spots appearing on his cheeks. She couldn't tell if he was angry or shocked. Probably both.

"I can't explain it all—I barely understand it. But from what you said about pheromones, this makes more sense than any other explanation. Parker, I didn't forget you because of a broken heart. I flat out forgot you existed. And considering the crush I had on you in high school, it had to take interference on an alien level to make me just forget about you.

"But dammit, I can't tell if anything we felt was real or if we were driven by the Sundry connections!" she concluded, massaging her temples. "Find one answer and get about six more questions."

Parker stayed silent. He sat heavily on the bed. "I don't know what to do with this information."

"Yeah, it's a lot," she said. Her eyes fell on the box. "I've got a damn murder to solve, and I can't even be sure that what I'm feeling or seeing with you is real." On a whim, she opened the box and took a vial, slipping it into her jacket pocket. She stumbled toward the door, slapping her hand on it before she opened it.

"Goddammit, Parker," she muttered. "What do I do now?"

"Mallory—" he said, but the door slid closed behind her, separating them.

18

THE HOT CHOCOLATE MASCOT

MALLORY DIDN'T GO far. After leaving Parker's room, she stopped outside Amy's door, across the hall, and knocked.

Amy answered it, a curious look on her face. Mallory pushed past her, saying, "Close the door."

"What's wrong?" Amy asked, closing it and facing her. She looked immediately concerned.

"It's Parker," Mallory said. "It's weirder than I could have imagined. He told you about what happened to the Sundry, right?"

Amy nodded.

Mallory told her about her conversation with Parker and his Cuckoo connection. She left out the part about the secret scientific work for the government. Best not to bring that up right away.

Amy, to her credit, didn't look surprised about the Cuckoos and Parker. "Max has been fascinated with him for years but couldn't come up with much explaining his weird luck. But when the news broke about what had happened to you with the Sundry, and I applied it to his situation, I wondered about the similarities. Insect sting, extreme reaction, and then a life of not impossible, but definitely weird, circumstances. It checks out. He would have figured it out, but I think he's been in denial. We don't talk about our mom much, or what happened back then. I think he blamed himself since he had found the nest and Mom ran out to help him."

Mallory took a deep breath and leveled her gaze at Amy. "I need your help, Amy. With Parker. I don't think he's the killer, but with his connection to chaos and the Cuckoos, I need to look at the party through a new lens. Think back if you can. Can you tell me anything about Parker at the party? Or about anyone, with the slightest connection?"

Amy sighed. "Well, there's Max, like I said. He's been watching Parker for years and asked for my help. I told him that observing my own brother wasn't scientific because of conflict of interest, but Max wanted my take on what made him tick, especially in this new environment. Hanging out with Parker is something I do anyway, but I made a point to do it last night, if only so Max could see me watch him. He doesn't understand that you can't just watch someone and identify what's going on at a quantum level. Things happen on the micro level that ripple out and may or may not affect the macro level. Often, they don't. But Max didn't want to hear that, so I was just watching him because he told me to."

"All right," Mallory said. "Go on."

"There's not much more to say. Nothing weird happened."

"Oscar died," Mallory pointed out.

"Well, that goes without saying," Amy said impatiently. "Nothing weird that you don't already know."

"But what did you see regarding Parker?"

"He was with me most of the night. He was concerned about you. He didn't realize the pheromones were affecting you. Then we had Max and Reggie fighting again"—Amy paused to roll her eyes—"or they were apart and Max was drinking. Poor Max just looked miserable. Reggie and Oscar talked at the bar, and Max didn't look very happy about it. Then Parker and I went to listen to the ambassador's speech. It was pretty boring, about being proud and excited"—here, Amy's voice took on a high, British accent—"that humans can join other sentient races in harmony on Station Eternity, and that she is so excited to be at the forefront of this exciting chapter in human history."

"She's not British," Mallory pointed out.

"I know, but she's very self-important," Amy explained. "It was a lot of self-congratulatory blah blah stuff. Most people checked out halfway through. When she was done, people started milling about, heading back to their rooms, but most of our group was still around. Your friend and the ambassador left together. Someone asked where Oscar was—"

"Hang on, who was in the dining room at this point?" Mallory asked. "Had it cleared out yet?"

"Max was all but passed out on the table," Amy said. "Don was looking at me, well, he just looked really tired, you know? I think that travel took it out of him."

"He's not that much older than we are," Mallory said, feeling strange defending him, but it was true.

"Where was Reggie?" she asked.

"Not sure. Bathroom, maybe?" Amy frowned.

"So if everyone hated him, who cared enough about Oscar to ask about him?" Mallory said.

"I don't know," Amy said, eyes widening in alarm. "I know it was a masculine voice."

Mallory laughed. "Easy to say since you're the only woman in that group."

She shrugged. "Anyway, the more sober of us started looking around for him. Reggie said he wasn't in the bathroom. The bartender said he hadn't seen Oscar leave. Then Don opened a closet door and Oscar fell out onto him. I screamed, Don fell down, then pushed the body off him and got back to his feet. He was white as a sheet. Then we heard the buzzing, then that's when Don tackled me." She rubbed her head. "And that's really it. I promise."

"And during all of this, Parker was what?" Mallory asked, thinking about Max mentioning Parker transfixed by the Cuckoos.

"He was quiet. Kind of melancholy. I think he was bummed about you." She gave Mallory a meaningful look. "I wish you guys had gotten it out of your system when we were kids."

Mallory felt a sharp retort struggling to get out of her throat, but she swallowed it back like sour bile. If weird Sundry effects had driven her teenage experiences with Parker, it was possible she couldn't trust her memory on how much Amy had kept them apart. Maybe they just thought she had done so. She smiled bitterly. "If we'd dated, we would be awkward adults for another reason."

"Would it be weirder to suspect your ex-boyfriend to be a murderer, or your unrequited love?" Amy asked.

Mallory stood up and stretched, frustrated and wanting to move. "I have to suspect everyone is a murderer until I clear them," she said. "I can't leave anyone out. Every time someone complains that they, or a loved one, is above suspicion, things get worse."

"But you said you didn't think Parker did it," Amy said.

"I know I said that," Mallory said, troubled. She looked at Amy's open suitcase for a moment, trying to find the right words. Beside her discarded blue dress from the night before sat a brown ball cap with a mug of hot chocolate embroidered on the front. "I can't really articulate why. I'm still watching him, but—" She frowned, then picked up the ball cap. "What the hell is this? Are you on a team with a mascot of hot chocolate?"

Amy looked startled, then laughed. "Something like that. A couple of us joined a winter indoor softball league. That's our mascot. It's a weird, cute thing, I guess. But you still suspect everyone? Even sweet little Max?"

"He has a strong motive, and medical knowledge means he

knows better how to kill someone than the average person," Mallory replied.

"The ambassador?" Amy suggested.

"I haven't talked to her much, but I know she was talking to a number of you last night," Mallory said. "I don't know if she has motive, but she has connections, and that's good enough for me. It's possible Oscar had dirt on her that would hurt her job here."

"What about me? You suspect me?" Amy said.

Considering you're probably with the CIA, hell yes. Mallory sat down again and took her friend's hand, remembering the times in their youth when they had confided in each other, or cried on each other. "You have motive. I have to suspect you until I am convinced, through evidence, that you're not the killer. I don't think you could kill someone, but I haven't known you for a long time. So yeah, I suspect you."

"But you're here alone in a room with me," Amy said.

"I don't think you have motive to kill me," Mallory said. "Although sometimes people kill when someone gets too close to the truth." She stood up and dropped Amy's hand. "Dammit, I had to talk to someone. And you're the only one who gets the Parker thing."

"I still can't believe you could think that one of your oldest friends could do that. I can't believe that you'd drop that bomb on Parker and then leave him alone."

Mallory stood up, feeling a thousand years old. "These are reasons why I don't have many friends anymore. If you're worried about Parker, go talk to him yourself. I can't right now." She straightened her jacket, wishing for a full-body reboot. "Thanks for your time. I have to go find a murderer."

"What if I'm right here, though?" Amy said, looking up at her with wide, innocent blue eyes.

"Then stay here so I'll know where to find you after I get the evidence I need."

19

. . .

MALLORY RETURNS, AS DO OTHERS

Xan woke up sore and stiff but feeling much less lonely than previous days. He had slept on something less than a cushion and more than a flat rock. More like a sculptor's idea of a cushion. Stephanie had given him a warm place to sleep that reminded him more of *Infinity* than Eternity's sterile room had.

"Thanks for letting me aboard," Xan said, yawning and stretching as best he could on the human-size bench that stuck out from the adobe-colored wall.

"Of course," Stephanie said. "Although I still don't understand it, I don't mind it."

"Yeah, well, I needed company," he said. When he'd come aboard last night, he'd filled her in on the bits of the night she had missed and explained he was too used to sleeping aboard a shuttle and his temporary room aboard the station had felt wrong.

"Did you know we're going to Bezoar?" he asked her, trying to get the kinks out of his neck.

"I found out when Ferdinand did, so shortly before you did," Stephanie said.

"And there's nothing you can do?"

"What would you suggest? The station is exponentially bigger than I am."

"Tina might listen to you. She did before, right?"

"Tina is queen of Bezoar now," Stephanie said. "She has chosen to continue to listen to my and Ferdinand's advice, but that doesn't mean that she will take it."

"It's just all chaos now," Xan said. "The Cuckoos took over the station, probably killed all existing Sundry by now, stung at least one person who was involved with a murder, and they only communicate with the least stable person we know."

"The station is taking her where she wants to go, so she sees nothing wrong with any of the current events," Stephanie said. "And Eternity—"

Xan laughed in disbelief, interrupting her. "She thinks there's nothing wrong with thousands of Sundry dying?"

"They live on a different scale than we do," Stephanie said. "For all their processing power, they are still primitive with the way they view their role in the world. The strong survive, even if the strong are the ignorant sneaky ones. Besides, Tina doesn't really understand regret. There's no going back to change decisions, so all you can do is look to the now."

"How very Zen of her," Xan muttered. "Anyway. You were saying something about Eternity?"

"Eternity is not listening to anyone right now except for the Cuckoos. What we need is the station's host, or at least *Infinity*. But I can't contact either of them."

Xan lay back on the bench and stared at Stephanie's ceiling. "I wish she'd come home. Tina said she should still be able to find us even if we're moving. Is that true?"

"Tina was right about something?" Stephanie said dryly. "Yes, the bond between mother and child is hard to sever. *Infinity* will find us."

"I guess it's good that Mrs. Brown took *Infinity* rather than another shuttle," Xan said grudgingly. "Although I can't even imagine what she's going to do when she gets back on board." He shuddered, thinking of the wrath of the formidable old lady.

"Who could have guessed Eternity would go walkabout?" he wondered.

"No one," Stephanie said. Gneiss didn't really do rhetorical questions. "Tina is coming aboard." Stephanie added the last part right before a pounding on the hatch made Xan jump.

Shortly, Tina was filling out the cockpit, head nearly brushing the ceiling. She carried a mug in her huge hand, something Xan knew that Ferdinand had created especially for her, since she was larger than any other Gneiss.

"It's early for day drinking, Tina," he said, nodding at the bucket-size mug.

"We don't have proper times to ingest fluids, that's just weird," she said. She took a slug of whatever she was carrying. "It's Ferdinand's best cauterize. Want some?"

Xan recognized the liquor that Ferdinand usually served in cups a quarter the size of that mug, the equivalent of a shot. "I don't think I can, but thanks. Uh, you doing okay?"

"'Tina, you're so smart, you know all about the Cuckoos, thank you for your illuminating information!'" Tina said, gesturing in a very human-like way. "'Tina, you've never been considered a valuable part of this team until now, thank you for contributing!'"

"Tina, you encouraged a rogue insect element to kill the hive-mind of the station and hijack it to a shithole planet," Xan said mildly.

"No!" she said, pointing a finger at him. "They had already taken control by the time I got aboard. And I didn't tell them to go there, I suggested that it would do us both a favor to go there. I can't tell them what to do. What I did do was tell everyone— including you!—what was going on, every time they asked. You just didn't listen."

"How did you get the apartment doors open?" he asked. "If you're not telling them what to do?"

"I asked them! Sometimes you have to just ask for what you want, Xan. And go away," she added, sounding petulant as she spoke into her mug, "if you don't really like me. I'm apparently unhelpful and next to useless."

Xan sighed. He knew Stephanie was listening, but she was staying quiet for now. "Whether the Cuckoos obey you or not, you're the only one who can speak their language," he said. "Right now you're one of the most powerful people on the station. We need you."

"And you're a queen," Stephanie reminded her.

Tina made a low rumbling sound but didn't say anything.

"Have you considered asking them to take us back home?"

"Where the home planet sent those goons to arrest us?" she asked. "I did ask them to take you back to Ariadne when they're done dropping me off. I wouldn't leave you abandoned. You're my friend!"

"Really? What did they say?" he asked in surprise.

"Nothing!" she shouted.

"Tina, we don't understand you when you talk to them. When you have had conversations, we only know what you've told us." He waited a second for that to sink in. "What I'm saying is, will you please tell us what you have talked about, even the stuff that didn't work out? Like, what else did you ask about? Do you know their plans? Do you know if Mrs. Brown and *Infinity* are nearby?"

"Oh. Um." She slung back another drink, and Xan winced at the heat coming off her. "I asked them to take us back to Ariadne to let you off, they said no. I asked them to help out the human they stung, they said yes. I asked them to stop killing Sundry and they said too late. I asked about Mrs. Brown and they said, 'Ha ha, if she can catch us.'"

"They've never met Mrs. Brown," Xan said grimly. "What's

going to happen after they drop you off at Bezoar? I can't believe they're just going to go into peaceful orbit."

"No, they're going to get all the other Cuckoos off the planet," she said. "It's time for them to take on the Sundry. Godspeed, little bugs!" She held the mug up in a toast and downed the rest of her drink.

The universe slowed down around Xan as he took in Tina's plan. "You're going to facilitate galactic war?"

"Oh, don't be so serious! They're just bugs!" Tina said.

Xan stared at her. "This just gets worse and worse. Does Ferdinand know?"

"No," Tina said sharply. "And I don't want him to. He's mad at me. He doesn't need to know this."

"But Stephanie knows," Xan pointed out, and the floor rumbled under his feet. She'd probably already told Ferdinand about this new disaster.

"Balls," Tina said. Which was another weird human statement since Gneiss didn't have balls, as far as Xan could tell.

"Tina, aren't the Cuckoos on Bezoar for a reason?" he asked. "Like they were killing too many hives? Hives of Sundry that other folks, even whole planets, depend on?"

"Sure, but most rules of war let the victor be the winner. But when the Cuckoos dominated everyone, everyone else got mad. Other conquering groups get to keep their spoils of war. War spoils. Stuff. But Cuckoos kicked ass and got nothing but trouble for it. Tell me how that's fair!"

"I can't," Xan said. He knew too much about the mind-set of countries at war, and the more he learned, the more he realized that he didn't want to have to handle that kind of ethical debate.

"And maybe the Cuckoos aren't so bad after all. You know that the Sundry lie. They didn't tell anyone about the Cuckoos. Who knows what else they're holding back."

"Mallory said they can't lie because they're a hivemind," Xan said. "They're basically flying computers, right?"

"Oh, Mallory," Stephanie said over the speaker. "I forgot sometimes she's as dumb as Tina. She has access to the hivemind and never uses it."

Tina ignored her. "Of course Sundry can lie. They're the best liars because they know so much, they know what little fact pebble can be changed to make the lie sound like a truth. My mother talked about hiring blue Sundry for public relations, you know, to make Bezoar a more attractive place for tourism. She even took a queen and some of her scouts on a tour of the planet, but they didn't take the job. They said they didn't do PR."

"Did they see any Cuckoos on the tour?" Xan asked.

"What? I don't know. Why?"

"They've destroyed themselves, haven't they? The Sundry would rather remain vulnerable to the Cuckoos than let the rest of the galaxy know they have this massive weakness. If they were honest with the rest of us, we could have helped."

"Sundry can make mistakes, just like anyone. Oh, and lie. Which is one of the reasons everyone is so nervous around them. Lies and mistakes and power." Tina's voice had a singsong quality at this last bit. How drunk was she?

"Mallory would have said if she thought she was sensing lying when she connected to the main hivemind last year," Xan said.

"No no no, she didn't connect with the main hivemind," Tina said impatiently.

"Okay, now I know you're wrong," Xan said. "What did she connect with if not the hivemind?"

Tina sat down in the captain's chair with a mighty thud. "This is great! I've never been the smartest person in the room before."

"Except for the room herself," Xan said. "But go on."

"There is not just one blue hivemind or one silver hivemind. They're not just one huge entity. There are hiveminds everywhere, and they send nodes to other hives to share information. This way if something goes wrong with one node, the whole hivemind won't be damaged."

"Which is why the Cuckoos couldn't wipe them out completely," Xan said. "It's like a branch circuit. If one is attacked, the branch gets hurt, but it severs the connection with the hive so there's no more damage done. Smart."

"I think that's right?" Tina said. "I'm not fully understanding what you just said. But anyway. What were we talking about?"

"Jesus," Xan muttered. "Where's Ferdinand? He can usually keep you on topic."

"Him? Oh, he ran away," Tina said. "I don't know where he went. He said he was mad at me, and then he said he was blaming himself for letting me down and bringing the Cuckoo queen here because she stowed away when he visited Bezoar." She slammed her fist onto the chair arm. "Hey, why didn't you notice a queen had gotten on board when you took him there?" She poked the chair with her finger then, as if to wake up Stephanie.

"I didn't take him to Bezoar," Stephanie said. "Remember? You wanted me to stay here and keep you company."

"Oh, right," Tina said. "Hey, thanks for that. We had some fun, didn't we?"

"Wait a second, he's gone? He just, ran off?" Xan asked, trying to picture the stoic, logical member of the trio doing an emotional rage quit. "He can't leave. He's the anchor to this group. But what was he doing on Bezoar, anyway?"

"He's been preparing various Gneiss worlds for Tina's coronation," Stephanie said. "He started a few years ago, ending recently with Bezoar."

"I thought she was only queen of Bezoar?" Xan asked, horrified at the idea that Tina would be in charge of more than one planet.

"She is. But other rulers need to be alerted to the fact that it's

Tina ruling the planet," Stephanie said. "We haven't had a lot of leaders like her."

"I've never heard you sound more diplomatic," Xan said with a grin. "But I've always seen Ferd as Ted Danson on *Cheers*. You know, a pleasant bartender. Why was he doing this diplomatic crown proxy shit?"

"I don't get the reference, but I want to," Tina said.

Stephanie vibrated around them, and Xan realized she was laughing. "Have we never told you? It's his job," she said. "He protects and prepares the world for Tina."

"He's her *herald*? Since when?"

"Since always," Tina said, shaking her mug upside down over her open mouth.

"So the bar on the station, is that there to pass the time?" he asked.

"Sort of. There wasn't a lot to do until Tina became queen," Stephanie said.

"So you're really going to live on a shithole planet?" he asked. "And keep Cuckoos and Gneiss and other prisoners company?"

Tina made an irritated huffing sound. "I have people to do things like that for me. Ignoring the surface details is a perk of the job of queen. I'll be living in Crystal Capital."

"That sounds really pretty for a shithole planet," Xan said.

"Oh, the underground areas of Bezoar are lovely," Tina said. "It's the surface that's terrible. But the surface is where most of the prisoners live. At least, the non-Gneiss ones do."

"But why would Ferd run off? Where did he go?" Xan said. "You said it yourself, Tina. No one told the rest of the Gneiss that the Cuckoos were still active. It wasn't his fault there was a stowaway. Did he even know about the Cuckoos?"

Stephanie was silent, and Tina took a moment, then stared at him as if surprised that he had asked her. "I don't know. Ask him."

Xan rolled his eyes. "My point is, people fuck up all the time. Look at Tina."

"Hey, look at me!" Tina said. "Apparently I've been hiding information from you. Even though I've been opening doors and carrying dying humans and stuff. I'm so tired from all the things I'm doing!"

"Yeah, thanks for that," he said. "But we need to find Ferdinand. Can't you guys just hum to find him?"

"Not if he doesn't want to reply," Stephanie said. "But I'll try."

"I've got to go," he said. "Thanks for the hospitality, Steph. And, Tina, try not to make too many decisions while you're drunk."

"I'm thinking clearer than ever in my life!" she shouted after him.

MALLORY NEARLY PLOWED into Xan in the hallway, her face set and her hair messy.

"Whoa, what happened to you?" he asked.

"Too much," she said. "You got some time? I need someone to talk to."

"I was coming to find you, so lead on," he said amicably.

MALLORY PACED HER room, Xan sitting in her chair and watching her.

"Pheromones. Parker and Amy were coated in fucking *synthetic pheromones*, and they worked on me like they work on the Sundry," she raged. "I don't even know what's real. I know I can't ever trust him again. I crushed on him for so long, but now, how can I tell if he didn't just cover himself in horny-queen juice to turn me on?"

Xan stifled a laugh and looked around her room. It was getting really stuffy in here, something that usually didn't happen aboard Eternity. "Why's it so hot in here?"

"But I know Parker didn't do it, because the Cuckoos were responding to his fear when they swarmed the restaurant. So we've eliminated one suspect. That's a bonus, right?" she said.

Xan grabbed her arm as she walked by his chair, stopping her. "Mallory," he said slowly. "Calm down. Take a breath. You can't make decisions like this."

"I can't make decisions at all! I can't trust any experience with Parker and Amy. I tried to connect with Eternity, but she'd make more sense if she were comatose. I lost the one thing that made me interesting, my connection with the Sundry. Adrian was right, what the hell am I good for now?"

Xan let her rant as he turned a few things over in his mind, mainly thinking of Mallory's first days on the station, renting herself out for medical testing to interested alien doctors and xenobiologists. "If the Sundry had been on Earth for longer than we thought, why did they study you so closely when you got here?"

She sighed. "After I left Parker, I went to confront Amy. I asked her the same thing. She said I was stung by an Earth-dwelling Sundry, a Sundry from a nearby node. Some of them stowed away with me when I left Earth, and then connected with the hivemind. They couldn't carry a lot of data. The blue knew I was one of them, but they still didn't have a lot of information on the humans until they could take a shuttle back to connect with the nodes." She wheeled and started pacing again. "Oh, and she also told me they don't think I'm the first to get stung and then have this weird murder sense. Some English priest in the 1800s got stung as a boy and then solved a bunch of murders as an adult. But his community loved him, while mine hated me."

She balled her fists and groaned in frustration. "I wish I hadn't lost my connection to the Sundry."

"Ironic that you want them now, when you can't have them," Xan pointed out.

She glared at him. "I know, I know, I held myself back by not connecting to the hivemind more. I'm an idiot and I'm completely impotent. I'm a Hemingway hero with one testicle. Are you happy?"

He stared at her, startled by her defensive tone. "Uh, I was just commiserating with you. You lost your connection, so did I. I didn't know how much I missed *Infinity* till I realized she was always, you know, there in my head. Did you ever feel that with the Sundry?"

"No, I avoided them. I was afraid they would try to flood my mind with data."

Xan thought while she paced, raging away. Something had returned to Mallory. He leaned his head back and thought about her figuring out her old friends were with the CIA. That had been some solid deduction.

He raised his head. "Mal," he said.

"And I can't even touch him!" she said, continuing some rant about Parker. "We probably would have electrocuted each other if we'd kissed as teens."

He whistled. "That would be a hell of a kiss, though. Anyway," he continued hastily at the look on her face, "did you realize you're back?"

"What is it?" she asked, looking behind her and batting at her shoulder like she was trying to swat a fly she couldn't see.

"No, Mal," he said patiently, "not your back, but *you* are back. You're sharp again. You're making deductions again. Have some faith in yourself. You've done this for years without knowing you had that connection with the Sundry. You don't know how it works. You could be somewhat connected to all the Sundry in the whole galaxy. You could have wild deductive skills and the Sundry only let you sniff out the murders. Stop worrying about what alien is or isn't affecting you and focus on the murder!"

She stared at him, mouth open. "Holy shit, you're right," she said, a grin slowly spreading across her face. "I have all the pieces, I just need to fit them together." She zeroed in on him, her gaze sharp again. "Tell me about the Gneiss."

"What do they have to do with the murder?" he asked.

"Tina is connected to the Cuckoos, who are connected to Parker, who's connected to the murder," she said. "I need to know what's happening."

"I didn't want to unload more on you, but here's what I found out," he said. Then he told her about the conversation that morning.

"Shit. Ferdinand gone is a real problem," Mallory said. "He's the only logical one left."

"And he's our friend," Xan reminded her.

She made a face at him. "That goes without saying, dude. Of course I'm concerned about him. He takes on too much responsibility. And he's accepted the job of Tina's herald? I knew he was patient, but damn."

"Now we know he probably does that because he protects Tina from the world. Or protects the world from Tina. I'm not really sure."

She paced again, back and forth, head down, thinking. "There's another missing piece. You were talking to the ambassador last night. I'll need to talk to her. Find out what she knows. She talked to Oscar last night, right?"

"Yeah, I saw them talking," Xan said. "She didn't mention him when I walked her home."

"Walked her home?" Mallory asked, startled. "Did this murder night turn into a date?"

"Don't you start," Xan said, his face warm. "She flirted with me, yeah. But it was no date."

"Shame," she said. "Someone should be getting laid around here."

He made a surprised scoff. "That sounds legit till someone you just met, and will probably be working closely with for a while, throws themself at you. Then it's just awkward."

"I can see that," Mallory said. "Anyway, can you contact her for me? I need a shower."

"Yeah, go ahead," he said, and walked to her terminal in the wall by the door.

He heard grunting behind him and saw Mallory wrestling with the bedroom door, which had refused to slide open.

"Problem?" he asked.

"Door's been sticking lately," she said. "And you're right. It's stuffy as hell in here. I need to get a drone to check the vent or something."

"Mal, automatic space station doors don't stick," he said, alarm growing in his chest.

Mallory grabbed the edge of the slightly open door and gave a mighty tug, then fell as it gave way.

She picked herself up off the floor and stared into her bedroom with her jaw unhinged.

Two incomplete paper nests had taken over most of the room. One sat over her bed, two Sundry crawling over the exterior, and the other one was on the floor nearly blocking the way to the bathroom, with three silver Sundry circling the top of the nest. Her books were all over the floor, ripped and ruined, their paper scavenged to make the barrel-size nests that adhered to the walls. Her bed was also in tatters, the linens and mattress repurposed to make the nest. A few Sundry stood atop her dresser, chewing the fabric in her shirts into paste, then flying over to reinforce the paper hive.

"Hello. Greetings. Welcome. We are all home. Together, united, reinforced, we must protect the queens."

Mallory's eyes were wide with fear as she backed up. Xan caught her by the shoulders and steadied her.

She looked up at him, then pointed at the nest near her bed. "Are those Cuckoos? I can't trust what I see anymore. Please tell me they're not Cuckoos."

"No, those are blue, and some silver over there," he said, pointing to each nest. "Some must have survived, and they're hiding out here." His eyes went to the vent in the ceiling, which was also covered in paste. "They blocked the airflow to keep their scent from going through the vents."

"How long was I away from my bed?" she asked in wonder. "And how many Sundry survived?"

"And I think it's official that you've got your mojo back," he pointed out as the Sundry hummed at them.

20

TIME TO INVOLVE THE AMBASSADOR

MALLORY AND XAN had checked the vents for any holes, then left the Sundry to do their work. After their initial freak-Mallory-the-hell-out greeting, they hadn't wanted to talk more than to confirm that each nest had a queen inside who was very busy laying eggs while her few subjects built the nest around her.

"Will they get along?" she wondered. "It's not really in their nature."

"They will as long as they have a larger threat," Xan said. "We should bring them some food, though."

"And more stuff to make into the nest. They got my favorite sweatshirt." She was happy to see them, despite the destruction to her apartment. She wondered if Xan was correct that not all her deductive skills were connected to the Sundry, since he said that before they knew some had survived. But it would take weeks before the hive became a viable force, and she really didn't have time to explore her connection to them. Right now she just had to keep these alive. When Mrs. Brown got back, and when this Cuckoo problem was dealt with, she could worry about her apartment again.

But that sweatshirt. Dammit.

"I feel like we should tell someone," Mallory said as they left her apartment. "Get the station security to protect them or something."

"Yeah, but protecting someone against swarming insects is nearly impossible to do, as every place on Earth has discovered. It's biblical. They're designed to get into places and overwhelm with their numbers. The best thing we can do is keep the doors closed and let them hide out in there and do their thing."

"And now we're both homeless," she said. "I just wanted a nap and a shower."

"You got a lot more than that," he said. "I've been sleeping aboard Stephanie, so you can have my room." He raised an eyebrow. "And hey, I bet Oscar's room is open."

Mallory glared at him. "Too soon, Xan. Although I do need to get in and see if I can find any records of these secrets he claimed to collect. I need to find Parker, too. We didn't leave on good terms, and I need to talk to him about his connection with the Cuckoos."

"You said he didn't know what the connection was," Xan said. "Go easy on him. You didn't take your symbiont news very well when you found out, and you had friends around you. The only person who can understand his situation is you, but his hive killed your hive, and then you walked out on him."

Mallory felt guilt flare, and then annoyance. "Xan, he used pheromones on me. Last night I was basically an animal reacting to instinct. That's humiliating."

"First, I'm not saying there's anything wrong with your reaction. I'd be pissed as hell, too. I'm saying he may not be open to a lot of interviewing right away because of all this. He may not want to see you at all." After a moment, he added, "Hey, at least he didn't use a sex pheromone. And you said he didn't know he would be affecting you. It's not like he targeted you. You know the guy; can you see him using these on purpose to manipulate you?"

"No, but I feel like everything we experienced as kids was colored by the Sundry influence. I can't trust my memories, or any reaction I have around him. I'll worry about his feelings after I solve the murder," Mallory grumbled. "In fact, I'd like to leave everyone's feelings at the door when I see him."

"I hear that," Xan said, thinking about approaching the ambassador again. "Do you want me to talk to the ambassador still?"

"Yeah. She'll need to know about the— what we saw in my room," Mallory said. "Also, we need to see if Devanshi can get into the station security files to find any personal info from the patient manifest."

"I'll get on that," he said.

They split at the next fork in the road and Xan stopped at a wall terminal to contact Devanshi.

"Xan. What is it?" The vidscreen was dark and the audio was very hollow.

"Where the hell are you?" Xan asked.

"We're in the guts of the station, be glad you aren't here," Adrian grumbled close to the microphone.

"We're trying to get a look at the Cuckoo nest," Devanshi said. "See if we can get a sense of the size, how many Cuckoos there are, and so on."

"And then what?" Xan said. "We've already established we can't take them out without a backup hive. We'll be dead in space if we do that."

"Getting information is never bad," Devanshi said. "Nothing bad can happen if we just observe."

"Says you. Your skin is too hard to sting, but they'll fill Adrian full of holes if you piss them off," Xan reminded the Phantasmagore.

There was a pause. "Good point," Devanshi said. "We'll send in the drones."

"That didn't occur to you first?" Xan demanded. He shook his head. "Never mind. If you ever return to the habitable areas of the station, we need some help. Mallory needs all the info on the visiting humans that security has."

"That's child's play," Devanshi said. "I can do that remotely."

"Thanks, just send it to me," Xan said. "And be careful, okay?"

"I didn't know you cared," Adrian sneered, but Devanshi cut the call.

"Jackass," Xan muttered. Adrian getting stung to death would be evolution in action, but it wasn't in Xan's nature just to let a guy wander into a hornet's nest and die.

He took a deep breath and asked Eternity to contact Jessica's suite. There was no answer. He tried to locate her, but Eternity was still in autopilot mode and not able to do anything complex. So he went directly to her suite.

Maybe she's wandering the station and forgot her watch. Or forgot to charge it. Maybe she's asleep. Space lag. Whatever. Maybe she had a bad reaction to the food last night. Maybe I should check the medbay. Maybe—

He couldn't fool himself. A new ambassador should be available at all hours, at least in the first week of her tenure. She very likely wouldn't be incommunicado if nothing was wrong.

At her door, he rang the bell, then knocked, then pounded. He waited about five minutes to see if Jessica was out and would come back to her suite, but the anxiety got to be too much. He contacted Stephanie.

"Hey, sorry to make you the messenger, but I need Tina right now. Can you tell her to come give me a hand?"

"Why?" Stephanie asked.

"I need her to open a door for me," he said. "It's important."

Tina arrived quickly and placed her hand on the door. She looked down at Xan. "Wanna see something cool?" she asked.

He wanted to shout at her to open the goddamn door but remembered he was dealing with essentially a toddler with a lot of power. "Sure," he managed to choke out.

"Abracadabra!" she shouted. The door slid aside.

Tina started telling him something about a word she'd picked out of Calliope's memory and how she'd told the Cuckoos that it would be the thing she said if she wanted to get into any door, but it was all background buzzing to Xan.

Right inside the door was the thing he had feared the most: Jessica's body, wearing yards of billowing silk in a lavender robe and nightgown, lying on her side in a pool of blood.

Tina stopped talking. "Messy," she said with distaste. "It's dead, isn't it?"

"Shit," he said, dropping to his knees. "I think so."

Blood had dried on her forehead to create a gory, tacky sheen on her skin. He touched her neck gently for a pulse. Even though her skin was cool, he felt a flutter like a heart struggling with its last few beats.

"Nope, she's still alive, despite someone's best attempt. Medbay it is," he said. He scooped her up in his arms. She was tall and muscular, but she still felt light. *Thanks, adrenaline*, he thought, and started to jog down the hallway.

"You want me to carry that?" Tina asked, walking behind him. "I'm faster! And I'm less disgusted by your disgusting bodies when they're all wet."

"Still safer for me to carry her," he said. "What you can do is tell Mallory that there's another attack and that I'm with the ambassador in medbay."

"Carrying messages isn't as fun as carrying bodies!" Tina complained.

"But less messy and more important," Xan said, holding tightly to his temper. "Much more important."

Tina brightened and lumbered off to the nearest air lock.

Since her size made travel difficult, she had started traversing the station outside via air lock. Much faster and less cramped than the lifts, she explained. Tina had an answer for everything.

On the elevator, a few aliens looked at him blankly. "Sorry about the mess," he said. "Heading to the medbay."

This seemed to satisfy them, and they even let him off the lift first.

Jessica stirred weakly in his arms, then groaned.

"Hey, calm down, you're going to be okay," he said automatically, holding her tighter in case she panicked. "We're almost to the medbay. Looks like you got into a fight with a Gneiss. Metaphorically, anyway. Who hit you, Jess?"

"Sho—" she muttered.

Whose name starts with "*Sho*"? he wondered.

"Sho—" she groaned.

"Yeah, I know," he said, and picked up his pace.

PART THREE

I've been playing at, I've been playing at
Self-worth again
Ain't it fun to play pretend?
I've been pulling for, I've been pulling for
Something different but the same is all we get

Don't get near me
I'll only sear your skin
In the state I'm in

Don't you free me
I know it'll happen again
My friends . . .

—"Needs of the Many" by the garages,
written by Yana Caoránach

21

. . .

TINA HAS A DRONE

DRAUGHN'S HEAD ACHED. He'd taken some Tylenol when the aliens slapped a bandage on his head and said the patch would heal his brain but not mask the pain from the concussion in the meantime.

He wondered if Amy was in pain.

He had gone to check on her, but she hadn't answered the door. He had done so three times, and then forced himself to stop so he wouldn't look too eager. But he had to know.

So now he sat in the park on a huge bench, his feet dangling like a toddler's, as he watched the faux sunlight creep across the purple grass. It really was lovely here.

The spousal support group had a strict no-dating policy, so when Amy had shown up to the group, he had kept a polite distance, even though he was inexplicably drawn to that blond hair. It shifted in color from almost brown to white-blond, a clear sign it was completely natural and the only color came from the sun and her genes.

He befriended her, awkwardly. They had a lot in common, it seemed. Both of them had crafting spouses; Draughn's wife had been a knitter and Amy's husband had programmed 3D printers to make amazing things. They both had learned to bake after being widowed. And they both loved the band Worm Quartet, only Amy liked the originals and Draughn liked the covers. They'd argued a lot about that.

The age difference in their friendship had never bothered her. She readily sat beside him in group, held his hand when he talked about Helen, and even invited him to dinner parties. Her friends didn't seem to know what to do with him, but they were polite enough. Work was turning out to be stressful, and he was glad for a new social group to spend time with.

"I wonder what she would have said," he said aloud, then jumped when a voice behind him answered.

"Who? What were you going to say?"

He slid off the giant bench and turned around, craning his head to see the largest alien he'd ever seen, the same one who had gotten into the medbay and vomited all the bees. Wasps. Whatever. It looked like a humanoid rock statue, so he knew it was a Gneiss, but it was taller and broader and . . . looked like a mech that Sigourney Weaver would just love to step into to kick some alien ass.

"Are you following me, dammit?" he asked, stumbling backward.

"No, I'm Tina," she said. "I'm here to clean up Sundry bodies." She lifted her left hand, in which she carried a slightly dented robot that looked like a spider. "Well, we're here to clean it up. Together. Dead bodies tend to upset the living, as I understand it."

"Aren't you living?" he asked, not sure what she was.

"That's a good question! But you were supposed to ask why I, Queen Tina, am picking up dead bodies."

He paused, expecting her to finish, but she stood there. "Okay, why—"

"Because I want my friends to like me again, and they like it when I'm helpful. They once told me I should do menial labor to humble me a little bit! Humble me! Like I need humbling. I'm a fucking metal queen and I don't need anything!"

She reminded him of a toddler who needed a nap.

"It's possible my friends just wanted to get rid of me so the smart people could talk. I'm smarter than they think because I figured that out."

She stepped closer, the thuds from her feet muffled by the grass, but still shaking the ground slightly. "Who were you talking about?"

"Uh, Amy, my friend. We both got concussions last night in all the chaos. I'm just concerned about her."

"Why don't you ask her what she would say? Then you would know before you asked the question," Tina suggested.

"That doesn't make any sense," he said.

"Did they fix your hand? I know they were going to cut it off, and that was apparently scarier for you because you won't grow back. Your system is so simple, you know, even if really wet and gushy. You didn't tell me your name yet."

"Oh," he said blankly. "I'm Don."

"Hi, Don!" she said brightly. "Are you a friend of Mallory's?"

"You know Mallory?" he asked.

"Sure! She's a good friend. She said she knew some of the people here from Earth."

"Yeah, I knew her back home," he said, then climbed back on the bench, hoping she'd get the hint.

"So what was the question you wanted to ask the other human?" Tina asked.

"Don't you have something to do?" he asked.

"Yes," she said. "But the drone is doing most of the work." She dropped it in the grass. "Go clean up bodies," she said, and it trundled off. "Let's talk!"

Christ, he had little to lose now. "I wondered what she'd say if I asked her out. She's thirty-one and I'm fifty-two. That kind of age difference is usually questioned in our world. We met at a dead-spouse support group, and you're not supposed to date people you meet there."

"Why?"

He sighed. "Because if you're focusing on your dead spouse and grief and healing, then you won't be looking for love. If you fall in love at group, then you're just avoiding the grief, not processing it. But I can't worry about what they say. You can't choose who you love."

He looked up at the artificial sky, which had taken on a pretty tangerine color. "As for the age difference, the assumption is that she couldn't be interested in an old craggy guy like me, so she must be after something else, like my money. They think I couldn't be interested in her personality because she's so young and I just want a pretty wife who will make me look good. No one ever asks about compatibility. Or the fact that she asked me over to her place for a party first."

"Oh, I can ask! Tell me about compatibility and the party place!" Tina asked. "I want love someday. But I'm not sure I'm allowed to get it."

"Allowed?" he asked.

"I'm queen," she said, as if that explained everything.

"But won't you want to have children to pass the throne to?" he asked. "Unless you aliens do monarchy differently."

"You're talking about babies," she said with a shudder. "I don't even know how they're made."

"But you're a queen. And you don't know about babies?" he asked, baffled.

"No, silly, I don't need to know about babies to rule!"

"That's fair, I guess," he allowed. "But sure, I'll tell you."

* * * *

THE SURVIVING-SPOUSE SUPPORT group had a few extra-curricular events outside of their official therapy groups. There were some intramural sports activities, some art museum enthusi-asts, and some people who just liked coffee or booze or both. Don dabbled in a few of these but ended up attending the ones that Amy liked to frequent. His favorite was when they would go to a bar after their meetings, happy hour in the local restaurant called Digby Dan's. He recognized a few people from the SBI there and had sat with his back to them, explaining that the anonymous part of grief was important.

Amy had sat beside him and was matching him beer for beer, her tiny frame processing the alcohol as fast as his did. He told stories about Helen, and she shared stories about Cal, and then the table would end up talking about sports or something and he would just be happy sitting next to her.

"We couldn't be more different," he told Tina. "She's Dr. Amy Valor, professor of physics. And I'm a promoted cop for the state."

"She must be smart," Tina said.

He frowned. "She is. I don't pretend to understand science, but still she wanted to hang out with me."

They kept sharing beers, and Amy would go to the restroom, citing her small bladder, and then come out dabbing makeup under-neath her eyes. He had wondered if she had cried about her husband in the bathroom, and felt bad about hoping that she would return his affections.

"We got pretty wasted," he said. "And I almost told her that night. I was pretty tanked."

"Tanked?" Tina asked.

"Liquid courage," he said. "I know y'all have alcohol, right?"

"We do, but I'm not allowed any," she said sadly. "Well, any more today, anyway. Ferdinand says I already have impulse-control issues. That makes alcohol more fun, though!"

Don thought about a sentient armed mech with impulse-control issues and figured this Ferdinand was smart.

"It can make humans relax and not be so nervous," he explained. "Do you have anything in your language that means 'far out of my league'?"

Tina didn't answer right away, but hummed quietly to herself. "I don't think so."

"It's an English phrase for when you're attracted to a person who's either more attractive or smarter than you. It implies you have no chance to date them. But that night I told her that I could really fall for someone like her." He stopped, remembering. "She laughed and said I was drunk. She ordered a ride home for us, stopping at my house first. I remember only wondering how she was so sober when I was trashed and we'd had the same amount of beer, but she helped me to the door, unlocked it for me, and then led me to the bathroom. I was about to return all the bottles I'd had that night," he said grimly. "She took care of me."

She'd left him a glass of water and a cold wet washcloth on his vanity. As he was draping the washcloth around his neck and brushing his teeth, his phone pinged with her text apologizing for having to leave and hoping his hangover wasn't too bad tomorrow.

He'd stared at his image in the bathroom mirror, at the little dots of red burst blood vessels around his eyes that always accompanied his vomiting incidents, wondering what she could see in him. They'd hung out at a bar, pro. He'd half confessed his feelings for her and she had laughed, con. But then she'd helped him inside when he'd been too drunk to do so, major pro.

She could also do all these things for her grandfather.

He went to bed miserable and woke up worse.

But then he had been gratified to learn that she was going to the space station where Mallory Viridian lived and was suggesting he try to get a ticket through work.

"What did you think would happen?" Tina asked. She was transfixed, or at least, she seemed to stare at Draughn while he talked.

He chuckled. "Well, not murder. But I should have, since Mallory is here. I had hoped that being in a new, weird location would help us reach for the familiar, and I would be here when she reached." He was being more poetic than usual, and the odd feelings made tears prick his eyes.

"I am getting old," he said, remembering his last performance review. "I really should have seen all this bullshit coming."

"Should have seen what bullshit coming?" Tina asked, looking around.

"The drama," he said, and then held up his fingers and counted off the grievances. "Oscar's dead, the ambassador is dead, I got a concussion and nearly lost my hand, Parker is acting suspicious, the Valor-Coles are fighting like cats and dogs, and I've barely seen Amy at all. It all points to Mallory Viridian."

"So many things happen around Mallory," Tina said, delighted. "She says this kind of thing happens to her a lot. Did you want all this to happen?"

He stared at her. "Good God, no! Of course I didn't."

"Oh. But you know Mallory and came to Eternity anyway. I'm confused."

Draughn shrugged. "When you fall in love, you make really stupid decisions."

"Oh," Tina said thoughtfully. "Maybe I am in love. I've been making bad decisions my whole life."

"That's not quite what I meant," he said, chuckling.

Tina paused. "Humans are weird. Anyway, who really killed those people? Come on, you can tell me. I won't tell Mallory." Tina leaned in, and Draughn could feel a heat wafting off her.

He shifted back, uncomfortable. "Do you think we *arranged* a murder for Mallory, like a murder-mystery party?"

Tina retreated, taking her furnace with her. "There are murder parties? I love parties! Mallory never talks about murder parties. Maybe she'd like murders more if there was a party."

Draughn dabbed the sweat on his forehead.

"I figured I'd ask if you knew the murderer," Tina continued. "I was lying; I would totally have told Mallory. I figured I'd do something nice for her, since I'm helpful now. But it was nice meeting you, Don. I hope Mallory finds your murderer. If anyone comes looking for me, tell them I went looking for love. After I do the corpse cleanup. I'm responsible!"

"Love?" he asked, frowning.

"I like to confuse people. It distracts them from noticing I'm not that smart."

"But you just told me you're not—" he began.

"Bye!" she said, and lumbered after the drone toward the dormant blue hive. The sound of ripping paper filled the park.

22

IT'S JUST AN ACADEMIC CRUSH

REGGIE AND MAX walked into Mallory's office. It still felt like an invisible wall traveled between them wherever they went.

The office was depressingly minimalistic. This woman was not a decorator. Metal walls, plush gray carpeting, a sofa, chair, and desk. Max itched to suggest someone to help her out. But maybe this kind of decor appealed to aliens.

Mallory sat behind a desk, smiling. Dark circles were under her eyes, and Max estimated that she'd had about as much sleep as he'd had.

She stood and held her hand out. "Hi, Max, Reggie. I'd say it's nice to see you again, but I'm not going to sugarcoat it. But thanks for coming."

"Always the charmer," Reggie said.

Max stared at him, feeling his jaw go slack. Reggie caught his eye and then stepped back, startled. "What?" he asked.

"It just hit me. What the hell did I ever see in you? You're mean, Reggie. Just plain mean." The words were out of his mouth before he could think about them, but he found he didn't regret them. Even when Reggie's cheeks went pale with shock, then red with anger.

He drew in a breath, but Max shook his head. "Never mind. We'll deal with us later. Let's hash out this mess first."

Mallory watched them carefully. When she had their attention again, she indicated the couch against the wall. It was orange and straight from the 1970s. Max sat down with distaste.

Mallory grimaced when she saw his face. "Yeah, I know it's awful. I'm working on it. Not a lot of human-friendly furniture here; I have to take what Eternity gives me. And sometimes she gets her view of what furniture should be based on Earth media. This"—she gestured to the office around her—"is her view of a human private detective office."

Reggie was still speechless, but he sat down next to Max, putting a full couch cushion between them.

Mallory touched the screen of a large tablet in front of her, and it glowed as it activated. "I've been reading about all of you. You're an interesting bunch."

"Reading about us?" Reggie demanded. "How? Did you get Oscar's data?"

"Although I would love to have that, I haven't found it yet," Mallory admitted. "But no. Eternity requests information about each visitor. Background checks. A safety procedure. I've only recently gotten my hands on them, what with the various station issues we've had."

"Then how did a serial killer get on board a few months ago?" Reggie demanded.

"She's not infallible," Mallory said, shrugging. "And that was what made her start to require the checks on incoming humans." She pointed to Max. "You've been an RN, but then pivoted to experimental psychology. That's really interesting. Why didn't you keep going in the messier medical fields, the ones with blood and vomit and stuff?"

Max laughed dryly. "You just answered your own question. But honestly I became more interested in psychology after"—he glanced at Reggie—"after a few years as a nurse. I became more interested in why people did things rather than what happened to their bodies."

"What year?" Mallory asked, cocking her head.

"I got my nursing degree in 2035 but went back to study psychology in 2043," Max said. "Why?"

"I know you got married in 2044. I heard you two met in the hospital after Parker got injured. When was that?" she asked, pointing from Max to Reggie and then back to Max.

"Twenty forty-four," Reggie said.

"No, it was 2043, right after our birthday. December," Max corrected. "What does this have to do with anything?"

"There are always interesting connections in situations like this. You two have this odd-couple thing going on, with the fun-loving flake Max and the tense stick-in-the-mud Reggie. Somehow you get along and fall in love and that's beautiful." Both men bristled, but she waved her hand at them. "Don't get mad. I'm not wrong, am I?"

"Doesn't mean you have to be cruel," Max said.

"I'm running out of time to protect feelings," Mallory said. "You two seem to be in a rough patch now, but I assume you loved each other once."

"Are you a marriage counselor? Why are you doing this? Don't you have my brother and sister to harass?" Reggie snapped, and then stood up.

"Sit down, Reggie," Mallory said, sounding tired. "Your storming off has gotten boring. I think it needs to come out that there was another reason Max was interested in you. This is something that Oscar had on you, right, Max?"

Christ. No one knew about that. Oscar wasn't smart enough to know . . . unless he got into my files. Shit.

Max held his head in his hands. "How did you figure that out if you didn't find his files?"

"Connections are kind of my thing," Mallory said. "I was off my game earlier. But I'm feeling better now."

"What the fuck is she talking about, Max?" Reggie said.

"Reggie, your brother is extraordinary. He is either the luckiest or unluckiest person I've ever met. It depends on your point of view. The truth is, when there's chaos around, he's going to be in the center of it." She held out her right hand and started counting the fingers. "Parker Valor was on a plane when he started to get appendicitis. He was sitting between an air marshal and an internal medicine specialist. Between the two of them, they forced the plane to land and got him to a hospital in time for an emergency appendectomy. Then the hospital caught fire, and he was one of four to get rescued amid massive loss of life. Then something happened in Iceland. Do you remember what it was, Reggie?"

"Was that the year the volcano blew and destroyed that town?" Reggie asked dully.

"Yeah. Mount Katla erupted and destroyed a section of a town before everyone could evacuate. Everyone who attended the conference died. Parker could have died on the plane of his illness. He could have died in the hospital fire. He could have died in Iceland. I'm betting if we had access to his medical files, we might find that the surgery was touch and go as well, but he got out of it all right. Parker is special, and Max saw it immediately. This is why he studied experimental psychology. He's here because Parker is here, right, Max? You wanted to see what happened with Parker in an alien environment. Because chaos happens around Parker."

Reggie looked pale and stared at Mallory, then Max. "That's ridiculous. You wouldn't have done that just for Parker!"

"There were other reasons," Max stammered. "I was interested in psychology. Meeting Parker was just the catalyst."

Reggie made a strangled noise. Max tried to take his hand, but Reggie yanked it away.

"Honey, I was already interested in luck, but I'd never met

anyone like Parker. It was like you both dropped into my lap that night. I had someone to study, and someone to fall in love with." Reggie kept his hands out of reach. Max sat back, distraught. "Spending time with Parker let me spend more time with *you*. That's what I wanted. You were the most real thing I had ever experienced."

Reggie shook his head vehemently. "I can't believe any of this! Everything I know is a lie. My business partner was corrupt and my marriage was built on a scientific crush on my brother!"

Max reached out again, but Reggie stayed out of reach and didn't meet his eye.

"Reggie, I can't believe you doubt his love for you," Mallory said, her voice strangely nonchalant.

Reggie focused on her, his eyes narrowed with dislike. "What are you talking about? You just dropped the bombshell that our marriage was built on a lie. You don't have anyone's best interests at heart."

A muscle twitched in Mallory's jaw. "I have Oscar's best interests at heart. Or at least, the desire to solve his murder."

"And what does that have to do with it?" Reggie snapped.

"Because Max has been trying since Oscar's death to imply but not directly state that *he* cheated on you with Oscar," Mallory said. "When really it was *you* who cheated. Max forgave you, but your own self-loathing kept you prickly about the situation. Which gives you both motive for the murder!"

Reggie looked at Max. "I can't believe you told her," he said, his voice soft with hurt exhaustion.

"I didn't tell her anything," Max said. "I said there were issues between us, but I didn't even say that anyone slept with Oscar. Much less me. Or you. She figured it out."

"I wanted to get past this," Reggie said, putting his elbows carefully on his knees.

"Do you?" Mallory asked. "You are still sniping at Max all the time, you chose to work with Oscar as, what, some kind of punishment, or to show Max you can be faithful?" She paused, and then the realization dawned on her. "No, you were showing yourself that you can be faithful."

"He has nothing to prove to me," Max said, his voice pointing at Mallory but his eyes stuck on his husband. "We talked about it. I got past it. He still hasn't. I don't know if he wants me to cheat on him to level the playing field or what."

"I can't deal with this," Reggie moaned.

"Don't deal with it," Mallory said. "Just tell me what happened at the party."

"I was at the party. I had a few drinks, but then saw Max was pounding the wine and figured I had to stay sober for him." He gave Max a resentful look.

"So you wanted to get smashed?" Mallory asked.

"Something like that," he said, shrugging. "We all need to let off steam."

"I've been there," she said. "Not the healthiest escape hatch. But do you remember what Oscar was doing before the party?"

"Oscar seemed really busy when he got aboard. He was handing out his card to every alien he could find."

Mallory interrupted Reggie with a laugh. "His card? He did know that no one here can read English, right?"

Reggie held up a finger. "He got them translated into a universal glyph system. That data has reached us. Do you not know it yet?"

Mallory opened her mouth, then closed it again. "Shit. But what did Oscar think a Gneiss would want with celebrity gossip on Earth? They don't give a shit."

"He didn't want them reading news on Earth, he wanted to expand the Trash Heap to alien worlds. He wanted to hire a new team of designers to connect our Internet with whatever aliens use for data transfer, hire reporters on other planets, and get the gossip for all over the galaxy."

Mallory sat back. "Oh, my God. That's brilliant. Too bad he was such a tool. Did he have sites all over the world?"

Reggie shook his head. "No. He said we could waste time going worldwide when there were already sites in other languages, or go galactic, where no one else was. His ambition knew no bounds. The tech he had already acquired was making his hacking on Earth effortless."

"That's something you're probably going to have to talk about in front of Congress," Mallory muttered. "Or worse, in front of Mrs. Brown. But anyway. I see why it was so important to have you on board since you were already looking into the law and aliens. Have you been studying the law of other species?"

Despite the tension in the room, Reggie relaxed a little and even got that look on his face that Max loved: the calm and happy look that meant he was talking about something he enjoyed. "As much as I can, anyway. Like you said, it's hard to read information in other languages, and there's a three-month wait for the one alien translation computer that the Gurudev lent us. Some folks at UNC say it's harder to book time with that translation computer than it is to book time on a telescope. But I got some audiobooks and I've been listening and transcribing them as best I can."

"Reggie, if you and Oscar had pulled this off," Mallory said, letting the first part of the sentence just kind of sit there.

Reggie shrugged. "Yeah, well, I hated working with him even though I loved the work."

"Who gets ownership of the Trash Heap now that Oscar is gone?" Mallory asked. "I doubt Oscar had a will. But then again, if you'd asked me five minutes ago if Oscar had a brilliant idea to corner the galactic market on gossip, I would have laughed, so I guess that guy was full of surprises."

"When I joined, he had no contracts in place, so I wrote him some to protect intellectual property and the like," Reggie said, looking at his hands.

He wasn't saying the rest of it. Max rolled his eyes. "Reggie, you have to tell her. She'll figure it out otherwise." Reggie glared at him.

"What, that Reggie wrote his own contract, which protected his own IP more than Oscar's?" Mallory asked.

"Uh-huh," Max said.

"Thanks for that," Reggie hissed. "That's another motive."

"It's your motive, and it existed before I said anything," Max said. "If you want to appear innocent, don't hold stuff like that back."

Reggie sighed. "Fine. Yes. I will retain ownership of"—he winced, as he always did before he said the name of the site he was in charge of—"the Trash Heap, Esquire, now that Oscar is dead. I have the right to take it, rename it, and go in any direction I want to." He glared at Max. "Are you happy?"

"Blame me all you want, it doesn't change anything," he said, using one of Reggie's favorite phrases when he used his legal mind and sharp logic to shred one of Max's more passionate opinions.

Mallory rubbed her lips. "That does establish a pretty big motive. But what about the site as a whole?"

"I don't know if he had a will or not," Reggie said. "I offered to write him one, but . . ." He winced, as if he knew how that would have looked.

At least you dodged that bullet.

"He thought he was young and immortal?" Mallory asked.

"And he thought his secrets would protect him," Reggie said, nodding. "He said there was a doomsday program set to release all the secrets he knew if he died. But I don't know if he was ever that organized."

Mallory raised her eyebrows.

Reggie shook his head. "He was ambitious, yes, but the details, not so much. That's why he needed me." He twisted his mouth like he had eaten something sour.

"So I'm guessing he had Max's secret academic interest in Parker on him?" she asked, looking at Max.

"That's the only thing I can think of that I didn't want my husband to know," Max said, feeling nauseated and hot.

"And Reggie? Did he hold anything over you?"

Reggie laughed bitterly. "I got fired from two law firms and the only job available to me was with the guy who I cheated on my husband with. He already had a pretty tight rein on me."

"Okay," Mallory said, writing something down on her tablet. "Let's get back to the party. What do you remember, Reggie?"

"I didn't see him beforehand. He said he was going to rub elbows, or whatever these aliens had, and he'd see me at the party."

"Didn't he want you with him? I mean, aren't you also representing the site?" Mallory asked.

"He told me not to come," Reggie muttered. "Said something about too many cooks ruining the broth."

Careful, that's another motive, babe.

"Too many cooks," Mallory muttered. "That's a weird thing to say." She chewed on her lip.

"But he came back early," Max said, remembering. "We heard him in his room, remember?"

"What did you hear?" Mallory asked.

"Just some moving around. A few things fell on the floor." Reggie waved his hand at Mallory's interested look. "He's a slob. He didn't respect anything, not his own belongings or anyone else's."

"But you didn't see him?" Mallory asked, eyebrows raised.

"Well, no, but we heard him," Max said. "Muttering, moving around, you know."

"Okay," she said, returning to her notes. "How about everyone else? Where were they before the party?"

Reggie shrugged. "Max and I were in our room. Parker said he was going to do a tour of the station."

"What about Draughn and Amy?" Mallory asked.

"I don't know," Reggie snapped. "I didn't think I'd have to keep track of everyone like a babysitter."

"I might remember," Max said slowly. What had Draughn said? "Amy wanted to explore with Parker. Draughn said he would tag along. He said he might run into you, and then Amy said she wanted to meet you."

"'Meet' me," Mallory said. "She knew me already. Why did she not want Draughn to know that she knew me?" She said it more to herself than to them. But Reggie spoke up anyway.

"Agent Draughn?" Reggie asked. "Amy said he had an unhealthy fixation with you, and it would be best if he didn't know our connection with you. And to not 'recognize' you till we saw you in person." He made quote marks with his fingers when he said "recognize."

"But why? Why should she care?"

"I have no idea, you'll have to ask her." His tired blue eyes stared pointedly at her. "I didn't see anything interesting at the party, I just remember Oscar falling out of the closet, and then all those wasps were everywhere. I grabbed Max and we ran."

"Oscar fell out of a closet, but who opened it?" Mallory asked.

"Agent Draughn," Max said. "We were looking for Oscar since the party was over. Oscar never left a party before it was over."

"You have to remember something more than that," Mallory said. She pointed to Max's hands, which felt better but were still red with burns. "There's Max's burns, and you keep rubbing that tooth. Is that chip new?"

Reggie winced and removed his thumb from where he had been unconsciously rubbing the chipped tooth. He glanced at Max. "Oscar said he wanted to talk to me. He brought me a mug of that hot sludge. He started being typical Oscar." He turned to look directly at Max. "Then you came over and knocked the mug out of my hands when I was about to take a drink. It hit my tooth, and then dumped all over your arms. You started screaming and I tried to get you cleaned up."

"Where was Oscar when this was happening?" Mallory asked.

"Laughing," Max said, the memory cutting through the haze with cruel clarity. "He thought it was hysterical. He sounded pretty drunk by then. That's about the last thing I remember."

Reggie nodded. "He kind of staggered away, and I didn't see him again."

"And you cleaned up Max and went home? How long did it take to clean up? Oscar needed time to get stuffed into a closet without anyone seeing him," Mallory said. She checked her notes. "Did either of you hear the ambassador's speech?"

"No, this was before her speech, but I think she called people into the main bar soon after," Reggie said. "I had to stay and babysit."

The memory was hazy, but it was there. "I remember Reggie propping me up." Max glanced at his husband. "You were really mad at me. You put me in a chair and told me you were going to get something to clean me up, but then you went into the bathroom to check your tooth. Oscar was in the room with us, at another table. He was really drunk. The ambassador was saying something in the other room, people were clapping, it got loud. My hands were hurting by then, and I started trying to get the goo off of them with a tablecloth, and focused on that for a while. Then—" He shook his head to clear it, but all he could remember was the sound. "Then there was only buzzing. Reggie grabbed me, and we ran."

"So Max was the last known person alone with Oscar," Mallory asked, focusing on Max. "That's interesting."

23

. . .

MANIC PIXIE DREAM HUSBAND

MAX'S BEDHEAD WAS the best part about waking up. It was as if his red curls had run rampant over his pillow at night, going out drinking, and coming home to nestle on his scalp, messy and hungover, not really caring what they looked like when they went to work.

"You're poetic when you're drunk!" Max had said, delighted, when Reggie had lowered his walls briefly to give Max this description. They'd been watching a movie on Reggie's couch, but Max had pulled Reggie over for a kiss, and Reggie missed the rest of the movie.

Max's wild Irish coloring, ginger hair, warm brown eyes, and freckled skin were so beautiful, Reggie flat out couldn't believe that Max found him attractive. When you look like a goddamn Irish fairy, you could date anyone you wanted. Why did he want Reggie?

Reggie knew he wasn't bad-looking. But he had no distinguishing features. He was like a picture-frame model. A woman Reggie had dated in college before he came out had called him "blandsome."

"You have the symmetry and the jaw and the Scandinavian blond hair and blue eyes thing going for you," she had said, studying him like he was an enigma. "But I forget what you look like the minute I turn my back. I couldn't pick you out of a lineup. You're like a mannequin."

The fool he was, he dated her for another month after that insult. At least it had helped him come out. No man had ever been that cruel to him.

He had cried the day Max proposed to him. A secret part of him was just trying to enjoy the relationship while it lasted, until Max found someone prettier to date.

Parker had tried to take credit for them meeting, which was cute, so he tried to let his accident-prone baby brother take whatever wins he could. The fact was, Reggie had met Max a few months before. He remembered, because Max was so memorable, but no one else knew about it. Even Max didn't remember. Reggie was very grateful for this.

Reggie had been gunning for partner at his law firm alongside Irving Rochs, who could kiss ass like no one Reggie had ever seen. Reggie preferred to get attention through hard work and didn't enjoy office politics. On a particularly bitter, cold Friday in late October, he heard Irving had made partner, and this was after Reggie had stayed up all night working on a brief. But no one had noticed.

The bosses called a meeting and, when everyone arrived at the common area, next to plastic plants and notes to clean up after yourself because Mom wasn't there, they announced their new partner. Everyone else clapped for him; Reggie just turned around and left the office.

Harry, the co-owner of the firm, ran after him. "Reggie, what's going on, what's the ma—" His hand landed on Reggie's shoulder, and something inside Reggie snapped.

Reggie spun and lashed out, punching straight into Harry's face. Harry gave a squawk and stumbled backward, eyes wide, nose streaming with blood.

Reggie went cold inside. He was surprised by his reaction, but also his lack of any sort of regret. This was justified. This was right. He didn't have to be okay with corporate bullshit anymore. He didn't have to pretend to like these money-hungry sharks anymore. He didn't have to kiss anyone's ass anymore.

Harry, unfortunately, was the fitter of the two (now three) partners, and stepped forward, his surprise turning to rage. He punched Reggie in the stomach, snarling, "You're fired. Get out before I call the police to report you for assault."

Reggie was doubled over, fighting to suck in breath, and he nodded weakly. Harry gave him a push and Reggie fell awkwardly onto the sidewalk. Something snapped in his left arm and he cried out.

Harry was already walking into the building with his face to the sky and fingers clamped on his nose.

Reggie fumbled around in his pocket and called a taxi to take him to the doctor. Stunned, blank, he gave the minimum amount of information to the receptionist, and then to the radiologist.

After getting images of his broken arm, the radiologist looked at his right hand. "You have some lacerations and bruising on your hand," she said, pointing. "We should get X-rays to make sure you haven't damaged anything. Can you open your hand for me?"

He couldn't. It felt as if his fist had closed, empty, around what had been his life. The radiologist tried to pry his fingers apart to lay his arm flat. He wouldn't budge. It wasn't conscious. He was just so tight inside that he couldn't relax anything. He positively vibrated with pain and rage. She gave a frustrated sigh and called for a nurse and a sedative.

"Hey there, what happened to you?" asked a mild voice. He turned his head to snarl at the newcomer, but when Max's brown eyes caught his, he melted.

"Bad day," he said. "I fell down."

Max's eyes took in the broken arm, the lacerations on his hand,

and Reggie's rumpled suit. "I usually don't get injuries like this until nine p.m. at least. You don't look like the kind of guy to join a fight club," he said. "Who did you punch?"

"I didn't—"

"Teeth marks right here," Max said, pointing to Reggie's fist. "Classic injury people get when they punch someone and they're not used to punching." He focused on Reggie again and saw how he was breathing shallowly.

"We're going to have to check him for internal injuries after this," he told the radiologist. "You fell after getting punched in the belly, didn't you?"

"How did you figure that out?"

Max shrugged. "I'm a nurse." He winked at Reggie. "Now they want me to sedate you so we can get an X-ray, but no one likes shots. Can I convince you to lay your hand flat for me? You don't need to punch anyone else today. I promise."

"Don't talk to me like I'm five," Reggie said.

"Oh, I'm not," Max said. "Five-year-olds tend to do what we tell them to. I'm talking to you like you're a grown man, and they're always the reluctant ones. But it's usually the threat of a shot that makes them comply." He grinned, lessening the sting of his insult.

And with that grin, Reggie's hand relaxed. The muscles spasmed briefly and then he was able to lay it flat so the radiologist could get an image.

After the X-rays, a doctor came and put a cast on his arm efficiently. Clean break, he said. Heal in no time, he said. He examined his swollen right hand, prescribed some antibiotics (because he, too, knew what a human bite looked like), then told him that a nurse would come and bandage his hand.

The nurse, Max, soon arrived with a basin and gauze. "I thought you'd be sick of me by now," he said.

"I don't have a choice, do I?" Reggie asked, trying to sound gruff, but failing.

"That's true. If people had a choice, they'd be asking for me all the time," Max said with an eye roll. "So who'd you punch?"

Reggie yanked his gaze away from Max's face and focused instead on the sink in the room. "Uh, I punched my boss," he said. "Former boss, I guess. Lost my job."

The nurse bathed his hand in the basin, warm water and pink soap stinging the cuts. Reggie finally looked at his hand. Teeth marks were clearly established on his knuckles, several breaking the skin.

"You punched your boss and assumed you would keep your job?" Max asked, smiling. "That's gutsy."

"I wanted to kill him," Reggie whispered. "But I only punched him. It was a bad day." The adrenaline was wearing off by now, and the pain became much more obvious. He hissed as Max put Betadine on his fist.

"Oh, hush, you big baby," Max said amicably. "Wanna hear about my weekend?"

"What?" he asked, startled. "Not really."

"That's rude, but I'm going to tell you anyway, because it's good to distract the patient," Max said, wrapping the gauze around his fist. "I saw my first alien at the mall. I think it was one of those Fantasms."

"Huh," Reggie said, baffled at the change of topic. Then, despite himself, he said, "What was it doing at the mall?"

"Driving the wrong way down a one-way road, which messed up traffic for the afternoon. I don't think they ever got to see the Cheesecake Factory from the inside."

"They don't know our traffic laws," Reggie said, his voice far away to his own ears. "How in the world was it able to rent a car without a driver's license? Did you meet it?"

"No, the crowd was too big."

"You didn't really meet the alien."

"I never said I met them." Max tied the gauze and looked him in the eyes. "Honey, if you punch someone the same day that you insult someone trying to give you medical attention, you're working with a common denominator, and that's you."

Reggie came back to himself abruptly and frowned at Max. "Just do your job," he said coldly.

Max removed his gloves and tossed them in the trash. Then he turned back to Reggie and searched his face, looking, possibly, for signs of humanity. Finally, he shrugged, packed up his supplies, and wheeled the cart out. "You're free to go. Follow the exit signs," he said, stopping to wash his hands at the basin. "Take all your antibiotics. Human bites are nasty."

On the taxi ride home, he wondered how he'd get another job, or if Harry would press charges. He wondered if he should go back to work tomorrow to hurt Harry more. He'd already lost his job—what else was there to lose? But his brain kept sliding back to those warm brown eyes and the story about the alien driving. He always ended up wondering about aliens and the laws of the various places on Earth.

Who was going to address this new, much more powerful, foreign threat to our legal system? What various laws would have to change to address interstellar visitors, all of them more powerful than humans?

He tried to hang out his own shingle, then applied to area law firms. He got a job for half his usual salary and tried to tell himself he got off easily. He spent his off-hours reading everything he could about alien visitations, and more importantly, how the US was responding on a legal level.

When he met Max again in Parker's hospital room, it was like it was the first time.

THEY'D BEEN ENGAGED and about to move in together when it all came tumbling down. It was two weeks after he'd been let go from his shitty law firm for focusing too much on alien law data. Max wasn't around because he was working double shifts and studying for exams. Reggie knew he shouldn't resent Max for carrying all the responsibility, but he wanted a shoulder to cry on, and Max was just too busy.

He met Oscar in the gym, and the charisma and looks and willingness to listen just led him to a bad decision.

The sex hadn't been great. For all his bragging, Oscar was selfish and fast in bed. Reggie lay there afterward realizing he had just possibly fucked up his life forever and it hadn't even been that great.

He confessed in a torrent of tears, hoping Max would punish him, let him do whatever he could to make it up to him, but Max forgave him and hugged him.

Reggie hated him for that. Because he would never have done the same. His confusion and guilt festered inside. He reasoned that if he, Reggie, the paragon of control, could lose control and cheat, then anyone could. Including Max, who had a bigger reason than most. He began to get suspicious of anyone Max talked to. Max withdrew in hurt confusion, which just fueled Reggie's suspicion.

Amy hadn't known of the strife between the three and invited Oscar to a party attended by Reggie and Max. Reggie stiffened, but Max took it in stride. He shrugged and said, "He's just another person. Let's not waste our time with him."

But Oscar was a loud other person who liked to be the center of attention. He had heard through the rumor mill that Reggie had lost his job. And that's when the best-paying job with the worst boss ever fell into Reggie's lap.

REGGIE LOOKED FROM Mallory to Max. "No, he was far too drunk to do this," he said. "I mean, he was piss-yourself drunk."

"Okay," Max said, glaring at him.

"What, you want me to tell her that you were totally sober and feeling great? I'm doing this for you!"

"And talking about me pissing myself"—he glanced at Mallory—"which didn't happen, by the way, is the way to be there for me?"

Mallory sighed. "Max, why don't you let me have this time with Reggie?"

"Sure," Max said. He stood up and rubbed his hands over his face like he was wiping away the anger and frustration. When he was done, his face was gentle and sweet again. "We'll get through this," he said softly, and leaned in and kissed him.

How does he do that? Reggie collapsed forward and buried his face in his hands. Max was going to leave. Reggie knew it would only be a matter of time.

Once Max had left, Mallory leaned back in her chair and asked, "Why are you so angry?"

He blinked at her. Resentment flared immediately. "Why? What the hell does that have to do with anything?"

"You've got a great husband, and you're doing really interesting work. Granted, your boss was an asshole, but everything else in your life looked rosy. I know things can look a lot different from the inside, so I'm trying to understand."

He was silent, glaring at the floor. This kid—as he would always think of people his siblings' age—was trying to ask him personal questions, shit that was not her business at all.

"Reggie, he loves you so much and it's clear he forgave you. Why do you hold on to the affair?" she asked. "It's like you want to hurt both of you."

"Are you a psychologist? You sound like *him*."

She was at least smart enough to know who *him* was. "What does he do that makes you so angry? He seems like a great guy."

He gritted his teeth so hard his jaw ached, then remembered

how Max's warm smile could relax him, back before things got tense. "Mallory, did you ever see that musical *Once*?" he asked.

She made a face. "God, yes. Manic pixie dream girl masturbatory dreck."

He nodded, surprised she cut so close to his own opinion. "Exactly. Perfect person comes into Guy's boring life and dazzles him, makes him turn his life around and excel creatively, and then she leaves. There's purity and yearning for what could never be. And through that feeling, they both grow."

"They both 'grow' into relationships neither wants. Doesn't sound like growth to me," she said skeptically.

"Max is my manic pixie dream girl," he said simply. "He came into my life and dazzled me. He is gorgeous and kind and forgiving and fun and he makes me want to be a better person and I didn't know how I got so lucky. I treated him badly and still he pushes me toward excellence. And every day I wake up and wonder two things: if I have taken his gift and used it for all it's worth, and if today is the day he will leave me and move on."

He laughed bitterly. "He inspired me professionally, but I'm working at a sleazy content mill. He inspired me personally, and I'm petty enough to wonder every day if he's leaving. I don't know what to do with this gift of a perfect husband."

Mallory watched him for a while. She didn't contradict him or tell him he was stupid or crazy, which both made him happy that she had listened, but also made him fear in his gut that his self-loathing was justified.

She finally leaned forward and waited till he met her eyes. "Reggie, you're a smart and logical guy. And I can tell by the look on your face that you know that all of this is fear talking. But when you wake up afraid every day, logic doesn't enter into it. Have you ever considered that the manic pixie dream girl trope is just a fiction trope and doesn't reflect real life? That real life is more nuanced? And that sometimes the people who love us just want to see us happy instead of maximizing our potential like zealous parents?

"You're holding on to your past mistakes as proof that you're forever worthless. You're deciding for him that you're not good enough for him, and you'll beat him over the head with that until you convince him. And when he leaves, you'll be alone in your cold satisfaction that you were right all along that he would betray you." She took a deep breath. "Every relationship in my life has ended with a murder except for one broody guy in college—who I wish had been around for a murder. It might have broken him out of his emo malaise. We went out for two wild, sexy weeks, and I thought I was in love. Then he dumped me, and I will never forget the words he said: 'I hate being alone, but I love hating it.' Dude dumped me because being alone and sad was better than being with me. If that won't fuck with your self-worth, I don't know what will.

"Max loves you," she said simply. "You confuse him, but he loves you anyway and won't let anyone say anything bad about you. Don't choose being alone and sad over being with the best guy in the world because you don't think you deserve him."

Reggie sat in silent numbness. "Why aren't you asking me about the party?" he finally said.

"I wanted to see what was making you so sour," she said. "What do you want to tell me about the party?"

THE PARTY HAD been a chaotic mess. Oscar was hitting on everyone at the same time, it seemed.

Oscar still found it hysterical that Reggie had agreed to work with him, and liked flirting with him whenever he could. Reggie would never go down that road again, and the flirting just disgusted him.

"Hey, remember when we slept together and then I gave you a

job like the little whore you are?" Oscar asked Reggie, bringing him a drink.

He'd been watching Max pound the wine and was alternately worried for and annoyed by him. His husband got up from the bar and wandered their way, distracted by someone at another table. "What do you want, Oscar?" he asked, forcing a bored tone to his voice. Emotional response was Oscar's meat and potatoes, Max had once told him. The biggest threat to Oscar was yawning in his face.

"Just bought you a drink, partner!" he said, handing over a warm stone mug.

"What the hell is this?" Reggie said.

"A peace offering," Oscar said.

"Most people don't begin a peace offering by calling someone a little whore," Reggie said. "Try again."

He tried to give the mug back, but Oscar wrapped both hands around his, denying Reggie a place to put it. "Sorry, habit. Sorry for calling you a little whore. You're doing good work for me, that I'm paying you for. That's not prostitution!" He laughed loudly, attracting irritated looks from folks talking nearby. Oscar cleared his throat. "Oh, and I'm gonna bang your sister tonight, and just wanted to let you know."

Max was talking to Agent Draughn over Oscar's shoulder, slurring his words slightly.

"Not likely," Reggie said, forcing a laugh.

"Jealous?" Oscar asked.

"Also not likely," he said. "You're crude and an asshole, Oscar. You didn't want me in your meetings today, so we have nothing else to talk about."

"I'll let you know how she is," Oscar said. "Drink up, it's good stuff. It'll apparently stop you from getting a hangover. Never say I didn't look out for you."

He wanted something to wash the taste of Oscar out of his

mouth, so he lifted the mug to his lips. Then Max was beside him, hitting the mug and tipping it back toward himself. The lip of the mug jammed into Reggie's tooth painfully, and the mug spilled all over Max.

Oscar just laughed. Agent Draughn watched them, a stunned look on his face.

"That lines up with Max's story," Mallory said. "Things are starting to come clear. Only, I need to talk to the ambassador." The last thing was said under her breath, to herself.

"Why? She'd left by then."

"She talked to several people on the suspect list. I like to cover all my bases."

"Good to be thorough," he said dimly, barely holding on to the conversation.

"Oh," Mallory added. "And I wanted to see if you knew where Parker was. I stopped by his room and he didn't answer."

"I can't keep track of my husband or my sister or my business partner," he said miserably. "What makes you think I know where my brother is?"

Her watch beeped to life. "Mal." Xan's voice was breathless, exhausted.

"What's going on?" she asked. "Did you talk to the ambassador?"

"Are you alone?"

"No," she said. "I'm here with Reggie."

Pause. "Meet me at the observation balcony, alone. And hurry."

"The obs—"

"Where you met my brother for the first time," Xan interrupted.

Mallory's eyes flicked to Reggie. "All right," she said. "I'll be right there."

"What happened?" Reggie asked.

Mallory looked at him as if she suspected he already knew. "I don't know. He didn't say. I have to go."

24

· · · ·

THE THREAT OF THE ONE

PARKER OPENED HIS computer with shaking hands. The truth that Mallory had dropped on him felt like a truck smacking into him, and yet hadn't he known the truck was there? All the pieces were in front of him, the bug expert, but he had chosen not to put them together.

He wasn't sure if he felt depressed to discover that he was indeed a walking disaster, or if he felt comforted to know that all the shit in his life hadn't been his fault.

Parker pulled up the files he had on the Cuckoos, then found the files Amy had shared with him regarding Mallory and the Sundry. In this context, their lives were frighteningly similar.

Although there was the irritating fact that the Sundry formed complex, gorgeous hiveminds. Capable of storing and processing data that Earth supercomputers couldn't approach. Near as he could tell, the Cuckoos were much closer to Earth insects, moving on instinct and basic needs.

Lucky Parker, he thought. *You're one of a few human symbionts to alien species, and you connect with the dumbest bugs in the universe.*

He really should have figured it out after Oscar's death. He'd been shocked and horrified to see the body fall from the closet, had been momentarily worried that Don was the one being attacked, since he fell underneath the weight of Oscar, but then Parker lost sight of the room as his vision filled with glittering green wings. First he felt a spike of fear, and then the realization that the pheromones hadn't worked if they were being swarmed. These insects weren't afraid of him. But as the green insects swarmed around him, he felt an immense sense of protection, of home. He lost all fear, because whatever had happened to Oscar couldn't happen to him; he was loved and safe.

Then the insects were gone. He snapped out of his daze and saw Oscar on the floor, dead. No one else was around him. Blood smeared the floor where he remembered Amy standing. Where had everyone gone? Why did they leave him behind?

A green wasp crawled over Oscar's body, probing his skin with antennae. It wasn't blue or silver. He didn't know any other colors of Sundry, not on Eternity, anyway. But he hadn't seen any of the other two colors, and this green color seemed to be the only one there.

A sick yet fascinating feeling landed in his stomach as he realized what these green insects likely were. *Could they be?* The word "cuckoo" came to his mind, and he felt a firm certainty, as if someone was patting him on the back. Were there cuckoos among the alien Sundry? That was very bad, but still, academically it was amazing.

Walking in on the discussion between Mallory and some of the aliens had confirmed it. He would have preferred if they'd come to him for more information, but no one had. Not since Mallory had stormed out after delivering the shattering information that he was symbiotically connected to these Cuckoos.

The computer offered no more information than he'd already remembered, so he closed his laptop in frustration and got up to pace the room. He needed to walk. Figure something out. This was too much of a mess.

What did it mean that he was connected with them? Part of their hive? Could he communicate? Was he in danger from them? Would he be in danger if he met blue or silver Sundry?

The pheromones had worked quite well, actually. They just worked on Mallory, who was part of an enemy hive. The Cuckoos recognized him as one of their own and ignored the pheromones, or perhaps they didn't register them at all. But he knew that Mallory had feared him, and the Cuckoos were protecting him.

He walked until he had reached the outer perimeter of the station, identified by the air locks and the portals through which he could see the stars. Some Phantasmagore startled him as they walked by, merging with the metallic gray of the wall and appearing only when they were right next to him.

He jumped away and stumbled, landing against the wall of the air lock. He heard what he thought was laughter.

The air lock controls were in front of him and seemed pretty straightforward. He got a sudden notion to see what would happen with his wild luck if he spaced himself. Would he be injured and then saved? Would the Cuckoos interfere to stop him? Would he finally die, his own stupidity beating whatever chaotic luck the insects had imbued him with?

He entered the air lock and closed the door behind him, liking the dichotomy of the close quarters at his back and the infinite nothing of space ahead. The stars were lovely and calming. His shoulders loosened as he leaned against the cool wall and then slid down to sit on the floor. He wasn't going to space himself, but he liked the sudden private clubhouse. He closed his eyes and relaxed, thinking of what he'd read about Mallory describing her connection to the hivemind.

The connection to the Cuckoos was there, obviously right there, like coffee shop conversation that he had been ignoring for his whole life. How had he never felt this nearly tangible thread that connected him to this wild energy?

It wasn't a hivemind full of knowledge and processing capability, but it was definitely a powerful entity. He could feel the systems of the station working around him, the intricacies of the different life-support systems, and the math involving the navigation to the planet Bezoar, the channels of communication open to thousands of conversations. He could touch all of these. He could join the hive. They would welcome him. Something would, finally, not see him as a mistake, a walking accident.

He retained enough of his humanity to resist. The intoxicating draw of acceptance was seductive, though. The Cuckoos were waiting on him.

He turned his head, his eyes still closed. He could see more colors, the streams of green running through the station. But there were some silver spots here and there, traveling erratically, and a bright blue spot on a deck below him. Instinct told him that was Mallory. Just like he always knew when her eyes were on him when they were in high school. He wondered if she could feel him sensing her, too.

Some smaller blue and silver dots were around her, but there was no centralized alarm going off. Insects worked with a different concept of numbers than humans. The individual only mattered if it was a threat (or, on their own side, if the individual had encountered a threat). Otherwise the Sundry and Cuckoos didn't worry about it until it had gathered enough friends to be really noticed. Clearly they hadn't killed all the blue and silver on the station, but the populations had dwindled enough for the survivors to not worry the Cuckoos.

Considering one Cuckoo queen was all it took to take down all these thousands of Sundry, they might want to worry more. Do insects experience hubris?

Still, a voice in his head said, the queen hadn't been a threat until she began to lay eggs and therefore increase her numbers. The one had turned into many, which had turned into a threat.

He got up, feeling resolve with this new information. He had to find the Cuckoo hive. He might be able to tell who had killed Oscar before anyone else died. He'd placed his hand on the air lock controls when a pounding thundered through the air lock, making him jump and whirl around.

A huge pink face was outside the window, staring at him.

25

· · ·

IT'S ONLY A THOUSAND DEATHS;
WHAT COULD GO WRONG?

CHRIST. WHEN DID this happen?" Mallory asked, her eyes on Jessica's bruised face.

"Last night sometime, from what I could tell from the mess in her apartment. Most of the blood had dried. I think the attacker assumed she was dead. Her apartment didn't look tossed or anything. I don't think she would have lasted much longer if we hadn't come by."

"I am tired of you humans and your injured brains!" a Gurudev doctor said, coming up behind them. He was short, about four feet tall, with bright red robes wrapped around him. "It's like someone wants to pulp your thinking organs."

"Bad day for human brains," Mallory said. "Thanks for taking care of her."

The alien looked at her. "Thanks isn't necessary when you're doing your job."

"I still appreciate it," she said. She motioned to Xan. "Let's go upstairs and talk."

They went to the balcony where they could look down on Jessica's bed, in the main observation area of the surgery so the doctors could keep an eye on her.

"I'm guessing she didn't say anything?" Mallory asked.

"Mumbled some syllables," he said, shrugging. "'Sho' or something like it. Sounds like a Gurudev name, but I can't imagine one of them getting the jump on someone as fit as her. Oh," he added, snapping his fingers. "We found Ferd."

"Is he okay?" Mallory asked, climbing onto a human-size stool that sat against the balcony railing.

"Yeah, he finally answered Steph. He was hiding in his back room and not talking to anyone, like a surly statue," Xan said.

Mallory crossed her arms and drummed her fingers on her elbows, unable to keep still. "The dude is the voice of reason against two unpredictable fugitives from justice. He's not supposed to fuck up."

Xan looked up sharply. "He didn't fuck up!" he started, but she stopped him.

"Hang on, I am just looking at it from his point of view. He sees himself as the big brother on a good day, or the babysitter on a bad day. He doesn't think shit is supposed to happen on his watch. He'll snap out of it. Likely whenever Tina does her next stupid idea."

"Steph said he's more melancholy than usual. But the Gneiss think we'll get to Bezoar in a few hours. Security is keeping things calm now that they have comms again. Navigation is keeping the shuttle bays closed. We're lucky the average person here doesn't know enough about astronavigation to look outside and recognize different stars. The pilots know what's up but have been asked to keep quiet while we work on things." He sighed, the sound a harsh wind coming through. "Now the problem is that Steph can't contact Tina. The last she heard was that Tina had a secret mission." He grimaced.

"Oh, Lord," Mallory said. "But that will give Ferdinand something to do. I'm afraid to ask what would be a secret mission for Tina. You'd think it would be impossible for us to lose something that big, but it's been a wild day."

"It always is," he said. "Speaking of wild, did you talk to Parker again?"

"Not yet. But I can't worry about him right now. I have to talk to the, uh, visitors in my room for some guidance."

He nodded, understanding. The new Sundry hives weren't anything close to a hivemind, but as long as the insects could form a four-person circuit, they could process and communicate basic things.

"What do you need from me?" he asked. "*Infinity*'s not back yet. I expect shit will seriously hit the fan when Mrs. Brown gets home."

"Protect the ambassador," Mallory said. "If the killer finds out they've failed, then they'll try again, especially if they think she saw them. If she wakes up and remembers anything, call me. I don't know if I will be able to answer, but I will if I can."

"Sure thing," he said. "Where are you going?"

"Home. Then I have to ask Devanshi a few things."

His watch pinged with an incoming message. "Speaking of which, she just sent the passenger manifest. She also found another file—whoa, Jessica had notes on all the shuttle passengers. You'll want to see this."

"Oh, definitely," she said, eyes looking hopeful and not exhausted for once.

"I'll take care of Jess. But I wish *Infinity* were home. We'd all be safer."

Mallory nodded. "Yeah, we would. She'll find you, don't worry."

"If we make it through this one, I'll buy the drinks at Ferd's," he said. "Be careful, Mal."

"You, too," she said.

"LOOK, YOU HULKING emo immovable object!" Xan said from his stool at the bar. "You have to snap out of this. If you feel so guilty, then there are things you can do to help out instead of just standing in the way."

The low rumble that preceded Ferdinand's words began, and he eventually said, "That's why I was in the pantry. To stay out of the way."

"Dude, Stephanie has done worse things," Xan said. "She stole a dead body and rapid-evolutioned herself into a shuttle. Tina nearly started a shooting war—that's not resolved yet, remember—with your own government. And you know what? You were the rock that got them through that. And you've helped us! You had someone take advantage of where you parked your shuttle. I can't even say you made a mistake, because how can you be blamed for one fucking insect being on your shuttle?"

"They needed containment; they were prisoners," Ferdinand began, but Xan interrupted.

"Okay, I agree with you. And whose job is it to keep the prisoners contained? Prison guards on the planet. Not a visiting diplomat! You know, humans have acceptable levels of shit that we'll put up with because we know no one is perfect. Where I come from, we don't eat insects, but food companies are allowed a small amount of insect parts in each box of cereal. The rule is not *zero* insect parts per box. It's an actual number that they will allow, despite the fact Americans would shit themselves to find insect legs in their Wheaties. It's because no one can be perfect and keep all the insect parts out of the food supply. You know why else it's allowed? Because insects are tiny, and we simply can't keep them out of everything. There are too many. So what does that say to you? You're bigger than any human, and you missed one insect stowaway."

Ferdinand stayed stationary. "That is a fair argument. Do the Sundry know that your people eat insects? Voluntarily and involuntarily?"

Xan rubbed his bald head. "I don't know, they probably do.

They were on Earth for decades before First Contact, right? I think we have bigger problems right now."

"We definitely do," Stephanie said through the wall speaker, making Xan jump.

"Is everything okay, Steph?" Xan asked.

"I just received communications that there is an armed escort waiting for us at Bezoar," Stephanie said. "They want to take Tina home."

"What are we going to do about that?" he demanded. "We don't have Mrs. Brown, or *Infinity*. The station is barely awake. We can't just let them take her."

"That won't be a problem," Stephanie said, "if we still can't locate her."

"Where did you last see her?" Xan said.

"She was trying to get a response out of me," Ferdinand said. "She was very upset. She said she was going to go on a secret mission to evolve into something I could be proud of."

"Evolve? Again? That's . . . bad. Really bad," Xan said, alarm bells ringing in his head. "Did you stop her?"

"No, because she wasn't serious," Ferd said.

Xan's mouth fell open. "You're fucking kidding. You've got to be. You know her better than most—Tina doesn't make wild threats. She is capable of doing any of the shit that she threatens to do!"

"No, she isn't," Stephanie said. "There have been very few deaths recently and the bodies are either preserved in the medbay or have been recycled through the station's methods."

"No, did you forget all the dead Sundry? The fact that the station is hijacked?" He slid off the stool. "Shit, we have to do something."

"Absorbing one Sundry body will not affect a Gneiss her size," Ferdinand said, sounding strangely like he was a vet telling an owner that one small Hershey's Kiss won't kill their dog.

"One? But we're talking about thousands! How many Sundry had to die so the Cuckoos could take over?"

They were silent.

"Oh," Stephanie finally said.

"Hell. When did she leave here?" Xan asked.

"About two hours ago," Ferd said.

"I really don't think she would do this without one of us," Stephanie said. "There's nothing to worry about."

"Are you two high?" Xan asked. "How many times has she listened to you since becoming queen? She's probably off chowing down on dead insects and evolving into something that she thinks will protect her against your entire government, like a Death Star planet killer or something."

The floor rumbled as Steph and Ferdinand discussed.

"You guys are leaving me out of this!" Xan said after a few seconds.

"We will find Tina," Ferdinand finally said.

He said something else, but Xan was distracted by a tickle at the edge of his consciousness. It felt like the first touches of *Infinity* when they linked.

We're on our way. Please respond. We're coming.

26

MATA HARI AND THE SCARAB TIE

WHY ARE YOU doing your hair like that? You look like a 1970s housewife," Parker asked Amy. He'd arrived early for the dinner party, ostensibly to help Amy get her house ready, but instead had stumbled upon something he shouldn't have. Now he sat on her bed, a paper file folder—containing data that could end her career—open on his lap.

Amy sighed from the vanity, ran a brush through her long straight hair one more time, and then grabbed the concealer, dabbing some on her nose where a zit was threatening. "I'm the hostess, and I want to look good."

He pointed to a line on a document marked CONFIDENTIAL. "You didn't tell me you're a video game character."

"What does that mean?"

"You're turning personal interaction into a friendship spectrum. You tell people what they want to hear and give them gifts, and then their friendship meter goes up and up and then you get what you want. Possibly after sex, depending on which game you're playing."

"That's not what I do!"

"Sure you do, it's a spy thing," he said, leaning back on the bed and putting his feet on the bedspread. "I'm still trying to parse how this happened, though. You got the education, you got the teacher job, you got recruited, you got more education, you got the training, and now you have the secret job?"

"It's like you wrote the CIA brochure," she said wryly. "Besides, I'm not a classified spy. I'm just letting them know some things I learn about what's going on up there."

"And do your friends know?"

"Of course not."

He tipped his head to the side, curious. "What will your spy bosses do if they find out you told me?"

"I didn't tell you," she pointed out. "You rummaged through my things like a dirty raccoon."

"Don't dodge the question," he said. "Will you get in trouble?"

She put down the concealer and glared at him in the mirror. "Probably."

"And you're telling me they didn't need an entomologist for all of this secret alien insect work?" he said. "Just quantum physicists?"

Amy began applying foundation. "We had an entomologist," she said, rubbing vigorously. "I got you into the program when I could."

He flipped another page. "So did you get any Mata Hari training?"

She dropped the foundation bottle, startled. She swore and began searching for a tissue as the viscous brown liquid burbled out of the bottle.

He laughed, surprised. "Oh, my God. I was kidding. But you did! What did they train you to do? Dance? Seduce men? Stab them at the point of orgasm?"

She didn't answer. Her face turned bright red. She finished cleaning up the mess and then tossed the tissue. "Twin brothers aren't supposed to talk about orgasms."

"You weren't supposed to tell me that part, were you? I cracked you that fast?" he asked.

"I wasn't supposed to tell you any part," she muttered.

"You won't last in the field at all! You're a science nerd, Amy! Who are you supposed to seduce?" He sobered as the reality hit him. "This isn't a good idea. This is dangerous."

She had regained her composure and was finishing applying makeup. "Do you think I don't know that?" While Parker read, she hunted for her earrings, small pearl studs. She winced as she forced a stud through an earlobe that hadn't held an earring since she was in high school. She popped it through with a hiss, then dabbed a drop of blood off the lobe with a tissue.

"I'll be fine. I've been trained. And I'm not an assassin. I'm not trying to get powerful men naked and then stab them or anything. I'm just supposed to flirt. Get close to some people. Learn what they know."

"You're bad at that, too," Parker pointed out. "Your last boyfriend—"

"We are not talking about him right now," she said through clenched teeth. "In fact, it's safer to never talk about him."

"Fine. So tonight, is this a date, or are you practicing your sexy spy shit?"

"It is a dinner party," she said. "These are our friends. I'm not flirting or seducing anyone."

She whirled around, fixing her blue eyes on his green ones. "That said, you say nothing about Washington, or the CIA, or any Mata Hari shit. I'm serious, Parker. I wouldn't have told you anything if you hadn't been snooping in my bag."

"I think the CIA will want you to keep your files a little more secure than that, by the way," he said, pulling out his phone and looking at his rival entomologist's social media pages. "I'm sorry I snooped, but you spooks are supposed to be better."

She glared at him again, her jaw set. "Nothing, Parker. You could really fuck this up for me."

He raised his hands in surrender. "I'll never say anything. You can count on me. I still have the idea that you are going to be a video game character, find the right person that is most advantageous to romance, and then start giving the right gifts and saying the right things to make him love you. Shoving present coins in the empty soul of a middle-aged man until an engagement ring pops out! For the US of A!"

"Are you done?" Amy asked, putting the final touches on her makeup. She had spoken with three stylists to find the exact perfect look to draw in different kinds of men. It was fascinating and horrifying, the shit these people had figured out about the human condition.

Middle-aged men liked women with the flush of youth but still with the comfortable, confident look of an older woman. Maturity. Past giggling about prom, but before the first crow's-feet. Thirtyish men usually looked for a bit of power, or a bit of vulnerability, depending on the man. They weren't as sure about attracting a woman, and weren't sure what they wanted anymore.

Young men and old men will still bang anything younger than twenty-five, one stylist had told her, laughing. But then she gave her some pointers anyway.

Amy frowned at her blue eye shadow, wondering if it was too far on the side of subtle maturity tonight. The one thing Parker hadn't found was the identity of her intended target, and she was determined to keep it that way. So long as Parker didn't mess it up.

"I'm not even close to being done," Parker said. "But you have hostess stuff to do."

"And you were supposed to help me." She pointed to his teaching clothes. "Are you going to wear that to dinner?"

"I wore my scarab tie!" he protested. "I am dressed up!"

She sighed. All the work she had done to herself to elicit the perfect response, and her stupid twin put on a tie.

"Seriously, are you going to hit on these guys at dinner? Do you have to make someone fall in love with you, or sleep with them, for your new job?" he asked.

"I don't know!" she said, losing her cool and snatching the file out of his hands. "I am prepared for a lot of things. I have to go with what happens. But you can't go all brotherly on me, and you can't give up my secret. You have to trust me."

He hopped off her bed and made a show of straightening his shirt. "Will you trust me, then?"

"With what?"

"The same stuff. Flirting, seducing, murdering, and not needing your bailout."

She laughed out loud, but he didn't join her. And for one second, she wondered if he was serious.

He couldn't be. "Sure. I'll trust you."

"Do I ever get to hear who your target is?" he asked.

"I don't have one yet," she lied, then immediately felt bad. Her gaze on him softened, and she realized it might be time to drop the information. He would need to know sooner rather than later. She took his hands and they sat on the bed, facing each other. "There's one more thing you need to know. We're putting together a team to go to Station Eternity to get closer to the Sundry. I'm going to try to get you added to the trip."

"Great!" he said. "Will I get spy training?"

"No, Parker, listen to me," Amy said, squeezing his hands to get his attention. "It's going to be Max, you, me, Reggie, Oscar, and Don, my SBI friend. But you should know that Mallory Viridian lives on the station now."

"Mallory. M-Mallory from high school?" He winced. "You can't be serious."

"She is another reason I got training. Don has been researching her and the murders she's solved for years. He's been in contact with her for the last decade or so," Amy said. "He knows more about her than anyone on Earth. I need that connection and I need what he knows; our childhood isn't enough."

"You want me to go into space on a covert mission, pretend that this SBI guy is a family friend, and face the girl I was in love with when we were sixteen who has ignored me for fifteen years. While we're surrounded by aliens."

"Is that a problem?" she asked, raising an eyebrow.

He fell backward onto the bed, holding his forehead. "No, no, it's great. Just as long as I get to meet some Sundry."

He was quiet for a moment, then made a face. "And Oscar's coming?"

"Yeah, just ignore him if you can," Amy said. "There was nothing I could do about it."

"God. Mallory." His voice held the hurt of years.

"This is bigger than your broken heart," she said. "Don't come if you can't handle it."

"I haven't talked to her since prom," he said. "Have you been in touch with her?"

"No, and she hasn't reached out either," Amy pointed out. "Parker. Can you handle this?"

"What does she have to do with anything you're working on?" he asked.

She pursed her lips, considering. Then she said, "That's classified. I just need to go to the station, reconnect with Mallory, and learn what I can about the Sundry. Don can't know we know her either, and we have to be surprised to see her," she added. "I don't want Don to think we're friends just because of his connection with Mallory."

"But you are, aren't you?" Parker asked. "Is that your target? That old guy?"

Amy hid her grimace by collecting her coat from the back of her desk chair. Parker knew her better than anyone, but she wasn't going to make it far if she couldn't keep secrets from him. Her computer monitor woke up at the slight movement, showing a red screen with a password prompt. Underneath the prompt, it said, "YOU HAVE 2/5 ATTEMPTS LEFT."

"Parker," she said, her voice low. "Have you been snooping on my PC?"

He sat up. "Of course I have. Why does that surprise you?"

"I'm not kidding when I say that this information is dangerous! You already know too much. I told you because I didn't want you to make up assumptions. I didn't intend to ignite your curiosity!"

"You told me because I found you out," he said. "And I wasn't going to try all five times!"

"If that fifth attempt fails, my whole system gets bricked. It will run an auto-erase program. A message will be sent to my boss to tell them I have been compromised. This isn't snooping just to fuck with my *Overwatch 3* inventory like you did when we were fifteen. Stop fucking around!"

"What's the problem?" he complained. "I didn't guess your password. You must have gotten better at setting them."

She put her hands on her hips. "Parker," she said dangerously.

He held his hands up. "All right, all right, I'll lay off. I'm sorry."

She glared at him, her heart hammering. Had she been wrong to trust him? She didn't know anymore. "Come on, I need you at dinner. I've got men to test flirting on."

"One is gay, one is your brother, one is your gay brother, and one is straight but married," Parker said, counting them off.

"That still leaves two, dammit," Amy said, and swept from the room, trying her best to exude 1940s bombshell energy.

OSCAR ARRIVED FIRST to the party, winking at her and leaning in for exaggerated kisses to both cheeks. His bald head was shiny and his grin was infectious. He wore a bloodred velvet track-suit, which was a super-expensive designer tracksuit—he made sure everyone knew—and carried a six-pack of beer.

"Good to see you, Oscar," she said. "Congratulations, I heard the team did well on the road last night."

"Oh, you watched, did you?" he asked, winking at her. "I thought I felt something." He handed over the six-pack. "I brought Rolling Rock."

"Classy. I'll put this in the fridge," Parker said from behind Amy, taking the beer.

"Parker, we have guests," Amy said, putting a disapproving tone into her voice. He smiled a great big fake smile at her. She didn't know if he was making fun of her or trying on his own persona, but he was messing with her mojo.

Oscar wandered to the living room, where he grabbed a fistful of peanuts and dropped them into his mouth like a backhoe dumping dirt.

Amy watched him from the doorway. Parker came up behind her. "Are you sure that's what you want to practice your flirting on?" he asked.

She pursed her lips, then straightened her back and walked into the room, all smiles. It didn't matter whom she had to flirt with. That wasn't the point.

Her superiors had trained her in the subtler techniques because that was standard for women going abroad, but they hadn't expected her to need it. Flirting her way out of a hostage situation with humans was one thing. They didn't think she would need to flirt her way out of a situation with aliens. She shuddered at the thought.

But the flirting was something she wasn't very good at; Parker was right. So if she had some training from the best, she might as well use it. Oscar was dumb, but Reggie liked him, or at least he worked with him, and he always seemed to be around when Reggie and Max came over. Then there was Don, who hung around in a hopeful-widower kind of way. Parker always wanted to know why he didn't get friends his own age, but at least he didn't say that in Don's presence.

Of course, the stuff she was supposed to be paying covert attention to was the movements of the various aliens, namely, the Sundry. She was also to be on the lookout for alien tech, gotten either through diplomacy or by other means. How was she supposed to steal data from folks when half of their computers were sentient? That was something she was supposed to figure out on her own.

She had already messed up big-time with Parker figuring her out, but there was nothing to do about that right now. Right now she had a dinner party to throw and some people to charm. She had a brother-in-law, who was a lot more fun than her stuffy brother, to hug, and the McRaes from the English department were always fun to talk to, especially when they started throwing nerd trivia at Parker.

"You've got a real housewife-from-one-hundred-years-ago energy going on right now," Oscar said, coming up to her from behind. "I didn't know you were throwing a costume party."

"So I dressed vintage, what's the big deal?" she asked, forgetting her flirtatious mask. She cringed internally and then smiled at him. "Or are you trying to say I look nice?"

He appraised her, leering slightly. "Well, you definitely do look like a snack," he said. "I just always imagined you as tougher."

"I can be tough in a dress, Oscar," she said reprovingly. "Do you want to see how tough?" She fluttered her eyelashes.

"The flower has thorns, eh?" he asked.

She poured herself a glass of Chardonnay. "Exactly," she said, screwing the top closed. "Can I get you something to drink?"

He held up the beer he had gotten for himself. "I'm good. I wanted to tell you something."

"Sure, what's that?" she asked, checking her wineglass for lipstick smears.

"I am launching a side project, doing a website, kind of a content hub. Reggie's on board. I'm doing some celeb gossip, some industry news, the like."

"Celeb gossip?" she asked. "You live in North Carolina. What celeb gossip are you going to get? Coach Laetner caught with another hooker? The mayor of Greensboro getting high during a town council meeting?"

He looked at her pityingly. "Such limited range, Amy," he said. "You don't need to be in Hollywood to spy on the stars anymore. Hack their phones, hack their digital assistants, hack their laptops. But I wanted you to know that I have been testing out my knowledge on my friends." He tapped his nose and winked at her. "And I got your secret. Don't worry. It's safe."

He walked away, guzzling his beer. Amy watched him go, fists balled so tightly that one of her fake nails popped off.

Parker swooped in and picked it up for her. "Uh, you dropped this. It's kind of gross." He saw her face and immediately stopped the teasing act. "What happened?"

"Nothing," she said with a bright smile. "Thanks for getting this for me." She sauntered away, dropping the nail into the kitchen garbage can.

27

. . .

RIP CALVIN SHUTTLE

THE PASSENGER MANIFEST didn't provide Mallory with a lot of information beyond names, addresses, and ages. Jessica's notes had more information, but the first glance through gave Mallory a bunch of information she didn't need. Despite having had background checks run through several investigative agencies, this group of suspects looked ridiculously normal.

She took a moment and slowed down, carefully reading a second time. Pertinent information started to appear. Amy's and Parker's work with the Sundry (post–First Contact) was well-documented. Amy's husband, Calvin Shuttle, was registered as dead—Jessica even had a scan of the death certificate.

Mallory looked at the name "Calvin Shuttle" and smiled.

Oscar's history with coaching and his online presence were there, too. So was a criminal record, but it was marked classified.

Reggie had stretched the truth on his past, since he didn't mention that he'd been disbarred after he'd been fired from his last job. So if he left trashy gossip work, there wasn't a lot he could do. Did Max know?

Max had an adoption application in with several agencies, but his was the only name on the application. That looked like someone who wanted a divorce.

Amy and Draughn were registered as members of a grieving-spouses support group, some of whom made up the intramural softball team called the Xocolatl.

She flipped to Jessica Brass's background, which was more extensive.

Xan was right to be impressed with this woman. She was captain of her college basketball team, captain of the WNBA team the Raleigh Audreys, Raleigh councilwoman, mayor of Raleigh, and US congresswoman before her job on Eternity. She had a reputation for being firm and fair, and it was advised not to stand in her way.

"But why try to kill her?" Mallory said aloud. "What did she know? Or see? Or did someone stand up to her and it got violent?"

Xan had said there was little sign of struggle or any kind of disruption to the apartment. It was like she had opened the door to a trick-or-treater and gotten hit with a blunt object.

She was no closer to finding the weapons either. Oscar had been stabbed; Jessica had been bludgeoned with one strike, with considerable force. A restaurant was the perfect place to stab someone since there were so many possible weapons just lying around. And bludgeoning was a spur-of-the-moment attack; any hard object would do if the person was hit in the right place.

Four Sundry buzzed through the small crack in her bedroom door to circle her head.

"What's going on, guys?" she asked.

"Denial. No. Impossible. We cannot get data for you in our current state."

Mallory put down her tablet with Jessica's background. "Where's this coming from? I didn't ask you to," she said.

"Desire, seeking, research. You want data." The Sundry hovered briefly in front of her.

"Well, yeah, I need more information about this murder, but

I'm not about to send you on a mission that will get you killed," she said. "You need every Sundry you've got right now!"

"Unity. Belonging. Hive. We help our own."

That's new. The Sundry she knew were not altruistic.

They buzzed back into her bedroom, where no doubt they were chewing her socks down to paste. She'd managed to convince them to give her a few pairs of underwear and a sweatshirt, but they'd taken nearly everything else of hers for the hive.

The idea of them offering help and wishing they could provide data was new. Was this due to the new queen? Or had they glimpsed their own mortality and had a Scrooge-like turnaround to change their ways? They didn't have a lot of processing power with their current population, but they had enough to communicate with her and show regret at not being able to help. Mallory didn't have the time to pursue this, but she wondered.

A knock interrupted her thoughts. "Who is it?" she yelled. She didn't want to share her Sundry secret with a lot of people. She wanted to ask Parker about his thoughts, but she couldn't trust his connection with the Cuckoos.

"It's Amy," came the answer.

Mallory manually opened the door and then closed it quickly behind Amy.

"Gosh, it's an oven in here," Amy said when she stepped into the room. She surveyed the apartment with her hands on her hips. "Do you always keep it this warm?"

"Not always," Mallory said evasively. "What can I do for you?"

"I can't find Parker," she said, her forehead creased with worry. "I don't know if he's just pouting in his room because of your fight, or went wandering, or—what if the killer got him?"

Mallory glanced toward her bedroom, her immediate thought to send the Sundry out to find him, but that would be too dangerous.

"Did you talk to him before he disappeared?" she asked.

"No, you told me what you guys had talked about and I didn't see him afterward. I figured I'd give him some time." Amy's eyes filled with tears. "I shouldn't have left him alone!"

"Come on," Mallory said, "he's the luckiest unlucky guy in the world. And the massive hivemind controlling this whole space station is looking out for him. I think he'll be okay. But—" She was about to say that the Cuckoos weren't sentient and therefore might not be as protective if instinct couldn't inform them that Parker was in danger, but she didn't want to scare Amy. Also, what if the Cuckoos had tried to bring Parker physically to their hive, the way the silver Sundry had tried to incorporate Mallory into their hivemind while her body was dying?

She sent a message to Devanshi, then told Amy, "I have a friend who used to be in security. She'll help us out if she can. Until I hear from her, can I ask a few more questions?"

Amy shifted from foot to foot, arms crossed tightly over her chest. She glanced around the room like a frightened horse.

"There's nothing else we can do right now," Mallory said gently, gesturing to the couch. "Have a seat. I only have a few things."

"Fine," Amy said.

"Can you tell me what you did yesterday before the party? I heard that you and Parker were wandering the station, but Reggie also said that Oscar was interviewing some of the residents of the station and Reggie couldn't come because there would be too many cooks. That implied that Oscar wasn't alone. Were you with him?"

Amy frowned and looked around the room as if trying to spot an exit. "Yes," she finally said. "Parker and I wanted to talk to some Sundry but we hadn't been able to secure interviews. Oscar apparently had." She took a moment to look disgusted, for herself or Oscar, Mallory wasn't sure. "I wanted to see if I could piggyback on his interview with the silver. Parker split off to talk to the blue."

Mallory nodded. "The silver don't have a diplomatic presence on the station, and they live in the shuttle bay." She thought of the hivemind of the station, the seething swarm of blue and silver insects. "Well, mostly the shuttle bay. On a normal day when the Cuckoos aren't taking over and killing everyone, I mean. What did Oscar say?"

"He grinned and told me it was a date. I lasted through two meetings with the Gneiss and the Silence before I couldn't take his comments and putting his arm around me. So much for the attempt to contact the silver." She grimaced. "He was so creepy."

"Why were you nice to him at the party?" Mallory asked. "He was hitting on you there, too, right?"

She shrugged, crossing her arms tighter. "I'd had some wine and told myself I could tolerate it to be friendly. I didn't want to blow him off in a diplomatic setting. So I went along with the joke."

"Was there another reason?" Mallory asked.

"What, that I really liked him?" Amy asked, finally meeting Mallory's eyes. "If I'd wanted to sleep with him, don't you think that our time alone before the party would have been the better place than the crowded reception?"

"I don't think you liked him," Mallory said. "But someone like that is good to use as a signal to tell someone else that you're not interested, or to make someone jealous."

Amy's face turned red and she pressed her lips together.

"You told me about your husband who died in DC," Mallory said. "I'm so impressed that you got Calvin Shuttle logged as a death in the public record, when we made him up in high school."

Amy looked stricken and then winced and smacked her hand over her mouth, defeated.

Mallory leaned forward. "Did you think I wouldn't notice?"

"It's not like you were anywhere near me when I did it. I didn't expect to have to lie to you about it," Amy said grimly.

"I have so many questions," Mallory said. "I am guessing you did it with a document forger—which I would bet Oscar dabbled in. Or he somehow found out about it. And that would be an interesting secret to hold over you."

Amy had grown quite tense, but then relaxed slightly. "Yeah, he helped me with the documents."

"I thought that might be it. But why did you need proof of a fake husband anyway? Lying would have been so much easier. Then the question of why you did it came up; what do you do with a dead husband? Be able to mark 'widowed' on your doctor forms. And . . . maybe enter a grief support group where a vulnerable SBI agent was mourning his wife. Clearly you were sent there to befriend him. But why? Why get solid proof of a dead husband to befriend an aging, cranky SBI agent? What did he have that you wanted? That no one else did?"

Mallory smiled bitterly and answered her own question. "Me. No one in law enforcement knew more about me than Agent Don Draughn. No one would have more extensive data on me. You needed access to his records, and possibly his opinions. The only thing I can take from this is that you, and probably Parker, are working with the government to find shit about me. This is why you acted all surprised that I was here. You didn't want Draughn knowing you knew me."

Amy assessed her coolly. "You think a lot of yourself, don't you? Why do you think you're so important? You're a middleman, Mallory. You're the link to the Sundry. Nothing else."

It hurt more than she expected it to. She swallowed it down. "But then you got here and all the Sundry were dead. That had to suck."

Amy pursed her lips. "Yeah. It did."

"But back to Oscar, and him hitting on you. Your plan backfired, didn't it? Draughn fell in love with you. Or you with him. Were you trying to warn him off? Make him jealous? What?"

Amy relaxed, slumping in defeat. "It doesn't matter. I've already said too much. I'm not cut out for this crap."

"Why didn't you just contact me? Why go through all of this runaround?" Mallory asked, baffled.

She didn't answer.

"You realize you look really bad here, right?" Mallory asked. "If Oscar knew you were CIA, that's a reason to kill him. If Jessica found out about you and saw you as a threat, that was a reason to kill her. Anyone could have picked up something sharp in the restaurant."

Amy rolled her eyes. "Oh, come on, Mallory, I was unconscious all night. How could I have stabbed Jessica?"

She thought Jessica was *stabbed*? The knot in her chest relaxed. She was about to correct Amy when four blue Sundry came out of her bedroom to circle them.

Amy gasped and ducked her head.

"Oh, real subtle, guys. I'm trying to protect you and then you just parade out here?" Mallory yelled at them.

"Where did they come from? I thought all the blue were dead," Amy said. The four Sundry landed on her arm. She flinched slightly but remained still.

"Relaxed. Trustworthy. Friend. Mallory trusts this one, so we trust her."

Amy glanced at Mallory, her arm held in front of her as if it were a bomb. "What do they mean?"

"Amy, did you murder Oscar?" Mallory asked.

"No."

"Is the CIA here to harm the Sundry?"

"No, just to gather data," she said.

"Fine. They say you're in the clear for the attacks." Mallory pointed to the insects tasting Amy's arm. "Which I already knew because you thought Jessica was stabbed. She wasn't," Mallory said.

"You're trusting me on that? I could have been lying," Amy said.

"They would have tasted the shift in your hormones if you were lying," Mallory explained. "So you've been cleared twice."

"Why not just bring everyone in here to question them?" Amy asked.

"Because no one is supposed to know about them," Mallory said pointedly to the Sundry. "Also, there aren't a lot of them. It's too dangerous to expose them to too many people. But since they're already okay with meeting you, follow me."

She led the way to her bedroom and forced the door wider.

It was impressive how fast the Sundry could build when spurred on by an outside threat. Mallory didn't know how many eggs the queens had laid, but both hives were noticeably larger. The pile of T-shirts had dwindled to about two. Mallory winced as she saw her favorite band's shirt being masticated by three silver Sundry, but she knew it had to be done. She would burn her favorite book for heat if she was freezing to death, after all.

"Holy shit," Amy whispered.

Mallory walked over to her bed, where the blue hive loomed. They had started destroying her pillow, having already destroyed her sheets. "Sundry. This is Amy Valor. She's from Earth and has studied your people for quite some time now. I thought you two might benefit from meeting. She might be able to help you."

A blue Sundry half the length of Mallory's forearm crawled from the hive, her antennae waving. She launched herself at Amy, who looked fascinated. Amy held her arm out like she was a falconer, and the queen landed.

Four workers came to hover behind the queen, and they spoke. "Curious. Bravery. Greetings. Mallory has said nothing of your appearance here."

"That was partly because I didn't know she was coming, and partly because I thought you all were dead, and I didn't know that she was interested in talking to you," Mallory interjected. "But you go ahead and talk."

"You are magnificent," Amy said, eyes wide. She studied the queen, gently turning her forearm from side to side so she could see the queen from all angles. At the same time, the queen tasted her, antennae probing her skin. They were both silent for some time. At last Amy said, "I'm so glad you survived the attack on your hive. I have some things to discuss, but I'd rather have my brother here. And I understand if this isn't the best time."

"Confusion. Defiance. Pragmatic. It's a fine time since we are only laying eggs and building the hive. Hunger. Annoyance. Desperation. We are hungry and can't afford to send scouts to feed us."

Mallory got the hint. "You sure you don't need me to stay?"

Amy looked at her, all business. "This is a confidential meeting, so you shouldn't be here anyway."

"You know I'm part of the hivemind, right?" Mallory said, annoyed. "Okay. Food. Got it." She was amazed at how quickly the teen emotions of being left out could return when high school friends came back into her life.

Mallory didn't have to go far. Her fridge had several pieces of fruit that she'd gotten from the Sundry themselves, and she'd also had sugar imported from Earth. She boiled some water to make a supersaturated solution and dumped the sugar in, stirring slowly.

The small kitchen table used to hold whatever book she was reading, or some notes she kept. It was cleaned off completely, and whatever notes she'd had were lost to the hive in her bedroom. She arranged the fruit around the table and put the sugar solution in a bowl to cool. Then she stared at the feast for the Sundry and realized that since she had discovered some had survived, she didn't feel askew anymore. She was still wary around them, but they were part of her, like it or not, and fighting that was actively hurting herself. Especially if she wanted to solve this murder.

Mallory went to her couch and lay down on it, closed her eyes, and relaxed.

THE SUNDRY WERE few, but close and loud. They were nearby, her hive was theirs. A few workers came into the room to investigate the food she'd set out, and the room was viewed through compound eyes. She touched the single hivemind gingerly, worrying about the deluge of information, but there was none. She saw what that Sundry saw, tasted what it tasted, felt its sense of duty as it grabbed morsels of fruit to return to its queen.

"Negative. Resistance. Refusal. The hive is in no shape to help the humans currently. Eggs. Males. Soldiers. Our priority is to build up our population."

"I understand completely," Amy was saying. "We are sympathetic. We want to offer the use of our chemical technology to help you while your numbers are weakened. My brother has developed several synthetic pheromones as well as essential oils with which to communicate. Your people will not be in danger of Cuckoo infestation while you're rebuilding."

Weren't the pheromones designed to work against the blue, to fool them? Why did Amy lie to them?

The buzzing sound in the other room immediately intensified. "Betrayal. Family. Danger. Pheromones for the enemy to infiltrate us, your sibling is a Cuckoo!"

"No, I'm not lying! Parker's loyal, I promise!" Amy's voice was tight but not panicked.

"Oh, shit," Mallory said. She rolled off the couch and ran back into the bedroom. "Amy, the queen already has everything she needs. She has food, protection, and a place to lay her eggs. The blue and silver are working together to stay safe. There is nothing else they need except time." She whirled and faced the blue nest. "If Amy were considering betraying you, she would have protected herself with the pheromones in case things went wrong. But she came in here with no synthetics on her skin; she is completely vulnerable to you."

The hive considered this, buzzing angrily but articulating nothing. "Unresolved. Twin. Parker. What of the brother, is he a threat?"

"Honestly, I don't know. I need to find him," Mallory said. "But I don't think either of these humans have intentions to harm you. Taste Amy to see if she's lying."

The swarm, small but angry, descended, and Amy tensed briefly as they landed. They didn't sting. They probed, tasted, crawled over her hands, face, and neck. She was a lot calmer than Mallory ever was when they did that to her. Then they took flight again.

"Truth. Apprehension. Insistence. Find the brother and bring him to us, Mallory." Then the Sundry returned to their jobs as if Amy and Mallory weren't there.

Mallory took Amy's arm and gently pulled her out of the room.

"Oh, my gosh, what happened there?" Amy asked, sagging against Mallory in relief.

"They figured out about Parker. I don't know if they got it from me or what. But I thought the pheromones were only to be used against the blue," Mallory said. She deposited Amy onto the couch, then flopped down beside her with a sigh.

"How did you know all that?" Amy asked. "How I was clean, no oils, et cetera."

"You and Parker were wearing the pheromones last night. I know that because I reacted strongly to them. Parker said you were wearing stuff to see how it worked. When you mentioned the essential oils, I caught from the Sundry that mint odors were part of the hated scents. If you're going to betray someone, you want to wear a bulletproof vest, so you would have been an idiot to walk in here without any protection. Anyway, I told you I'm part of the hivemind," Mallory said, leaning her head back on the couch. "By default they're going to know a lot of what I know. You should have figured this out if you studied about me. Did you think that you could have hidden that from her for the whole of your discussion? I'm connected to the hivemind and I have trouble hiding shit from them!"

Amy rubbed her upper arms, hugging herself. "That was scary." She shuddered as if shaking off the last of the crawly feelings. "I need Parker here."

"If they'll talk to him," Mallory reminded her. "They might just see him as a Cuckoo."

"Great," Amy said. "Let's find him and then we can see how they react."

Find Parker. Despite feeling tense and annoyed at Amy, she wanted Parker found, too. Especially if he was where she thought he was.

Devanshi messaged Mallory back. She was ready to help find Parker.

"Go back to your room," Mallory said. "You don't want to stay in here more than you have to. It's an oven."

"Also, you don't trust me alone in your apartment with the Sundry."

"No, I don't. You may not be a murderer or mean the Sundry harm, but that doesn't mean you can't fuck stuff up, and I think we have some trust issues to work through."

"If you think it's worth the time," Amy said with a shrug.

"Be careful out there," Mallory said, ignoring her jab.

"Just find him," Amy said. "Don't worry about me."

28

TINA APPOINTS A COURT ADVISER

TINA HOVERED OUTSIDE the air lock, holding on to the handle so Eternity wouldn't fly away without her. She wished again that she hadn't grown so large. Perhaps she'd made a mistake. Moving around the station was a pain, having to duck through everything. Flying around the station was much better, if lonely. But when she went outside the station, she could think.

Thinking was hard. Several centuries younger than her friends, and frankly, more positive and friendly than all of them put together, she didn't have their talent for thinking through boring, detailed things. She'd rather think about hosting parties on Bezoar.

She tried to talk to the station drone that she had grabbed earlier from its job doing an outside repair. But she didn't make any noise in space. She always forgot that.

The drone sat in the hollow cavity on her back that she had grown to carry smaller beings. It had seemed like a good idea at the time, but she was surprised how infrequently Mallory, Xan, or any other human wished to ride there. But now it held a drone and its precious cargo.

Her finger hovered above the air lock button. If she flew on her own, Eternity would slowly outpace her, but they were close enough to Bezoar for her to make the rest of the trip alone.

A small figure appeared in the air lock. He put his face up to the window, spotted her, then jumped back. It was a human. He was tiny, like Mallory's size. He had dark hair and green eyes. He looked up at her with interest.

Sound didn't travel through space, no matter how loud she screamed. Tina knew this. She also knew what explosive decompression was, and what it could do to a human. She remembered this from Mallory's patient lessons. But she needed to tell the wet little person to get out of the air lock so she could come in. She pounded on the door a few times. His eyes got bigger, and he stepped back so the air lock could close.

Her door opened and she drifted inside until she was within Eternity's gravity field, and then she dropped to the floor. She closed the exterior door and waited for the room to fill with air so she could exit.

Air. So much time and energy wasted on something no one could see.

The human was still there. He looked up at her, craning his neck back. "Hi, Tina," he said.

"Yes. Should I call you tiny human?"

His face moved. Human faces were so busy! They moved constantly like worms crawled underneath their skin. Mallory had once told her that human faces telegraphed emotion much more than words did, but it was like trying to learn the Silence's sign language. Who had time for that? Just say what you feel!

"We met yesterday," he reminded her. "I'm Parker."

"Oh, yes! You know Mallory. And you know all about the Sundry."

"Yes," he said. He stopped looking up at her, which frankly relieved her since she didn't have to try to figure out what all his facial movements meant. "Mallory was an old friend of mine. But not anymore, I don't think."

"What happened?" Tina asked. "Maybe I can help. I like fixing things. I'm really good at it."

"I betrayed her trust, but I didn't know I was doing it," he said. "I don't know if she'll ever forgive me."

Tina thought for a second. "I'm not sure I understand what you mean. I mean, I understand all the words, but not them together. But my friends get mad at me all the time, and we're still friends! My friend Ferdinand? He left today! But he'll forgive me and come back."

Tina looked around the air lock. "Wait a second. You shouldn't be in the air lock. Your little wet bodies shouldn't be outside without a suit on. If you space yourself like this, it might be exciting for a little bit, but you'd get cold very fast. And then probably freeze to death."

"It's tempting," he said with a large breath. "I came out because I saw you and was worried about you being outside. I forgot that Gneiss can survive in a vacuum."

"What would you have done?" Tina asked. "You don't know me, and you're tiny."

"Well, anything I could, I guess. I hadn't thought it through, just wanted to make sure that you were okay."

"If I'm okay," Tina said thoughtfully. "I hadn't thought of myself like that. I am queen, that's metal. I have a limousine ride to my home planet, which is really fucking metal. But using the limo made a lot of my friends really angry, which is less than metal. And the Cuckoos, well. That's a big mess right there. That's too complicated. I don't know if I'm okay or not!"

"Sounds about like me. I found the girl I loved from high school, I made a huge scientific breakthrough, my science made the girl not trust me ever again, and, oh, yeah, she told me I was symbiotically connected to the chaotic bugs driving the station." He leaned against the wall and slid down until he was sitting on the floor.

This really irritated Tina, since he was even farther away from her. With a grunt, she went through the process of sitting on the floor next to him. It took a while. "So you're symbiotically connected to the Cuckoos? That's so metal!"

"Is it? I don't see the upsides to it."

"Not a lot of humans have connected to the Sundry."

"Are Cuckoos considered Sundry?" he asked. "There are obvious similarities, but the Sundry seem vastly more intelligent."

"They want to be, so I'm trying it out. If they can spin it right, they can be the green Sundry!"

"I'm not sure that will make people overlook the fact that they have to commit mass murder to build a home," Parker said, frowning.

"Stop interrupting," Tina said. "I was talking. Oh, right, connections to the Sundry. First Mallory, then you, then . . . I don't know of anyone else. Maybe there will be thousands someday. You'll figure it out." She reached out a hand to pat him on the back the way she had seen humans do it but remembered what Xan told her about touching humans and withdrew it. "I mean, one bonus is you can talk to them, right? And right now, I'm the only other person on the station who can do that. It's like we're in a club!"

Parker laughed. "A club I didn't expect to be in," he said. "But what do you mean, I can talk to them?"

"You should be able to understand them if you're linked to them. If there are four or more, you can talk to them. If you connect with the hivemind, you can learn a lot of things! I can't do that yet since they can't sting me, so I don't know any more to tell you."

"Yet?" he asked. "When do you plan to?"

"Oh, I don't know, it's just something I say. I don't like saying things are impossible," she said idly.

"What were you doing outside the station?" he asked.

"I'm very large, too large for these halls, and I wanted room to stretch out. I definitely can't ride the elevators anymore, so I found moving via the outside of the station faster. It's a bonus that vacuum doesn't bother me. Getting some alone time was good for me, too, since I have my own problems." She felt very important having problems beyond "not knowing what people are talking about."

"What are your problems?" he asked.

"My central government is mad at me for turning into a fucking metal battle mech," she said. "Then they were mad at me for escaping the planet after they tried to imprison me for being a fucking metal battle mech. So now I'm going to the planet where I'm in charge, where at least I'll be safe. I'm just hoping to beat them there. Oh, and my best friend is really mad at me. Oh, and even though the Cuckoos are doing me a favor by taking me back to Bezoar, they wouldn't do it if it didn't help them. They help me when I have requests on the station like 'open that door' or 'bring comms online dammit because the other sentients need it or they might die,' but I can't control them. Once we get to Bezoar and they send a shuttle down to get the rest of their people, they might then take Eternity and then take over the galaxy and kill all the Sundry. And people will blame *me* even though they had already taken the station before I got here!"

"Wow. I have no idea how to respond to any of that," he said.

"Oh, go on, try. Stephanie and Ferdinand are always telling me to appreciate others' opinions, which I do when they match my own. You fix my problems and then I can fix yours. Then we'll be friends."

"All right," Parker said thoughtfully. "You can't change the fact that you're a battle mech—"

"A *fucking metal* battle mech," Tina interrupted. "And I can change it, but I don't want to."

"—sorry, a fucking metal battle mech. You don't want to

change that, so your government is just going to have to get over it. If they haven't stripped you of your title already, then you probably will be safe on your planet."

"But you can't guarantee that."

"Well, you already knew that! I just met you and don't know much about the Gneiss. I'm just trying to think logically. As for your friend, you should apologize to him if he's mad at you."

Before he could continue, she interrupted him with a fist to the floor. He jumped.

"Apologize? I'm a queen," she said, knowing that would explain everything.

"You should always respect your friends," he said. "If you stop admitting when you're wrong, then your friends can't trust you. Then they won't really be friends."

"Oh," she said. "But I like my friends."

"Exactly," he said.

She rolled the idea around her head for a bit, then wondered if she should apologize to Ferdinand. Stephanie had been messaging her constantly to find out where she was, and she ignored her, tired of explaining herself. But Ferdinand was still angry.

The real question was, would the station be going to Bezoar if she hadn't asked it to? She wasn't sure. She'd like to think so, but she'd like to think a lot of things. She wanted to apologize to him right then but realized she was already in the middle of something important. She felt very proud that she recognized that she should wait to talk to him, so proud that she told Stephanie how proud she was that she waited. Then she decided to apologize to Ferdinand anyway, so she sent a small thrum of apology to him through the floor.

Stephanie immediately sent a message demanding to know where she was, but she didn't answer. If they didn't know, then they couldn't tell her what to do. That wasn't the same as not respecting her friends' advice, she was pretty sure.

"Are you okay?" asked Parker.

"Oh, yeah, forgot you were there," Tina said. "Thanks, little human. I should have you as one of my advisers. Want me to try to fix your problems now?"

"Sure," he said.

"That apology thing is a good idea. Apologize to Mallory. She gets mad and yells about murder a lot. But she doesn't have a lot of friends, probably because of all the murder. A lot of people leave her. If you say you're sorry, maybe she won't want you to leave, too."

"Hey, you're just taking what I suggested and turning it back on me!" he protested.

"Not so easy now that it's you, is it?" she asked.

"Fair," he admitted. "I apologized, but she didn't take it well. She doesn't think she can trust me."

"You'll have to prove it to her. Jump off of something very tall."

He shook his head and his eyes grew wide. "What are you talking about?"

"Your media always seems to have big grand gestures involving jumping off of things. They often involve trust. I viewed a video with two humans linking hands and driving a car into the Grand Canyon. That was trust."

"That was Thelma and Louise committing suicide so they don't get caught by the cops in an unfair system," Parker said flatly.

"See? Trust!"

"Okay, let's put that as a maybe. You didn't solve my Cuckoo problem."

"And you didn't solve mine," she said. "They tend to be rather large problems even though they're such tiny beings. But there are a lot of them. I just wish they would listen to me. Or you. To someone. Like we could just say, 'Hey, Cuckoos, stop being assholes!'"

His eyes got wide, so wide Tina was worried there was going to be another mess on their hands. "Holy shit, Tina. Holy shit. I've got it."

"You do?" she asked eagerly.

"Yes! I just need a few things. Can you meet me in the shuttle bay?"

"Fucking metal, I'll beat you there! We're going on an adventure!" She sent a quick message to Stephanie telling her that everything was going to be okay and she would fix everything. Then she lifted her hand the way she had seen humans do. Since she had absorbed the human Calliope, these human actions felt more and more natural. But she remembered to let Parker make the move to actually high-five.

He shrank back as her hand rose, but then he saw that she was waiting. He carefully smacked her immovable stone, then shook his hand.

"Let's go."

She took two lumbering steps out of the air lock, but a buzzing sound filled the air. She turned and saw the human engulfed in a swarm of green bodies. He didn't yell in pain or fear, which Tina was very used to, so she just watched, confused. Parker then slowly left the air lock, turned the opposite way from Tina, and walked, still engulfed in insects.

"So, I'll meet you there, then?" she called after him. "The shuttle bay! Don't forget!"

29

. . .

Devanshi &
Adrian &
Mallory &
Parker &
Tina

"Tʜᴀɴᴋs ꜰᴏʀ ʙʀɪɴɢɪɴɢ Adrian," Mallory said sardonically. They'd been crawling through the vents for what felt
like hours. Mallory's back was aching and her knees were bruised
from all the toddler movement. Adrian's constant commentary
spurred her along, giving her the strength of spite, if nothing else.

"Aren't you supposed to stop things before they get this bad?"
he whined.

"When did I ever claim I could do that?" she said. "I'm not
even solving the murder right now. I'm doing an errand!" She bit
back the part about doing it for the queen.

"So you're not running after your boyfriend?"

"Fuck, Adrian, you sound like you're thirteen. Gonna do the
K-I-S-S-I-N-G song at me next?"

"I'm so glad I befriended humans," Devanshi said from ahead, barely visible in the vent. She sounded like the tired mom of six-year-old twins.

One thing Adrian didn't do was complain about the crawling, and he was the king of complainers; he had a whole book of complaints. So when it came to her aching body, she just bit her tongue.

The buzzing ahead intensified, as did the heat. "Is this safe?" Mallory whispered when she caught up to Devanshi.

"Of course it's not safe," Devanshi said. "We're crawling through an artery of a living space station, about to disrupt her Heart. What made you think this is safe?"

"Fine, fine," Mallory grumbled.

"We can turn back," Adrian said from behind her. "I'd love a hot bath about now."

"No. Parker's in there."

"Are you absolutely sure?" Adrian said. "I thought since the Sundry were dead, you don't have your special voodoo powers."

"Grow up, Adrian," she snapped.

After escorting Amy out of her apartment, she had slipped back in and tried to see if she could sense Parker. She'd been able to do it in high school, but she just thought it was her imagination plus hormones. But if she'd wanted to find him, she always could.

In her living room, she sat on the couch with some Sundry scouts beside her. "Don't sting me," she warned. "I'm just going to try something."

She closed her eyes and sought the Sundry in the other room, feeling a solid connection with the blue and a nearly recognizable connection with the silver. Contacting the silver felt like having a passable knowledge of Spanish and hearing Portuguese. It felt like she should understand it, and it sounded similar, but she struggled.

With her eyes closed, she could sense the other Sundry entities on the station. A few blue and silver sparked here and there. Either scouts sent from Mallory's room or solo, lost insects who were seeking a hive, but probably would meet their doom if they found the Cuckoos first.

The Cuckoos were hard to pinpoint, but they were there. All she had to do was look for more "blue" Sundry, and she found their camouflaged presence at the Heart of the Station, where they had taken over the hives and station operations. And amid that mass of blue was one gleaming presence, a searchlight above a city, a member of the hive that wasn't a Cuckoo. Parker was definitely with the Cuckoos. Why, or how, Mallory didn't know. But she could find out.

She'd asked Devanshi if she would escort Mallory if she had to go through the vent shafts, and Devanshi had arrived with her ever-present companion. But Mallory needed the help.

Sweat dripped down her nose and fell onto the vent floor. "God, it's hot," she said.

"Can't they smell us coming? You're sweating buckets," Adrian said, disgust coloring his voice.

"They would have already smelled us by now," Devanshi said. "It appears the synthetic pheromones you took from the other human are working. It helps that we're not presenting as a threat yet. So don't be a threat."

"I'll do my best," Mallory said. "I'm so glad I walked into this unprepared."

"What could have prepared you for this?" Adrian asked.

"An epinephrine shot, for one," she said. She didn't know if she was allergic to Cuckoos, but she was allergic to Sundry and didn't like taking the chance. She had been in such a hurry to save Parker that she hadn't thought about her shot. She could easily die down there with one sting.

"Oh, yeah, that was stupid to leave behind," he replied.

She rolled her eyes. *Count on Adrian to be helpful.*

The buzzing was louder, reverberating through the floor. They came to a chute that went straight down. They had crossed vents like this before, but at this one, Devanshi stopped at the edge. "Down there, about twenty feet," she said, pointing with her long, spindly finger.

"It's dark," Mallory said. "Why is it dark?" She had a disturbing mental image of a cavern stuffed so full of Cuckoos that light couldn't penetrate.

"The nest is attached at the ceiling, covering the vent. There are openings at the top for them to get into the vent, and at the bottom for them to access the cavern," Devanshi said. "How did you think you were getting inside the nest if it wasn't readily accessible?"

"I planned on figuring that out when I saw the nest," Mallory grumbled.

"That would have been something else good to prepare," Adrian said helpfully.

"What if I get into trouble?" Mallory said. "Can you pull me back up?"

"No rope," Adrian said. "If you get into trouble, try reasoning with them. Surrender as a prisoner of war. Pretend to be one of them, like they did to the blue."

"Are you enjoying this?" Mallory asked, the small penlight she had thought to bring swinging at her neck, casting light that bounced off the gray vent shaft and made Adrian look otherworldly and sinister. "You look like you're happy that I'm going alone into danger that I'm not sure how I'm exiting."

"Oh, get over yourself, fall guy," he said with a harrumph. "Of course we'll get you out. We've got some drones coming with some rope. I called them a few minutes ago."

"I have trouble believing that."

"Relax, Mallory, we're on your side. If you'd mentioned your shot earlier, we could have brought that, too."

"Learn some timing, Adrian," Mallory said. "But thanks."

"Are you sure he's in there?" Devanshi asked, peering into the darkness. "This is a big chance to take."

"He's in there," she said.

SLIDING DOWN A vertical vent with no climbing gear looked a lot easier in the movies. Her arms started aching immediately as she pressed against the sides of the vent to keep herself from falling.

"Channel the Grinch," Adrian called down. Mallory realized he could see her through his drone's eyes, and she paused to give him the finger.

Freeing up one hand made her slip, and she swore, losing her purchase and tumbling down the chute. She remembered how massive Eternity's cavern was, and had a sickening fear that she would just fall and fall until she—

—fell only a few feet before landing on the soft, papery surface of the nest's roof. Adrian's laughter echoed above her, but she didn't rise to his bait again.

She carefully poked around the top of the nest, feeling for an opening. The Cuckoos were smaller than she was, but still they needed a sizable exit hole if they wanted to travel anywhere in a swarm. The blue Sundry had shown her around their nest once, and she knew where the top exit was. And it was highly unlikely that the Cuckoos had built this nest themselves.

She found the opening and ripped a larger hole, listening carefully for a change in the buzzing noises outside. But the droning continued.

She finally was able to slip her legs through the roof. She thought she saw light inside but didn't know how far away the floor was. She closed her eyes and held her breath and slipped through the hole.

Her ankle made a painful twinge when she landed, but she tried to roll to avoid major injury. She bumped into a body, then jumped back and scrambled to her feet.

The cavity in the hive was a simple, rounded room. Dimly lit by a slit in the paper wall, it was large enough to fit a few people. Which it now held, as Parker sat on the floor, looking up at her, his face unreadable in the shadows. But she knew it was him. She'd know him anywhere.

"Mallory? What are you doing here?"

"I'm trying to find you," she said. "You disappeared." She forced lightness into her voice. "Were you expecting someone else?"

"Actually, yes," he said, coming to his feet to face her. "You really shouldn't be here. How did you get in here?"

"Devanshi, my Phantasmagore friend, helped me through the vents," she said. "How did you get in here?"

"I was talking to Tina. Then there was another swarm. I blacked out, and then I was here," he said, sounding far away. Then he raised his voice and pointed toward the hole in the side of the hive. "I don't like blacking out, for the record," he shouted into the buzzing storm. "But how did you get in undetected? Isn't my hive kind of deep enemy territory for you?" His voice was bitter.

"Ah." Mallory rubbed the back of her neck. "Those pheromones I took from you. They were the no-threat ones. I didn't know if they would work on Cuckoo if a blue wore them, but it was worth the risk. I thought that might get me in."

"Oh!" he said, surprised. "That's why I feel like I should be angry, but I don't really have the energy." He paused. "I really do want to be mad at you. You cracked my worldview like an egg and then left me because *you* were upset."

"I—" she began, but he kept talking.

"But I wanted to apologize. If I had put two and two and two together, I would have figured out both that the pheromones might work on you, and that I had a similar link to the Cuckoos. The facts were right there. I just chose to ignore them."

"It's a mindfuck when you realize it, isn't it?" Mallory said. "I'm sorry I left you. It just made me question everything you and I have ever experienced together. Anything I ever felt."

"Why would that change anything?" he asked. "If our symbionts make us ignore or dislike each other, we should have stayed farther away from each other, not been attracted."

"True," she said with a rueful smile. "If only we had some symbionts to explain it to us. It doesn't make a lot of sense." She shook her head and got back to business, moving past him to look outside the slit. "Are you all right?"

"Of course I am," he said, puzzled. "Why would I not be?"

Mallory recognized the cavern Mrs. Brown had shown her, only now from the perspective of being in its topmost corner. Wasps—appearing blue, but which she now knew were green— flew around them, buzzing and computing to keep the station going. She looked down and saw how far they had to fall. "I hope this is anchored well," she said nervously. Then she faced him, finally looking at him in the slim shaft of light.

"Why would you not be? You've been captured by the mind-less insects that took over the station!"

"They're not mindless," he said, "they're just not sophisticated. They make a functional hivemind, else we'd all be dead. They just can't communicate as easily or perform some of the higher processing that the other Sundry do."

"They brought you here against your will, didn't they?" Mallory said flatly. "They killed countless other Sundry. They hijacked the station."

Parker shrugged. "Would you call a tiger evil? Or a hawk? The Cuckoos are doing what comes naturally. They are gathering their own to bring back to the hive. They are taking over hives like they've evolved to do. They don't want to kill anyone who isn't a threat."

"What about people who have something they want, like a hive full of Sundry?" she challenged.

"Fair," he said. "But that's instinct again. It's not like they fly around looking for anything they want and then kill to take it. It's in their nature to take what someone else built. It's not admirable the way we look at things, but they don't move with an evil intent."

Dark circles surrounded his eyes, and his hair was messy. He looked unharmed, but not happy to see her.

"Why did you come here, Mallory?" he demanded. "Those pheromones will wear off eventually and then what will you do? Inside the hive they'll definitely see you as an intruder, and I can't protect you."

"Why did I come here?" she echoed, baffled. "Parker, there's a murderer still out there. The station's been hijacked. Then you disappeared. I didn't know if you were missing, or dead, or injured, or what! I was worried about you! Amy's worried. I—" She bit her lip. "There are things I have to tell you, but the Cuckoos shouldn't know."

"And you don't trust me because I'm connected to them," he said, jerking his head to the Cuckoos flying outside. "And because I made those pheromones you suddenly found useful when you needed them. You said they were too dangerous to test, and here you are, using them when they're convenient."

"I'm not *experimenting* with them," she said, struggling to keep her angry voice low. "I was using whatever I had to come get you."

"Why?" he demanded again.

"Because you're Amy's brother, and an old friend, and I feel like I owe you!"

"That's why? Because you owe me? Because of Amy's friendship?" His voice was cold. He had retreated into the shadows again.

"No, dammit, it's because I care about you! I hate all the time we lost because of these damn bugs." Her voice was hoarse with the struggle to keep quiet while wanting to shout at him. "You are dominating my every thought since you got on the station. I can't think about hardly anything else. And I have shit to do! Someone's murdering people out there! But I can't deal with it until I know you're okay."

"I could be the murderer," he said.

"No, you couldn't be," she said. "When Oscar died, you had a fear reaction; you were scared for your own safety and the Cuckoos came to protect you. If you'd killed him, you wouldn't have had a strong fear reaction and they wouldn't have swarmed. I doubt anyone would survive a murder attempt. They'd sting the hell out of any threat against you. They protected you, and they saw Amy as your family. So she's part of the hive by proxy, I'm guessing."

"You care about me?" He was in shadow again, and she wanted to grab him and pull him so she could see his face, but she clenched her fists to stop herself.

She took a deep breath to calm down. "Parker, I can't trust the reality of things that happen between us; I don't know what's real or what's pheromone manipulation. I can't know if someone stripped us of our connections to the Sundry, that we would still notice each other. I'm not sure we even know each other. But despite all of that, yes, I care. So much."

He shook his head and pushed his hair away, but his face was still dark. "I have never felt for anyone like how I felt for you. Not before we met, not after high school. I've dated people, thought I'd fallen in love, but no experience has matched how I felt at that time. Have you?"

"No, but that was probably just teen hormones amplified by Sundry influence. We haven't felt that with anyone else because we haven't encountered anyone else who's like us, affected by the damn insect brain chemicals."

"God, you frustrate me!" he said, clenching his hands in the thin beam of light. "You can't say that the alien connection both pulls us together *and* pushes us apart. You're blaming everything you've ever felt for me, good or bad, on the Sundry instead of on your own emotions. You have to have one or the other. Which one are you going to own? Is it the hivemind connections that made us fall in love, or that made you forget about me entirely?"

The buzzing outside got louder, and Mallory thought fleetingly of her EpiPen back in her apartment.

He made no move to touch her, but she felt him move closer. "Brain chemicals, all emotion is chemical in one way or another. That feeling of falling in love, it's just dopamine. Does that mean no one falls in love, ever?"

Mallory's throat felt dry and incapable of speech. She sputtered something awkward, but he stepped into the light again.

His deep green eyes shone in that way that had always unnerved her. "Stop. I need to say this. I held back in school because of fear, or these alien forces, or my sister, whatever you want to call it. But I have regretted it ever since. Now we've been apart for years, but you're still you. Kind, brilliant, empathetic. You have a way of talking to someone that makes them feel like you've been old friends for years. How many real conversations did we have in high school? Six? Seven? And yet you were all I could think about. I was desperate to talk to you, to tell you everything I was feeling, to kiss you. You consumed me, even with so many things pulling us apart. When you look at me, the whole world goes dim and all I see is you. In high school, the best days were the ones where I could catch your eye and you'd smile. The worst days were the ones where I would catch your eye and you'd look at me so intensely that you made my throat close up, and it took everything within me to not grab you and kiss you.

"I've spent most of my life being the accident-prone, frequently injured, and strangely lucky guy. I'm a joke to most people. They call me a chaos magnet or walking disaster—even my own family calls me that. They may love and trust me, but they're always worried, always on alert when I'm around. But the only time I really thought myself unlucky was when I lost you. You've spent your adult life running from people. Keeping out of their way. You have trouble with people trusting you, trusting that your proximity won't ruin their lives, like they were blaming you for just being around violence. But I'm right here. I'm not afraid of you. And you're the only one who doesn't flinch when I'm around. You make me feel like I'm more than this chaos. Like we are more than these chemicals. I trust you." He laughed slightly. "And I'm right to trust you, because even though you were mad as hell at me, you still parachuted into a giant wasp nest to find me."

"I don't feel like I've earned your trust," Mallory said, tears burning her eyes. "I flat out said I don't trust you—how can you trust me?"

He reached out his hand and offered it, palm up. "You trust that your alien friends won't sting or crush you, right? Even though they could? We have to trust friends not to betray us even though every day it's a possibility. If something was a sure thing, we wouldn't need trust." He moved back in the shadows, leaving his hand outstretched.

She took the offered hand hesitantly. She had wanted all of this when she was a teen—his attention, his words, the touch of his skin—and his proximity as an adult caused her emotions to form a confused swarm.

She gasped when their hands met. Her vision lost the little light that lit the room and she saw teen Parker, face still delicate, green eyes watching her, and felt what he had felt for her. She saw them together, as adults, with blood dripping over their clasped hands. She saw the hospital fire that nearly consumed him, when her memory was the last thing on his mind before he was rescued. The images flared bright in her mind, then faded, leaving imprints on her memory.

"Wait a second," she whispered, then tugged him into the light. He came, reluctantly. He had tears shimmering in his green eyes, and she finally got it.

"Your eyes are blue when you use those synthetic hormones. Blue like blue Sundry." She smiled in relief.

"What color are they now?" he asked.

She stepped forward. "I don't know if this is a good idea. But I haven't allowed myself to feel anything for a long time. Caring for someone involved overwhelming hope and pain until I was sick of it. When you got here, when I realized what you were, compared to what I am, I got scared. I know there are a lot of things I can't trust. But, I think, I can trust you."

She reached out and took his other hand, marveling at the burning sensation that came, like when he touched her face. "Whatever held us apart in school had to have been pretty strong, because I was wildly in love with you back then."

She looked up at him. For a moment she could believe this was just a simple romantic moment instead of happening close to imminent death. "What about now?" he asked, his voice nearly drowned out by the buzzing.

"Now all I want to do is kiss you," she said. She was about to say something else, but Parker's lips were on hers. The electrical feeling was instant, slightly painful, but that sensation was far away in her mind, eclipsed by the longing of years and the connection of people who had found the one person who might understand them.

She was no longer alone.

He let go of her hand so he could touch her face and bury his hands in her hair, deepening the kiss. The burning didn't intensify, but mellowed as she relaxed into him.

Outside, the buzzing continued, then slowed.

A ripping sound intruded on their space, and then a voice interrupted them. "You humans are exchanging wetness? That's even grosser than you existing!" The voice came from the new hole in the paper nest, a massive gash that had been ripped open by giant stone hands. Tina peered inside, her jets firing to keep her in the air.

Mallory reluctantly stepped back but held on to Parker's hand. "Tina, the Cuckoos won't like you messing with their prize."

"Hah!" she boomed. "The Cuckoos are my bitch now!"

"What did you do?" Parker asked.

"Well, you got swarmed and wandered away, and never got to the shuttle bay, which made me kind of angry. I went looking for you and found your sister, and we started talking and I said I just wanted to be able to tell these insects to obey me like the others on Bezoar will. So she helped!"

The swarm surrounding them was more placid now, lazy like a solo honeybee on a hot summer afternoon instead of an angry swarm of wasps.

"Helped? What did you do?" Mallory asked, staring at the sluggish bugs.

"Amy gave you the pheromones!" Parker said, pumping his fist. "Yes!"

"You gave her pheromones? But won't they wear off?" Mallory asked, going up to Tina and peering at her jet pack, which still fired awkwardly to help Tina get through the hole.

"No, I drank them! When I absorbed all the dead Sundry bodies that I collected, I also absorbed the pheromones!"

Mallory stared at her. "You experimented with . . . Tina, that was really dangerous!"

"It had to be her," Parker said. "They can't hurt her."

"But drinking Earth-made synthetic Sundry pheromones?" Mallory demanded. "How many things could go wrong here?"

"Nah, things are great. I have new bitch-queen perfume, and they will totally listen to me!" Tina said. "They'll do anything I want!"

Mallory's eyes widened as she took in her friend. The perspective was odd since they were high inside a vast cavern in Eternity's depths, but she was pretty sure Tina was even larger than she'd been before.

"You guys planned this?"

"I was there for half of it," Parker said. "Amy and Tina went the last few miles on their own."

"Why didn't you tell me?" she demanded, smacking Parker's arm.

"I wasn't thinking very clearly, since I wasn't expecting someone to fall through the ceiling and then have to declare my love for them!"

She focused on the waiting Tina, then blinked and took a step closer. "Jesus, Tina. Did you change your form again?"

"Of course I did!" Tina said. "I had to, in order to be full bitch queen."

"So all the Sundry bodies were enough to transform you?"

Tina's jets fired harder, pushing her farther into the hive. "Oh, just enough to become awesome! Look!"

Parker and Mallory jumped back in alarm as she ripped the hole bigger and started firing her jets to force herself inside. They made as much room for her as they could, and when she finally was able to sit on the floor, Mallory could tell that Tina was definitely different.

Tina had kept the jets but lost the weaponry on her back. Her chest had rounded hugely, giving her a bulbous appearance. A wasp—still looking blue to Mallory—crawled over Tina's shoulder and then disappeared. It was hard to tell, with the Cuckoo sounds outside dominating, but from her chest cavity came a low, deep buzzing sound.

"I'm a hive!" Tina said happily.

Mallory approached and inspected the area and found a small, nearly hidden hole, just large enough for a Sundry-size body to slip inside.

"Holy shit," she said, shaking her head in disbelief. "Why?"

"Stephanie and I know a little more about evolution and ascension now, and since Parker and Amy brought these pheromones, we did a little experiment," Tina said. "I've been interviewing females on my way here to decide who gets to live inside. I want only the best."

Parker caught Mallory's eye. "The queens can't be interviewed, as such," he said, his voice low and amused.

"I thought the pheromones were supposed to work on rival insects," Mallory said.

Parker shrugged. "The queen pheromone was different, meant to make any intelligent alien insect obey. It's not perfect, but Tina wanted to try it out."

"You did an experiment with your own evolution?" she asked. "No, wait, I don't know why I'm surprised. So what now?"

"Now?" Tina asked, her voice baffled. "Now I go to rule Bezoar with my own Cuckoo hive along with me. They can be my spies and my scouts and friends that will never leave."

"Tina, your friends would never leave you," Mallory said. "Ferd just needed some time, and as much as Stephanie complains, she'll never abandon you. You should know that by now. But, hey, new friends are great. Congrats."

"Will the Cuckoos listen to you now?" Parker asked, looking out at the insects.

"Duh," Tina said. "I'm bitch queen."

"So you can take them back to the planet? All of them?" Mallory asked.

"Sure, if you want me to remove the hivemind driving Eternity," Tina said. "Is that what you want?"

Mallory winced. She couldn't tell if Tina had included sarcasm in her communication, but the point was still valid. "I think we might be able to deal with that, but it'll take a few weeks," Mallory said carefully.

"You need to catch the murderer still, don't you?" Tina asked. "They've already killed two people."

Her head snapped up. "Did Jessica die in medbay?"

"I guess so," Tina said. "Don told me she did."

Something about Don. And Amy. And their time together. Mallory looked at Parker, her face in a panic. "Parker. What language did you take in school?"

"Four years of Spanish," he said, looking confused. "Why?"

"What's the Spanish word for 'hot chocolate'?"

"Technically it's *chocolate caliente*," Parker said, frowning. "But the actual drink is *cacahuatl* in Spain, and in Mexico they call it *champurrado*."

Mallory hit her forehead with the heel of her palm to jar the answer loose. "No, that's not it. Is there anything else? Portuguese? Anything else in Latin America?"

"Amy's softball team was named after what the Aztecs called it, *xocolatl*, for some reason. Spelled with an X," he said. "Is that what you mean?"

"*Xocolatl*," Mallory muttered. "It starts with an X but has a 'sho' sound."

And then she had it. She looked at Tina. "Can you get us out of here? And I need you to open a door. There's going to be another murder very soon if we don't move."

"I love helping!" Tina said, and grabbed them both.

"Wait—" Parker said, but Tina gave a primal whoop and leaped out of the hole in the wall.

"BITCH QUEEEEEEEEENNN!"

30

· · ·

THE OPAL CONFLICT

XAN TUCKED THE blanket around Jessica. The Gurudev nurse, a grumpy alien by the name of Vel, stood beside her bed, grumbling to herself.

"I don't like it any more than you do," Xan said. "But it's necessary."

"You're putting her, and me, in harm's way. How is that keeping her safe?"

"It's a long story," he said. "But trust me, I've got to be here and I've got to protect her, and so she has to be here."

His watch pinged to life, Mallory's voice and a lot of wind coming through.

"Xan!" she yelled. "Are you safe?"

"Yeah, where are you?" he asked.

"No time to explain," she said. "Is Jessica dead?"

Even though he had just secured her blanket, he looked down at the prone ambassador. "No, she's doing okay. There are some other developments you should know—"

"That seals it. I know who the killer is. I need you to watch Amy. Don't let her out of your sight."

He frowned. "But Jessica—"

"She'll be fine. You need to pay attention to Amy now. I'll be there as soon as I can!"

"But I can't, I'm—" In the background, an all-too-familiar primal yell reached the mic, drowning out whatever Mallory said.

Xan could just make out "—ch queen in the motherfucking house!" before Mallory's comm went dead.

He glanced at Ferdinand, who sat in the captain's chair, and then at Stephanie's diamond portal, where Eternity, Mallory, and the woman he was supposed to be watching were receding rapidly. Then Steph's screen flickered and showed a different angle, a telephoto view of the planet Bezoar, where a Gneiss fleet waited in orbit.

"Watching Amy will be difficult," he muttered.

"But Jessica is still protected," Ferdinand said.

"Great," Xan said.

He'd thought it was a great idea to put Jessica and a nurse aboard Stephanie for safety, since Steph wouldn't open her hatch to anyone without Xan's clearance. And it had been, until his mission parameters changed.

"Can we go back?" he asked, although he knew the answer. He'd been trying to offer a win-win scenario to the Gneiss—protect Jessica while they meet the Gneiss fleet for some diplomatic talks before Tina could talk to them and ruin something. They hadn't done Stephanie and Ferdinand's mission yet.

The whisper in his head again. *Almost there.*

"Steph, are you also talking to her?" Xan asked.

"Yes, I've been getting updates," she said. "I have been trying to keep everyone on both sides calmed down. Maybe I should go into diplomacy."

"You've already gotten into the shuttle career path, Steph," Xan said. "I'm not sure you can change majors at this point."

"You do not know my dreams," Stephanie said, making him laugh.

The new ambassador was safe. Safe from the murderer, anyway. He glanced down at her again. "Sho," she muttered.

"I wish I knew what you were saying," he said with a sigh. "What's our ETA, Steph?"

"Ten minutes," she said. "I hope to beat Eternity there by at least four minutes."

"And then what? What do the Gneiss plan on doing?"

"They will demand that Tina surrender and come with them," Ferdinand said from the massive chair. "Then they will demand that Eternity turn her over to us. As it's a place of sanctuary—"

"—and driven by a hivemind running on instinct instead of reason," Xan interjected.

"Yes, that. Those reasons indicate Eternity will not turn her over. Then they may try to board the station or simply attack."

"They'd attack a space station to get at one rogue Gneiss?" Xan said. "Wouldn't that be an act of war with a number of governments?"

Ferd's voice was grimmer than usual. "There are rumors in Gneiss politics that the government wants exactly that. Tina isn't the real focus here, she's just a convenient scapegoat. But we have no proof."

"And the best way to get proof is to have Tina surrender herself," Xan said. "Which ain't gonna happen."

"No, it ain't," Stephanie agreed. "She's been silent since telling me she was going on an adventure."

"She apologized to me and then was quiet," Ferdinand said. "I was surprised to hear it, but gratified."

"What can we do against a Gneiss fleet?" Xan asked.

"Not much," admitted Stephanie. "But we're one more thing they have to go through before they get to the station."

"So we're cannon fodder?" Xan asked in disbelief.

"I believe so, yes," Ferdinand said. "I think Stephanie supplied some safety belts. You might want to strap in."

Steph's view switched back to Eternity, which had nearly disappeared as Stephanie accelerated. "Good luck, Mal. Hope you keep Amy in your sights," he said.

All awareness of Eternity, Stephanie, the Gneiss, and Jessica faded with the sudden bright, all-encompassing sensation of *Infinity* being nearby. She was close, she was fast, she was with him.

I missed you.

XAN'S HEAD FILLED with information, and he staggered back and fell into his chair. He was dimly aware of the Gurudev strapping him in.

This must have been like what Mal experienced connecting with the Sundry.

Infinity tried to tell him everything that had happened on her end, in about five seconds.

Travel to November / tour the sentient ship nursery / Brown getting training / Brown attempting to communicate with Eternity / Brown angry / Brown very angry / receive Stephanie's message about Cuckoos and Gneiss conflict / Learn about Cuckoos from November historical database / fury so much fury / hurry to Bezoar / prepare for Gneiss / reconnect with Xan

He held his hands on the sides of his head to keep his brains from leaking out his ears. "Jesus, slow down," he said.

You are within comms distance. You will be here soon. Mrs. Brown is angry. The Gneiss are here.

"Stephanie told me. Is it a big fleet?"

No, except for one warship named Premee. She's a four-thousand-year-old behemoth who, according to Mrs. Brown, "suffers no fools and takes no shit, so everyone on Eternity is in trouble."

"Sounds like she'd like to take this old lady to tea instead of fight with her," Xan said.

Accurate.

"Are they attacking?"

No. *They are waiting for Tina.*

"Get in line," he muttered, then attempted to sum up what he knew about the murders and the Tina issues aboard Eternity, including no one knowing her whereabouts.

Stephanie informed us about the destruction of the Sundry hives and the Cuckoos. Mrs. Brown wants to know why Mallory didn't stop it.

"I'll let her fight her own battles, but just remind Mrs. B that Mallory thought the Cuckoos were blue Sundry since she's linked to the blue hive. They didn't see the Cuckoos coming in, and neither did she. Also, there's been a murder, so she's been distracted."

That is acceptable, although irritating, says Mrs. B.

"I think Mallory would agree with you," he said. Then he realized there was one thing Mrs. Brown wouldn't know because he hadn't even told Stephanie yet.

"Everyone should know that the blue and silver Sundry are rallying and laying new eggs to take back the station," he said. "Also, Mallory will probably need a new apartment soon."

If we're alive to grant it, that's not a problem, Mrs. Brown says.

"WHERE . . . YOU?" MALLORY shouted over the comms. The distance was making communication difficult, and he got mostly static. ". . . can't find . . . or the . . . Gneiss."

"Gneiss and I are going to Bezoar. Jessica's safe," Xan said slowly through his watch.

"Don't mention the nurse," Vel said from her seat beside Jessica's bed. "I'm of no consequence. Just kidnapped and brought aboard a sentient ship who's not smart enough to conjure up some cushions."

"You want me to call her back and tell her you're here, too?

That you're okay?" Xan snapped. "I appreciate you being here, but this is not mission-critical information."

"Wait till someone gets hurt, then I'll be the most mission-critical person there is," Vel replied. "I served in the Opal Conflict. I reknit crushed limbs and other countless injuries."

Ferdinand looked over at the little Gurudev for the first time. "You served in the Opal Conflict?"

Gurudev were the aliens Xan had the least amount of experience with, so he didn't know anything about their body language, but still, the room got very quiet as all focus turned to the Gurudev, who had apparently dropped a big truth bomb.

"What was the Opal Conflict?" he asked, looking at everyone in turn.

"Well, yes, they needed medical personnel, and . . ." Vel trailed off. "I was following orders!"

"Are we really doing this? Now?" Xan asked desperately.

"The Gurudev decided to mine one of our nurseries for opals," Ferdinand said.

At the same time, Vel said, "The Gneiss had laid claim to a planet in our space without telling us. We didn't know they were there when we started mining."

Dawning horror crept over Xan's skin. "Are you telling me that you harvested Gneiss babies as gemstones?"

"Yes," Ferdinand said.

"They were only opals when we mined them," Vel said quietly. "They look like rocks! Everyone looks like rocks in this species!"

Ferdinand started to get out of his chair and advance toward Vel, who shrank back.

Xan unsnapped his restraint and ran forward to get between them. He didn't know what technology the Gurudev had to fight a war, but in hand-to-hand combat, a Gneiss would beat them in an instant. "That was history, y'all. We have something else going on right now. You don't want to say that we lost the Gneiss-Eternity skirmish because of ship infighting, right? That's not a good story to tell at a bar, trust me."

"They murdered children!" Ferd yelled.

"You were trespassing and we didn't know!" Vel yelled back.

Stephanie's voice boomed over the speaker. "If you're done fighting, we've arrived. Even if you're not done, we've arrived."

31

. . .

LOVE AND LUCK

AT THE WELCOME-TO-THE-STATION reception, full of blowhards and rich assholes, State Bureau of Investigation agent Donald Draughn sat on a massive barstool and wondered if he'd finally gone off his rocker.

He didn't want to be at the station. He didn't want to have spent most of his savings to get here. But you had to gamble for what you wanted, right? At this point in his life, it was all or nothing.

He had purposefully chosen a barstool built for those huge rock dudes. It was a pain to crawl up there, but not as hard as he'd expected. All that softball had actually been paying off. He'd chosen that stool because it kept him away from everyone. Mingling was not his thing. The conversations were starting to bore him.

It had seemed like a great idea to come here, when he'd first had it.

Most men just buy a sports car. Why did your midlife crisis have to be this?

Those UNC professors he traveled with were either boring or infuriating. Most of the academics argued over pointless shit, and Oscar just sneered at, or hit on, everyone. What a waste of air.

Amy was the only one who was different.

"Agent Draughn?"

He jumped at the voice, nearly falling off the stool. "What?" he snapped, wheeling around.

The woman sitting there looked relaxed and beautiful, her hair upswept in a bun and secured with two straight metal sticks. She was far too young for the confidence she radiated. She smiled at the rock statue, who had no doubt lifted her onto the stool. "Thank you, Ferdinand," she said. Like they were on a first-name basis or something.

He cleared his throat. "Ambassador. Having a good time?"

"It's wonderful," she said. "Everyone is very nice and welcoming. I wanted to make sure all of the humans were feeling positive about this visit. You're one of our few tourist visitors, and you were sitting alone, so I was concerned."

He took a drink of his beer, grateful for whoever had brought it aboard the shuttle so he wouldn't have to drink whatever weird alien swill they served here. "I'm fine. That trip wore me out, you know?"

"What are your plans aboard the station?" Her voice dropped the smooth diplomatic tone and was sharp and direct. "I hope you're not here to start any trouble."

He glanced sidelong at her. "What do you mean? You said it yourself; I'm a tourist here."

She shook her head. "You think I didn't look into everyone who was coming aboard with me? I know your story, Agent. I know your history with Mallory Viridian. I know your grudges. I know how hard you worked to get into the SBI, and I know what a colossal fuckup you were to get kicked out. And now you're spouting some 'PTO vacation' bullshit. You were fired, *Mr.* Draughn. Why are you really here?"

The spit in his mouth dried up, and he took another drink. "That's a lot of intel, Ambassador. Where did you find it?"

She gave a tight smile. "Typical. More concerned with where

the secret came from rather than what the secret revealed. Or maybe you're just misdirecting."

"Or maybe you're just wrong," he said nonchalantly. "You should double-check your sources."

"I've got eyes on Mallory Viridian," she said. "And eyes on you. If you make one threatening move toward her, I'll have you sent back to Earth immediately."

"Eyes? Who do *you* know here?" he demanded. "You're acting like you're top dog, when we're really all bowing to the whims of that old woman and that AWOL soldier. When they say 'jump,' you're gonna say 'out what air lock?' You don't have any power on the station."

"Yet," she said. "And who said my eyes were on the station?"

He thought about one person who stood out as not belonging on this trip. He hadn't seen Oscar talking to the ambassador, even though she had made social rounds to almost everyone at the party. Was she purposefully avoiding the idiot coach?

"I see," he said softly.

"In fact, I'm not even sure how you got this ticket," she said. "I would have thought you'd be deposed to talk about the unfortunate slaughter in Spruce Pine."

He rubbed his chin. "No charges were filed."

"I'll bet that's because you agreed to early retirement, right?" she asked. "Besides, who's gonna miss a bunch of hillbilly meth dealers? And. Their. Families." The last three words were harsh, cutting through the pleasant restaurant banter like a shiv bypassing ribs to get to his lung.

THE MEMORIES CAME, unwelcome and horrific. He hadn't had a bust since Mallory had left the planet. It had only been a few months, and his superiors weren't even bringing it up, but he could feel his own work sliding. He went into a spiral, drowning in the realization that he had needed her, and had ridden on her skill at solving crimes. He had used her to leapfrog into the SBI, but after she left, everything dried up. Maybe he'd never had any ability to be a detective.

Helen had died in October, the cancer taking her fast. She went into her grave thinking he was a screwup.

After bereavement leave, he'd gotten a lead on a meth lab in a tiny town in the North Carolina mountains. Excited to prove himself, he did minimal research and organized a raid. The raid was short and brutal. His intel had failed to mention that the meth lab owner's extended family—not to mention several other families— lived and worked in the trailer park that hid the lab. He and the agents had raided the whole area. He had taken down the lab, sure. But the gunfight and subsequent fire took twenty-seven lives, including eight children, four spouses, and ten residents who had no apparent connection to the lab. Five officers had also died: three local, two SBI. It was a colossal fuckup, and the blame had come directly down on him.

In the late night, he had fixed it in his head that it was Mallory's fault all of this had happened. In the years that Mallory had been on Earth, his skills had atrophied because of her meddling. She had made him lose the keen sense of sniffing out crimes. Once he had fled his controversy by making a quiet exit into early retirement, he could think of little else.

The only bright spots in his life were the time spent with Amy Valor. The support group meetings, lunches, dinner parties, and softball games. The ball games were the best, with Amy's cheeks flushed with the exertion and excitement of the game.

Most of the time, other support group members, her weird twin, or other professors would be nearby, but even then, being around her was a breath of fresh air when he hadn't even realized he wasn't breathing. He couldn't help but wonder if she could ever love him. His wife was only a few months in the ground, but if he was honest with himself, they hadn't been close in years, and their sex life had died sometime in the 2020s. But when Amy's blue eyes had locked onto his, he believed he might feel young again.

He worried about the inevitable May-December jokes, everyone who assumed being an SBI agent got you "Sugar Daddy Moneys." ("SDM" was apparently the hottest hip-hop song nowadays by a group called Rich D4D. Draughn's nieces had sung it to him last Christmas and he'd been horrified.) But SBI agents didn't make a ton of money, and fired agents even less so.

Even if she did go for him, what would people think? Everyone who looked at his old and craggy face and her bright blue eyes would have the same thoughts, hidden behind a polite smile if he was lucky: he was chasing youthful tail and she was after aging money.

It's not even May-December. More like June-September. Only twenty years separates us, after all. It may not even matter to her. I won't know until I ask.

He'd lied to her and her friends. He had already been fired from the SBI when he told Amy he was investigating some computer crimes on campus and they should have lunch. She brought some friends along and then lunch had become a regular thing. He would keep up the ruse, lying about what he was investigating, bragging about his classified work, and then manufacturing his "PTO." When he heard there was a chance to go to Eternity with her, he took it. Perhaps it would be the best way to get her alone, to confess his feelings.

Perhaps he could also work some things out with Mallory while he was there.

None of this he would confirm for Ambassador Jessica Brass, who sat there looking younger than Amy and smarter than Mallory and better than Draughn. Grandma had said butter wouldn't melt in his father's mouth, and it took him a while to figure out what that meant. He thought it meant "cool," which didn't make sense, since his father was a digital grifter, scamming men and women alike out of their life savings by posing online as people in need. But he got it at last, and knew that Jessica Brass also fit the same slick, unflappable mantle as his dad.

This could be a vacation. He could just relax, see the station, meet weird aliens, then go home and get a job in a library or something. But he wanted the next phase of his life to go in a different direction, and he wanted Amy with him. He gathered his resolve and surveyed the crowd to see if he could spot her from his perch.

That slimy piece of shit Oscar was talking to Amy's brother and Mallory. Even up here, Draughn could hear him bragging about his gossip site and how he had found out secrets about people on the trip. What if Jessica hadn't been privy to bureau information but had learned from the gossip king? What if those were her "eyes" now?

She wasn't the only person who could watch.

He looked back up to Jessica, who waited for him to respond to her accusation about the meth lab. "I don't know what you're talking about, Ambassador. I'm just trying to enjoy my beer."

"That's fine. We don't have to talk about it. You're not accused of any crime." She wrinkled her nose as if she had already tried him in her head and found him guilty. "I have a speech to give. It was nice talking to you."

"Remember. I have eyes on you," she said, then slipped off the stool and gracefully landed as if she hadn't just fallen several feet. He had forgotten she was a former basketball player.

He hadn't even planned on doing much more than talking to Mallory and confessing his feelings to Amy.

But then.

Oscar went over to where Amy was talking to someone. He wrapped his arms around her from behind and kissed her cheek. Instead of shoving him off her, as any self-respecting woman should have done when embraced by literal human slime, she laughed and awkwardly put her arms above her head to hug him back.

He would like to say that he saw red, became enraged, and lost his mind in mad passion. But it wasn't the truth. Everything went cold then. A light inside him was extinguished, and the only thing left was the small bottle of "medicine" he had brought with him in case he felt the need to deal with Mallory.

But it would work for Oscar, too.

Something shiny caught his eye under the stool that Jessica had occupied. He slid off his stool, landing solidly if not gracefully. A stick that looked like a sharp metal chopstick lay on the floor. He looked around and saw the new ambassador's bun was coming down, her remaining silver hair stick unable to keep it together. She was unaware of this, laughing and flirting with Xan Morgan. He picked it up and fingered it. This was a brilliant weapon, strong, metallic, and sharp, and easily concealed in a thick head of hair. He considered giving it back to her and then heard Oscar laugh again.

Not yet.

He went and eavesdropped on Oscar and Reggie, hearing Oscar's donkey laugh when he talked about screwing sweet, beautiful Amy.

Spiking Oscar's drink was laughably easy. No one was paying attention, and Oscar actually put his drink down to go to the bathroom. Jessica called everyone into the bar area to hear her speech, and Draughn had spent his own time in the bathroom, just missing passing an angry Reggie, who came into the bathroom and slammed the stall shut. He slipped out of the door as Reggie furiously talked to himself.

The sedative had worked quickly, and he found Oscar and Max both passed out at different tables.

"Hey, Max," he whispered, and when the guy didn't stir, he sat Oscar up so that he leaned back, his face up to the ceiling, and then dragged the chair toward the wall. He kept careful watch, making up his cover story as he dragged, and then found the little alcove full of cleaning supplies. He contemplated making Oscar drink something from the alien cleaner but didn't know what that would do to him. It might not be deadly, he might scream, he might reveal Draughn.

No, the direct method was best. Carefully measuring the spot between the ribs, Draughn drove the hair stick into Oscar's chest and into his heart. He could feel the muscle spasm once and then go still. He removed the hair stick and slipped it into his back pocket. He would plant it on the ambassador later. He then picked up the loathsome deadweight and shoved it into the alcove, jamming the door shut.

He hadn't even gotten any blood on him. He returned to Jessica's speech and clapped politely. When she was done, Amy approached. He smiled as he always did, wondering what she was going to do with her night now that Oscar wouldn't be warming her bed.

"I haven't seen you all night," she said with a smile. "Are you having a good time?"

"I thought you and Oscar looked like you didn't want to be disturbed," he said. "I'm feeling jet lag, or spaceship sick. Whatever they call it. I should have turned in hours ago."

"Oscar is a charmer, but I have room to talk to my friends," she said. "Let me get my stuff at the table and we can walk back to our rooms. I'd love to hear your take on the party."

"Sure," he said with a frozen smile.

Reggie was at the table with Max, trying to coax him awake. Parker was sitting alone with a melancholy look on his face, as usual. Then he blinked and looked around. "Where did Oscar go? Did he finally succeed in seducing someone?"

They all started to look for him. Draughn panicked for a moment, realizing that if he left the scene now, he would be the only one who acted like Oscar was dead.

"I think I saw him leaving with someone," he ventured.

"No," Reggie said grimly. "He was here and pretty drunk just a few minutes ago. He was sitting there." He pointed to the table where Draughn had returned the chair.

Reggie went back into the bathroom; Parker went to ask the bartender. Draughn stood with Amy, Max, and Reggie, then started moving around the room. Finding the body would look sudden and unintentional, he decided. He found the little closet and knocked on the door. "Anyone know what this is?"

"Looks like a closet," Parker said. "Is it locked?"

Draughn steeled himself and then opened the door. Oscar's body toppled on top of him, and he allowed it to knock him over. He gave a disgusted cry and scrambled out from under the body.

Amy screamed, Parker swore. Reggie looked at the body and couldn't hide the relief on his face. "At last," he said quietly.

Max woke up and blinked at the room. Then the buzzing began.

Amid the screams and chaos, the goddamn green bugs came into the room and made everything worse. Or better, since the chaos benefited him. But Amy was in danger now, and he still cared about her. He leaped at her, covering her from the stinging insects. Alarmed, she backed up from him, and he tripped and fell forward, grabbing her. They both hit a table as they went down, and the insects swarmed over him, and then there was pain like no other. He screamed and writhed, his exposed hand taking sting after sting.

That was the point where everything turned red, and he didn't remember anything after that. He had apparently gone to Mallory for help. Mallory. The thought disgusted him. Why not just alert a detective to your own murder scene?

He woke up a few hours later in the medbay, his head bandaged, his hand tightly bound to the point of pain.

Parker was there, fussing over Amy, who was still unconscious, with a bandage on her head, too.

"Is she okay?" he muttered.

"No," Parker said, distracted. "Whatever hit you both knocked her out."

He paused, trying to remember. "So you didn't see what got us?"

"No."

Draughn was annoyed at the lack of information. He remembered that Parker had said he knew Mallory. He wondered how much he knew about her. "Whatever happened, Mallory will probably figure it out."

Parker looked back at him, green eyes troubled. "I don't think so, not this time."

Mallory off her game? "What do you mean? Isn't she connected to those bugs or something?" Draughn asked. He dared let hope flare in his chest, just a spark.

"She was," Parker confirmed. "But there's a problem. There aren't any blue Sundry left."

"How do you know that?" he asked, alarmed.

"I don't know," Parker said, frowning. "I just do."

"So Mallory's whole murder-magnet ability, or crime scene bloodhound, or whatever she has, that's gone?"

"I think so, yeah," Parker said. "I—I should tell her."

"No," Draughn said hastily. "You'll just upset her. It's been a stressful night. Give her a little time before you deliver more bad news." He smiled. "Trust me. I've known her a long time."

He'd been granted the good-luck window of opportunity that he couldn't let slide. With Mallory out of the picture, the only person left who could figure out what had happened was that ambassador. They'd said that people couldn't even contact security. He had a golden opportunity.

Speaking of Mallory, she was there, wanting to talk to Parker, taking him out of the room. Draughn's head was swimming still, but he had to take this chance. Jessica wanted to fuck with his life and mock his departure from the only career he had ever cared about. He hadn't thought about her when he had killed Oscar, but if Jessica's little informant turned up dead, she would figure out pretty damn fast who had the best motive. She had to go.

He returned to his room and retrieved the novelty bat he'd kept in his suitcase because it had amused Amy when they'd gotten them after winning their softball championship. It was the size of a police baton. He also got his Xocolatl hat and carefully put it over his bandaged head in case anyone saw him and was alarmed at his injury. He considered stabbing Jessica with her own hair stick, but it was a lot easier to stab someone neatly when they were passed out.

The ambassador opened her door with a flourish, wearing a sultry nightgown that clung to every curve, her hooded eyes clearly expecting someone else. She stepped back in shock and then set her jaw in annoyance. "Jesus, Don, what the hell happened to you?"

"Do you know how it feels when someone tries to ruin you in the eyes of the woman you love?" he asked, gripping the bat tightly.

"Do I what?" she asked, closing her robe around her.

"It hurts!" he said, and brought the bat down, aiming for her temple.

She crumpled immediately without even a cry.

It was harder to club her with his left hand, but he managed to do okay, even getting minimal blood on him—the trick, he had learned in his years of law enforcement, was to hit only once. Then there won't be blood spray. He cleaned off signs of his own passing: his fingerprints, his own blood that had seeped from under his bandage like a bead of sweat, any footprints. He left her body right inside the door, pulling it out of the way so that the door could close when he left. Then he tossed the hair stick, wiped clean, back in with her as a bargain. Maybe she'd be blamed for Oscar's murder.

With a groan, he slipped the novelty bat into his sling and under his bandages, which went up to his forearm. The stings throbbed even more as the bat rubbed against them, but he couldn't risk having it found before he could get rid of it.

Then he ran back to the medbay, landing on his bed right before the nurse was returning to check his hand and announce that they couldn't identify the venom in his hand, nor could they localize it. Which meant their only recourse was to amputate.

The concussion made his head pound and blurred his vision. He wasn't sure, but he thought he might have puked on the way back to the medbay. But this news drove all the pain, the worry about getting caught, even the concern for Amy's health out of his head.

He sat up in bed, cradling his throbbing hand against his chest. "No, no, fuck no, you're not taking my hand. I thought you had the best health care, better than anything Earth has! What kind of barbaric alien just chops off your hand if they can't heal it?"

The alien—Gurudev? short, insect-like, creepy hands with bark-like skin—reached out unsympathetically and took his arm, pulling with ridiculous strength. His swollen forearm pulsed with increased pain as he fought, but it was no use. Luckily he didn't pay attention to the bandages, as he was looking at Draughn's upper arm.

"See here," the alien said, pointing to his arm with the claw that didn't have a death grip on him. There were striations going up his arm. On Earth, they would have been red, indicating a growing infection. And, admittedly, the fix would have been to amputate before the infection reached an important organ.

But these streaks weren't red. They were a glowing green.

"Oh, no," he said, the breath leaving his lungs in a slow wheeze. "What the fuck is that?" He looked around the room at the doctor and the attending nurse, seeking sympathy and finding only alien stoicism.

"We don't know. That's why we may have to amputate," the Gurudev said.

His eyes flew open. "May? You mean I have a chance of keeping my hand?"

The alien let him go, and he immediately cradled his arm again. "We are going to run more tests overnight," the doctor said. "But the odds are very low that we will find anything. We will amputate in the morning if we don't learn what this venom is."

It reached into a pocket in its complex wrapping of cloth around its body and brought out two dark gray patches. Its other hand produced a scalpel from somewhere. Faster than Draughn could react, it reached out and sliced through the gauze on his head with terrifying precision. The bandage fell away except where it was attached to his temple, where the laceration was. He flinched.

The alien put the patch on his forehead, where it stuck and immediately began to get warm. "We do have good news. We have studied your brain enough to know what it needs to heal from its trauma. You'll feel better shortly."

It went over to Amy's bed and did the same thing, but removing the bloody bandage instead of leaving it to hang from her head like a piece of sunburned skin that hadn't peeled away yet.

It dropped the gauze into a slot on the wall where Draughn had seen it place other biohazard materials. "Get some rest," it said. "Don't worry about the amputation. You won't feel any pain." It dimmed the lights in the room, then left, proving that bedside manner didn't exist in other species.

"Jesus," he said, his lips numb. He had forgotten everything that had happened that night, except that he was going to lose his hand in the morning. He had just enough mental capacity to toss his hat and the bat into his own room, lock it, and then struggle back to the medbay.

Parker returned, and Draughn feigned sleep while the nerdy professor got himself settled in a chair by Amy's bed so he could sleep near her. *That's my spot, you incestuous freak*, he thought.

As Draughn's headache lifted, he watched Amy in her bed, the pinched look on her face slowly relaxing as her own patch did its work.

I may lose a hand for you, he thought. *And you will never appreciate it. It's your fault I'm like this.*

He began to plot. His love for Amy had evaporated, leaving nothing but bitter salt behind. She would never appreciate what he had been willing to do for her.

32

THE FINAL BATTLE, FROM THREE PERSPECTIVES

TINA HAD WANTED to take them outside the station for speed, but Mallory pointed out that the vacuum would kill them, and they didn't have time to find suits.

"Fine, I'll take the outside route and meet you there!" she shouted, and headed for an air lock.

"We also don't know where we're going," Parker said.

"We need to find Amy. She'll be the next target. So we start with her room, if we can get Eternity to let us in."

"She said she was going to give me access, but I didn't get a key. And how did you know it's Draughn?" he asked. They sprinted toward the lift as a few Gneiss got aboard.

"Amy was targeting him for intel," Mallory said. "I've been wondering if her attention would make him fall for her, and I was right. Oscar was hitting on Amy at the party, and she was letting him. To keep Draughn from making a move, I thought. Or to make him jealous."

"I wondered why she was letting him do that," Parker said, disgusted.

"Amy and Draughn are on the softball team, the Xocolatl. He must have been wearing their mascot hat when he attacked Jessica. Who knows, maybe he did it with one of those novelty bats.

She's been trying to tell Xan 'Xocolatl' because that's probably the last thing she saw before he hit her."

Parker tapped his feet impatiently as the lift moved. "But you could apply all that to my sister. She didn't want her secret out, she hated Oscar hitting on her, she was on the softball team, too."

"Three things," Mallory said as the doors opened and the Gneiss pushed past them to get out.

"First, Amy was unconscious when Jessica was killed. Did you spend all your time in the medbay last night?"

"No, I went back to my room for some things," he said.

"That gave him his window. He was injured, but conscious."

The lift zoomed along, Mallory praying that it wouldn't stop again. It opened on the human residential area. They began running again.

"The second thing was, Amy thought Jessica had been stabbed, not bludgeoned. She could have been trying to throw me off, but with the other two reasons, I think it's solid.

"Third, when the Cuckoos came to protect you, they left Amy alone and stung Draughn. I thought they left her alone because she was your sibling and an honorary member of the hive, but I don't think it had anything to do with her. Draughn was the murderer, and Parker thought he was in danger as well, so they swarmed to protect him, but they also attacked the person they thought was attacking one of their own. They've known all along who did it."

"I still don't know—" Parker said.

"I haven't had time to spread the word to the other humans about Jessica's attack, and I know Xan hasn't. But Draughn knew she'd been hit and assumed she had died because that was his intent."

"So why will he go after Amy if he loves her?" Parker said.

"Murdering the woman that he can't have is unfortunately a common motive for male killers," Mallory said. "Oscar died, which didn't make Amy leap into Draughn's arms, so now she has to die."

"But why attack Jessica?" he asked.

"From her files, I think she was watching him closely, and I think she was using Oscar to do it. If Oscar died, Jessica would accuse Draughn, or at least tell me what she knew. He wasn't counting on me finding her notes."

They stood in front of Amy's door, Parker staring at it awkwardly. "You said she gave you access, so you just put your hand up to the bio-scan," Mallory said mildly.

He grimaced in embarrassment and held his hand to the door, which slid open.

Inside was Amy's room as Mallory had seen it before. It was relatively neat, but the mirror over the sink was cracked, with a novelty bat spotted with blood lying on the floor nearby as if it had been hurled.

"What's going on now?" Mallory muttered to herself. "And I was actually kidding about the bat."

"Hey, Mallory," Parker said from the desk where he'd sat down and begun scrolling through his twin's laptop. "Shouldn't Tina be here by now?"

TINA THOUGHT HER new hive body would protect her friends if she had to travel in vacuum. They seemed to have plugged up the holes to avoid leaks. This made sense; the silver Sundry could make space-worthy paper nests.

Tina thought Mallory was being silly by worrying so much.

They buzzed away in Tina's chest, creating a pleasant vibration that was entirely silent due to the weird no-sound-in-space rule. She engaged her jet pack and started to fly around Eternity.

She pulled up fast, staring at the scene before her. Planet Bezoar, the shithole planet, the brown rock, the home of prisoners across the galaxy and the descendants of prisoners like the Cuckoos, lay in front of her. It was a terrible place, but it was hers and she loved it. She was home!

There were also her friend Stephanie, *Infinity*, and a matriarchal battleship facing off above the planet, but that didn't take away from the majestic view.

She wondered what they were doing.

She flew a little closer. *Infinity* wasn't facing off with the Gneiss; she was trying to dock, but Eternity wouldn't let her. The Cuckoos were probably meddling here. Those darn Cuckoos!

She wanted to tell the Cuckoos in her chest to tell the ones on the station to let *Infinity* in, but they couldn't read her mind, and she had no way of speaking in space. She'd thought of other species as weak for needing helmets in space, but at least they could communicate with each other.

She flew over to *Infinity*, not sure if anyone could see her, but then extended her hand to the ship. *Come on, send out a grappling hook or whatever you have! You're too round to grab!*

She shook her hand impatiently, then *Infinity* extended a hook. Tina grabbed it and began tugging with her jets. She and her cargo inched forward, slowly gaining speed.

The shuttle bay doors remained closed.

This is stupid and a waste of time, she thought. She let *Infinity* go and approached Eternity instead. She held her hand out and touched the metal of the shuttle bay doors, allowing her vibrations to go into the ship.

The vibrations weren't of the polite variety and had many swear words that she had learned from the humans. But she had the extra power of the Cuckoos behind her, or more accurately, inside her, and those on the station finally bent to her will. The shuttle bay doors opened and *Infinity* prepped for landing.

Who else can I help?

MALLORY PUZZLED OVER where Amy could be, and if she was in danger or just wandering around.

"What files does Jessica have?" Parker asked, looking at a station map.

"She has documents on all of you," Mallory said. "She has as many secrets as Oscar did, if not more. I'm pretty sure Oscar was working for her, since she knew that Draughn had lost his job with the SBI. She was highly suspicious of why Draughn was on the station. It's an expensive ticket for someone who'd lost his job."

"So all of his snooping wasn't about the website at all? He was spying for the ambassador?" Parker asked.

"I have no idea," she admitted. "Maybe if Jessica wakes up she can tell us. But Draughn's MO was: remove Oscar so he couldn't sleep with Amy, remove Jessica because she was most likely to figure it out, then remove Amy because he couldn't have her."

"And remove Mallory for meddling in every damn area of my entire life," came Draughn's voice.

Amy's door hadn't slid closed after they entered. So many things had gone wrong that Mallory hadn't thought much of it, besides blaming the Cuckoos for something else that went wrong. Now she wished she'd thought to close it.

"Move!" shouted Parker, then he slammed into her and she fell, hitting the carpet with a painful thud.

She was unharmed, but Parker was going white with shock as he stared at the intricate handle of a Gurudev table knife sticking out of his right shoulder.

Before Mallory could react, Draughn reached down and yanked the knife out with a snarl. Parker cried out in pain, and the blood started to flow.

Mallory scrambled to her feet. Draughn stood there, pointing the knife at her, wet with Parker's blood.

"You just couldn't leave anything alone," he said. "You have to be around all the death, and solve it all, and be a hero, and make everyone around you look like a moron." He lunged and she danced to the side.

"What, don't you have something clever to say?" he asked, a wild grin on his face.

Mallory backed up. She didn't have a huge area to evade him, as Amy had a small room, but she had to stay out of his grasp. "There's nothing left to say, Don. I've defended myself to you countless times," she said, trying to keep her voice from shaking. "Nothing I say right now will change your mind about me." Her thighs hit the bed, and she fell backward on purpose to roll across it.

Parker still lay on the floor. His eyes were open, his face gray. *He's going into shock.* A stray thought demanded her attention, but she couldn't identify it over all the other panic.

The Cuckoos. *Where are the Cuckoos?* Parker had been attacked directly, badly injured, but the cavalry hadn't come like the night Oscar died.

"I haven't figured out where Amy is," she told Draughn. "You flummoxed me there. All my sleuthing and meddling, and I couldn't find her."

She edged toward the bathroom door, keeping Draughn at a distance. When her foot came up against something hard, she fell to her knees and grabbed the novelty bat. A small makeup case inside Amy's open suitcase caught her eye when she dropped down. It held several vials with colored stickers on them. She took one, trying to remember what Parker had told her, and hoped she had it right.

"You think the worst of me," Draughn said. "I love Amy. I couldn't kill her."

Mallory made a strangled noise that she meant to sound scornful but just sounded like a frightened bird.

". . . until I made my case," he added with a leer. "I took her to one of those disgusting alien restaurants." He lunged again, and Mallory hit his hand with the bat. His dominant hand was still swollen from the Cuckoo stings, and he swore.

"I confessed to her," he said, tightening his grip on the knife.

"Did she leap into your arms when you said you were a murderer?" Mallory asked.

"I confessed my love, you bitch," he snarled, and swiped at Mallory's face. She barely dodged in time, feeling the sharp point slide across her cheek. She went with her momentum and hit the floor and rolled, ending up under the bed.

"Since you asked, I don't know her answer. After I said my piece, they closed down the restaurant. Some kind of incident happening outside. I looked around and Amy was gone."

"I think that's your answer, dude," Mallory said.

She shifted under the bed enough to get a look at Parker's face where he lay on the floor. He met her eyes, and she had a sense of déjà vu. She'd been here before.

Where the hell was Tina?

"SHE WHAT?" XAN asked.

She demanded the station open its shuttle bay doors in the name of Tina, Bitch Queen of Bezoar, Infinity said. She had a hive of Cuckoo wasps inside of her. The station did exactly as she commanded and we were able to land.

"What does that even *mean*?" He relayed the message to Ferdinand, who was still glowering at the Gurudev nurse.

"I don't know. It's Tina," Ferd said, then returned his focus to the waiting battleship.

"Is that battleship spinning faster?" Xan asked nervously.

Yes," Stephanie said. "We are getting messages from Tina now. She has"—the Gneiss equivalent of a sigh came over the speaker—"absorbed thousands of Sundry bodies, plus pheromones, and changed her form to become a hive for Cuckoos to live in."

"And it worked," Ferdinand said.

"Jesus Christ, Tina," Xan said. "Becoming a literal hive for someone. Has that happened before?"

"Not to my knowledge," Stephanie said.

He brightened. "I have an idea. Can you get her back out here so she comes aboard?"

After a pause, Stephanie said, "She's coming."

NO TINA, NO Cuckoos, and Parker was down. Mallory had tried to put faith in other people and it had gotten her nothing.

But that was unfair. Every one of her friends had helped her. She was just so used to being alone that she slid into that poor-me mindset whenever she felt down.

Xan was outside on Stephanie. She wasn't sure why. Tina also might still be outside the station. She had to handle this alone, but she wasn't lonely. She looked into Parker's stunned eyes and winked, then rolled out from under the bed.

She rolled toward Draughn, catching him by surprise. She rolled straight into his shins so he fell backward with a surprised yelp, dropping his weapon and flailing for purchase. She scrambled to her knees and lunged for the knife, but he was faster. Now they faced each other on the floor, with the pointy weapon in his hand.

"I can't tell you anything else, Draughn. Except I lied all those times. All of the people I put away were innocent. I just liked to fuck with people."

His face went slack with shock for just a moment before he reverted to rage. But the moment was all she needed. She unstopped the vial and threw the clear liquid at Draughn.

He flinched as if expecting something painful, but when he discovered he wasn't hurt, he touched it. "What the hell is this?"

"You'll see," Mallory said, dropping the vial and running toward Parker. She grabbed his left hand and pulled him out of the room into the hall. Her eyes fell on their hands, and the full sense of déjà vu hit her. Their clasped hands, stained with blood.

"What did you do?" Parker asked weakly as she pulled him along.

"Well, they didn't come when you were attacked. Probably something to do with Tina and whatever she did, I don't know. So I thought we should send a strong message."

And that's when the buzzing began.

A full swarm of Cuckoos came down the hall from both directions, and through the ventilation shaft.

"Which one did you use?" Parker asked weakly.

"I just put a name tag on him," Mallory said. "Huge Threat."

He smiled and closed his eyes. Screams came from the room as the Cuckoos dispatched the threat to their hive, then they flew serenely away.

"We need to get you to medbay," Mallory said, applying pressure to his wound. "You've lost a lot of blood."

"I think I'll be okay," Parker said.

"No, don't be a hero," she said.

"I'm not," he said. "But Sundry venom has restorative ability if used the correct way."

"Yeah?" she said.

He closed his eyes and passed out. Mallory ran to the nearest terminal and called for medbay, but stopped when another group of Cuckoos came down the hall. They landed on Parker and began busily inspecting his wound, the blood, and the taste of his skin.

"Okay, but can we get him to medbay for this? The middle of the hall isn't a good place."

A groan came from Amy's room, and Mallory peeked inside. Draughn was nearly unrecognizable, his eyes swollen shut and hundreds of stings over his exposed skin.

"I didn't think you'd survive that," she said. "I'll tell medbay to send two stretchers."

Draughn died on the way to the medbay. She followed Parker's gurney, driven carefully so as not to dislodge the Cuckoos, who had already stopped the bleeding, until she heard a familiar voice that filled her with both happiness and dread.

"Mallory Viridian. Get your ass to Mrs. Brown's office, or, if you prefer, behind her barn for a whuppin'."

"I LOVE THIS idea!" Tina said.

"I hate this idea," Ferdinand said.

"This is a terrible idea," Stephanie said, but she sounded thoughtful. "But it has a chance to work."

"No, it's great. Now, did everyone meet all my Cuckoos? There's Tom, Jerry, Marmaduke, Garfield, Snoopy—"

Instead of asking why all her Cuckoos were named for American cartoon animals, Xan pointed her toward the battleship, which spun faster. Small pods, individual fighters, had appeared along the edge of the huge flat saucer.

Infinity had also come from the station along with Tina, and circled Stephanie in a guarding position.

"Tell us their names later, you have a war to stop," he said.

"Comms are open, and may we all survive this," Stephanie said dubiously.

"Oh, I didn't tell you my queen's name. It's Calliope," she said to Xan.

He felt unexpected tears spring to his eyes, which he wiped hastily to focus on his Hail Mary throw.

"Gneiss family!" Tina boomed through the comms. "I welcome you to Bezoar."

"Queen Tina, you are guilty of the following crimes against your people," came the droning reply.

"Yeah, yeah, I know," she said. "But here's what I'm also guilty of. The Gneiss have never bonded with another sentient species. We didn't think it was possible because they're so different from us. Until now." She raised her arms, and from her barrel chest came the buzzing of hundreds of Cuckoos. "I provide them a home. They provide me with the ability to communicate with Cuckoos, a parasite that has done untold damage to sentient beings across worlds. This communication is something no one in the universe—in *the whole fucking universe*—has been able to do. I can take them off this station and take them home to Bezoar. They'll listen to me. I am a unique being. And if you want to lock me up instead of allowing me to reign, you're just stupid."

She paused as if waiting for applause. "Oh, and then I won't take the Cuckoos back to Bezoar," she added. "'Cause you want me to go with you right now and stuff. Also 'cause I'll be mad at you."

"Tina, stop talking," Xan hissed. "You've made your case."

The reply took five minutes. In that time, the granny battleship kept spinning but didn't get any faster.

Xan was sweating by the end, but Stephanie and Ferdinand didn't seem concerned. He had to remember that Gneiss moved at a slower pace than everyone else.

"Your terms are acceptable. You are queen of Bezoar and queen of the Cuckoos, and responsible for both." The booming voice dropped the gravitas. "That means if prisoners escape, it's your fault."

Granny battleship slowed her spin, and her fighters slipped back inside her edge.

"I can't believe that worked," Ferdinand said.

"I can," Xan said. "Tina's going to be a great leader. We just have to make sure she's in the right position to lead."

33

. . .

BEHIND THE BARN

THE STATION WAS back up and running, with Mrs. Brown guiding the systems run by the Cuckoos. Now that they had a strong hand at the wheel, the Cuckoos weren't going on base instinct, which was bad timing for Parker, who had needed that instinct when Draughn stabbed him. But the synthetic pheromones did the trick.

Mallory and Xan had gotten their talking-to for allowing, among other things, the station to be taken over and the new ambassador to nearly be killed.

"Couldn't see them is no excuse," she said when Mallory tried to explain Cuckoos. "You saw Sundry dying. You should have done something. You should have been in constant contact with your hive in the first place."

"Yes, ma'am," Mallory said with a sigh.

The fact that new blue and silver populations were being created at the moment was a positive thing in Mallory's defense, as she was partly responsible for getting the station up and running again.

Xan's facing the Gneiss down ahead of Eternity was a gold star on his record as well.

With the scales balanced between pride and anger, Mrs. Brown told them to get some rest.

After Mallory and Xan, Parker and Amy had their turn to speak with Mrs. Brown. Parker was much improved, and they talked to her about the Earth's research.

"I really wish they'd stop sending government spooks up here; they know it makes me mad," Mrs. Brown said. "You two seem like good kids. You're not going to damage Earth's diplomatic relations with alien governments by reporting all the Cuckoo nonsense, right?"

"I am not cut out for CIA work," Amy said grimly. Mallory had found her hiding in the vacant blue Sundry hive, where she had fled when she realized Draughn was dangerous.

"Sometimes the body is trained to kill but the mind can't get there," Mrs. Brown said, patting her hand. "Some of us have the opposite problem."

Amy smiled, then looked startled, but Mrs. Brown had moved on.

Stephanie, Ferdinand, and Tina had taken some of the Cuckoos planet-side to see if Tina could control the ones there, while the few scouts that the blue and silver Sundry had were busy scouring the crevices for any Cuckoos not directly involved with powering the station's operations.

Xan had moved back aboard *Infinity* and already appeared happier and more content. Mallory hadn't realized how much *Infinity*'s absence had affected him until the ship had come back. But still, he'd come up with the script on how Tina could stand up to her government—and won.

As for Eternity, they'd decided that they would orbit Bezoar until the blue and silver Sundry populations had grown to the point of taking over the station again, and the Cuckoos could return to the planet.

* * *

MALLORY SAT WITH Parker in his room, their hands lightly touching.

"You're going back," she said.

"Yeah," he said. "I have a lot to process. And Amy and I are probably going to be called to report on this, with Draughn's death and everything." He grimaced. "That won't be fun."

"That's why I'm not going back there. I'd be in congressional hearings for weeks," Mallory said. "Do you think you can carry a letter back for me? I need a care package with the next shuttle. The Sundry ate all my clothes."

"Yeah, no problem." His voice was far away.

"I don't think I'll forget you," she said. "Not this time."

"Good," he said. "But if you do, I know where you are, and I'll come find you."

"Just don't bring more synthetic pheromones," she said. "Mrs. Brown will not be happy if they hit the station anytime soon."

"Right," he said. He rubbed his neck. "I'll miss you."

"I'll miss you, too," she said. "Being with you has made me feel like I got a piece of my soul slotted into place."

"Same here," he said. "I'll write. Tina wants me to visit Bezoar and study the Cuckoos, so I'll be back in your neck of the woods. I'll see you."

"I'll see you," she repeated. They linked hands again, and the vertigo hit.

"I don't know if I could get used to that feeling," she said shakily.

"I talked to Amy about it," he said. "She thinks the Cuckoos use something similar to quantum tunneling. They sometimes make lenses that can look into the past or the future."

"They can tell the future?" Mallory said flatly.

"Not exactly," he said. "Take a big flock of birds, the murmurations. They all fly independent of the others, but it looks synchronized. Or a swarm of wasps, actually. It looks like there's a lot going on there on a macro level, but each bird on a micro level is just flying. They're not trying to make these beautiful images with their murmurations, but to humans, it's like art. The brief glimpses into the past or future are just that. Art. Unintentional."

"But it affects the luck you have," she said.

"Yeah, I think so."

They sat for a moment longer. Mallory sighed. "Well, if touching you is dangerous, I guess I might as well make it count." Then she kissed him.

AMBASSADOR JESSICA BRASS'S office was the opposite of Mallory's, Xan thought as he entered. The walls were a warm lavender, with a white carpet and a mahogany desk. She had an Earth computer on the desk, and a new legal pad and fountain pen on top of it. Her guest chairs were antique-looking and cushy. A potted vine sat on the edge of her desk with a small watering can neatly beside it.

Jessica was at her desk, Mrs. Brown in a cushy visitor's chair. Jessica looked like someone had wired her mouth shut, while Mrs. Brown calmly accepted the coffee that Xan brought them.

"I see you two have met," he said cautiously.

Jessica had mostly healed, although some bruising still colored her face.

"Jessica is angry that she missed everything," Mrs. Brown said. "I told her to join the club."

Jessica's angry eyes flitted to Xan. "You and your friend made several high-level decisions that you had no right making."

Xan laughed. "Oh? And what should we have done in the meantime? Told everything to be on hold until you got better or Mrs. Brown got back?"

"You had no right," she repeated.

Xan shrugged and put a travel mug of coffee on the edge of her desk. "Keep telling yourself that. I'm not going to say I'm sorry for holding down the fort."

He nodded to Mrs. Brown. "Mrs. B, good to have you back."

"Good to be back, Alexander," she said pleasantly. "Thank you for the coffee."

"Xan," Jessica said before he left.

He looked over his shoulder. "You going to yell at me some more?"

She winced. "No. I wanted to invite you out for a drink this afternoon."

He thought for a moment. "I can do that."

"ALEXANDER IS ON a date," Mrs. Brown said as Mallory entered her office, which looked like a greenhouse by now.

"Is Eternity doing better?" Mallory asked, wincing at the scrape of her shirt against her skin.

"Much. She's speaking in full sentences again," Mrs. Brown said. "Are you not going to comment on my earlier piece of information?"

"What is there to comment on?" Mallory said with a shrug. "Good for him."

"And your young man from your past? Is that a relationship that will continue?"

Mallory winced again. "It would be difficult to manage on a day-to-day level," she said. "I'll see Parker when he visits the station. It will have to be enough."

"Companionship is important. You've been a lonely woman," Mrs. Brown said.

"Not so much anymore. I have Xan and the Gneiss still."

Mrs. Brown plucked a dead leaf off a bright purple flower.

"The Gneiss are leaving us. Tina must rule Bezoar and control the Cuckoos. Stephanie will be her adviser and her shuttle. Ferdinand will always go where Stephanie goes."

"Why?" Mallory said.

"He's in love with her," Mrs. Brown said. "I thought you knew."

"He is?" Mallory frowned. "It's so hard to tell what emotions they're having. So they're all three going?"

"They are," Mrs. Brown confirmed. "We'll be in this orbit for a few months more, still, but we'll be leaving eventually.

"I have brought you something," she added, rooting around in her massive old-lady purse. "It's part gift, part experiment."

"Okay," Mallory said, guarded.

Mrs. Brown pulled out two paperback books, a notebook, about seventy-three tissues, a packet of butterscotch, and finally a small metal box. "Ah, there it is," she said, and handed it to Mallory.

Mallory almost dropped it; its weight was much more than she'd expected.

Mrs. Brown smiled. "There's a lot of there in there. Before you open it, give me your hand."

Mallory stretched out her free hand while she held the box on her lap. Mrs. Brown reached out with a small blade and cut the side of Mallory's finger.

Mallory jerked her hand back, hissing.

"Oh, you big baby," Mrs. Brown said. "In the last twenty-four hours you've had a cut on the cheek and a full-body sex burn. This is nothing."

Mallory's face turned bright red. "Stop spying on us, Mrs. B. It's really gross."

"I did no such thing!" she said. "I know that you and Parker have trouble touching each other because of your connections to different Sundry. The way you're walking clearly communicates that you tried anyway. Was it worth it?"

"It was worth doing," Mallory said carefully, her face still hot. "There were a lot of pent-up feelings there. But he doesn't want to live here, and I'm not sure it's safe for us to be, ah, intimate too often. I'll miss him, though. I've never felt— Never mind." She blushed again and looked down at the box.

"Anyway, open your box, with the wounded finger." Mrs. Brown leaned forward like a grandmother on Christmas morning watching her grandchildren open the present that their parents didn't want them to have.

Inside was a small green-gold orb made of metal. Mallory picked it up, her blood streaking its surface. The orb wiggled in her hands and fell free of her fingers, but instead of bouncing on the floor, it hovered in midair and then bopped around her in a circle like a puppy.

"You got me—"

"This is another of Eternity's children," Mrs. Brown said. "His name is *Mobius*."

"Of course it is," Mallory said, smiling.

"She wanted me to bring him home, but he needed someone to take care of him."

"But I'm already connected to the Sundry," she reminded Mrs. Brown. "What will that do to my relationship with them?"

Mrs. Brown exhaled through her nostrils, pursing her lips together. "Can't take a moment of pleasure, can you? Fine. This is part experiment. The Sundry wanted their own ship and Eternity refused, but she said she would allow you to have one. What you allow the hivemind to do with it is your call."

"But it won't fracture my brain or anything?" Mallory asked, uncertain.

"Doesn't seem to have done that. Not so far, anyway."

"You didn't know what would happen?"

"I had a pretty good idea. So did Eternity." Mrs. Brown smiled at her, all kindly grandma energy. "But you're fine. Aren't you?"

"I don't know how to take care of a baby sentient ship," Mallory said, watching the orb fly high until it brushed the vines across the ceiling, then fell alarmingly like Icarus. Mallory jumped forward to catch the orb. It wriggled in her grasp. "What do I even feed it?"

"I'm sure Alexander and *Infinity* can help you out there," Mrs. Brown said, smiling. "And Eternity, once she gets her full capacity back."

"Thank you," she said. "For the ship, but not for experimenting on me."

"We're all experiments, honey. I'm surprised you don't know that yet. And don't thank me now; you have to do all the nighttime feedings and walking and all that. I just gave you a chore and a half."

"I'll do it," Mallory said. "Little *Mobius*."

EPILOGUE

. . .

ARE YOU SURE it's been enough time?" Mallory asked, peering up at the swirling Sundry, the blue and silver hives finally back where they belonged. The number looked so small compared to the first time she had seen them.

Mrs. Brown stood beside her in a long, puffy coat. She cocked an eyebrow up at Mallory. "Does a pig love slop?"

"Yes . . . ? I guess that was a stupid question," Mallory said.

"And are you sure you don't want to do this in a more intimate setting?" Mrs. Brown asked. "It's awful chilly in here."

Mallory shook her head. Mrs. Brown had suggested she try to connect with the Sundry from the safe confines of the station's Heart, where Mrs. B had made her living space. But Mallory had wanted to be close by. Physical proximity wasn't necessary, but she felt closer to them.

Mallory went to the far end of the catwalk and sat down to lean against the closed elevator doors. "Just don't let them sting me, okay?" she asked.

"No one will sting you if I have anything to say about it," Mrs. Brown said in a firm voice.

Mallory closed her eyes and tried to relax her mind and open it to the entities around her.

I'm here.

Though her eyes were still closed, she had a strong sense of a massive presence turning to focus on her, then coming nearer.

You come to us, not against your will, nor under duress?

Yeah. How come you're not talking like you usually do when you're talking to me?

We don't have to form words to be translated when we're here. It's less effort. We welcome you.

The sensation was . . . "Respectful" was the best word she could come up with. It was a different sensation from any other feeling she'd gotten from the hivemind.

You seem less like an asshole. The words formed in her head before she could stop them. But it was true, the Sundry had always seemed to lord their knowledge over others, making them less than pleasant to work with. Even as they claimed to welcome Mallory into their hive, they would do little to help her unless it also fit some agenda of their own.

We have a different queen now. The voice sounded like it was obvious.

I guess that makes sense. I just am not used to you being nice. Especially since I have something you want. She gripped *Mobius*, dozing in her jacket pocket.

We are not at full capacity yet. And the ship is not old enough to gain our attention. When those are both remedied, we expect to find a way to fit the ship into our hive. Metaphorically. The voice in her head now sounded like it expected no pushback, which Mallory was more experienced with.

We'll see. We have to ask him what he wants, too, remember.

We are all connected. It will happen.

You sound like it's inevitable.

Is it not?

Humans have free will, you know.

A singular entity having free will, the voice said thoughtfully. *That would destroy a hivemind. Sundry do what is best for the hive.*

Then maybe you shouldn't have included non-Sundry in your hive.

We all have something to learn about each other, then.

Mallory's eyes opened in surprise. The entity was still on the edge of her consciousness, but fading as her eyes took in the swarm above her. "They're willing to compromise with me."

"Hallelujah," Mrs. Brown said, shivering. "Now I have to get these old bones somewhere warm." The elevator doors opened, making Mallory fall to the side.

She struggled to her feet, taking one last look at the swarm, then followed Mrs. Brown into the elevator.

Visit us again, Mallory. I think our relationship will have more benefits than penalties.

"It's good to have powerful friends, Mallory," Mrs. Brown said as the elevator closed. Her hard brown eyes met Mallory's in the shiny reflection of the elevator wall. "But it's also important to not let them push you around."

"Understood," Mallory said. This fit with both the Sundry and Mrs. Brown herself, Mallory thought, but she'd never tell the tiny woman that.

"Are you going to the goodbye party for the Gneiss?" Mallory asked.

"Of course. I want to send the queen off with the respect she deserves," Mrs. Brown said. "I think she'll be a fine leader."

"She'll certainly shake the Gneiss up," Mallory said. She pulled the dozing orb out of her pocket. "You have to grow up fast, little one. Then we can visit the queen whenever we want."

Mobius wriggled in her palm as if trying to burrow underneath her skin. She put him back in the darkness of her jacket pocket.

"The next time I leave the station, try not to get into any more trouble, all right?" Mrs. Brown asked with a sigh. "I could have dealt with this Cuckoo problem so much easier."

"Actually, they were already here when you were aboard. That's how sneaky they are. You didn't know because Eternity didn't know because the Sundry didn't know." She bit her lip thoughtfully. "I hope Tina took them all back to the planet."

"Eternity says she did," Mrs. Brown said. "But I've got full permission to swat any remaining Cuckoos with a rolled-up newspaper if I catch any more on my station."

The elevator opened to the shuttle bay, and the noise from the party aboard Stephanie was already raucous. "I've never been to a Gneiss party before," Mallory said.

"The party doesn't start until we get there," Mrs. Brown said.

The party went quiet as they approached and was entirely silent by the time they reached Stephanie's open hatch. They climbed aboard, Mallory helping Mrs. Brown up the steps built for a Gneiss-size person. When they got to Stephanie's main hold, large enough to fit many Gneiss and their tiny human friends, Mallory gasped.

Tina lay on her back on the floor, green Cuckoos circling her head. Everyone else in the room—Xan, Ferdinand, Adrian, Devanshi, and several Gneiss Mallory vaguely recognized—was still, staring at the body on the floor. Mallory walked forward, her heart hammering.

Then she saw that someone had drawn on Tina's pink face two Xs where her eye sockets were, and she was vibrating quietly with laughter.

Mallory laughed. "All right, asshole, you got me."

Everyone around her laughed, even the stoic Gneiss, although some sounded like they weren't sure what the joke was.

The lights inside Tina's face lit up as she did the Gneiss equivalent of opening her eyes. "What do you think? I am going to have my first official meeting as queen starting out like that. Did you like it?"

"We're really going to miss you, Tina," Mallory said.

ACKNOWLEDGMENTS

. . .

I need to add some regrettably late acknowledgments here for *Station Eternity* before I get started on acknowledgments for *Chaos Terminal*.

I am known as a pun hater, but it's not entirely true; I just hate *lazy* puns. Clever wordplay is great, and my good friend Daniel Solis is excellent at it. He was the brain behind naming this series Midsolar Murders. Thanks, Daniel!

Second, we have Christiana Ellis, an old friend of mine through podcasting. During a lunch at Boskone several years ago, she helped me untangle one of my main plot problems with *Station Eternity* and I've been grateful ever since.

Before the release of *Station Eternity*, I produced a dramatic reading of an audio drama of the first few chapters of the book, and the people who helped out with that were amazing (and each is a much better actor than I could ever be): Brian Gray, Joey T. Badger, Marissa Farmer, Bridget Copes, John Serpico, John Cmar, Jim Van Verth, Numbersninja, Tim Minneci, and especially Amanda Berry, who came in at the last minute to fill our starring role. The audio drama is still on YouTube—go check it out!

Now to the *Chaos Terminal* acknowledgments:

Yana Caoránach, Tim Crist, and Tom Rockwell continue to inspire me with their music, and kindly let me quote their songs in this book. Long live the garages, Worm Quartet, and Devo Spice!

Drs. John Cmar and Pamela Gay continue to offer medical and space advice, respectively, and I will always be grateful to them.

Thanks to Ursula Vernon, who is always available for a sushi lunch, drowning sorrows in sake, and weird animal facts. In addition to her friendship and support, she also helped lead me to a lot of the cuckoo facts used in this book. Anything I got wrong was either intentional for the sake of the story, or my own oversight, not hers.

Thanks to my agent, Seth Fishman, for his guidance, and to Anne Sowards and the team at Ace for making this book the best it could be. Thanks to Will Staehle for the unbelievably gorgeous covers for this series.

Thanks as always to my parents, stepparents, podcast supporters, and of course Jim and Fiona. I'm luckier than most.

Anyone I've forgotten, well, I'll remember for book three.

Photo by Karen Osborne

MUR LAFFERTY is an author, podcaster, and editor. She has been nominated for many awards and has even won a few. She lives in Durham, North Carolina, with her family.

VISIT MUR LAFFERTY ONLINE

MurVerse.com

Twitch.tv/MightyMur

Ready to find
your next great read?

Let us help.

Visit prh.com/nextread

Penguin
Random
House